"Swelling fever," she says to the darkness or the wall, "and the wasting away, and sties in their eyes, and the wildfire. And gravel in their urine, and the palsy. That's what they're afraid of." Her hand, lying atop the pages of her black-bound volume, curls and clenches, digging ridged white nails into a yellow palm.

"The idiots. Afraid of sickness instead of the pit they've dug themselves. Black as their souls. We'll show them, won't we?" Her bulging eyes focus, fervid, in the darkness. "They'll get theirs. All of them. Every one of them in this reeking town."

NANCY SPRINGER

APOCALYPSE

BAEN FANTASY

APOCALYPSE

A Baen Books Original

Baen Publishing Enterprises
260 Fifth Avenue
New York, N.Y. 10001

ISBN: 0-671-69819-2

Cover art by Tom Kidd

First printing, August 1989

Distributed by
SIMON & SCHUSTER
1230 Avenue of the Americas
New York, N.Y. 10020

Printed in the United States of America

*For all the women who
showed me trails.*

PROLOGUE

The one-room apartment over the Tropical Beauty Tanning Salon: the heat came up through the old floorboards, in winter, when it was wanted, for winters in the Pennsylvania mountains are gelid; but also in summer, when thunderstorms raised steam from the potholed pavements and flat tar roofs of Hoadley, turning the days more sweltering than before; when any increase of heat was a perversion.

In the darkness of a May night and in ungodly heat, in the rented room, a black candle burns. She, the denizen, studies perversion by that shadowy light. She reads the works of Albertus Magnus, Aleister Crowley, the prophecies of Nostradamus, the erotica of Anaïs Nin. She likes the darkness.

If she could read with less light, she would. The dim candlelight softens but cannot straighten the skewed contours of her face. Her nose and cheekbones, squashed and awry. Her head, her skull, bent to one side, as if her maker had gotten temperamental in the molding and had thrown it against the wall. Her mouth, a harelipped rictus. No chin. Her eyes—

1

the candlelight catches on the whites, which show all around an iris the color of mud and algae. Huge eyes. Enormous. Like a frog's.

This night she reads that infamous work of Pennsylvania German pietistic witchcraft, John George Homan's *Der Lang Verbogne Freund*, "The Long Lost Friend."

She lifts her frog-eyed stare from the printed page and smiles at the wall—she sits with her back to the one window, and keeps no mirrors in her darkened refuge. She does not close her mouth to smile, for she breathes through it. Her nose is an excrescence on her face, of no use.

The candlelight flickers on the hollow moons that are her eyes, on the young skin lying pallid over the pathos of her face, on her aspiring mouth. The mouth moves and speaks.

For some years she has practiced reading aloud the poetry of Donne and Dylan Thomas and Sylvia Plath. Her voice is low, silky, thrilling in spite of the slight distortion due to the harelip, the nasal blockage. Her enunciation is precise from long practice. Her tone, intense.

"Swelling fever," she says to the darkness or the wall, "and the wasting away, and sties in their eyes, and the wildfire. And gravel in their urine, and the palsy. That's what they're afraid of." Her hand, lying atop the pages of the black-bound volume, curls and clenches, digging ridged white nails into a yellow palm.

She scrapes back her chair and stands up. Even in the candlelight the stains on her thrift-shop clothing show. Her body deserves no better. Though young, it moves lumpishly, not fat but unhealthy looking, mushroom-colored from living too long in the dark. She takes a step or two, reaches across the small confines of the rented room and from a hiding place on a high shelf lifts down a shoebox. At her touch, the occupant rears its head out of its bed of shredded newspaper: a tiny snake with a human head, conceived from a spell and springwater and a hair plucked from near the vulva of a mare in heat.

She places the shoebox on the table, in the candlelight, and the snake, no larger than an earthworm, turns its androgynous face toward her and awaits her word.

"The idiots. Afraid of sickness," she says to her tiny ally or to the darkness, "instead of the pit they've dug themselves. Black as their souls. We'll show them, won't we, Snakey?" Her bulging eyes swivel and focus, fervid, on this friend of sorts. "They'll get theirs. All of them. Every one of them in this reeking town."

CHAPTER ONE

Hungry. Even on horseback, even out in the wild birdsinging carnival-sweet springtime, still hungry. Since marriage and childrearing and the other accidents of life, Cally Wilmore had a theory that horseback riding released druglike substances in the brain, suppressing all discomfort whether physical or psychic, but this time it wasn't happening for her. She still felt the hunger, not just the pinch in her gut but the hunger hanging in her whole body like the haze in the yellow Hoadley sky.

She pulled her horse to an abrupt halt, staring up. The black brim of her headgear got in the way of a view of the high sky, where a true-blue remnant might yet survive. No matter. Blue sky would not feed her. She saw canned-pea green shading into banana yellow—more of a chicken-gravy hue toward the horizon. Those colors did not feed her either.

Sunlight filtered down as if through cheap kitchen curtains. Even on a cloudless day Hoadley lay under a shadow.

Cally heard a roaring in her ears and felt vertigo,

though her eyes remained wide open. She slowly lowered them to the abandoned strip-mine site and the woods, the scraggle of stunted trees rising beyond her horse's ears. Outside her nothing ever seemed to change, yet within her mind she felt a whirling, a turning, relentless, like the wheeling of time. And a pressing sense of doom. . . . The sensation was a familiar one lately. "What the hell," she muttered. "Who cares." In thin hands she gathered the reins. With her booted heels she nudged her horse into a walk.

The roaring sound had not stopped.

Far away yet all around, as if it had had no beginning and no end, though Cally had just become aware of it: a humming, a mighty, muted phenomenon of sound, glassy, constant, lonesome, like the hollow roar on the empty telephone wire long distance, a sound hollow as the coal mines under Hoadley, hollow as Cally's belly, hollow as a defeated heart. Cally's eyes widened, for she had heard that hungry sound before, she knew it in deep memories, almost palpable, she could almost smell it, almost taste it in the scent of white warm-weather flowers, bindweed, honeysuckle, blackberry, heavy in the air all around her, but she could not recall.

It was not the yammering, flatulent roar of the mine down in the woods. That sound she knew well. It was far louder, and far less eerie. In this sound, somehow, were intimations of mortality.

Even the horse seemed to feel unease, and balked, reluctant. Cally kicked the animal to keep it moving across the clay and shale toward the woods. I know how the deer feels, she thought, when the hunters hang out the fluttering strips of plastic. I just have to go closer. Have to look. Have to see.

Then she saw, and understood.

Weeds stood at the edge of the strip site, thriving on the ravaged ground where nothing else would grow, tall and bright green except for—on every stalk, bending the crabgrass, clustered thick on the woody stems of chicory, a brown blight clung. Cally thought at first that she saw many small dead leaves hanging from the broad, fleshy milkweed leaves like leeches. Then she signaled her horse to halt and looked more closely: the things were hollow shells, tan husks out of which had crawled—

"Cicadas," she said aloud.

In a single May night they had come bubbling up out of the ground by the thousand, by the hundreds of thousands, and now they hid in the scrub trees somewhere and shrilled. Closer now, Cally could hear within the humming roar the individual voices. Amid the buzz and chatter, something that sounded like a sigh. Or a scream.

"What in God's name . . ."

And again, and again, many times, from many voices, the cries: wailing, dying, chilly smooth cries cold as flute music, yet heartbreaking.

"It sounds like babies!"

Demon infants, descending to the pit . . .

"Lost souls," Cally murmured. She knew the things were cicadas, yet she had never heard cicadas pine so. Their song cast a shadow on the day like the shadow of yellow smog.

"Huh," she muttered. Her bony shoulders moved, shrugging off the mood. She rode on, taking the trail that ducked dark as a low mine tunnel into the green scarp of the woods.

A grown woman who rode horseback was considered peculiar in this part of Pennsylvania. Riding alone in the state game lands, even more so. Cally knew the women back in Hoadley, the ones she thought of as the "cows," talked about her. God forbid what they would think if they knew what she was hearing: the cicadas, in the lettuce-green leaf shadow all around and above her, sighing "Doom . . . Doom . . ."

She looked around at the trash woods that stretched for mountainous miles, state land and logging land and mining land and rocky farmland gone back to half-dead scrub dense with grapevine. Rotting logs, bare groping snags, rocks hulking and desperate saplings reaching for light. No sound but the cicadas and the sharp protests of chipmunks. Nothing to justify the taut, portentous feeling in her back and buttocks.

Her horse broke into a trot.

Momentarily Cally was so delighted by surprise that she let the mare go. A ponylike dun named Dove, the horse was customarily placid. Dead safe, to Cally's pique. Boring. Trust Mark to buy her a horse that was safe and boring. . . . The mare's unexpected rebellion heartened her as if it were her own. She let Dove veer off the trail; meekly she braced herself in the saddle and ducked branches as Dove slalomed down a steep slope between trees, then plunged over a weedy embankment, almost on her haunches, to a logging road. On the dirt road the little horse speeded to a bobbing canter. "Okay, enough," Cally said, and she tightened the reins.

Dove laid back her mouse-colored ears, tossed her head and fought the bit, cantering faster, though Cally's efforts to stop her turned her almost sideways. "Dove!" Cally exclaimed, more astonished than afraid. "Where do you think you're going?"

As if in answer the horse's ears came up and pricked forward. Cally stared and slackened rein. On her own Dove slowed, walking with dignity toward the presence that drew her. A red-tailed hawk swooped overhead, bound in the same direction. Cally grew aware of rustlings in the underbrush to both sides: animals of some sort—but she did not turn her head to look. She stared at the person sitting on the road's edge in front of her.

Cally prided herself on her intellect, her sophistication relative to the bovine women among whom she lived. The fact that this man was thoroughly naked in and of itself would not have made her gawk. There was more, much more. . . . The hawk sat on a crooked finger of deadwood near his shoulder. A black snake lay in cryptic loops at his side. Deer stood near enough for him to touch. A red fox sat flame-bright under his stroking hand. Birds chittered along with the cicadas in the trees all around, and squirrels flounced, and tick-ridden rabbits crowded around his bare strong feet. At night, Cally knew with unreasoning certainty, there would be black bear and wildcat and maybe even larger beasts out of the depths of the woods.

She came toward him until Dove stood with the deer, and then the horse stopped of her own accord and Cally sat on her back, looking down into caramel-brown eyes and shaking.

He was young, or ageless, and ridiculously beautiful, so much so that Cally knew he was unnatural, a fetch, what her Folklore in Literature professor used to call, erroneously, a doppelganger. Face and body, both were too beautiful for a human as Cally knew humans in Hoadley. His eyes were too bright, glass-clear, unveined, like hard honey candy. His body was that of a carved Greek hero, all the color of alabaster, no, butter-cream icing, too sweetly flesh for her to think long of stone. This is my body, take and eat. . . . She noticed his lips—there was no restraint, no morality about the way he held his full-lipped

mouth, and though he did not move, suddenly Cally
understood the meaning of the word "pagan" as the
old farts in her Sunday School used it. There were
Christians, and then there were the unbelievers. . . .

He sat at ease, leaning on one forearm, his knees
bent and lazily spread. Despite herself, Cally shifted
her gaze down his broad shoulders and chest to his
genitals, so casually displayed. They bulked large
even at rest. She had never seen the penis of an
uncircumcised man before, and her lips moved; at
once she wanted to swallow it into her mouth, tast-
ing it, the new thing, the exotic fruit. . . . Her reaction moved hot and tight through her groin, ruining
the depth and relaxation of her riding seat, and for a
moment she thought, hit-and-run, of Mark. She loved
him. She loved him. But it had been so long since he
had moved her the same way, and another word for
pagan was infidel. . . . She hoped she did not blush,
but on the weird stranger's sculpted-sugar face she
thought she saw the flicker of a smile.

He wet his lips with a slow, probing tongue, then
spoke. "Prepare," he said.

Cally's hand left Dove's reins and faltered to the
buttons of her cotton shirt between her flat breasts.
"What?" she whispered. "What do you mean?"

"Prepare," he said again, the single word.

Though he had not moved, even his hand had not
paused in its stroking of the red fox, though the
snake had not uncoiled from its place at his side,
though no part of him had roused, as Cally could
plainly see, she could envision only one immediate
event for which she might prepare, and think only
one thought, half-frightened, half-thrilled: He Is Not
Nice.

"Go away," she said to him, since even on horseback she herself did not seem able to do so. "Let me alone."

He grinned wickedly at her, then wavered like heat haze in the air, thinned and disappeared. On the ground where he had been lay a massive stub of log, three feet thick and oddly hacked and gouged as if someone had gone mad with a chain saw.

The deer, the fox, the hawk and snake remained, momentarily. Then the deer leaped away, the hawk wheeled into sky, the others darted into underbrush. The snake sluggishly coiled, regarding woman and horse with an impersonal stare. Dove seemed to see it for the first time, shied and snorted at it.

Cally turned the mare, kicked hard and sent her galloping back toward the stable. But Dove had reverted to her deadhead self and would not gallop long on the steep trails. Cally let her slow to her customary walk. What, in fact, was there to run from? She could not be hearing what she thought she was hearing in the cicada chorus; she could not have seen what she thought she had seen. She had to be going insane.

The thought did not trouble her. Insanity seemed reasonable under her personal circumstances.

The trail led past the coal mine, not running on that day, or she would not have been able to ride a horse past it, even so tame a horse as Dove. It made an appalling noise; it would have vibrated the woods like a gigantic purring cat. A huge beast hidden in blackness, buried and shaking the world.

She turned Dove onto the black-gravel mine road, bound for the rough-timber mine tipple that reared above the scrub woods.

The mine hermit was out as she came clopping through, Dove's hooves striking crisp beats from the brickle. "Hi, Mr. Zankowski," Cally called, because as a tenet of etiquette she was pleasant to everyone always, no matter what her own state of mind. But she spoke too early, because Mr. Zankowski made her nervous.

She had seen him a few times before, and he had always answered her greeting with a shy smile and a tentative lift of the hand, nothing more. A small, scrawny man dressed in work clothes too big for him, he ran the mine alone, defying dozens of government regulations, and lived alone in the shack at the tipple. On its plywood walls and low, rusting roof he had spray-painted messages: "Repent!" and "Kilroy was here," "Eternity Awaits!" and "Do Not Harm Snake."

"Hi, Mr. Zankowski," Cally said again when she got nearer.

He was standing on the mine road, apparently waiting for her, and he did not smile or lift his hand, but called out in a high, anxious voice, "Have you seen my black snake?"

She started to shake her head. Then her eyes widened, and she halted Dove. Mr. Zankowski took a few impulsive steps toward her.

"Keeps the rats out of the house," he said. "Sort of company for me, too. Missing. Ain't drunk his milk. You seen him?"

Mr. Zankowski twitched all over when he talked. He had a sister named Rose, Cally had heard, and one named Lily, and one named Daisy, and his first name was Bud. Parents did awful things to their children sometimes. Cally sympathized.

"I saw a black snake," she said. "Might not have been your snake." Mr. Zankowski was so much more on the fringe than she was, she forgot to feel insane. Maybe the twitchy little recluse knew something about the naked manifestation she had seen. "It was lying by a sort of wild man out along the logging road."

"What? What man?"

Finding she could not admit how eerie he was, and how beautiful, she grew terse. "No clothes. Kept saying, 'Prepare.' "

Too late she realized she should have kept the details to herself. Mr. Zankowski turned ashen. His eyes rolled, and he folded to his knees on the hard black gravel and started to shout.

"Arr-mageddon!" His scrawny face turned skyward and seemed to catch the high-heavenly color; it looked blue. "Prepare to be raptured! Oh, Lord have mercy on me a sinner, men gonna wail and gnash their teeth. The moon gonna turn to blood! The streams gonna run wormwood! It's a sign, it's a sign!"

His shrilling voice blended into the cicada chorus. His wailing cries were of the same essence as theirs. That or his words jarred Cally's already shaken nerves so badly that she hurried Dove away, foregoing etiquette.

"It's the Judgment coming! The horses gonna trample in blood up to their bridles on that day of wrath. And the Beast, the Beast—"

Cally kicked Dove into a gallop and left the frail screaming voice behind her. She knew the words, even so. She was a churchgoer. The Beast was going to come up out of the bottomless pit.

The cicadas she could not leave behind her. They were everywhere.

Halfway up the next steep slope Cally let Dove slow to a walk, and found that her hands held the reins in shaking fists, and felt angry at herself for running away. It was because she had not eaten that she was hearing things, seeing things, that was all. Because of her rigorous diet, to which she would adhere no matter what. She would show some control of her own body, her own mind, her selfhood. She would never become like the napkin-tucking, narrow-minded, credulous, superstitious, omnivorous boors around her. Never.

"Ignorant," she muttered, turning her anger against Mr. Zankowski. The simpleminded man had a bad case of millennial fever, obviously, and saw the end days in everything. A lot of the uneducated people had it as the end of the century drew near, especially the people in Hoadley, and absurdly so: Hoadley seemed permanently mired in the 1950s.

"Hysterics," she grumbled, quieting and softening her hands on the reins.

Cally Fayleen Anderson Wilmore, intellectual, neurotic, and aspiring anorexic, was one of the few people in Hoadley who had not lived there all her life. Mark Cornelius Wilmore had brought her there after they were married, and for the ten ensuing years she had hovered, in her own perception and that of the townspeople, she had floated on the surface of Hoadley, moored only at the one point of marriage. She was a naught, a cipher; how was anyone to read her and comprehend her when they had not known her parents and grandparents and what vices ran in her family, her original church affiliation, her brothers and sisters and what pattern they had set in school? She was an oval zero-face in a slot labeled "Mark's wife."

She rode past two junked cars and thought, I graduated with honors in English Literature from the University of Pittsburgh, and now my mind is becoming like this woods, full of people's garbage, their junk, their leavings, and I am seeing their ghosts. She rode past an inscrutable, yawning structure of concrete built into the hill, its gape full of

coffee-black water. On clumps of mountain laurel the
new leaves looked succulent, substantial, meaty to
her, like little green steaks. She rode past a pile of
twisted sheet metal, a slag heap, a springhouse buried in poison ivy, a ruinous stone farmhouse, all
pierced by reaching trees.

She had seen an apparition, and all she remembered clearly was its sexual equipment. Very well.
No one had to know.

Her back and thighs relaxed, surrendered to the
rhythm of Dove's walk. This was why Cally rode
horseback: this pleasant lassitude, this sense of letting go. Self lost in journey, even though journey
circled and came back where it began, going nowhere
—it didn't matter. Very little mattered. Cally began
to hum as if a small mine worked in her innards, and
after a while she began to whisper words remembered from the Yeats unit of Modern Poetry 201:

> "Turning and turning in the widening gyre
> The falcon cannot hear the falconer. . . ."

Elspeth lay amid the grazing horses, sketching a
picture and not unconscious of the picture she herself
made, lounging there in the pasture in her vivid
dashiki, her bare legs taking on umber shadows from the
spring-green grass. After a month's sun her tea-colored
body would darken to raisin brown, but her face
always stayed ecru and exotic. It pleased Elspeth
that she looked like an artist, that people turned
their heads when they saw her. She had her sense of
individual style and her mixed blood to thank for
that. Her mother was native American and Black,
her father Chinese, Irish and Hispanic. Out of this
mulligan stew Elspeth had somehow emerged with a
dainty, graceful body, lustrous dark hair and eyes, a

strikingly beautiful, full-lipped face, a confused mind and a blazing temper.

She sketched, not the grazing horses or the Pennsylvania hillsides or anything so pretty—a pejorative word—but scenes from her mind. Often scenes of warfare, primal warfare, hard, bloody and honorable, with the sword.

Overhead the Hoadley sky spread mottled with vague, inchoate clouds. Yellow ochre, Elspeth thought (her thoughts hazy as the sky), a watercolor wash of yellow ochre overlaid with a mottling of Payne's gray. Nearby, a butterfly bright as her dashiki alighted on a pile of fresh horse dung and clung there, sipping sustenance. Elspeth gazed, pleased not by the beauty but by the irony, the conceit. She was the butterfly, she considered, and everyone knew what Hoadley was. But to Hoadley she clung, and in Hoadley she somehow found what she needed to nourish her, because Shirley had brought her there.

Shirley had repaired the farmhouse, put up the fences and the prefab stable. Shirley had torn down the sagging old barn but built a castle: to the glazed-brick silo she had added flat roof and floors and spiral stairs and small, slotlike windows, crenellating the top, all because Elspeth wanted it that way. It was Elspeth's own tower keep now. It was her private retreat, her recompense for being brought to this place of horse dung, and sometimes, with Shirley, her love nest.

Elspeth signed her sketch with a flourish copied from the signature of Queen Elizabeth I, the powerful and pseudovirginal virago who had influenced her choice of a name. Elspeth used no surname. As it had taken her practice and artistry—if not artifice—to settle on the signature, so it had taken her some thought to settle on the name itself. Trying to belong in a WASP world, perhaps—though her motives were mostly hidden even from herself—she had discarded the name her parents had given her and called herself Elspeth, a quintessentially British appellation, when there was not a jigger of British blood in her. She used no other name, no family name, since she could not use Shirley's.

The doughty Germanic, Anglo and Slavic folk among whom she found herself were not impressed by her pseudonym. No matter what she called herself, Hoadley people could not take kindly to a racially unclassifiable young woman who rode cross-country to the post office on horseback.

Yet Shirley, whose name and provenance were no less open to question than Elspeth's—these same tight-assed people seemed to like Shirley well enough. Elspeth tried to appreciate that irony, and succeeded only in feeling bitter. It did not trouble her so much that everyone liked Shirley as that Shirley seemed to like—

Cally Wilmore on horseback crossed the artist's field of vision, coming back to the boarding stable from her ride. Elspeth did not wave, though it pleased her that there was someone now to see her, to see the picture she made in the meadow amid the horses with her private castle rising in the background.

Without conscious thought she turned to fresh paper and sketched in all its poignant agony the head of a crying baby, then attached to it the clumsy winged body of a cicada.

"Yo, Cally!" hailed Shirley from a straddle-legged stance atop a small mountain of manure, where she had just emptied the latest barrow load from the stalls. Her voice rang out, as always, and her short, bleached hair, the color and often the texture of binder twine, caught the eye even against the yellow-smogged sky. Everything about Shirley Danyo was big and golden; brassy, almost. Big, bell-like voice. Big, clever hands, shins like two-by-fours, big work-booted feet. Six-foot body, strong enough to shovel stalls to the bare clay, fling bales of hay, string fence wire, muscle horses. Big, plain-featured face. Big grin.

She abandoned her wheelbarrow and came down to help Cally with Dove, not because she had to, or even to keep a boarder happy, but because she liked horses and people who liked horses. All her life she had wanted nothing except to have a place with some horses on it, and if running a boarding stable was the way to do it, then that was what she was going to do. Even though Hoadley was hardly the place to do it. Not many people who lived here could afford to keep a horse, even at her rates.

On the other hand, the land was cheap. Though in fact Shirley had other reasons for coming to this unlikely place to try for her dream. And it had been time to try. She was nearing forty. Not getting any younger.

"Good ride?" she asked Cally, swinging the saddle off Dove.

"Okay."

"You ran her a lot." Shirley was feeling Dove's hot, wet chest and neck, looking at her wide-open nostrils. Cally just nodded, and Shirley looked closely at the younger woman instead.

"Somebody bother you?"

"Not really." To say something, Cally added, "The cicadas are out."

"Yo! I thought I heard them locusts!" Shirley seldom lacked for enthusiasm. "Well, ain't that a kicker! Lots of them?"

"Scads. Everywhere."

"Ain't that something. Is this the year for the seventeen-year locusts? Can't be." Shirley's generous mouth veritably flapped when she talked, as if vibration of the lips was necessary to maintain her customary volume. "They was out in seventy and eighty-seven, and this here's only nineteen-ninety-nine."

"Well, they're out." Cally shuddered.

Cally, Shirley knew without censure, was wired too tight. Without reason, for she was not an unattractive woman. In a town where most women turned fat, Cally was still slim, had a body like that of a prepubescent boy, in fact. There was no need for her to be so hard on herself, to fuss and diet. Cally was okay if she'd just know it. Had a pretty little cat-face, pale now—had the cicadas given her the creeps, was she phobic about bugs? Sure, she was nervous, squeamish about blood and danger, and not a very good rider, not always in control of her horse, though she usually managed to stay on. But none of that made Shirley think any of the less of her. They were women who rode horses in a town and a culture where women were supposed to outgrow their own dreams and desires as soon as they bore children, if not before. Shirley and Cally were two who had kept hold of something the others had given up. It was bond enough.

"Dove go okay for you?"

"She acted up for a change. It was almost fun."

They took the mare into the cool, shadowy stable, where cats lolled in clusters, like mushrooms. Gladys "Gigi" Wildasin was in there, in the aisle, grooming her expensive appaloosa, Shoshone Snake Oil. The thick-bodied Pennsylvania Dutch woman nodded but did not speak, and Cally and Shirley accepted this in her. They knew Gigi. A gray-haired rebel, that was Gigi, an aging adolescent with a frothy nickname. Gigi patronized no beauty parlor, attended no church, sat in no coffee klatches, and watched Hoadley with cynical pebble-tan eyes that spared no one. She would converse or not converse, just as she chose, and this day she chose not to chat.

Cally and Shirley talked while they groomed Dove. After a few moments in the dim light Shirley hugely yawned. "Lord, I'm tired," she apologized. "Didn't sleep worth a shit." This with great cheer, as if it were a blessing. "God damn coal mine pounded on my ear all night. Shook the bed, it was so loud. I swear, the fucking thing sounds like it's right under the house."

"Probably is," Gigi put in, suddenly unbending enough to speak. Shirley turned to her without missing a stroke of the brush in her hand.

"Not supposed to be."

"It doesn't matter." Gigi did not look up from polishing Snake Oil's speckled flanks. Her words, while never sharp, were as blunt as the nose on her dry old face. "The mine owners don't care. They go where they want with the mines. And those fat-ass politicians won't pass a law against it."

Of course Shirley knew this, but she showed no annoyance. "What I mean," she explained, "Zankowski told me it wasn't."

"Zankowski isn't any different from the others. I remember when I was a youngster, day after day and night after night how the mine noise would shake Hoadley. They were mining right under the town. Nobody slept for years. Windows broken, houses going crooked, foundations cracking, and the mine owners didn't do anything about it. And then they never fill in, you know. Ground under the town is wormy with mines yet. It's a wonder the whole town doesn't fall in."

"Might be a good idea," Cally said.

"Aw, Cally!" Shirley protested, laughing like a big bell. And Gigi barked out quite a different sort of laugh, the hard, brief laugh of a woman with a secret.

A slender, jealous shadow drifted in out of the sunlight: Elspeth. Shirley saw her coming without surprise. Having seen Shirley go into the barn with Cally—though Elspeth was not jealous of the older woman, Gigi—having heard Shirley laugh, of course Elspeth would pry herself loose from her sketching and come, prickly, to stand guard. Elspeth rode horses, but perceived them only as an extension of her own ego. She would never understand the bond between women who loved horses; she could not understand that her lover's friendship with Cally was no threat to her, and Shirley did not know how to reassure her.

Shirley said, "Yo, Elspeth, how's it going?"

The artist glowered and did not answer. The little, spoiled, self-centered, high-breasted brat, how could she be so exquisitely, incredibly beautiful, and know it, and still not know it? And still not know how Shirley loved every droplet of sweat on her fawn-colored forehead?

Good Lord, Elspeth. Cally's so straight she probably thinks we live together to share expenses.

"Hot out there," Shirley tried again.

Elspeth shrugged, no more.

Cally was as accustomed to Elspeth's silences as to Gigi's, and neither liked nor disliked the strange artist, and trusted her as she trusted Gigi and Shirley, simply because they were women. Nevertheless, in the still air of the stable aisle she sensed a tension she did not understand. She threw down her brushes and put Dove in her stall. "Old man Zankowski says his black snake is missing," she blurted into the smog of her own discomfort.

"Just so it don't come here," Shirley retorted without blinking. "He can keep his damn snake." An awkward pause. "Hey! I gotta show you people what I got for the barn." She strode to the tack room, anxious to put the three alarmingly disparate women at ease with each other.

"One of them guys was pulled up along the road," she explained as she came back out carrying a large paper bag. "Selling them hex signs, like. Lookie what I got."

With a flair she revealed a circle of masonite. Crudely pictured on it in oil paints was a thick-bodied black insect with orange wings outspread and hard clawed feet groping at air.

"Lord," said Elspeth, utmost disdain causing her to break her silence. "What did you get that for? I could do you something better with my eyes closed."

"I should hope so," said Gigi.

"Now you know you don't want to waste your time doing barn signs," replied Shirley with great good humor. Then she glanced down at what she was holding, and her wide, flexible mouth pulled into nearly-comic dismay. "Whoa! What the hun? This ain't the one I bought!" She turned the barn decoration toward her and glared at it. "I got me one of them distelfink luck birds setting on a heart. Somebody tell me I ain't going crazy!"

Elspeth looked merely bored and annoyed, and Gigi returned to her grooming of Snake Oil, but Cally edged away. In no way could Cally know how Elspeth's faintly pouting pose hid dismay, how Elspeth, also, had brushed elbows with the unaccountable that day. "I'd better get home," said Cally in a pallid voice, and she fled.

CHAPTER TWO

Because she had cut her ride short, Cally got back to Hoadley's Perfect Rest Funeral Home, which was her home also, in time to say hello to the funeral director, her husband, before she had to go pick up the kids at school.

Mark Wilmore, already in his sober-toned three-piece suit for the evening's proceedings, was standing in the Blue Room, one of the viewing rooms, trying to get a corpse to assume the perfect rest position. The man, or quondam man, was stout, and his thumbs, which had stiffened straight, refused to hold his hands clasped atop his ample belly. They kept sliding down to his sides. "Glue," Mark muttered, his handsome brow creased. "These people aren't going to want to cuddle him." The grieving family was too civilized to want to hold the deceased's hands, Mark meant, or climb into the coffin with him, as sometimes happened. Sometimes it was a real problem to keep the mourners from mussing the deceased, especially a deceased who had died in a tragic accident and had needed to be patched together with wax. But with a stately, peaceful *paterfamilias* such as this one, nobody was going to pull at the hands. "Cally, go down cellar and get me the glue out of the embalming room, would you please?" Only then did Mark look at her. "Cal!" he complained. "Do you have to come in here in your riding boots?" Mark was meticulous about his deep-carpeted premises. "You'll get manure on the rug!"

"No, I won't," Cally lied. "I checked." She would have worn the boots all day if she could have gotten away with it. She hated low shoes, women's shoes, skimpy, flimsy, flabby, insubstantial flats, crippling heels; she hated it when she had to put on a dress and dressy shoes to go to church or a funeral or viewing. Women's shoes made her feel helpless, susceptible to cold and weather, unable to run from danger; flat or not, the things were designed so that she would twist an ankle if she so much as tried to stride out in them. And the heels made all women walk like waterfowl, in her opinion. Cally loved boots. She could stride and swagger in boots. She fantasized of men, muggers, rapists, foolish enough to attack her when she was wearing boots. One hard booted kick to the crotch, or a crunch of a heavy leather heel on an instep, and she would show them.

She fetched the glue, running downstairs and up again. She always ran wherever she could to use up calories. She wanted to be thin, youthful-looking, and loved. . . . She watched, belly growling, as Mark positioned the dead man's hands. Deceased, rather. Never say dead.

She wished Mark would thank her, notice her, maybe kiss her, but he was preoccupied by his work.

"He looks nice," she said, doing the duty of a good wife. Mark took pride in his business. He pinked out his bodies well, applied cosmetics to them with artistry, displayed them in beautiful layouts (arranging the flowers himself), and he could even sculpt convincing facial repairs with wax when necessary. These accomplishments were not such that he could brag of them at Rotary meetings, so only Cally knew how much of him was artist rather than businessman. How he had struggled, for instance, with the body of a manic-depressive who had jumped off an overpass onto the concrete four-lane in front of a tandem truck. Most funeral directors would have simply closed the casket, but Mark had made the man look nearly as decent as a church deacon for his burial. Though the ungrateful `corpse had ruined the effect by leaking. No matter how well you patched up jumpers, they always leaked.

No glue showed when Mark had finished with the stout body's hands. "Very dignified," Cally approved. "His own manicure?"

"I freshened it."

"Very classy."

Mark nodded in acknowledgement, and Cally felt her heart hunger like her aching gut. He was such a good-looking man. She wanted to take that monkey suit off him and put him back in jeans, the way he belonged, the way he had been when they met—or better, just take it off him, and take him to bed. . . . How long had it been? Far too long. Funeral directors (never say "undertaker") often had to work at night.

"Go on over to Peach," Mark suggested, "say hi to Barry, see what he's doing."

The Peach room, he meant: his ultimate in decorating achievement, with its heavy, fringed, gold-damask curtains and crystal-beaded lampshades and the three-tiered fountain mumbling nasally to itself like a priest. Business was good, if Mark had two layouts going at

once. The funeral home (a term Mark preferred to
"mortuary," which had a cold ring to it), must have
been one of the few businesses doing well in Hoadley,
and no wonder. The town was full of old people who
were busy dying. Generally at inconvenient times,
Cally thought, thrilling herself: such a daring, such a
cynical thought. Gigi would be proud.

She was not yet daring enough to wonder why
Mark seemed to be pushing her away, or to stop
obeying him. Cally went to see what was going on in
the Peach Room.

"Hi, Barry."

"Hi, Mrs. Wilmore."

Another man of that age, early twenties, would
probably have called her by her first name, but Barry
Beal always called her Mrs. Wilmore. She was the
boss's wife, and Barry was serious about such things.
About most things. He worked slowly with blunt
white hands. She saw his face profiled over his work;
the half she could see was as lump-sugar white as his
hands, and ruggedly beautiful, like a weathered marble statue, scarred and pocked as it was from a past
battle with acne.

Then he turned toward her.

She knew, of course, what she would see. But she
could never entirely escape the shock. The other half
of Barry's face was mottled a livid bruise red varying
from plum to purple grape to strawberry to screaming raspberry pink. The birthmark started above Barry's hairline somewhere and spread downward like
spilled jam, taking in eye, temple, cheek and jaw, as
well as one nostril and the corner of his stoical mouth.
It made him a man of two faces, one pleasing, the
other hideous.

"I still ain't got it the way I want," Barry said, but

he stepped back to show Cally what he had been doing.

Fine caskets (never called "coffins") came with pastel-colored linings of tufted silk, and most often with a thin, soft blanket of matching dinner-mint hue to be laid over the "sleeper" within. Barry was slow of intellect if not actually retarded, but like many less-than-gifted people he possessed one inborn talent, and his was the knack of arranging these blankets. More than knack or talent: his was a genius and an obsession. With stubborn, relentless hands he formed the limp fabric into tucks, pleats, intricacies that let go into folds and draperies worth weeping over. He took hours about it, and Mark did not mind paying him for as many hours as cared to spend.

The present sample of his work lay over the still form of a middle-aged woman with a ghastly hairdo, courtesy of Wobbles Enwright, the only hairdresser in Hoadley who would work on dead people. She made all her late lamenteds sport pompadours stiff with perfumed spray, regardless of what their former style had been. It took Cally a moment to shift her gaze from the horror of that rigid hair to the marshmallow-pink blanket, softly puckered and pleated à la Barry Beal.

"Looks good to me," she said. But though it was, in fact, impressive by any ordinary standards, she knew it was not quite up to the level of Barry's best work. He had not been able to concentrate very well for the past week or two. Ever since the Musser girl had run off, in fact, he had been quietly, doggedly unhappy.

His misery showed only in the quality of his work and in the question he asked every time he saw her. Which he asked now.

"Mrs. Wilmore, you heard anything about Joanie?"

Joan Musser. His girlfriend since high school. Cally had seen her a few times, and to her chagrin had found herself wincing away and staring back again, repelled and fascinated, just like a Hoadley yokel. Joan was incredibly ugly, far uglier than Barry, and all the more freakishly so because she was female. From the town grapevine Cally had found that Joan had been called "Frog Face" (mostly behind her back) almost since she was a baby. The consensus of Hoadley opinion was that she and Barry Beal had ended up a couple because nobody else wanted either of them. Maybe. Maybe she hadn't cared for him. But it certainly seemed as if Barry had really loved her.

"No, Barry," said Cally, keeping her tone gentle and civil even though she had answered the same question a dozen times before. What could the poor innocent do but ask his gods, the adults in full possession of all the regulation smarts, to help him? "I haven't seen her since I took you and her out to the stable that time."

At Barry's request. He had said Joan wanted to see the horses. And Cally had been astonished when placid Dove had kicked at Barry's girlfriend. What in the world had the frog-faced woman been doing to the mare while Cally's back was turned? Even when she was in heat, Dove was usually trustworthy.

As Cally spoke to Barry, she faced the head of the pompadoured corpse, the dead woman; he faced its feet. Therefore he did not see what Cally saw. Afterward, she tried to tell herself that she had imagined what happened, that it was a trick of the light, a shifting shadow, something in her head, though she was not one to imagine things about corpses. She was accustomed to being around them. She brought Mark coffee to the embalming room when he was working late. She slept every night in the upstairs apartment without a thought for the sleepers-never-to-wake down below.

"No, I have no idea where Joan can be," Cally said.

And the dead woman opened her eyes.

Just a blink, a glimpse, a leer out of the blank implants that covered her sunken eyeballs to give their closed lids the appearance of peaceful repose. The eyelids had been glued shut; how could they move? But move they did, fluttering up to reveal lifeless plastic orbs more horrible than any skeletal stare. Then gone. And Cally stood ashen, wobbling in her riding boots, and Barry Beal was saying, "Mrs. Wilmore? Mrs. Wilmore? You okay? You remember something you heard about Joanie, Mrs. Wilmore?"

I'm Barry Beal, and I knowed Joanie practically since we was born, and I didn't like it when she went off that way.

I didn't know her that good till we was in junior high together. Thing was, we went to different elementaries. She lived in Hoadley, and I lived about ten miles out. Course I knowed who she was. Everybody in the county knowed who she was from the first time her mom brung her out on the street. You took one look at her face, you didn't forget. She looked like a squashed frog instead of a little girl. A squashed frog with long yellow hair. Her mom used to comb that hair nice and put ribbons in it like to try and make people look at that, but it didn't work. The face was what people remembered.

The kids called her "Frog Face." Kids was mean in junior high, meaner even than in elementary. These kids, their daddies worked in the steel mills or the coal mines, they all think they got to be big and tough. What I mean, they always called me Retard and Tardo and Jamhead and like that, and done Indian rope burns and noogies on me, but in junior high they stole my money and stuff, locked me in closets, tripped me in the hallway, like that. Them hallways in junior high, with all the kids punching and shoving no matter how much the teachers holler, they're like hell.

Even the girls was mean. They hit on me and scratched me when they got a chance. And them boys older than me, think they're tough, they beat me up one day after school. It took a bunch of them, and they only done that once. I got big brothers, see, took care of them.

But what I mean is, nobody in junior high wants nothing to do with a tardo or weirdo or a puke face. And there's a sort of rule people who ain't what they call normal get stuck together. The kids nobody much talks to talk to each other. I noticed that from little on up. So me and Joanie, we was the two ugliest kids in the school, we seen each other a lot, in lunch and in study hall and just around.

Joanie wasn't a retard like me, though. Joanie was real smart.

I don't think she showed it in class much. Times I seen her, she was always sitting kind of curled up, like she didn't want nobody looking at her. And she didn't hardly say nothing the first few times I set with her at lunch. But after I ate with her two-three times she started talking to me, and then I knowed she was smart.

"That mark on your face," she says. "I know what it is."

Thing is, I got this big purple splotch on my face. I'd be just average ugly without it, but with it I'm a damn freak. Plus I had zits on top of it back then.

"I've been doing some research," says Joanie. "It's called a hema—hema something, a port wine stain. You can get it taken off, you know that? They can laser it right off."

"Don't want nothing to do with no laser doctor," I said.

"That's ignorant. I'd sure get my face done if my mother would let me."

Sentences like that I got to take one thing at a time. "Them laser doctors can fix your face?" I says. Her face didn't look like nobody could fix it with anything.

"Not laser doctors. Plastic surgeons. They can move the bones around, put new bones in, like that."

I guess if they would've done that, she could've breathed through her nose and been nicer to eat with. She was awful to eat with. Chewed with her mouth open and snorted air around her food. I didn't care because I ain't no winner when it comes to table manners myself.

I taken the next thing. "Your mother won't let you get your face fixed?"

But she sort of scrunched up and wouldn't talk to me no more that day.

I can figure things out if I want to. It takes me a while, but if I decide I want to, I can do it. So I done it. I listened to the teachers in the hallway talking, people talking around town, my mom gabbing on the phone with her friends, and I figured out some. And then later, when she knowed me better, Joanie told me some more.

Joanie's mother was Norma Koontz. Them's the Koontzes that sells insurance. They sent Norma to college and all that, and she married this sort of artist fellow named Roland Musser and come back to Hoadley with him. They was going to have an art gallery, but it didn't do no good. Not hardly, in this town. Even I would've knowed that. People ain't got enough to pay the bills, they ain't going to buy no art. So the gallery went bust, and Joanie got born about the same time, and Roland started drinking. He been drinking ever since, pretty much, and after a few years Norma's folks got tired of helping out. They moved to Florida and stopped sending money. Joanie's mother worked different places, but it's hard to find good jobs around Hoadley. And then she went and got mixed up with this cinderblock church outside of town. And they tooken all her money Joanie's father didn't drink. So Joanie never had nothing.

I guessed it took a lot of money to get your face fixed. But then I found out even if she had money Norma Koontz wouldn't have got no face job for her daughter. Joanie's mother had some weird ideas.

By ninth grade me and Joanie was good friends. My bus got to school early and she usually come to school early too. She wouldn't of had to because she walked, but she come early anyways. We'd stand around and talk about all kinds of stuff. Sometimes I thought she liked me because she come to school early when she wouldn't of had to. But mostly I knowed better. She come to get away from home. I knowed where she lived, in one of them trashy row houses between the river and the railroad tracks, right by the slag heap. It wasn't the house Joanie was getting away from, though.

"My mother gave up on me when I was ten," she told me.

"What do you mean, gave up on you?" I says.

"She just gave up on me. She sat me down one day and told me I was bad, sunk in sin, had a devil in me, and that was why my face was the way it is. And she didn't know what was ever going to become of me, but she was done with me. And she's hardly talked to me since."

"Jeez!" I couldn't believe what I was hearing. To me back then it almost sounded kind of good, because my mom was always on my back for something. "You mean she don't care—"

"She doesn't care where I go or when I come home. She doesn't fix food for me. I get myself something to eat. She washes my laundry because I put it in with the rest, but she doesn't fold it. She just dumps it in a mess on my bed."

I guessed it wasn't no good after all having a mom like that. No wonder Joan always looked like hell, and not just her face. I mean, I was no beauty myself and where I come from we ain't picky, but Joanie didn't take proper care of herself, I guess because she didn't get no encouragement. Her hair was greasy and the rest of her was kind of flabby, not really fat but just sort of dumpy, and her clothes was ugly and sometimes she smelled. I didn't know much about being a girl but I knowed there ought to be something she could do about the smell. She usually had food on her, too, on account of she couldn't chew right because her face was bent.

When we got to high school, tenth grade, we was in a different building and Joanie took Academic and I took General. Most of them bookworms hadn't got much use for us farmers, and Joanie probably wouldn't of been no different if it wasn't for her face. But as it was, she still ate lunch with me every day.

Them school lunches was awful, but she ate most everything because she wasn't likely to get much at home. After a while I knowed what foods she really liked though. She loved bananas and I didn't care much about them so I would give her mine. She would peel the whole thing at once and get all the hairy stuff off it and take the little black thing out of the bottom. If it didn't come out she wouldn't eat the bottom.

"That won't hurt you," I says.

"How would you know?" she says. "It reminds me of a worm or something," she says. "Black. Ick."

Sometimes other kids would offer her the food they didn't want, but not so much to be nice. Mostly they did it to make fun. She wouldn't take their food.

"I hate normals," she says to me one day.

"Huh?"

"People with regular faces. Girls with fluffy hair and nice clothes, think they're pretty. Boys who think they're God's gift. Teachers who think they're so smart, know all the answers. People who whisper behind their hands. The do-goody women in the thrift shop. The old farts loafing in the park. I hate them all."

"Yeah," I says. I didn't understand much, but I figured I better keep quiet about her greasy hair or she might end up hating me too."

She says, "Someday I'm going to get them."

She scared me, the way she looked. Like she might really do something. I kept quiet, and so did she for a while, like she was thinking.

"I've stopped going to church," she says then.

I didn't know much about church one way or the other. My folks was decent but they didn't go to no church. All I knowed was most people in Hoadley was Catholic and the rest was pretty much all Brethren or Lutheran, and Joanie's mom wasn't neither. That place where Norma Musser went, a guy named Culp was the preacher, and some people said he was crazy. Preached hell and Armageddon all the time. My folks said he was crazy like a fox, had people under his thumb, taking their money from them.

"I've had it," says Joanie. "I don't care what Mom or Culp do to me."

"Why, what would Reverent Culp do?"

"Pray for me! Bar, it's terrible the way he prays. He thinks I'm so bad—I might as well be the Antichrist." She was talking funny. She looked a little crazy. "He better let me alone or I don't know what I might do."

I says, "How would you know what he says if you ain't there?"

She says, "I'd know. That snake. I'd feel it. He's been praying his poison over me once a week practically since I was born."

"Every Sunday?"

"Every Sunday he has a go at healing me."

"You sickly?"

"Lord, no! My face, Bar, my face! It's supposed to be all my fault. God is punishing me. I'm stubborn in sin. Well, God can go to hell. I'm not going back. I don't care if my mom kicks me out of the house."

Her mom didn't kick her out, but she sure didn't get no happier, neither, and Joanie changed after that. She started smoking pot, for one thing, when she could get it. She never had enough money to get much, but then along about tenth grade she had problems with boys. I guess some of the guys thought she was so ugly she'd be easy. They started hanging around her house, driving by and beeping their horns, hollering, stuff like that.

I guess her mom thought the same. "Mom says I'm a whore," she tells me.

"I wouldn't know it," I says.

"Shit," she says and laughs at me. She'd got into a habit of saying swear words a lot. What with her sneaking reefers and all, she was getting into trouble in school, teachers sending notes home to her mom and like that. I think she liked making her mom mad. I think she even liked being called a whore. I don't think she never done nothing with them guys though. I don't really know. I just don't think so.

"The old lady says I'm the Whore of Babylon," Joanie says. "Says I'm going to get struck down by God and go straight to hell. Someday I'd like to tear her tongue out and show it to her."

I was used to the way she talked, but that turned my stomach. "*Joanie*," I says.

"I would! She's hateful. She thinks every time she goes out to church I've got ten guys in the house, fornicating on the kitchen table."

"How come the kitchen table?"

"Bar . . . Just never mind."

"Well, don't your dad say nothing about all this?"

"Him? He's no use." She laughs again. "He's a vegetable. Pickled. Even when he's there, he's not."

I should have knowed that. I'd seed him.

It really bothered her, what her mother said. "Shit, she thinks I'm rotten to the core. Whore, whore, rotten to the core. I might as well make her happy," Joanie says. "I sure could use the money. And some people say it's fun."

"Don't do that," I says, and she got mad.

"Don't you try to tell me what to do now!" she yells at me, and she stomps off. So I went home in the bus that night and got three of my brothers and we come back in town. Her house was the kind with them asphalt shingles falling off the sides and the wooden steps with the paint gone. There set her father on them splintery steps with his bottle, and there was real rude guys hanging around, but Mr. Musser don't mind none. Me and my brothers piled out of the car and started pounding away on them guys to send them off, and Mr. Musser set there grinning like a lit pumpkin. Me and my brothers got cut up a little bit but we sent them bastards on their way. My brothers give me a hard time about it but I felt we done right. Then we went on home.

The next morning in school Joanie come up to me steaming. I was surprised. I thought I done good.

"Who the hell do you think you are!" she yells. "You don't own me!"

I was real surprised. "You want them guys back?" I says. "Shoot, I'll round them up and send them back."

"Heck, no!" She cooled down a little. "I'm just trying to figure out how that—that saurian mind of yours works, that's all. What's your right? You've never even asked me for a date."

"I'm asking you now," I says. I never even thought of it till then, but I should've done it before. It worked out good. She was my girl, so the wise guys let her alone after that.

We went to a movie. It's dark in movies. But we still had to put up with some stares and snide comments from ignorant people. "Why would they come out in public!" some lady says. So we didn't go to movies much after that. We dated two-three years, once a week every week regular because nobody else wanted neither of us. We went different places—out to my house to watch TV, or for a drive in my Chevy when I got it, or to the library. The library, for cripes sake! Joanie made me drive her to every library for miles, and she got a card at each one.

Little libraries ain't no use, but I got to admit, big libraries are nice private places, especially back in the shelves.

Sex was something you got to do when you're in high school. My brothers was all after me about what base was I at with Joanie. I didn't say nothing and I didn't really care, but after a while I figured I better give it a try. Joanie didn't really attract me that way and I didn't want to mess with her because of all that Whore of Babylon business, I didn't think she'd like it, but then sometimes she'd step close to me to talk and I didn't think she'd mind after all. Like I say, sex was kind of a duty, so one night back among them library shelves I tried kissing her. Right away I knowed she wasn't no better at this than I was. We both bashed our mouths together, and I wondered why that was supposed to feel good. I got excited anyway, it was the idea of the thing, and I rubbed against her and got hold of her jug in my hand, and all of a sudden she pushed me away.

"Bar, you are gross!" she says, and then she was mad and wouldn't talk to me. But next time I seed her, damned if she didn't start standing close to me again.

We went on like that for a while, fumbling around and bruising each other's lips and me getting slapped off. Joanie couldn't seem to make up her mind whether she liked sex or not, and after a while I give up, like I figured my mom and dad done a long time ago. It just didn't seem worth the bother. We never got no clothes off or nothing. I didn't hold it against Joanie, that she didn't have no more enthusiasm, because the girl was suppose to try and stop you. After Joanie got her own place I guess maybe we could've tried again, but that was later and I was comfortable the way we was by then.

Joanie dropped out of school soon as she turned sixteen. It didn't surprise me none, because I done the same. Course she was better at school than I was. But she couldn't wait to get a job and her own apartment and get away from her mom. She couldn't get no good job—even the normals couldn't get no good jobs in Hoadley—but she got a job selling by phone and done okay at that. She always had this really classy voice. So she had her phone and her room over the Tropical Beauty, and she didn't hardly ever go out of it, except she still wanted me to drive her to libraries. She was always reading, long as I'd knowed her, poetry and storybooks and like that. Once she got her job, she made just enough money to live on and the rest of the time she'd read, and when I looked over her shoulder I could see she was reading some real strange stuff, with pictures of stars and snakes and eagles and horses and strange letters and naked people in it. But the naked people wasn't having sex, usually.

Like I said, maybe good old Joanie and me could've had sex better after she got her own place. But I'd been to some real whores by then and I knowed what they did and I liked Joanie and I didn't want to bother her with them things. I figured she was a nice girl and wouldn't be interested, and she never done nothing to show me different. Maybe I was wrong, though.

I was doing construction work for my uncle then, and just about every night after work I'd stop by Joanie's place. Just like when we was in school, her nose was always in a book. I'd ask her what she was reading, trying to get some sense out of her, but she said I wouldn't understand. Said it was mostly all about magic and witchcraft and spells. Pretend stuff. She didn't hardly seem to take no interest in real stuff at all.

"You're going to wear out your eyes reading all the time," I told her.

"Right, Bar."

"Don't you never go out of here?"

"After dark."

"That ain't no good for you. What you been eating?"

She didn't answer me. She wasn't paying no attention.

"I know you been eating junk. Here, I brought you some bananas. Have a banana."

"Bar," she says, "let me alone."

"You're alone too damn much."

"Barry," she yells at me, "you don't understand! I've got it almost figured out, how I'm going to—" Then she stops short and clams up.

"Going to what?"

She won't tell me.

It was a nice night out for tardos and puke-faces, nice and dark. "Buy you a Coke?" I says.

She just shakes her head. I didn't really expect no different. She didn't hardly ever go out no more. So I says goodnight and left her alone.

Couple days later, all of a sudden she came to see me out at work. We was pouring a new concrete porch for a house where the old wooden porch got rotten. Construction was real slow in Hoadley, and I'd started working part time at the funeral home, but this day I was working with my uncle. He didn't mind when Joanie come to see me, though.

"Bar," she says, "I got to borrow five hundred dollars."

"What for?" She'd quit pot a couple years back, about the same time she quit school, said she didn't need it no more, so I wasn't worried about that. I just wanted to know what for.

She didn't say. She just says, "I'll pay you back."

She would, too. I knowed that. She'd borrowed lunch money from me all through school. Her mom didn't give her no allowance, so if she didn't get no babysitting job she didn't have no lunch money. And she didn't babysit that often because her face scared the kids. But she always managed to pay me back somehow. She shoveled snow, scrubbed floors, stuff like that. My mom and other people would give her clothes. She always looked like hell in all them dumb old clothes.

"Can't you get no money saved up now?" I says. Her room couldn't be costing her that much.

"It's my mo-ther." She said it like that, *mo*-ther. "Every time I get a little bit stashed away, she comes around and claims she's got no food in the house, she's hungry."

"So don't give her nothing," I says. "You don't owe her nothing."

"I know! I hate her!" Joanie stamped. "But I can't— seem to—help it. . . ."

She stopped with a kind of sniffle. I stood with my mouth open, because I couldn't remember that I'd ever seed her cry, not with all the mean things people had said to her when I was around, and now she was going to cry about her mother? But she didn't cry. She stiffened up and looked at me straight.

"Can you loan me that much money?" she says to me.

"Sure I can." I was living at home yet, didn't have no expenses to speak of except my car, I got plenty of money. Well, not plenty, but enough. "But it ain't for your mother, is it?"

"No," she says, and she never did tell me what it was for.

I went to the bank after work and come by Joanie's place and give her the money. "One more thing," she says. "Can I borrow your welder's mask?"

"Sure." I didn't use it no more. I was going to be working full time at the funeral home soon. Reason I didn't ask her what she wanted the welder's mask for, I knowed she'd always liked it. She used to play

with it and put it on sometimes and say she ought to
wear it on the street, people would stare at her less.
I just figured she was going somewhere she wanted
to hide her face.

I keep a lot of my stuff in the trunk of my car, and
the welder's mask was in there too. I got it and gave
it to her. "Thanks, Bar," she says, and she looked at
me kind of strange. Like she was taking a picture of
me with her eyes. "I'll get this thing back to you,"
she says.

I didn't have no reason to disbelieve her. I never
took notice till afterwards that she didn't say she'd
give it back. She just said she'd get it back to me.

"Well, I got to go home and get my supper," I
says. Dumb. Here I'd just loaned her enough money
to leave me and that mean little town behind, and I
says I got to go home and get supper. Dumb! She
just nodded, still looking at me funny, and I went on
home.

And like a moron I watched the feature movie on
TV, then went to bed, then went to work in the
morning. And I guess she took the noon bus. Because when I stopped by that night she was gone. All
the way gone. Took her name off the mailbox even. I
never heard no more about Joanie Musser, not by
that name. Me or anybody else in that town.

Anybody who asked, her mom told them she
guessed the girl had run off to be a prostitute. The
girl had always been bad news.

A few weeks later I got a box in the mail with that
dumb welder's mask in it. The thing looked like it
had been through a fire. There wasn't nothing else.
No letter, no nothing. And no return address.

CHAPTER THREE

When Cally got to the school, a bit early, to pick up Tammy and Owen, the children were undergoing the weekly lice check. It was a small, informal school; Cally walked in and chatted with the teachers and watched as the nurse, who resembled a white sausage, lifted the neck hair of one youngster after another, each time with a fresh popsicle stick. Never did she touch a child with her hands.

Cally kept up a wincing smile, scratched herself reflexively, and watched. Odd, how children always managed to look sweet and pretty, no matter where they came from. In all the assembled children there were no truly ugly ones, except perhaps the boy called Slug, the hefty one with the buzz haircut—but even he had petal-fresh skin on his pudgy cheeks. And the girls, the little Irish or Polish or Italian girls in their long soft beribboned or barretted hair and their sweet petulance—knowing their parents and their older sisters, Cally understood that they would grow into breathtaking young beauties, all dark eyes and boyfriends and bone structure, until they married and turned nearly overnight into cows, beefy, bovine, dull and beautyless cows. Hard to believe it, looking at the ethereal little girls, one of whom the nurse was screening for lice at that moment.

The child sat in the designated chair, head bowed in a semblance of penitence, while the nurse pushed her heavy hair to one side and combed with her wooden implement the fine strands at the nape of her neck. The nurse wore white plastic gloves; they glistened on her strong, bulging hands like gut on fresh pork.

"There's nits," the nurse announced. "Look here."

All the teachers and waiting parents stepped forward—the community, validating the find—but not too near, stretching their necks to look at the small thickenings, like specks of bread dough, adhering to the hair strands. They nodded and murmured agreement, and several started to scratch.

"Makes me itch just to think of lice!" exclaimed the kindergarten teacher.

"Hey, we found a live one on a kid last week!" The fifth-grade teacher, a man, seemed to have acquired some of the bumptious volume of his students. "We put it on a slide, put it under the microscope. Want to see?"

"No, thank you!"

"I'd like to see," Cally offered. She did not want to watch the nurse give the child the requisite paperwork to take home, quarantine her from the other children, call her parents. Lice were a shame on the family, no matter how the propaganda tried to say they had nothing to do with poverty and dirt.

She climbed (rapidly; use calories) the steep old stairs to the fifth grade classroom on the second floor. (Put the bigger kids up there, she imagined some teacher saying, Hope they'll be responsible

enough not to push each other over the railings splat
on the foyer floor. And some other teacher saying, I
can think of a few we can splat.)

She found the microscope set up on a windowsill.
She looked at the louse.

And gasped, a small sound, quickly stilled. And
gawked. She had expected something like a flea,
some sort of insect, but this was like nothing so
easily apprehended. Under the microscope it seemed
to come at her, looming out of a black porthole,
swimming, translucent, and entirely too leggy. Though
she was not sure whether the numerous long protuberances were legs, or hairs, or feelers of some sort,
or . . . Something like the clinging tendrils on a
squash plant, but many, many, and Cally did not
look long enough to entirely decipher what she had
seen. She turned away with a shudder, remembering
the dish of cold spaghetti in the Boy Scout Halloween House of Horrors—"Feel here, these are his
guts!"—remembering the long tentacles of a childish
old nightmare, feeling the memory as she sometimes
felt the bloodsucking touch of Hoadley.

Or of family.

Cally's father, a frozen-meat salesman, had made a
modest success of himself, had grown prosperous,
supported his wife and children in a manner to be
proud of, and died before his time of heart failure.
He had been a decent, hard-working man, entitled
to rest and be let alone when he was home. He and
Cally's mother had slept in twin beds. She had never
seen her parents argue, never seen them kiss. Cally's
mother, clinically depressed all her adult life, had
perturbed her adult children by regaining her mental health with alacrity shortly after her husband
died. She lived in the Finger Lakes district of New
York state, wintered on the Gulf coast of Florida,

and devoted her days to cards, clubs and luncheons as she had once devoted them to doctor's appointments, self-help books, counseling, isometrics, religion, aerobics, health-food catalogues, psychiatry, bee pollen pills, revival meetings, astrology, and the I Ching. There had been little time and no energy in her for her children beyond the basics of their physical upkeep. Though adequately fed, Cally had grown up hungry for her parents. Her hunger for them was their hold on her. That grip clung, leeched, threw out long tentacles around her even at the distance of death and time and place.

Cally's childhood daydreams had been of beatings and torments. Sometimes, in the fantasies, her father and mother had been the perpetrators of torture. The dreams had been pleasant, because after suffering she had felt that she deserved love. The imaginary abuse had its bittersweet pleasures; the real neglect had none.

Suffer, her Cinderella mythology had said, and someone will rescue you and love you and take care of you forever. And make you happy. And there had been Mark, and he had brought her to Hoadley. Her new family.

And she turned away from looking at the louse and shivered, for the new family had much the same slithering feel to her as the old.

In the evening Cally took the children to her in-laws for supper because of the viewings. When mourners were in the Home, no cooking odors could intrude their tactless presence from the apartment upstairs, no childish thumpings and scamperings and vociferations were allowed overhead, and even ordinary footsteps were discouraged—when she had to be around, Cally laid old pillows on the floor and walked on them. But generally she and the kids cleared out.

On this May day, warm at last after the long Hoadley winter, the beautiful day the omens began, there was no hurry; they walked. Ten-year-old Tammy and her younger brother Owen, full of the pent-up energy of schoolchildren, careered ahead. Even in boots Cally could not keep up with them. And she could not keep up her usual rapid calorie-burning stride; she felt dazed, dizzied, either by the events of the day of her own end-of-day hunger. Warily she watched everything around her, half expecting the sparse traffic on Main Street to turn into an invading army, the plastic bunnies and flat-ceramic kissing Dutch kids and wooden propeller-wing ducks on the lawns to change before her helpless eyes into something horrific.

(Though in fact she found Hoadley's lawn kitsch horrible to start with. She did not much care either for the massive concrete paired lions and urns and three-tiered fountains with which Mark adorned the outside of the funeral home, but she was grateful that his sense of the dignity of the place kept him from decorating it with plastic pinwheel daisies.)

A few doors up street from the funeral home Sojourner Hieronymus was sitting on her front porch waiting for suppertime. Cally stopped to talk. She could not have gone by even if she had wanted to. A strict though tacit porch etiquette prevailed in Hoadley. In emergency cases of extreme hurry a person could hustle past with a flap of the hand or a shouted greeting, but an explanation was due afterward, and such cases had better not occur too often, or their perpetrator would be suspected of unfriendliness, liver problems and subversive sympathies. The accepted behavior was for children to stop and say hello respectfully before escaping about their own business, and for adults to stop and talk for at least five or ten minutes from the sidewalk or leaning on the porch railing, depending on the degree and warmth of the acquaintance—but never to presume actually to come up on the porch and sit down unless invited. The porch was an extension of the porchsitter's home, and was treated, like a foreign embassy, as a sovereign territory.

Cally would have stopped to speak with Sojourner Hieronymus in any event. She was interested in the old woman, if only because Sojourner kept no ceramic skunks, no whirligigs or cutout wooden tulips, no Mexican donkey planters or wire-legged flamingos or reflecting balls or pistachio-green seahorse birdbaths in her yard. She did not even plant petunias. The lines of her house, innocent of ornament, scrupulous and Heavenward-aspiring as the long lines of her face, rose austerely from her flat, clipped lawn. A broom and a shovel hung against the side of the house, on nails big enough to last. In front of the porch a small, smooth-raked, severely rectangular garden awaited three tomato plants in three tidy wire cages. The two porch chairs were of chilly metal many times painted. By the door stood a lean dapple-gray milk box. Cally appreciated Sojourner Hieronymus and her total lack of sugar-coating.

"Good evening," she called.

The old woman looked gray all over, smooth prayer-bonneted hair, housedress—in fact the housedress was a faded, flowered blue, but it looked gray as old meat. Sojourner nodded and motioned toward the empty chair beside her. Cally came up and settled herself on the porch. The metal chair was of the sort with diamond-shaped cutouts and only two legs, in front, made of pipe bent to form a U-shaped stand rearward. It gave springily when sat upon, and could be jiggled to resemble a very staid amusement park ride. There should have been a metal glider to go with the chairs, but Sojourner had sold it.

"How are you?"

"How are you?"

Neither woman listened or answered. This ritual needed no response. Their eyes watched the children capering on the front sidewalk, clapping and calling to the friendly mutt who lived in the neighboring yard. Cally felt no temptation to tell Sojourner about the crazy perceptions that were troubling her. Sojourner would have listened; Sojourner was not self-centered on her own ailments and bodily functions as so many old people were. Nor, in spite of the prayer bonnet, did Cally think Sojourner would scream "Armageddon!" and fall down in a fit. Sojourner was far too tough and stiff-backed for that. But she knew Sojourner would not approve of her seeing strange manifestations. Sojourner scarcely approved of anything.

"Don't you know better than to kiss that dog?" the old woman called to Tammy. "You don't know where that dog's nose has been!"

Tammy smiled reflexively, her own snub nose confronting the suspect canine one, and paid no attention. At one point Mrs. Hieronymus had told her that if a cat gets into a crib with a newborn baby it would smell milk on the baby's breath and suffocate the baby trying to lick the milk out of its mouth. Tammy had repeatedly introduced various neighborhood cats to her baby brother as he napped, with no satisfactory results. Mrs. Hieronymus had also told her that a child who bit on a banana peel would get leprosy. At various times Tammy had tested this statement by inserting banana peel into her brother's mouth and forcing his teeth closed on the yellow, bitter skins. Again, she had observed no satisfactory results except Owen's passionate aversion to bananas. She now knew better than to listen to Mrs. Hieronymus.

Cally changed the subject. "Did you know Mrs. Zepka?"

This was the deceased woman in the Peach Room, the one who had leered at her, as a corpse was not supposed to leer, however briefly. Cally's question was a veiled request for information, which Sojourner promptly provided.

"She was divorced and an atheist." Mrs. Hieronymus lowered her voice to keep the dangerous words from the children. "It's a sin she's being buried in holy ground. I don't know what Reverent Berkey can be thinking of. Just because her daddy is on the Council."

"Atheist," in Hoadley meant nothing more than that the woman refused to go to church. Gigi Wildasin was an "atheist." Cally often wished she could be the same. But Mark's business depended on churchgoers.

"They say she died of one of them aneurysms," said Sojourner, "but I heard different." The old woman lowered her voice yet further, to a hollow, husky whisper. "I heard she slept naked. And I heard a bat come in the room while she was sleeping. You know how a bat will go in any little hole. It went right up her vagina, and she didn't know it when she woke up. She thought she had a dream." Sojourner placed a disapproving slur on "dream," then reverted to horror. "And it rotted there," she whispered, "and poisoned her, and she died of it."

Cally was saved from responding to this revelation by Oona Litwack, who emerged smiling and fluffy from her house onto her porch next door.

Within arm's reach, almost, because the two old

houses formed part of the same structure, a duplex. Oona's porch, cheek and jowl with Sojourner's, sheltered a waist-high white pachyderm planter containing a large, dead prayer plant, several white plastic parson's tables holding potted coleus, a huge ceramic frog serving as a doorstop, and a wicker koala bear next to the porch swing, cradling magazines to its varnished bosom. In the small front yard, Oona had indulged in her usual springtime dementia, digging garden with dirt-strewing abandon until only an irregular patch of lawn remained, then putting out a random exuberance of miniature windmill, plastic chipmunks, impatiens, cosmos, recumbent Bambis, gnomes, dahlias and snapdragons. Later in the year, Cally knew, the yard would resemble a jungle as the flowers and weeds outstripped Oona's good intentions. Out of the riot the blue-eyed, butt-sitting fake chipmunks would peek, grinning. On Sojourner's side of the property line, three tomato plants would nod meekly in their cages. The double house could not have presented a more antithetical face to the world if it had been Barry Beal.

Oona Litwack was a plump, gray-haired woman with polyester slacks and poodle curls that reminded Cally of shredded coconut. "Look what I got me," she chirped to Sojourner and Cally, displaying the object dangling from her hand. An obvious garage-sale find, it was macrame-and-ceramic wind chimes in the shape of owls.

"You listen to them things all the time," said Sojourner darkly, "you'll go deaf."

"Then I won't be able to hear Gus call me," Oona retorted, and with more eagerness than prudence she clambered onto her porch swing to hang her find amid an already-impressive display of pendant macrame planters, other wind chimes, and nameless whirling *objets d'art* made out of two-liter Orange Crush bottles. She swayed with the swing, grabbed at a porch post, then paused, staring down the street.

"Is that somebody riding a horse?"

Cally smiled. "Haven't you seen Elspeth going to check her post office box? She loops the reins over a parking meter—"

Cally's smile faded as she looked, then peered. It wasn't Elspeth.

"Don't know what anybody would want to ride horses for," said Sojourner severely, knowing quite well that Cally rode several times a week. "You don't never know what a horse is going to do. And it puts you up too high. The birds fly too close to your head, they get tangled in your hair and peck out your eyes."

For no reason Cally got up and went down the porch steps to stand with her children on the sidewalk, a hand on each of them to protect them against she didn't know what danger, as the rider went past like a dreamwisp plucked out of deep time.

A woman, a young woman, so beautiful Cally knew without asking that she had never been seen in Hoadley before: Cally would have heard talk of the stranger if she had been anybody anyone in this town knew or had ever known: the fine-molded beauty of her face was that unforgettable, that symmetrical, that eerie. Her long hair, moon blond, rippled down her shoulders to the back of the white horse so that for a moment Cally thought hazily of Lady Godiva, though this young beauty rode fully clothed, in a simple dress like a flame that flowed down over her feet. Her eyes, amid a haze of blue shadow, seemed enormous. She, the stranger, whoever she was, did not turn her head or glance at the people standing on the sidewalk gawking at her—for Cally and her children were not the only ones—but gazed straight ahead. She did not speak. Down Main Street she rode, holding her bit-champing horse to a spirited walk. After she rounded the curve under the railroad bridge, Cally could see her no longer.

And though her children were tugging at her and exclaiming, Cally turned first to Sojourner Hieronymus and demanded, "You saw her, right? You saw her too?"

"I saw some sort of hussy on a white horse," Sojourner snapped.

"The horse," Cally muttered. The strange, far-too-beautiful woman had not just happened into Hoadley, Cally felt sure of it. Her ride had been staged. It took hours of work to get a horse looking that white. The animal had been prepared as if for a parade. Had the hussy in question truly been riding it sidesaddle? Or had that been an illusion of the shimmering flame-red draperies, the elaborate trappings? Cally remembered a jeweled bridle with a bright circle of bronze at the cheek. With that bridle, the matching breast-plate, tossing mane, polished hooves, the horse had looked like—like—like no living sort of horse Cally had ever seen. Its conformation did not match that of any breed she knew. Straight of profile, high-headed, short-coupled and slender and so white—

"It looked like a carousel horse," Cally said aloud.

Of course. The bronze circle had been the number plate. The horse had even rolled its eyes and gaped its mouth like a carousel horse, showing its teeth. Had there ever been a carousel horse carved with its mouth closed?

"I wouldn't never let my children go on no carousel," Sojourner declared. "Them horses start to go up and down, snakes come out of their mouths. A child I knew once got on a carousel horse and whole nest of copperhead snakes come out of its mouth and stung him. Death took him right there."

Cally stood speechless. Over the years she had gotten accustomed to the fact that Sojourner didn't approve of ice cream ("You don't know what they put in it!"), books, butterflies, bells, trees ("You don't know what's going to drop out of them next!"), puppies, garbage disposals and permanent press clothing, but she had just reached the limits of her belief in the negative: no one could not like carousel horses.

Oona Litwack, who had long since learned, like a good neighbor, simply not to listen, chirped tangentially, "We used to have a wonderful carousel, right here in Hoadley. At that trolley park."

"Trolley park?"

"Didn't you know Hoadley used to have a trolley? And they always put a park at the end of the line, out in the country, with a carousel and everything, so's people could go out on a Sunday afternoon with their families and have a good time."

"So's the trolley company could get rich," retorted Sojourner.

"You know nobody cared so much about money back then. Free and easy, that was us when we was on the trolley, on the merry-go-round. Oh, them days felt good. We felt like there was going to be a future for us."

"Trolley wasn't good for nothing but for young girls to go out on a Saturday night and get ruint," snapped Sojourner.

"They didn't get ruined, they got married," said Oona merrily. "That's how I got married. Right, Cally? You know what they say, the first one comes any time, and after that they take nine months."

Cally wasn't listening. An evening breeze had come

up, and her eyes were caught on the spinning of Oona's many whirligigs, round and round and round. She waved to the ladies on their porches and started on her way, thinking hazily of Yeats and his turning gyres, of the giant carousel of time. . . . She looked up at the sky, where a display of sun rays, dusty gilt spokes in a celestial wheel, shone down through the clouds over Hoadley. Cally had been a sky-looker always, since she could remember. No matter what dreary bit of concrete her feet stood on, the sky was always there to look at. She gazed up often, on her way to the shopping mall, the mid-week Bible class, the dentist. The sky made her feel like riding a flying horse, like stretching out her hand for a brass ring always just out of reach. The sight of wild geese flying over in autumn, the sound of their piping, were enough to fill her with a pleasant longing. It was the very song of sky. A sunset, if she had time to lose herself in it, could bring tears to her eyes. And the sun rays, wheeling, always wheeling, tokens of passing time . . .

Her children tugged at her hands.

"A person looks at the sky too long, they'll lose their mind!" Sojourner shouted at her back.

Gigi Wildasin was the first one to say that something peculiar was happening. She was not afraid, not tough old Gigi, the clear-eyed cynic with the frou-frou name—"Gigi," she had explained to Cally and Elspeth and Shirley out at the stable, stood for "G.G.," Gladys Gingrich, her maiden name. ("And who the hell would want to go by Gladys?") She did not mention that in certain high-school and nursing-school circles she had also been called "H.B.," for "Happy Bottom," a paraphrase of "Glad Ass," a pun on "Gladys." And not for nothing had her ass been called glad. But those memories of sexual escapades, though they delighted her, were no one's business but her own. She spoke her mind about most things, but she had her private affairs, the hidden matters she kept to herself.

Cally knew something strange was happening, but was afraid to say it. Her children knew, and were not afraid, but merely watched, their heart-wrenching eyes veiling their alien thoughts, in the manner of children everywhere. Gigi, however, as was her habit, saw what she saw and spoke her mind about it. To Homer, when she finally got home to fix him some supper.

She had spent her day at the stable, of course. She liked it there, and often went there at odd hours: dawn, dusk, late in the day when young wives like Cally Wilmore had to rush home to meet the children after school and make dinner. Gigi had decided some time back that her husband could fix his own supper if she was not around. Her husband, Homer Carville Wildasin, protested only by not eating, not so much as a sandwich, going on a sullen, silent hunger strike when she was not home to feed him. He went hungry a lot.

The young wives, they didn't have the gumption to stand up to their husbands. "How did you get Homer to buy you Snake Oil?" that little twit Cally had asked her, out on the trail one day. Cally's husband, Mark, insisted that she wear the silly velveteen-covered hard hat and ride only the "guaranteed dead safe" horse he had bought her, and the poor thing didn't know what to do about it. The goose. Gigi knew the younger woman liked her; Cally's admiration amused her because it was based on misapprehension. There were quite a few things Cally didn't know or understand about her. Cally was a nose-picking square, and an innocent. Gigi took sour pleasure in coaching her on the facts of life as she perceived them.

Women out riding together, blessedly, did not talk coffee-klatsch chat, did not talk of recipes or carpet cleaners or diaper service or any of the usual church-supper topics. They conversed more deeply, about husbands, children, horses, husbands, rides past, things seen, things felt. And guilts, joys, childhoods (their own), adolescence, maturity and hope. And husbands. And men in general. Men were fair game, for horses were the domain of women bold and crazy enough to claim it. Some of the boarders at Shirley's stable were vacuous teenage girls, but none were men or boys. Gigi knew what men were for. Men provided the peripherals—photos, tack boxes, admiration—and the support services—horseshoeing, vetting, oats and hay and money.

"Did Homer take much convincing?" Cally had asked, kicking at her plodding Dove, while Gigi floated ahead on Snake Oil's airy trot.

"Nope."

"The man must be a saint," said Cally.

"Not hardly," Gigi shot back. "If I didn't have cancer I wouldn't have no five-thousand-dollar horse. But I do. I've got six kinds of cancer, and I can have anything I want."

Shirley and Elspeth, riding beside her, turned widened eyes and did not speak. Cally, who was more accustomed to death and talk of death than they were (though reticent about sex), whispered, "Cancer?"

"There's nothing like it for getting your own way. AIDS don't work, because it's your own dirty fault, the way you get it. But with cancer you're just a poor soul." Gigi glanced around at three stunned faces

and bowed her mouth in a droll inverse smile. "My
word, women! No need to faint. I been dying since I
was born."

Cally gave her a startled glance. "You've been
reading Dylan Thomas?"

But the blunt, hard-bodied woman was simply
stating the truth as she saw it. She had been born
with malignant tumors on her infant body. Doctors
had cut them off, and then some few years later had
attempted to improve her yet further by removing a
large, bright-red birthmark from her arm. They had
put radium on it—this was in the time when medical
science had used wonderful new treatments for the
skin, such as X-rays for acne—Gladys still remembered the grip of her well-meaning parents restraining her during the painful radium applications. Some
of them had burned, leaving her arm with white
marks and scar tissue she still carried. And of course
her body cells still carried the potential of her own
destruction. Every time she saw the boy with the
dreadful birthmark on his face, Berry Beal, she thought
of telling him how lucky he was that he had not been
cured to death.

She had told Cally, "I believe I got more parts
missing than left."

Like a tough old tree, lopsided, hollow, rotting
inside, half the branches dead and falling, but still
the roots deep and stubborn, still that touch of green
at the top. And still rough of bark and hard as iron.

She had said, "Every time I went in that damn
hospital and the doctors took another piece off me, I
promised myself something to make up for it. And
then I wouldn't take no for an answer. One good
thing about cancer is, makes everybody around you
feel guilty for not having it. And that's how I got my

first horse, and that's how I sold him and got Snake Oil."

The appaloosa was beautiful in body but not in color. Snake Oil was the mottled, nondescript roan of a dirt road in midsummer, tan with dust and speckled gravel-white. It did not matter. Gigi adored the gelding. He had cost Homer a great deal of money.

And that is the way things are. Gigi thought, facing Homer across the late supper in the little house on Railroad Street, Hoadley, where they had lived since they were married. *Things are the way they are, and the way things are right now is peculiar.*

She said, "Homer, the cicadas are out. But they shouldn't be."

Homer merely grunted over macaroni and cheese. He sure would have liked some good homemade macaroni and cheese once, not this damn stuff out of a box. All his life he had worked hard in the steel mill, double and sometimes triple shifts to put three kids through college, and all he'd ever wanted of his wife was that she'd mind the house and kids and fix him good meals. She was trained a practical nurse, because that's what her parents had made her do, but he knew she hated it, and he'd never made her work at it. Now he'd finally got to retirement—and he'd only just reached retirement age before the mills were closed for good—and there he was, like the laid-off, unemployed younger men, hanging around the house with nothing to do but go fishing, could have spent some time with her, and she had him playing second fiddle to a goddamn horse. It had choked him up once to think he might lose her—the first few times she had gone in hospital, it had about killed him—but it sure didn't choke him up any more. And he sure didn't want to hear her news from the stable.

"And Shirley said something strange happened to her. She bought herself one of those barn signs, thought it was a distelfink, and when she got it home here it had turned into a blasted locust. And now it's turned back again. She says she feels like she's losing her mind."

"Wouldn't surprise me none," Homer grumbled. Even though he had never met her, he had a low opinion of Shirley. Gigi ignored him.

"And she said Cally came in from riding looking like she'd seen a ghost. And then there's that woman just rode down Main Street—"

Homer interrupted. He had already heard enough and far too much about the woman who had ridden through Hoadley. "I guess a person can dress up like Robin Hood and ride a horse down Main Street if they want to," he complained. Homer played the role of civil libertarian only if he didn't want to hear any more about someone.

"It wasn't like Robin Hood. She wore a gown. And that's not the point, Homer. The thing is, nobody knows who she is. I know all the horse people for miles, and I can't imagine who she is."

"Last I heard, there were still people in the world you didn't know."

"And what would any of them want in Hoadley?"

That silenced him. Alone in its pocket of the Pennsylvania Appalachians, Hoadley could hardly have been more isolated or forgotten. The coal barons had raped it and passed on, leaving behind them only black-lung death and the heaps of slag the miners called bony piles. The steel mills were turning to rusting skeletons. The land lay poisoned. The streams ran orange. But the community lived on, feeding on government largesse and, cannibalistically, on itself. For most of those who lived there—they had lived there all their lives, often in the same house all their lives, with the same friends, the same enemies, the same annoying bonds of kinship and religion—for Hoadley people, the town stood still at the hub of time and space, while just beyond the mountains the world spun on its way all around, faster and faster toward the close of the millennium.

Gigi pressed her advantage. "You know as well as I do, nobody comes here."

Homer snorted. "It's probably some sort of promo. Some new product they're pushing."

"Who would start something like that here? There's no money here. Homer Wildasin, you know better."

He rolled his eyes.

"Something very strange is going on," said Gigi softly.

Homer pushed himself back from the table; though he did not consider he had had enough to eat, he could see there was not going to be any more. He went off to look at a gun catalog until bedtime. Homer Wildasin had the skewed pride of a martyr. He would not speak his mind when he could suffer in noble silence—especially when a woman was neglecting him, and especially when a woman was showing her stupidity.

Ma Wilmore's house, though not as extreme an example as Oona's, typified Hoadley taste: there was a cactus in the window wearing a crocheted hat Ma had made especially for it. The cactus's name was Fred. Flanking Fred stood a silver-wattled Avon bottle in the shape of an amber-glass turkey, and a ceramic horse head with plastic roses sprouting between its ears. Ma Wilmore herself, meeting Cally and the kids at the door—unsurprised, for she phoned her son the funeral director several times a day—Ma Wilmore herself wore a crocheted hat much like the cactus's, for her neuralgia. She wore it winter and summer, indoors and out. But her name was not Fred. It was Ma. Cally knew her by no other name. Perhaps she had no other.

"Did you see that girl on a horse, Cally? Wasn't she pretty?"

Only Ma Wilmore or some other Hoadley woman of the older generation, Cally reflected sourly, would have called the apparition a "girl" or "pretty." Ma would have called a bougainvillea in full, heady, incredible bloom a "posy bush," just as she did the hydrangeas by her basement door, papery flowers which changed color, like litmus, depending on how the dog pee struck their roots.

"Can you ride as good as her?" Ma Wilmore never waited for an answer, giving the impression that her questions were mostly rhetorical, intended to inspire thought in the listener. They generally succeeded in Cally. Ma Wilmore would not have believed how she inspired her daughter-in-law's thoughts.

Inside, the TV was on with no one watching it, as usual. Cally glanced at the Smurf rerun on the screen, then away again, remembering wistfully how exciting television had seemed to her as a child, before censorship. Ever since the fundamentalists took over there had been nothing good on TV or in the newspapers, either. Oddly, considering her liberal beliefs, she found the censorship of her TV watching more annoying than censorship of news and ideas, though less frightening than the loss of civil liberties.

Ma Wilmore knew nothing of freedom of choice. Cally had never asked—Cally had been taught early in life not to rock the familial boat—but she felt reasonably certain that her mother-in-law approved of the anti-abortion law.

Ma served dinner without turning off the TV. Over the cartoon clamor she insisted, "That girl on the white horse, Cally, do you know who she was?"

She worked the same vein throughout supper. As she chattered, Pa Wilmore smiled across the table at Cally and teased the kids with his hand, with which he could convincingly portray a werewolf, a bat, and other diabolical beasts; he had lost most of his fingers in a corn-picker accident as a boy, and apparently had loosened some joints as well, for he could manipulate the stubs in a most ungodly manner. Tammy and Owen never failed to squeal for him.

"Elmo, stop that," commanded Ma Wilmore without heat. Her husband's wing-shaped eyebrows showed him to be a puckish character, and she had known it when she had married him. "Cally, have something to eat. I worry about you. One of these days you're going to starve yourself into nothing and blow away."

Dinner was meat loaf and mashed potatoes and gravy, none of which Cally was eating. She saw the children gulping the food and knew it was tasty; Ma Wilmore's cooking was always good. She felt the pinching of her empty stomach and her smothered anger. The pain rewarded her more than food would have. She was Cally the Master of her Self, superior to all this. She would never be like these bovine Hoadley women. She would never be fleshy and complacent and gossipy like them. She knew how Mark detested his mother. He would never detest her the same way. She would be thin, a princess, and he would love her.

Family was family, and from that there seemed to be no escape. But her body was her own. And the more Ma Wilmore urged her to eat, the more politely she refused.

CHAPTER FOUR

Shirley stood at the fence, waiting—not at all the usual pastime for her, not when she could have been doing something. But there was a waiting feeling in the yellow air over Hoadley.

She leaned against the house fence: her show-them fence, not an ordinary pasture fence. She had built it out of posts and chicken wire, and the wire served no purpose to keep anyone or anything in or out, least of all chickens—Shirley might as well have put up the posts alone and had it done with, because on the posts were the soul of the structure. Atop each one she had placed a horse: molded plastic horses with their cowboy saddles and studded bridles as much a part of them as their serrated manes and knife-edge tails. Dun, dapple, pinto; wide-eyed, savage-toothed, head-tossing, wildly galloping horses salvaged out of junkyards and attics and weedy back yards all the way from California. Tiny, pudgy, fierce-looking horses little kids had once whooped and bounced on. Shirley had carefully patched the holes in their shoulders and flanks where the springs or the rockers had gone. Elspeth, complaining, had repainted them for her with an expert airbrush. Now they surrounded the farmhouse, five feet in the air, each with a post set in its stretched, flying belly. Beautiful.

Shirley had gotten the idea from a place she had seen somewhere out west, a shack with cows' skulls set on each of its fenceposts, alternately school-bus yellow and Rustoleum black. To Shirley the sight had seemed somehow ominous, depressing, tipping the balance of things in the world toward the dark side, and instinctively she had set herself to provide a counterweight. The yellow and black cow skulls had been ugly. Her horses were beautiful. She had placed herself in the line of battle. In her mind, it was that simple.

She leaned, shoulders against a fiercely galloping little palomino, and watched Elspeth riding her tall red bay mare around and around the training ring.

Having Elspeth around the place was like having an exotic pet, a jaguarundi. Elspeth wasn't good for much except to watch. Shirley mostly on her own had built the place up out of sumac and blackberry and scrub cedar, had strung the electric pasture fences and built the ring out of scrap pipe and black rubber mining belts, had scrounged old bathtubs for watering troughs, had dug drainage ditches and hauled hay, while Elspeth sat cross-legged atop her castle and sketched, looking down to where Shirley was working. And all of this was all right with Shirley. She liked to be out in the wind and sun, working, and the harder and heavier the work the better. And she liked having her jaguarundi around, keeping her talented pet who painted in watercolors and acrylics and oils. Docile, adoring, she lived somewhat in awe of Elspeth, wary of her claws.

She watched the artist ride with somewhat more than ordinary love in her eyes; yet her wide mouth twisted in amusement. Elspeth had got hold of another kooky outfit somewhere. She was wearing some sort of tatterdemalion tunic too big for her, and reddish tights, and soft brown leather boots that came up over her knees to nearly meet the hem of her Robin-Hood top. She hitched at the belt of the oversized thing, trying to keep it under control, while the mare snatched the reins from her other hand, getting out of control in her turn. Elspeth swore like a truck driver, and Shirley's smile faded as she observed, hoping Elspeth wouldn't lose her temper with the horse. Elspeth had plenty of patience for her painting, but she didn't have much for people and animals.

With a spurt of dust and a clatter of gravel, Cally Wilmore pulled down the lane and parked near the barn. Shirley bestirred herself from her unaccustomed lassitude and headed in that direction. Self-conscious as always in Cally's presence, Elspeth quieted in mid-curse. A moment later, Gigi Wildasin blew in like an autumn storm in her big car.

Weekdays, if their schedules worked out, all the women got to ride together without having to put up with the giggling teenagers. Shirley went to catch and groom Shady Lady, her rawboned gray thoroughbred mare.

From her seat behind the leather-covered steering wheel, Gigi watched Cally walk into the stable and smiled, setting her teeth edge to edge. She knew exactly what Cally was thinking about as she strode along in those pipestem boots. Every time she, Gladys the Happy Bottom, pulled on her skin-tight, buff-colored riding breeches and tall black boots, she felt her own sagging backside ever so slightly begin to swing, her stride lengthen a few arrogant, seductive inches. Gigi knew how Cally walked past her husband Mark on her way to go riding, hoping he would notice. She did the same to Homer, and she could have told Cally it was no use. Men shriveled up to life and love before a woman got well started. But that didn't stop her from swinging her ass, and she knew it wasn't likely to stop Cally either. Hers with hardly any meat left on it. Not much bigger than two coffee grains sitting on a yardstick. Little fool, starving herself that way, thinking it would make her man love her. Gigi could have told her the score as far as men were concerned.

Gigi liked Cally in her callous way. She thought no more of Homer than she did of his simple-minded hunting hounds, but she liked Cally and Shirley. She was just old-fashioned enough that she would not allow herself to swear hard or to like a man other than Homer, since she was married. But she was allowed to like women. The way people of her generation thought, there was no unfaithfulness in a woman's liking other women. She wasn't an innocent like Cally; she understood what Shirley was, and didn't mind as long as Shirley kept it between her and Elspeth. It was natural enough. Gigi didn't care what the preachers said; she had watched the horses in the pastures and the dogs in the yards, and she knew it was as natural as the other way. Free thinking, she was, so much so that she had no friends of her own age. So she liked the women she rode horseback with (except for Elspeth; she didn't think much of a jig who wouldn't be honest and *be* a jig); she liked Shirley and Cally.

And she loved her horse. Only people who have stopped loving their mates and children loved their pets the way she loved that horse. She knew Homer loved his dogs the same way. And she could tell Cally still loved Mark, because Cally didn't love that sweet little dun mare of hers, Dove. She just rode it. But Gigi could understand that. Gigi didn't mind using animals, or people.

She had loved Homer, she recalled, up to a point. Maybe as recently as ten years ago she had still loved him. But like all the men she knew, Homer thought of nothing but his job and his hunting and his beer, and wanted her to take care of the rest. And she despised housework. Lord Almighty, but she detested it, just as her mother had hated it before her, the hatred making a shrew out of Mom when she might have been a sweet woman otherwise. . . . Gigi would have been glad to take a job. She wouldn't do nursing; her parents had forced that on her, nursing school, and then turned around and forbade her to take the position in Baltimore because it would have meant leaving Hoadley. Wouldn't let her leave home—and she had wanted to go to Baltimore, and see some of the world, see the ocean, see the capital. But they had kept her tied to the apron strings. So she had married Homer, and refused the job in the local hospital, and to hell with them.

All her adult life, she would have been glad to work some other job, in an office or the mills or wherever, even stand out on a road in the hot sun and flag the traffic for the construction crews the way some women did. But nothing would suit Homer but that she should stay home and "do" for him. Well, she had stayed home, all right, and found herself a way to make money right there in the house, and that money was hers, because he didn't know what she was doing while he was at work and the kids were in school. And her parents never knew how she was using the nurse's training they'd shoved down her throat.

For all Homer or her parents knew, Duty had been her middle name all the time the kids were growing up. Now the ungrateful youngsters were gone, and Homer had retired, hanging around the house, in her way, and like an overgrown kid he thought she should be there to babysit him still.

Too bad for Homer. She had her horse, six miles out of Hoadley, out in the country, where a person could breathe. And she had her car to get there. And she had her cancer, so that he couldn't take either away from her.

She swung out of the car, swaying her hips, swinging her ass. Too bad there were no men around to see her. She knew better than to think Snake Oil would be impressed. Shirley was leading Shady Lady in from the pasture; Gigi flashed her hard little grin at her and strode into the stable, where her gelding was waiting, and put her scarred old arms around his neck, and kissed him on the smooth, aromatic fur of his face.

After the others were out of the barn and mounted, Elspeth rode in from the ring to join them. It was typical of her not to join in the talk beforehand. She had her pride. On this day, though, she had further reason for staying aloof, so trenchant a reason that she had hidden it in the tall grass near the riding ring at first, where Shirley would not see it until the last minute. Once she put it on, it felt far heavier than its actual weight, hanging at her waist.

She rode in with flat-faced bravado, showing none of the uncertainty she felt. Lashed to her leg, the thing did not get in her way as she had feared or hoped.

"Whoa!" Shirley exclaimed at once, as Elspeth had known she would. "Where'd you get that?"

Like a bizarre fashion accessory pendant from Elspeth's belt, in a scabbard covered with Prussian-blue velvet, hung a sword.

"Flea market," Elspeth replied, purposely not answering the unspoken questions: Why a weapon? What for? She drew the sword and brandished it briefly. A lightweight, slashing extension of her arm, it responded to the twisting of her wrist. The blade flexed and flashed, spooking the red bay—"Blood bay," Elspeth always called it, insisting that the others do likewise in her hearing. The color was dense and lustrous, every bit as bright as red chestnut, but richer, not as coppery. Aside from her color the mare was no beauty: heavy-headed, rough-gaited and sour-tempered. Elspeth did not care. She let the horse shy and jump sideways, bumping into the others. She had bought the blood bay for the color, and named her Warrior.

The other women spooked from the sword much as the mare did, and from Elspeth, with her blood-colored Warrior, her sardonic stare, her weapon. For a moment the apron outside the barn was a picturesque melee of mounted women, milling horses and shining, uplifted sword. "God's sake, Elspeth," ordered Shirley with far less than her usual serenity, "put that thing away."

Elspeth obliged, sheathing the long blade, and the scene quieted.

"What you want that thing for, anyways?" Shirley demanded.

"You're always saying how the trails are getting grown over."

It was a flip, quick, easy answer, prepared in advance. In fact, Elspeth herself did not know why she had bought the sword. A genuine Sudanese kaskara, it had not been cheap, even at a flea market, even in Hoadley. But she had felt the bone-deep pang of some odd, dark, nameless yearning when her hand had touched the thong-bound grip. . . . Her glib words were enough to reassure Shirley so that the big woman flung back her head and laughed uproariously at her own fears.

"You got that there for the blackberries!"

The brambles, Shirley meant, always reaching with thorny fingers, grasping at riders on the trails. When the fruit was in season, it would stain the blade of the sword blood black.

"Name it Berrysmiter," Cally put in. Name the sword, she meant. How did the little snot know a sword needed a name? How dare she? It was a private matter, what Elspeth named her sword. Hard-eyed, Elspeth stared at her. Cally met the look, unsmiling.

The little turd. Elspeth wanted to detest her, because Shirley liked her too much. But there was some quality, some quiddity about Cally that made her something more than just another neurotic woman. Perhaps it was only her extreme thinness making her seem somehow more than self, as a whippet seems somehow more than just a dog. . . . Perhaps all such perceptions were merely in Elspeth's mind. Despite herself, Elspeth thought often about Cally. Wondering.

This time, clutching the hilt of a still-nameless sword, Elspeth wondered about Cally's name. What was "Cally" short for? Calypso? Calliope? Once in Elspeth's hearing Gigi had asked, but Cally had given an annoyingly inadequate laugh and not answered. Now she had the temerity to suggest a name for the sword. What did Cally know about names, about what to call things? As if she expected the weapon to be used on nothing but blackberries. . . .

Shirley still laughed like a great brass bell, but Cally was not laughing. Damn her, she knew, somehow, that—what? There was nothing to know.

Elspeth dropped her grip from the sword hilt. "Certainly," said Elspeth coolly. "Berrysmiter it is."

So they went riding, four women far too old for that sort of thing: gray-haired Gigi with her own death riding inside her, and full-breasted, brassy-curled Shirley, and Cally, whippet-thin and neurotic, and an absurdity in pseudo-medieval garb who called herself Elspeth. But even as they mounted and moved away from the stable they felt themselves expanding with the swaying of the walk, the primal rhythm of the trot, the rocking canter, so that they were no longer Shirley, Cally, Gigi and Elspeth, but something more, something ancient and powerful and uncaring.

It was good, even better than most days, to be on the move. There was more than usual to be left behind. The talk in the stable as they readied the horses had been constrained, not as pleasant as usual. Something unspoken had lurked like a rat in the shadows of the aisleway.

Elspeth, usually the silent one, blurted, "Where shall we go?"

Elspeth looked to Shirley, but it was Cally who spoke. Already, after the first jog down the pasture line, her taut face, haggard with constant dieting, had smoothed and softened. "Back behind the mine," she said. On horseback, with her fellow riders, she was ready to face the same things that sent her fleeing in her nightmares, in the nuptial bed at home. She wanted to return to the place where she had seen—him. The naked one whose face she could not recall nearly as plainly as she did his crotch.

Cally led off. She took them the roundabout way, which no one minded; the longer the ride the better. Ridge trail to what they called the Periwinkle Path to the old Seldom road, then up the Grapevine Trail . . . Even though the grapevines looped low, Elspeth did not offer to use the sword. No one mentioned it.

"Where are the cicadas today?" Cally asked suddenly.

Elspeth stiffened, because in her sketchbook was a drawing she had not made; something had taken control of her hand. But she covered up her discomfiture with scorn. "Gone away. Where were you expecting them to be?"

"I'm expecting something else," said Cally. Being on horseback made her brave, comparatively. The comradeship of the ride, the bond of women on horseback, made her able to tell the others about the eerie encounter she had mentioned to no one else. They let their horses browse and listened: Shirley intent, Gigi dourly smiling, Elspeth hiding as always behind her sulky, beautiful face.

"He was buck naked?" asked Gigi, salacious rather than shocked.

"There were animals all around him, and it was like he was another animal. But he looked at me like he was thinking."

Even Gigi did not snicker. The feel of the day was too shadowy for that. Cicada silence hung heavy as the saffron haze over Hoadley.

"All he said was 'Prepare'?" Shirley had been a bus driver, a plumber, a forklift operator, a short order cook. As a longtime manager of practical affairs, she wanted to make sure she had the message straight.

"Prepare. That's all he said. Then he disappeared."

"I want to see him," said Gigi, who plunged her horse down cliffsides and into rivers, the boldest rider in the stable, always, even though she was by far the oldest. Perhaps because she was the oldest. She had the least to lose.

"I don't," said Elspeth, honest for a change. She felt chilled as if by the shivery stare of eyes weirdly bright as a wolf's.

"Now, it ain't likely to be up to us, whether or not we see him," Shirley put in, quelling argument before it could start. Even more than most women she spoke mildly and strove to keep peace. This was the role of a Hoadley woman in her family, to smooth things over, and to Shirley the world was family. "We can at least go to see where he was," she added like a good mother to disappointed children.

The women bullied their horses away from their browsing and sent them forward again. And for a while, riding the narrow, vine-choked trail, they kept an unnatural silence.

"Do you suppose it could be the, you know?" asked Gigi when finally they came out onto the logging road. "The Second Coming we're supposed to prepare for?"

"The millennium? The Last Judgment?" Elspeth spoke with trembling scorn and a voice that rose in pitch with every word.

"Don't have to be that," Shirley soothed. "Could be something else."

"Like what?" Just as sharply Elspeth turned on her.

"Like, I dunno! Like them crazy people out in California with their coven."

"A witch." Elspeth began suddenly, too shrilly, to laugh. "That's all we need. A witch hunt."

"Plenty of people in this town who might qualify

as witches," said Gigi with her own peculiar dry, blunt zest. "Anybody know Sojourner Hieronymus?"

Cally thought of Sojourner Hieronymus sitting on her pristine porch and hating butterflies. Sojourner had once told her that there was a woman who had got a butterfly up her skirt and stuck in her underpants in a public place and it fluttered her to death. Gave her such a strong orgasm that she got a heart attack from sheer exertion and embarrassment. Died on the spot. Wherever Sojourner went, she carried a cane for striking away butterflies and mice and whatever small creatures might assault the sanctuaries of her skirt. Sojourner never wore slacks. She didn't approve of them.

But instead of saying she knew Sojourner Hieronymus, Cally said, "Listen." She stopped her horse, and the others, who were following her lead, necessarily stopped theirs.

"Huh?" Shirley complained. "Listen to what?"

Then they all heard it. The primal sound, empty, angry and yearning, hollow as Cally's belly, lonesome as her childhood heart.

"Locusts," Shirley answered herself.

"Cicadas," said Cally, "all around."

Elspeth said with unnecessary force. "So what?" And Cally shrugged her thin shoulders and sent Dove forward again.

The road narrowed to a grassy trail. Woods closed around like felons in an alley, and the women began to hear within the hollow mob-roar the individual voices, the shrillings and snickerings and tiny screams. They began to see the sere husks clinging by the thousands to the twigs.

"It's locusts, all right," said Gigi.

"Cicadas," said Cally.

"Whatever," Gigi retorted. In each woman's voice

was a stretched harp string of tension. Shirley, also, looked uneasy. "They don't hurt nothing," she offered with far less than her usual volume. "Not even the trees. I heard someplace where they don't chew, all they do is suck. They come up—out of the ground. . . ." Her voice dwindled away. She had tightened rein on her horse, stopping where she was, and the others stopped with her. They did not let their horses browse, but sat with the reins in their clenched hands, listening. From the woods on either side and all around them sounded the voices of thousands upon thousands unto millions of—what?

Something was crying. Or, many somethings. Amid the clickings and chucklings and hum and clamor they heard the wailing cries.

"It sounds like babies!" Elspeth exclaimed.

"That's what I said, the first time I heard them." Cally controlled her voice, but her body shook, a fine vibration, at one with the mobbed and trembling trees, the cicada resonance.

Shirley, more prone than any of the others to say whatever came to mind, blurted, "Did you ever hear about the woman died a few years back, over in Mine 27? They went through her things, they found babies in her attic. Five babies, all brown and dried up, wrapped in newspapers and stuffed in a box. Can you imagine? They said one of them was almost a year old before she—"

"I don't want to hear it," Cally interrupted, shaking harder.

With more anxiety and less sense than was usual for her, Gigi put in, "I've heard that deer make a noise like that sometimes. Like humans."

"That's not deer," said Elspeth flatly.

And with a twiggy sound, a dry, rattling buzz of wings, the chorus made itself visible.

In spectral colors, Halloween colors: black bodies, orange legs, orange veining in their crisp, translucent wings, spherical orange eyes on their blunt, black heads. They were little more than an inch long, the size of the first joint of Shirley's work-callused thumbs. With a plangent shriek one flew past Cally's ear to the crest of Dove's mane—seemed to topple there and stick in the coarse hair, rather, like a winter leaf in a storm wind—and with a noise of disgust in her throat and heaving stomach Cally struck it off before she realized.

The cicada had a human face.

A round, flat face like that of a baby, though still of that dead black-rubber-eraser color and still with those beadlike orange eyes, as if someone had stuck them into the infant sockets with pins. Cally did not at first comprehend; only as her hand, a huge doom, came down and swatted the clinging body into oblivion did she see the tiny triangular suckling mouth open to wail. Then her own mouth came open and screamed panting cries that made no sense, though they tried to form a word.

It finally came. "Babies!" she cried.

And the babies, bugs, cicadas, whatever they could properly be called, were swarming in such numbers that their pudgy bodies and frail wings darkened the world. Whether for revenge or for loneliness or love, there was no telling, but they lurched through air until they encountered big, warm, soft, and that they embraced. They caught hold on the horses and on the women, on their clothes, their collars, their hair; Shirley and Elspeth and Gigi, like Cally, had seen the pathos of their chinless, fumbling mouths, their tiny upturned noses, and tried to remove them gently, but they could not be gently removed. Their clawed hands stuck like thorns, like burrs. They flew toward faces. They clung to soft, whiskered noses, invaded flaring nostrils; the horses reared in protest. They crawled down collars, through plackets, searching for breasts—finding little enough on Cally and Elspeth, and only polyurethane on Gigi—and big-breasted Shirley screamed, a struggling, unaccustomed sound from her, alto in pitch, at variance with the soprano screams of the cicadas.

For scream the cicadas did, as they clung to bodies and faces, as they were struck down, they squealed and rasped and shrieked the hungry, demanding cries of babies, and all the women were fighting them with hard hands and swinging arms, and struggling to stay on the horses, and the horses were running wild, unreined, away from the fearsome place, toward the sheltering stable, where Shirley would give them food in the evening.

Gigi got control of her horse and herself first, for she was a steely old woman, and Snake Oil was accustomed to obeying her. She stopped him once he had run clear of the cicada swarm, and she batted away the bugs who had ridden with her, and pulled a fistful of squashed ones out of her post-mastectomy bra, and looked at them curiously, then dropped them with a muttered curse. Cally came straggling up and stopped beside her, for Dove was slow and calmed quickly. Cally did not calm so quickly; she was shaking thinly, like teazels in winter.

"Did you see!" she cried out to Gigi, more in plaint than in query. "Babies!"

"I saw."

"But what the hun is going on? What are we going to do?"

There was, of course, no answer.

Shirley and Elspeth had been longer stopping their horses. Once they had collected the animals and themselves somewhat, they rode cautiously back down the trail, looking for the others. Shirley's ample face showed wholehearted relief when she saw Gigi and Cally safe, neither thrown by their horses nor savaged by anything weird and unaccountable. Elspeth, as usual, showed nothing, but she said, without embroidery, "Hoadley babies."

The others all stared at her, and Cally cried out in the same aggrieved tone, "There aren't that many babies in Hoadley!"

"Dead ones. Out of the ground." Elspeth stared over their heads with the glaze of intuition in her eyes. "Aren't the dead supposed to come up out of the ground?"

This came close to speaking something none of them wanted to say. Shirley gawked, and even Gigi seemed shaken. But Cally, oddly, turned suddenly serene. Death procedures were familiar footing to her.

"Not that way, they're not supposed to come up," she said.

"Well, that's the way I'd do it," said Elspeth with knife-edge of envy in her voice. And with a shadowed awe, the admiration of an artist for another—for a mystery artist, work exhibited but identity unknown. "If I were taking Hoadley down, I'd do it with a chorus, a swarming of the dead. That's just the way I'd do it."

Shirley said, "So who's doing it? A witch, or—or God, or what?"

"How the hell should I know?" Elspeth reverted to her customary peevishness. "And what the hell can it possibly matter?"

"It matters." Shirley tried, ineffectually, to explain herself. "It's not like we're just talking here. It's *happening*."

"We don't really know what's happening," said Cally.

"Don't we?" said Gigi.

The four horsewomen rode back to the stable in silence. Elspeth's sword chafed against her leg; she had not touched it since leaving the barn, and no one seemed to find it odd that she had not used it on anything, not even on blackberries.

There were plenty of dead babies in the ground around and under Hoadley. Aboriginal babies, among others. The town had been founded on blood-soaked ground. The first settlers, stalwart Pennsylvania Germans, had massacred or driven away all the savages they had found in the area, in retribution for an Indian raid (distant, probably by another tribe) on another frontier settlement. With the natives duly dispatched, they had set themselves to making the place a new Eden.

It was an Eden slow in coming, as the stony hills did not take well to farming. The growing season was short, the winters long, the labor hard. More babies died, babies white as wheat flour, joining the red ones under the ground: pale babies dead of pneumonia and "teething" and scarlet fever and "paralysis" and a hundred other diseases, and sometimes of starvation, neglect or abuse. Whole families died or moved to more fertile ground.

But wherever any folk at all remained, food had to be grown. By the nineteenth century, Eden had at last been established. Hoadley was a country village, an isolated hamlet, picturesquely located amid the Canadawa Range of the Appalachians on the banks of swift-flowing, crystalline Trout Creek; just below the village, the river plunged over fern-draped falls into a gorge that ran for a mile and a half, every inch of it lovely with moss and cliffside and huge old trees and leaf-sifted light on the sweet water. The place was known as far away as Pittsburgh as a beauty spot. An artist's colony of sorts became established there, and in the summer society people came to improve their minds in the peaceful contemplation of art, nature and each other. There were a few rooming houses, a general store, and one good hotel for the summer visitors, where downstairs the artists drank ale.

Then someone discovered coal.

Within the year the village had turned to a wildly thriving boom town, with new buildings thrown up daily as the mines bored down and the money flowed the way the stream once had. All the trees for miles were gone, cut down to make tipples and railroad ties and mine timbers, and the smoke of burning debris filled the air. Trout Creek ran choked with mud, its course diverted under new roads, around new buildings. Concrete supports stood atop the waterfall, carrying the black railroad bridge overhead. On every available inch of the valley the mine-town row houses were going up for the immigrant workers flooding in, the Irish, Italians, Poles, Lithuanians, Slavs, Greeks.

For fifty years Hoadley experienced unparalleled prosperity and appalling poverty. There were twelve tailors in what had once been the place where the road crossed the creek, and twenty barbers, and doctors and lawyers building great gingerbreaded houses on the hillsides only a little below the mansions of mine owners. In the row houses down below the tracks, down by the sulfurous stream, where the black bony piles shut out the air, lived the coal miners' women, the dun-skinned women the "natives" called "foreigners," barefoot women who sometimes out of desperation ended or hid their pregnancies, strangled their newborns, entombed tiny tan bodies in the walls.

Then the many-branched deep mines reached the end of the coal. And the mine barons moved out of the mansions on the hilltops, leaving behind miles of rusting railroad, acres of slag, row on row of sparrow-brown mine town houses beneath hills scrubby with second-growth woods. Trout Creek, orange and life-less with acid mine runoff. The waterfall and the gorge, junked with discarded machinery. The air, polluted enough to turn even new-fallen snow black with the smoke from the steel mills roaring farther down the valley.

Then the steel mills closed also, and the air, sul-lied only by house coal, was somewhat cleaner again (though not the earth or the creek), and half the row houses in Hoadley were boarded up and empty, and the people who remained supped deep of the mys-teries of Unemployment Compensation and Welfare and Food Stamps and Government Surplus Cheese. There was a flood like the wrath of God, coming to wash the refuse out of Trout Creek gorge. A dead baby floated down the bloated stream. The people who remained in Hoadley learned the ways of the Red Cross and Federal Disaster Aid. Rebuilding, they went about their business with cautious eyes and no poetry in their souls, not daring to hope in anything. These were the sons and daughters and grandsons and granddaughters of the Irish and Italian and Polish and Lithuanian and Slavic miners. Some few were the Pennsylvania German descendants of the the original settlers, and went to the Lutheran and Brethren churches instead of the many Roman Catholic ones, and gave themselves airs. But they all remembered a time when men had worked twelve hours a day in the dark and couldn't ever get ahead of the Godawful gouging rent, the constant debt at the overpriced company store. They remembered men dying under the guns and clubs of strikebreakers. They remembered men going berserk and killing their wives, each other, their babies. They remembered all the babies dead, the stillborn and those who lived a few days or years, all the little ones for whom there was seldom milk and sometimes no bread.

Much evil had been done in Hoadley.

A council of such cautious-eyed citizens met the fourth Thursday of May: the borough council sat at its regular monthly meeting. Seven men, mostly substantial and oviform, and two high-coiffed women in rhinestoned glasses sat around the long table. One of the women took notes. All church councils, school boards, library boards and such governing bodies in Hoadley had to include at least one woman to be secretary. Men, apparently, did not know how to write minutes, though they sometimes made coffee.

A motion had been proposed that an ordinance should be formulated to ban pit bull terriers from the borough. No one in the area owned such an animal, nor to any council member's knowledge did anyone in Hoadley plan to own a pit bull terrier, but a council has to have something to do at its monthly meetings. The motion had opened a far-ranging discussion on dogs and dog ownership, and the council was discussing the banning of chronically barking dogs, and how many woofs over what period of time defined the term "nuisance barking," when council president Gerald Wozny thought of yet another possible pet ordinance.

"What I mean," he said, "we ought to forbid dogs

and cats from defecating on anybody's property but their own. Their owner's, I mean."

"What about urinating?" one of the women, the one not taking notes, wanted to know.

"Defecating leaves a pile. Urinating don't matter."

"If it's on shrubs it does," challenged the woman. "Kills the shrubs."

"My neighbor's dog used to come and piss on my eggplants," complained the only thin man in the gathering. "Would you like to eat eggplants had a dog pee on them?"

"All right, then, defecating and urinating both. Producing bodily wastes. The dog or cat is only allowed to do it on their own—their owner's property. What do you say?"

The council was saved from discussion of the impact, constitutionality and enforceability of this proposal by a knock on the door. A tall, husky woman no one recognized came into the room, followed by a smaller young woman everyone knew by sight: the breedy oddball who rode her horse to the post office.

"Shirley Danyo here." The first one loudly announced the reason for her visit. "Me'n my friends want youse guys to know about some plenty strange things been going on."

Though Elspeth had come with Shirley, she did none of the talking. She stood by, quietly and contentedly conscious of her exotic beauty, as Shirley explained, in Shirley's own inimitably voluminous fashion, about her hex sign, the cicadas out of season, the naked fetch in the woods, the baby-faced bugs.

Without surprise Elspeth observed the council members glancing at each other, then growing too uncomfortable to glance at each other. They had, of course, already heard about the mysterious far-too-beautiful woman on the white horse. She had appeared again, on foot, at dusk, to speak to some ignorant people in Hoadley park. Tacitly the council had agreed to ignore her presence in favor of the more pressing problem of dog excrement. The national government could have learned from Hoadley natives; the latter had used censorship for generations. Entire scenes of Hoadley history had been erased from the books and had therefore never happened. Council discussions often went unnoted, to be denied if necessary. The woman on the white horse, undiscussed, therefore did not exist.

Instinctively, then, the members of the council did not want to hear any of what this fool Danyo was saying. They rooted their hind ends deeper into their chairs, stared down at their hands and composed elaborate arrangements with their fingers. The president poked discreetly at nose and ears with his pinkie, finding nothing to distract him from his ordeal. Danyo had to be a jackass, a screwball at best, and at worst downright dangerous to say such things.

Knowing that Shirley had never been afraid of being considered a nuthead, Elspeth allowed herself to feel darkly amused.

"What I mean," Shirley concluded earnestly, "it looks like the end of the world, unnatural things happening."

"We were discussing business before you came in," hinted the council president.

"I won't take but a minute longer. What I wanted to say, what if it ain't God? What if it's a witch? If that's what it is, youse guys ought to be able to stop it."

A few of the council members actually blushed, as if Shirley had ripped open her work shirt and exposed her breasts. All except the woman taking notes looked profoundly discomfited. The latter (Zephyr

Zook by name), as secretary, found Shirley somewhat more bearable and less offensive to her sense of parliamentary procedure than President Wozny.

"Ahhh—we will refer your concerns to the appropriate departments," said that gentleman, and he got up and laid a hand on Shirley's elbow, as if he could steer her out of the room that way. Shirley looked down at him, and he removed the hand.

Elspeth spoke for the first time, with wry pride in her voice. "C'mon, Shirl. These people have other business to discuss."

Shirley acknowledged Elspeth with a nod, then looked hard at Wozny. She was not stupid; she had known before she came that whatever she might say would do no good. But being Shirley, she had to try anyway. "Them was babies crying," she declared to the round man before her. "Ghost babies. Something's bothering their rest, I tell you." She left without waiting for a reply, and Elspeth left with her.

CHAPTER FIVE

I told you libraries is nice places. I ain't much of a reader, but after Joanie went away I started hanging around the Hoadley library anyways. It wasn't but a little ways from the funeral home down past the hardware store and a couple boarded-up stores and the Goodwill to where they'd put the library in another of them stores, and I'd go down there when I was done with the bodies. In there with all them books I felt like Joanie wasn't so far away. Anyways, old Beulah Coe the librarian knowed Joanie. I kept asking her if she'd seed her.

"Barry," she says, "you think she's folded herself up inside a book, or what?" But I still kept asking. I didn't know what else to do.

There was another boy, Garrett, hung around in there too. I guess he wasn't really a boy. He was a lot older than me, probably as old as my mom, but he didn't act old. He always brought lots of dominoes with him in his pockets, and he'd pull them out and set them all up on their ends on the big library table, around and around in circles. He'd take maybe a couple hours doing it. And then he'd take and touch one and knock them all down in a minute. It was real pretty to watch, the way they all rippled down. Sometimes he let me touch the one to knock them down. Or he'd let the little kids that come in the library do it. He liked it when the little kids paid attention to him. That was all he come for, was to set up his dominoes and knock them down and make them do flips and like that. He was real smart with dominoes. Other than that he was dumb like me. The little kids liked him because he looked normal except his head was big. That seemed funny to me, that Garrett was dumb like me with his head as big as it was. A person would think he should have been smart. But his face looked okay and he set his dominoes up good so the little kids liked him. They was scared of me because my face was marked up and ugly.

Garrett and me talked sometimes, hanging around the library, and when he found out I worked for Mr. Wilmore he started making dumb undertaker jokes. "Hey, Barry," he'd say, "how's business up there? Dead, huh? Going in the hole?" And then he'd hee-haw laugh. "Hey, Barry. Didja hear the one about the undertaker had two bodies at once, a bank president and a lawyer? And he got them in the wrong caskets? And when the families complained, he said he'd switch them? And in them three-piece suits nobody ever noticed he just switched the heads?" Hee-haw, hee-haw. "Hey, Barry. Didja hear the one about the undertaker got married? And on his wedding night he told his bride take off all her clothes, but he couldn't get it up? So he told her go in the bathroom and get in a tub of cold water for a while, and when she came back to bed she should just close

her eyes and lie real still?" Garret snorted when he
laughed, too, in between hee-haws.

He tried to call me "Digger," too, but that didn't
work because I didn't dig graves. They got backhoes
to do that. It didn't make me mad none, the way he
talked about undertakers. Mr. Wilmore was a funeral
director, and funeral directors is different from
undertakers.

So I talked to Garret different times, and I'm glad
I did, because I guess I must have told him about
Joanie, and he's the one told me to go see Ahira.

"You gotta go look at her," he says. "She'll get
your mind off that Musser girl." And he laughs like
he said something smart.

"I don't want my mind off Joanie," I says.

"Then go and ask her about your sweetie, for
crying out loud, and quit asking everybody else."

Ahira knowed about stuff like that, he says.

So I went that night. Garrett told me where. There
was this little park between the post office and the
bank, don't hardly deserve to be called a park, just a
patch of grass and a couple benches for the old
geezers to loaf on and a statue of some army guy on a
horse. But there was this little round building there
too, sort of a picnic pavilion, pointed like a circus
tent only it was made of wood. Every year at Christmas the town put lights on it, and it looked real
pretty, like a carnival ride. Except they always forgot
to take them down till about the fourth of July, so
half the rest of the time it looked dumb.

Anyways, this was May, and the lights was still
hanging on the bandstand—people called it the bandstand, but Joanie always said that wasn't what it was,
it was a gazebo, but I never heard nobody else say
gazebo, but I never seed no band on it neither—
only them lights wasn't lit, and they looked dumb.

They looked like that junk old ladies hang around the tops of their porches. But Garrett says this is the place where Ahira comes every night.

So I hung around, and after a while she come. And as soon as I seen her I knowed she was the one Mrs. Wilmore kept talking about, the lady on the white horse. She didn't have no horse with her, but no two people in Hoadley could be that beautiful.

She come at dusk, in a white dress down to her feet and kind of floating around her, and her hair was down her back and lifting like soft yellow wings each side of her face, so she come like a white-and-yellow butterfly. And her feet was bare, and just as beautiful as the rest of her. Don't ask me how that could be so, because feet is generally ugly, but hers was nice. And her face was beautiful like an old painting, wide at the top where her big eyes was, then coming down to a little chin, like her face was a heart. But strong. Like them schoolbook pictures of Joan of Arc or somebody. And her mouth was full and sweet-looking and real still. Right away, before she even opened her mouth to talk, I felt like she was somebody who *knowed*, just from looking at her. Not just thought she knowed, but really knowed, like God.

She went up there on that bandstand, and there was already people standing around waiting for her down below, like Garrett and me, and she called out over our heads, "Misfits! Come to me! All you people who sleep alone and fondle yourselves and have messy dreams in the night, come to me! All you bent-out-of-shape, stomped-on people, all you thumb-suckers, bed-wetters, the ones the world looks down on, come here; I am Ahira, and I want you."

And they come, too, more every minute. I hadn't thought till then how many freaky people like me there was in Hoadley, because we mostly all hid ourselves away. But they come out that night, like bats coming out in the dusk, out of places can't nobody believe, them little narrow places under the eaves. There was the old woman who always smelled like a hamster, and the skinny one whose back was so bent she looked at the ground all the time when she walked, and her head went back and forth like she was sniffing her way with it. She had to sit down on the ground to look up at Ahira. And there was the man who walked on the stumps of his legs and wore big leather feet on them, like elephant feet. And there was the blind guy with the paper bag on his head. His face looked okay, not ugly like mine, but he hardly ever showed it, only on real hot days. Most of the time he kept a paper bag on. I guess it didn't make no difference to him if he had a paper bag on his head. I guess he wore it to keep warm.

And there was all the ones that picked their noses and pulled out big wet boogers in public and talked to themselves and wore stripes with plaids. There was people with crooked teeth long and gappy like fence pickets and breath like hound dogs been eating road kills. There was a woman so fat I guess she couldn't go to movies no more, and the bald girl who went to the high school. She'd got cancer and lost her hair, and the kids was mean to her, kept stealing her wig until she didn't bother wearing it no more. I guessed soon as she could she'd quit school, like Joanie and me done. I wished Joanie was there. She should've seed it, all those people misfits like her and me. It made me all excited that there was so many of us. I felt almost sort of proud and strong, like we could have done something.

"Misfits, come to me!" this Ahira woman calls out to Hoadley. "All you others, stay away! No people with second homes and tax shelters allowed here. No fat-ass bankers, no lawyers, no preacher men with nicey-smiles on their faces and larceny in their hearts, no housemamas serving up green vegetables and guilt. None of you people in designer clothes here. All you ones who think you've got it made, go away! Ahira doesn't want you."

Nobody went away, even though there was some people there looked normal to me. There was a couple young guys in long hair and jean jackets and tattoos and earrings, and some just regular fat people, and even the pretty blond girl with the cast-iron eyelashes from down at the drugstore. What she was doing there I didn't know. Maybe it was some sort of disease, made her do that to her eyelashes. Then I started to think, maybe some of the normals was misfits too, inside where it didn't show, instead of on their faces like me.

"Misfits," says Ahira to all of us listening, "I am a misfit too."

She was, sort of. She was too beautiful for a regular person.

"I am Ahira, child of the sun, and Estrella, daughter of the stars, and Amaris, moon child, and Anona, born of the earth. The people with big cars and swimming pools, none of them know me."

Then she started telling us what was going to happen, and just listening to her voice I knowed it was all the truth.

She said the people who thought they were big was going to find out what it was like to be small. She said the ones who beat us to death with their Bibles was going to find out what was really in the Bible. She said if they knowed the secrets, a misfit could do healing better than any preacher who ever lived. She said strange things were going to happen as a sign that we should listen to her.

Her voice was like them blankets in the funeral home, silky with just enough roughness to make it warm. I could've listened to her forever.

She said for us not to be afraid, because we was her misfits and she'd never hurt us. Then all of a sudden that gazebo thing she was standing on started to move, spin around, and them stupid Christmas lights flashed on all green and red and yellow, up and down the poles and around the circle roof and up in candy stripes to the point where the metal-horse weathervane was, and there Ahira stood on the bandstand going to town like a merry-go-round, but she didn't move. She was like a real still, white-and-gold place in the middle of it, and it was going crazy all around her. And the crowd was yelling, and some of them was falling down like Garrett's dominoes, except he hadn't pushed them none. He was standing next to me shaking and gaping like I was. I guessed this Ahira woman hadn't made the bandstand spin before.

Then she lifted up her arms like wings, just about the time I thought Garrett would pee his pants, and that merry-go-round stuff stopped, though them lights was still on.

Ahira says, "Listen to me, misfits. You are my people. You are my family, and I love you. There are six hundred sixty-six of you in this town, and I am going to find you, and not many days after I have found the last one of you the great backturning will begin. And every one of you will wear my mark."

Then it seemed to me that she looked straight at me. But them big, greeny-dark eyes of hers, it seemed like you always felt them. They latched onto a person like her voice.

She says, "On that day I will come gather you, and I will take you to the good place where the world began, the spinning place, while the rest of them go down into the pit."

Then she closed her eyes, but even when her eyes was closed I felt like she was still looking at me and holding me that way. And she started to say words like out of the Bible, but they wasn't no Bible words I have ever heard. They was from something she called Yeats. She says:

"I hear the Shadowy Horses, their long manes a-shake,

"Their hoofs heavy with tumult, their eyes glimmering white;

". . . The West weeps in pale dew and sighs passing away . . .

"The Horses of Disaster plunge in the heavy clay."

She didn't open her eyes when she was done, she stood like she was dreaming, but she lifts her hands like to tell us that was all. Some in the crowd was going away, and some was heading towards her.

Garrett says to me, "Go ask her about your Joan girl."

I says, "No," because something is bothering me and I don't know what it is yet. So I turned around and went on home.

One thing I saw when I was leaving: that sort of black girl, the one that rides into Hoadley on her horse, standing there in her funny clothes staring, not going away or going to say hi to Ahira either. She was one of the misfits all right, I figured, on account of her being the only halfway-black person in Hoadley. This town got a Jew or two, but no blacks except this one. But she didn't look happy about being there with us other misfits. Course she didn't hardly never look happy, even though she was so beautiful, most as beautiful as Ahira, except dark like creek water and Ahira was all milky pale.

So I went and drove my Chevy out them black, twisty country roads, not trying to think, because that don't never work for me anyways, but just waiting, because I knowed something was coming. When I got home my mom and dad was in bed, but my brothers was still up, and they teased me some when I come in. "Where you been?" they says. "You got a girl? About time you had yourself some fun." And I looks at them and wonders if they're like me or if they're what Joanie would've called normals, what Ahira called "the others," and I guessed that's what they was.

I went to bed and laid there in the dark and sort of dreamed about Ahira, and Joanie, and asking Ahira about Joanie, and Joanie and Ahira, and the darkness over the bed looked like it was spinning around, 'cept that was stupid. Darkness can't spin.

Mark Wilmore came back from his most recent burial and post-funeral social to find that Cally had put the kids to bed early and was waiting for him in the apartment, wanting to talk. At the sight of her he felt a spurt of anger, quickly smothered and quite inadmissible, since all was as it should be: she depended on him, and she had patiently waited until he was free to turn his attention to her. Why, then, did the deer-eyed look on her thin, boyish face annoy him? She did what a wife should do; she was exactly what a wife should be.

Nevertheless, he shouldered past her toward the bedroom, saying, "Let me get out of this damn pimp suit, Cal."

The three-piece, dove-gray wool flannel suits he

wore for funerals resembled those worn by top-flight procurers in the cities, especially when combined with a fawn-colored greatcoat. The irony was not lost on Mark and Cally, though likely no one else in Hoadley knew or cared; but he wore the expensive neutrals because he would not wear the black "preacher suits" of the older death specialists or the navy-blue polyester pinstripes of those who exhibited less taste than he.

Cally followed him and perched on the bed. Carefully hanging the suit, standing in his jockey shorts, he remarked to her, "I hate it when it's babies. Everybody feels so bad. I dread doing babies worse than anything else except maybe burn victims."

"I forgot it was a baby," Cally said.

The Bender baby, born with multiple defects, and nobody had expected it to live as long as it had: five days.

"Another Hoadley baby," said Cally faintly, "in the ground." A strange thing to say: Mark saw how she swallowed hard, as if swallowing at the words, and how the effort convulsed her throat. Such a frail flower-stem of a throat, he noticed wearily; he could have put one hand all the way around it, and sometimes he would have liked to, put one hand there and choke her. . . . He could see her searching her mind for something nice, wifely to say to him. But the best she could come up with was, "Did the family like the layout?"

"I guess they were satisfied. The mother said something about the blanket."

Barry had done well with the blanket. Half-a-brain Barry Beal, that was another one he sometimes wanted to choke, just to shut him up from always asking about that pitiful Musser girl. But it would have taken more than choking to silence Barry. An ax, maybe.

"Did the service go smoothly?"

"Fine."

She was a good wife. She was a good wife. Why did he feel so irritated at her when she was such a good wife? It did not occur to Mark to connect this phenomenon with his loathing of his mother. He considered that a discrete difficulty between Ma and him, and his mother's fault, because she happened to be whining, back-stabbing, manipulative and a martyr. He had never wondered how she got that way. He had not had occasion to notice that most of his mother's female peers exhibited the same unattractive traits when in the bosoms of their families. But as a young man he had seen with a lover's leaping joy how utterly different Cally was from his mother—at least, had been until he married her and brought her home to Hoadley. . . .

Most of his life, as far back as he could remember, Mark had wanted to run a funeral establishment. At the age of five or six, going from his linoleum-and-Lysol home into the hushed, thick-carpeted, high-ceilinged, swagged-damask-and-pilaster-heavy sanctuary of the former Lentz Funeral Parlor for the viewing of a great-aunt, he had known at once that this, this velvety-rich, flower-scented dimness and elegance and ritual, this was where he belonged. As a teenager he had gone to work for old Lentz and spied on some of the mysteries of the embalming room; they had not troubled him any more than the dissecting of a frog in biology class, heady with the odor of formaldehyde, had bothered him. Dead humans were not very different from dead frogs; he could handle dead humans. And he had liked the idea of service, heroism in fact, of being of use to people who needed him at a difficult time, almost as much as he liked the gold-flocked wallpaper and the thick tassels on the fringed and scalloped window blinds. He had prevailed upon his parents to send him to the Pittsburgh Institute of Mortuary Science for education; they had borrowed from the bank, and his father had worked extra shifts to pay the way. It was in Pittsburgh that he had met Cally.

By a marvelously romantic accident they had met; she had literally fallen at his feet on a slippery campus sidewalk and sprained her ankle. Mark had picked up her dropped books, helped her to the infirmary, sat with her while she waited. Hoadley men, at least those who didn't drink themselves silly every weekend, thought of themselves as protectors, defenders, strong providers for women and children; this mindset ran so deep in Mark that he accepted it without being conscious of it, as a premise and essential of male existence, like wet dreams. Atop it he had added his own bright myth of Mark as hero, helper, friend in time of trouble and death. He had fallen in love at once with Cally, with her childlike good looks, her helplessness. Yet what he liked even more in a way was her spirit, that she sometimes slapped away his hands from her books and crutches and her life, that she never thanked him. That she wore boots and jeans and went her own way, and saw him only when she wanted to, even after she agreed to marry him.

She still wore boots and went her own way, on horseback—though Mark had insisted on a safe horse and proper headgear, as befit his role of concerned protector. She sometimes refused to wait on him or the kids at mealtimes. She still protested when he became officious, as he knew he often did. Yet in a deeper way. . . . Something essential had changed, and not for the better, once he had married her. Once he had brought her home to Hoadley.

He did not question the pattern of life that had brought him back there. Of course he had come back to Hoadley. It was unthinkable to go anywhere else. His parents were there, his family was there. Family above all else; this credo of duty had echoed through his childhood to the determined exclusion of all siren songs of Elsewhere.

Nor did he ever question the idea of marriage. Like newlyweds everywhere, he and Cally after the wedding had at once discarded the fatiguing intensities of courtship and begun to imitate the marriages of their parents. There was little in her parents for Cally to build on, but Mark admired his hard-working father for the most part. He acted toward Cally as his father acted toward his mother: strong, protective, working hard to provide.

God, he felt tired.

"So, Cal," he said, sitting down on the bed, "what's up?"

"Cicadas, mostly. Up in the trees." She ducked her head like a five-year-old about to bare her heart. "Listen, Mark. There's something scary in the air around here."

"Spooks?" he teased. "Somebody been telling ghost stories?"

"I'm serious. Strange things have been happening."

She told him, in a disjointed, fumbling way, picking at blanket fuzz with thin fingers—it was hard to believe that this hesitant woman was the person who had taken the Expository Essay Prize her senior year. Mark listened, hearing all the words yet absorbing only snatches of the meaning. A naked man in the woods—an exhibitionist, a sexual pervert, a danger to her? Should he forbid her to ride there? A changing picture—superstitious nonsense. Somebody had imagined something. When Cally was upset, she was quick to draw confusions. . . . Bugs with baby faces—more excited imaginings. The strange woman on the white horse, Ahira—a crackpot. Everyone had been talking about her, and he didn't want to hear any more conjectures. He didn't want to hear any part of what Cally was saying, and so in a sense he did not, although he listened and nodded until she faltered to a stop.

"What are you getting at, honey?"

She hesitated, then forced out words. "I think—I think it's just what Mr. Zankowski said, Mark."

He saw her soft mouth shaking, a subtle tremor barely visible above her chin. He saw how the bone showed white through her taut face, through her twiggy hands now lying clenched in her lap. He remembered briefly, though not in any felt way, how he had once desired that ever-so-slightly pouting mouth, that gamin face, those hands, back when they were younger, before he felt so tired all the time. The memory softened the scorn in his voice.

"For God's sake, Cal. The end of the world?"

"Something like that, yes."

Her seriousness, her fear, thrust him into the role of strong protector and made him feel simultaneously exasperated, superior and amused. "Why in the name of heaven would the world want to end in Hoadley?"

"Why not?"

Mark snorted. On the water tower looming above the town somebody had once spray-painted, black on the blue metal, "Everybody knows this is nowhere," and truer graffiti had never been vandalized onto public property. Everybody did know that. Mark, the native, knew it; the knowledge informed the loyalty and inverse pride that had drawn him back to the place where he was needed. Why couldn't Cally, the outsider, know it too?

Cally said, "I don't know why it's happening here. But the point is, something weird is going on—"

"Millennial fever. They're trying to downplay it, but it's going on everywhere." Mark listened to the government-censored news reports from the outside world.

"What's going on here is more than just people's imaginings, Mark! Do you think I'm imagining things?"

Yes, he wanted to say. It was the easiest thing for him to think, and he saw no reason not to. He had not known Cally to be irrational in the past, but, well, she was a woman, after all. Nearly every woman he had ever known in Hoadley had "nerves." And ever since she had had the kids, Cally had been wired too tight. It was good for her to get out of the house on that horse of hers. When she was home she hovered around the apartment with that haggard face, those bony, shaking hands. . . . Mark knew she didn't eat right, but it did not occur to him that she was starving herself. So she didn't eat much at meals; his mother had never eaten at meals. She had "snitched" in the kitchen all the rest of the time, and got fat. Women were strange. Like an alien species, almost. They didn't think like men.

So to be honest he should say yes, he thought she was imagining things. But then she would be angry at him. His father would have said yes, would have teased, would have told her she was cute when she was angry. But Mark didn't feel he had the energy. He was tired. People had been crying on his shoulder all day. Most likely more people would come and cry on his shoulder tomorrow. God knew there were enough poor souls in this town.

He said with a more than a little edge in his voice, "What do you want me to do about it?"

It went without saying that she wanted him to do something about it. That was his function in life, to comfort the weeping, take care of the details, serve on the church council, join the Jaycees, do things for other people—and then for her yet. But that was the hell of it, she was entitled to expect it of him. He was her man, her defender, her protector, and he should have said, Sure, I'll look into it, it'll be all right, I'll take care of it. She just shouldn't have talked to him about it at bedtime, was all. She knew he was always tired at bedtime.

"What do you want me to do about it?"

She shook her head, looking at him with a flash of white in her eyes, sensing his mood. Wouldn't tell him, or didn't know, and that irritated him more. She said, "Nothing. Forget it. Let's go to bed. We can talk about it in the morning."

Great. He had that to look forward to, then. And in the bed, she would want him to do something, too. And he wasn't going to.

Cally rode alone the next day, with a purpose in mind. She was not afraid of the cicadas, she decided, though if their wailing voices advertised their presence, she would stay away from them as best she could—but ride she must. If Mark was not going to look for answers, she would. For that reason, and perhaps for others, she wanted to see the naked whatever-he-was again.

She rode to the mine tipple first. As she had hoped, Mr. Zankowski was not at the shack; he spent most of his time down in the mine, puttering with his unreliable machinery. But the black snake lay on its sunlit stone by the door, near a chipped china bowl of yellowing milk. With irrational sureness Cally got down from Dove and picked up the snake—her hands for once quiet, steady, soothing, for she was going on her own to do something, an action more calming and buoying than any drug a fatherly Hoadley doctor could give her. She draped the snake around her shoulders as she mounted Dove, then rearranged it so that it rode on her left arm, where she could best observe it. All of this the snake placidly accepted, for there was a hypnotic confidence in her touch. She had had a dream, or a half-waking insight in the very early morning, to tell her how this project had to be carried out.

She said to the reptile, "Show me where he is," and it lifted its lean black head and pointed the way.

She rode. The snake guided her. Down in a valley-bottom hollow hidden by maple saplings (their bark thinly striped like mint candy), amid the parasol leaves and white-cup blossoms of mayapple, she found him.

He sat naked, partly hidden by the mayapple leaves and nearly as buttercream-white as its flowers. She looked down on him from Dove's back and said to him, "I want you to tell me what's going on."

He said, "That is not all you want, or lack."

His voice, dusky and liquid and prickly, like the taste of whiskey. On Cally's arm, the snake raised its head. Under the mayapple (lime-green luncheon-plate leaves), another blunt head roused, raised. Without seeing Cally knew, for she felt the liquor of his voice warming its way through her.

He said, "Come here."

She got down, let Dove wander off to browse, let the snake slither off her arm to disappear into the ferns surrounding the hollow. The one with a body too beautiful for words awaited her. He was right;

this was what she had come for, in part. Mark . . . she remembered how only a few years before Mark had devoured her presence, her conversation, her availability, sometimes mouthing her body inch by sweet inch with the same concentrated attention he now gave to devouring peanuts in front of TV football on Sunday afternoons. If Mark would no longer eat of her, would no longer give her what she wanted, needed, hungered for, then by damnation, by whatever force was moving in her world, she knew one who would.

She turned, looked at him. Calm and confidence left her, and she shook. Just to look at him was to feel the tingling whiskey-rush from her breasts to her crotch, feel wet, feel the black hole that was Cally yearn for him. He was the white thing that might fill her, white as sunlight, white as half-sucked Christmas candy. He was—what was he?

"Where did you come from?" she whispered to him. "What is your name?"

In an easy movement he stood up to talk with her, muscular and unblushing, a parody of parlor courtesy. She stared. He—or the part of him that defined her perception of him—it was colossal, magnificent, fit for a god. Her mouth moved, spasming. She felt herself ready to implode with desire for him.

"You name me," he said.

"You don't have a name?"

"She wouldn't name me. She made me and she is frightened of me. She will not come to me. You come to me."

She went; she could not wait any longer or think any longer of the answers to her questions. She went, and he opened her shirt, caressed her only briefly before he pulled down her riding breeches and laid her in the mayapple. Vivid spring-green shade on her face, sweet cream in her mouth, in her mind taste of *crème de menthe*, no, absinthe. By midsummer, the milk-white blossoms would bear pepper-red, plump round poisonous fruits. . . . It was very quick, over in the duration of one deep kiss. She did not care. She knew she was too achingly empty, too hungry, too starving, for anything else, even had he wished to play. Which she doubted. He serviced her, nothing more.

She looked up at him, clear-eyed, a moment after the climax. "Eros," she named him.

"As you wish," he said. He got up and slipped off like a wild thing into the scrub woods, leaving her there.

An hour of searching later, she knew to her heartfelt chagrin that Dove, also, had gone back to the stable and left her stranded. Wobbling up the steep trails in her riding boots—not meant for hiking, those boots, they chafed both at heel and behind the knee—passing cicadas in the underbrush, hearing them snickering at her, she knew herself for a pitiful, wantlove object. True, she had been filled by the phallus of a god. She felt—replete in body, one small, dark portion of her body—but ravenous as ever, elsewise, wailing like the hungerbugs. . . . Eros could not fill her. He did not—he did not care about her. She knew somehow that what this—this bizarre stranger had done for her, he would have done for, or to, anyone of her gender.

"Thin," he had remarked to her at one point. "You are very thin." That, at least, she could cling to; she took it as a compliment.

Sleeping next to weary, indifferent Mark that night, Cally dreamed of the naked youth in the woods, at first of his effortlessly potent and pleasing body, vividly recalled, and later, more serenely, of his face.

To which she had paid little attention at the time. . . .

She awoke with a gasp and a shock of recognition. The face, handsome, no, more than handsome; strong-featured and poignant of pale skin and eerily beautiful: it could have been, in some unblemished other-world, the face of Barry Beal.

CHAPTER SIX

Elspeth thought of herself as a small animal peering from the thickets with wide eyes, a butterfly drifting on the winds with sensors fully extruded, nothing more. Therefore it did not trouble her that she did not know how to side in the holocaust Ahira was brewing. She had never in her life chosen a position or a direction. She was the artist, all eyes, focus, observation and waiting; neutral, like a small country in a great war. If she wore a sword, it was for—for . . .

For blackberries.

She turned her mind away from the uncomfortable thought of the sword (a thought often lurking in her mind, just beneath consciousness, just beyond seeing, as if under the shimmering surface of deep water) to watching. She was herself all shimmer and shine, she thought, a polished shield reflecting the world back to itself, of the one who crouched behind the shield showing nothing; she did not perceive how much she revealed through her art and her own silence.

Observing, she stood in the stable aisle in swordbelt

and indigo tights and leather jerkin and a tunic of her favorite color, crimson: ready to ride, holding Warrior by the reins and watching the way the slanting sunlight through the doorway struck the hay-colored stable dust and the gray cobwebs, and watching the others. Principally watching Cally, as always. Something about Cally . . . Not sexual, either, for sure not in the least, not in that toothpick, but there was something. . . . Most of the time Elspeth wondered why she bothered thinking about Cally. But the skinny wimp was worth watching today. Cally was mad.

"I could kill!"

"I always said," Gigi remarked, "when it came to Homer, I never considered divorce. Homicide, often, but never divorce."

"Does Homer treat you like you're stupid?"

Gigi retorted, "Was there ever a man who didn't kiss himself?" At Gigi's elbow, Shirley stirred uncomfortably. Uncomfortable about the quarreling tone of the conversation, probably. But Elspeth didn't mind. Cally, the little nerd, it was fun to see her so furious. Her bony hands were shaking so that she could not tighten her saddle girth. She gave it up and stood gesticulating.

"I don't know. I thought when we first talked about it—Mark wasn't too bad. I just thought he didn't understand. But now he as much as tells me I'm feeble-minded. Me, the lame brain, the airhead, the dumb broad who got him A's in all his courses, did his reading and his papers as well as my own. Finally this morning I really got mad—"

Cally choked up and couldn't talk any more. One of her windmilling hands hit Dove in the face, and the gentle, dun-colored mare spooked, rearing against her tie ropes. Shirley stepped forward and caught her, quieted her and stood as silently as before.

"Don't that make you mad," said Gigi with wry tenderness, "when you cry?"

Cally found her voice. "It sure does! I could scream. When they're mad men can make all the noise in the world, but when I want to yell I always go and bawl."

"I used to do that too," said Gigi. "It's because you still love him." She spoke matter-of-factly, as if saying to a youngster, It's a phase, it'll pass.

Cally gawked at her a moment, then turned and ran, awkward in her high black boots, her small ass bobbing, ran outside and behind the barn to hide. Not in the least discomfited, Gigi turned and continued to tack up Snake Oil, and after a moment Shirley began to tighten Cally's girth for her.

"What do you think he called her?" Gigi addressed the silent barn. "Irrational? Hysterical? I know." She snapped her fingers with a dry sound, as if bones instead of flesh had clicked together. "He told her she was cute when she was angry."

Elspeth, contentedly watching, saw how Shirley glanced up at Gigi with an uncharacteristically tense and grim and puzzled look, saw the fine lights in Shirley's brass-colored hair, saw the soft line of Shirley's big breasts, and of Shirley's feelings understood only the puzzlement, which she felt herself. Was Gigi a normal or not? Elspeth comprehended in an artist's slantwise way what a normal was. Enlightenment had come to her in the post office a few days before, as she had stood in line to buy stamps. Ahead of her, bullying the clerk, had been an overweight woman wearing a crocheted hat even in the warm May weather, a warty, whiny, gossipy older woman like hundreds Elspeth had seen before. *Somebody loves this woman*, Elspeth had thought unexpectedly. Her parents might yet be living and perhaps loved her. Probably her children loved her. Possibly even her husband loved her. If she had a dog, in all likelihood it loved her. According to the Christians, God loved her. The thought had caused Elspeth an astonishment which of course she could not show. So this was what it was to be normal! To be so sublimely unaesthetic, so far from beauty or perfection, so piggily wallowing in love . . .

But did anyone love Gigi?

Cally came back into the stable, face reddened and rubbed, looking nearly as repulsive as any woman Elspeth had ever seen in Hoadley. Perhaps Cally was a normal.

She stalked, black-booted and limpkin-like, to where Shirley stood bridling Dove for her, and glowered, and refused the reins Shirley offered.

"I loathe that horse!"

"Dove didn't do nothing to you," Shirley said, more serious than usual, and Cally quieted somewhat.

"What I mean is, Mark made me get her. She's not the kind of horse I wanted. Look at her!" Cally windmilled again. "It's a wonder she doesn't crawl instead of walk. She's a worm. And she's the same pukey color as my hair."

Elspeth laughed, a baiting laugh flung into the angry air of the stable. No one looked at her to either approve or reprove the laugh, not even Shirley. Elspeth felt cheated. She knew none of Shirley's stable boarders particularly liked her, but they all tolerated her because she was Shirley's—friend. "Friend" spoken with a leer. Was Shirley a misfit? If so, did Shirley's love count? Could it make her, Elspeth the exotic pet, a normal?

Gigi, the aged adolescent, said to Cally, "I told you how to get the horse you want. If you don't have cancer, I understand a nervous breakdown works just as well."

Shirley put in quickly, "What sort of horse do you want?"

"Anything that's not so damn safe." With that disclaimer, Cally took Dove's reins and headed outside. Gigi followed.

"Cally! You want to see something that's damn unsafe?" The older woman called.

Gigi knew of a horse they could all ride to see, across the paved road, farther away than they usually rode but not impossibly far. There would be roaring coal trucks on the road, and the drivers would jake-brake and blare their horns and yell obscenities, deliberately trying to scare the horses and send the women ass-over-teakettle. There would be hostile dogs and other obstacles as well; in Gigi's eyes Elspeth saw the manic sheen the old hot stuff always showed when she smelled a risk. And for once Cally's mood matched Gigi's. Shirley, who had some sense, mentioned the dangers, the uncertainties, but no one ever doubted she was coming. A misfit on horseback, she rode hatless, in jeans, in a western saddle on her big English-trained thoroughbred, and jumped fences like a wild Irishman, which she ineluctably was not. Shirley was—Shirley. She would come along to help the others out of whatever trouble they got themselves into.

Elspeth took no part in the discussion. She watched, serene in her certainty that whatever was decided would make no difference to her. She would ride along wherever, like a bright brown-and-crimson leaf on an autumn gale. The end of the world would make no difference to her.

So they rode off, the four horsewomen. The mount she wanted Cally to see, Gigi told them, was a renegade, and all the talk turned toward this rebel equine, this coal-black crossbred, this tall and hulking proud-cut gelding, utterly unreliable, with no further thought for the ominous events that had caused Cally to quarrel with her husband in the first place. No particular thought of danger from weird cicadas; it is the business of horsewomen to meet and overcome the dangers of the trail. No further talk of what action to take, how to resist or (in an uneasily remembered word) prepare. They were in a way powerful, in a way impotent. On horseback they would do what they had decided, on any given day, to do. Elsewhere and otherwise, they had done what was expected of women: they had spoken to their menfolk.

Mark had just had a death call when Cally got home. The day was taken up with the stricken family, arrangements and legalities, and he didn't get a chance to talk with his wife until late at night, down in the basement embalming room, where he had asked her to bring him some coffee while he processed the former Mr. Lehman.

The late hour, plus the routine, soothing procedure of transferring bodily fluids through the carotid artery, always made Mark feel relaxed at this time. Some of his best memories were of long talks with Cally through the embalming room door while the electric pump ran and a corpse pinked out. This night he especially wanted to talk with her. He was beginning to be worried about her, and lately his worry had expressed itself in irritation. He had said some things he knew must have hurt her. Normally he would never have called her stupid; he knew for a fact that she was smarter and more level-headed than most women. He had never noticed her to get carried away like his mother did. Even so, if he had to choose between believing there were baby-faced bugs haunting the woods outside Hoadley and believing that Cally was imagining things, he much preferred to believe the problem was with Cally.

Speak of angels. She brought his coffee to the door, and he had a look at how Mr. Lehman was progressing, then left the pump to do its work, stripped off his surgical gloves (a protection against AIDS and other diseases) and came and took the warm, steaming cup of affection from her, never guessing how she detested bringing it, how she perceived the act as servitude.

He was trying to think of something both witty and conciliatory to say, some sort of smiling semi-apology, not abject, not unmasculine, a Humphrey Bogart line, and he was slow about it. Cally spoke first.

"I got a new horse," she said.

Mark (only afterward realizing with disgust how much like his mother he had become) thought first of money. "How much?" he asked.

"Traded Dove."

His next thought was as his mother's would have been also. "Safe?"

Cally said flatly, "No." Echoes rang in that word as if in the depths of a mine pit, reverberations . . . Mark felt dizzied, as if facing a plunge. She was going off, Cally had slipped over the edge. . . . When he spoke—not for a few moments—it was softly, delicately, as if to a madwoman.

"Why not?"

"I want safe, I can go on a merry-go-round," Cally said. "I got the horse I want, and I got a job to pay for his keep."

"What!" This shook Mark closer to where he lived than the news of the unsafe horse. "What job?"

"Church secretary. I can do the typing here, in the evenings, and it'll pay for the horse board."

Mark knew what Hoadley would think: that Cally had taken a job because she mistrusted his ability to support her, she perhaps contemplated divorce. For the time being he stayed away from what he himself thought. Hoadley came first. "Honey," he protested, "what did you do that for? Business is good! I sold a sofa!"

(Though the days were gone when the sign over the door had read, "Funeral Parlor and Furniture Emporium," the tradition since the days of the first cabinetmakers/casketmakers/undertakers had been that "diggers" sold furniture, and tradition still held. Mark was able to furnish his viewing rooms in the sumptuous fashion of his childhood dreams by ordering wholesale and affixing price tags discreetly to all pieces. Mourners coming to pay last respects to the dead could console themselves between bouts of sorrow by peeking at the costs of end tables and lamps. Mark sold furniture between, and sometimes during, viewings. Hoadley admired his taste. The living rooms of many of the town's elite were furnished from his Blue Room, Peach Room and Rose Parlor.)

"The aubergine plush camelback," added Mark, watching anxiously for her smile, her pride in him. "More than makes up for what we didn't realize on that shoe-box infant's casket."

Cally said, "I don't care if you sold the whole place. This is my horse, Mark Wilmore, and it's going to be supported with my money so you can't say you gave it to me and you can't take it away."

Mark stared at her a moment, hoping he kept his face flat while the pyrotechnics popped and crackled inside his mind. Good God, what had he ever done but try to take care of her . . . ! He handed her his emptied coffee cup and went back into the embalming room to manipulate Mr. Lehman's extremities. He said to Cally, "Come here."

He imagined she blinked; this was different. Usually he made a policy of keeping her and the kids out of the embalming room, as a safety precaution against germs. And also, he admitted in his more contemplative moments, to preserve the integrity of his private turf.

She stepped to his side, silent, rather stiff; he knew she knew he was smoldering. Wordlessly he pointed at the dead man's face, erubescent but still ghastly above the tubes in its neck. "Lehman," said Cally. "I knew that." The man had been president of the First Bank of Hoadley, chair of his church property committee, one of the town's most solid citizens both physically and morally, an egg-shaped individual privately known in a few iconoclastic households as "pomposity on wheels" for his bicycle-riding proclivities during the past few years, his late-date attempt to strengthen a weakening heart. It would be a profitable funeral.

"Just checking," said Mark. "Look here."

He lifted Lehman's drape, taking care not to expose the man's genitals but revealing the swelling torso to below the waist. Cally gasped and clapped a hand to her mouth to stifle an undignified giggle. At least she wasn't too far gone to have a sense of humor. . . . Around and incorporating the navel of that important belly, where for years it had jiggled under all the white, starched Brooks Brothers shirts, was a tattoo. A large tattoo. A wonderful tattoo. Despite her restraining hand Cally burst out laughing.

"It's a—it's an asshole!" she cried.

Mark did not laugh. He had laughed earlier, though not to the widow's face when the woman had dolorously asked him if the work of art could be excised and preserved, by tanning perhaps, for her to frame and hang in her home as a memory of her departed Lester. He had excused himself and gone to laugh himself silly in his soundproofed private chapel. But now his straight, tight mouth felt no inclination to twitch, because he was angry with a very strengthening, satisfactory anger and it was time for the punch line, with a tough-guy Bogart delivery. "And an asshole," he said, "is exactly what you are acting like."

Cally's laughter stopped as if he had flicked a switch. She turned her back on him and pushed past the slab, out of the narrow room. Once beyond the door, she turned on him. "You aren't even trying to understand," she accused. "I need to do things on my own. I need to feel that I have some control."

"If the world is ending, the way you say," he shot back, "what can it possibly matter?"

She gave him a killing look and strode away in those damn black riding boots of hers, black as a wet coal pit in the dark of night. . . . Mark felt disappointed and uneasy; he had expected her to weep at him, but she did not cry.

Cally looked out the next morning on a town that seemed somehow ineffably changed to her, as irksome and familiar and as inexorably strange and distanced as the face of a doting old aunt once she is dead and laid out in hairdo and rouge and wedding gown. The water tower, its blue paint clashing with the chicken-soup colors of the polluted sky, seemed to crouch over Hoadley like a huge bulbous insect on spindly steel legs. Or like a light-bulb-shaped cartoon of a fat woman trying to get into a girdle. Or like a horse's behind, over its absurdly thin supports.

Cally had seen it every day for years, and on that morning it looked incomprehensible to her. And the two old slat-legged women down on the sidewalk, their oversized black granny shoes nearly longer than their flat skirts were wide—every fair-weather morning she saw them, sometimes in their almost-matching coral-pink raincoats, sometimes in their lacy cardigans and beige-print dusters, sometimes in their fake-fur headwarmers, never an exact match for each other but always close enough so that she knew they had consulted. She did not know who they were. On that morning, she did not know what they were. They might as well have been something from the zoo to her, rare oriental fluffhead cranes, no, something even more alien. As alien as the woman she had read about in the newspaper, who had been told by an unidentified man on the telephone that he could diagnose cancer if she held the receiver to her breast, and who had done so, while on the other end of the line the man had hummed contentedly . . . or as alien as the weirdo who had so harmlessly duped her.

For no reason Cally put on her best shirt, a polyester silk-look paisley print. "Mommy, you've got your fancy tadpoles on," Tammy said to her over sugar-frosted corn flakes at the kitchen table. "Where are you going?"

"To ride my new horse."

"New horse! What horse? When did you get him? Can we ride him?"

Mark, silently standing and drinking coffee by the counter, took his cup and left the room. Cally didn't care. He was a stranger, as inscrutable and out-of-focus as all the rest of the dying world, as alien as that other male, his fat-cheeked son Owen, sitting and making farting noises with his cereal-stuffed mouth. To Cally only Tammy seemed real: the little girl with a child's ethereal pathos of profile and the watercolor blue-gray hues, sky hues, in the whites of her eyes.

Because Cally was ravenous, she cooked a healthful scrambled-egg breakfast and made the children eat it. As soon as she had seen them off to school she went to the stable, far earlier than usual, leaving the breakfast dishes on the table, egg hardening on the plates and milk souring in the cereal bowls. With the same floating feeling, or lack of feeling, as when she had awoken she led the giant black horse from his stall, not reacting when he threatened her with bared teeth. Tazz Man, the seller had called him. Gigi had joked on the way home that it was short for Tasmanian Devil. Only the presence of the other horses had enabled Cally to ride him from one stable to the other. She had kept the name Devil for him. It seemed apt not merely for the black horse, but for her world and, indeed, her soul. The Devil had arrived. . . . She put the bridle on him, using the same snaffle bit, Dove's mild bit, that she knew he had utterly disregarded the day before.

As soon as she swung onto him he reared and lunged and rocketed into a headlong gallop, and with a rapt, faintly frowning look on her thin face she let him go. She was a passenger, nothing more. Perhaps mildly suicidal . . . but she would hang on, a child on a wild carnival ride, she would wait and see where he was taking her.

Down the steep, wooded slopes at the same racehorse pace . . . Baby-faced cicadas screamed in the trees. The screw-loose gelding plunged as much as ran, and Cally felt herself falling blind into the pit, her bony shoulders hunched over the black devil's neck and her head ducked to pass under tree limbs, her eyes shut, lids whipped by black mane; she didn't mind. The horse lost his footing, rebounded over boulders (the Mafia car, run off the cliff in the chase scene, about to burst into flames), took to the air for a moment, then righted himself and ran on. He hit the valley bottom like a ton of coal falling into a chute. But then his demented plunge altered to a steady, thudding gallop, and Cally lifted her head slightly, opened her eyes to find herself already passing beyond the trails she knew into strange terrain.

Devil ran like a black avalanche, black bowel-fire out of a volcano, a black sun exploding, and like the relentless passing of time he showed no signs of slowing down. Through a stony river, stream lifeless and rocks orange with mine waste. Up the steep rise on the other side, looking down at a tiny town Cally could not name, a cluster of houses trapped between river and wooded mountain, a place whose existence she had not suspected. . . . Atop the rise, shadowed by trees, the inevitable old cemetery, grass growing rank in hillocks, headstones leaning. Without hesitation the black monstrosity leaped the sparse ranks of bone-white stones, flying a man's height above them, like a huge flesh-eating bird, and glancing down Cally saw a flash of eyes meet hers; the sepia-toned photographs inset behind oval glass atop the headstones looked up at her, at the massive dark presence shutting out their eternal view of the sky, as if at the black belly of hell.

Then on in a flash of fear, through the heavy scent of white flowers, lovesick honeysuckle, plangent black raspberry, the white violets swooning amid the graves, the thick mock orange aroma wavering up like heat haze from the town below. Running . . . The black renegade hurtled Cally into wilderness again, onto a road overgrown with briar and poison, pressed narrow by ever-groping trees, a raised road that had once been graveled, once been going somewhere. . . . A fallen tree blocked the way, trunk huge by Hoadley standards. The black horse leaped it. Cally felt the ropy, exhausted muscles of her legs give up their struggle to keep a grip, felt her body lurch onto the horse's neck; in a moment she would hit the ground—

Devil slowed to a gentle, rocking canter, then a soft trot, then stopped within a few strides, pulled the reins from Cally's hand (fingers hardly thicker than soda straws) with a single casual jerk of his jaw, dropped his head and began to graze. Cally stared around her, then shakily got down and turned her back on the black horse without another thought for him.

Around her, what had once been a clearing, a park, studded now with half-grown trees. Silent. No hungerbugs up here. Rudimentary, boarded-up buildings stood among the treetrunks seemingly at random, shadowed by black locust, half-hidden by sumac. Shed-roofed edifices—Cally recognized them from country fairs, firemen's carnivals. Hot dogs and popcorn and vinegar fries and waffle-and-ice-cream sandwiches had once been sold here—her tortured stomach spasmed at the thought. And funnel cakes thick with powdered sugar, and whoopie pies, and hot pretzels . . .

And spins of a wheel of chance. She forced her thoughts and her wobbling, booted steps onward.

Beyond the small ones, a much larger building, rags of white paint still peeling from its graying sides. . . .

Cally walked closer. The building, round, or rather octagonal, rose to a single peak, like a circus tent. A sizeable padlock secured the door of the deserted structure, but it did not matter. Something had burst a hole in the nearest boarded-up side. Singed black, as if by an explosion, the wood lay splintered outward amid obscenities—vandals had at some time immortalized their obsessions on the plywood. "Bobie Jacobs eats cold weiners," "Mary Utz was laid here," and a detailed invitation to a lesbian act. Cally read it twice. It sounded good. Mark hadn't done anything like that for her in a long time. And the big dick, Eros, hadn't done it for her either. Though he might if she went back and asked him.

She wasn't going back. Her gut crawled with guilt at the thought, and all her anger at Mark blew away as if by a deep miner's dynamite blast, along with all her drifting detachment; she felt ready to bawl and run to him.

It was a baffling bond, marriage. She could not have sworn at that moment that she loved Mark. She knew only that he was mixed deep in her, deep, pretzeled into her insides, part of her, like bone marrow, like memories. That like sacramental wine on white linen he had stained her soul, never to wash out. That she would maybe hate him, but never be without him. He and she had long since become an us; he was always with her, a rider in her heart.

He was with her as she stood and read the graffiti. In her mind she could hear his reactions, his impatience as, with the compulsiveness characteristic of a former literature student, she read them all, every message that was still decipherable. In much the same way as she had given herself over to the black horse's ungovernable back she read them, looking for—something. Only when she was sure she had missed nothing, that there was nothing there for her, did she look onward again, set her booted foot through the shattered boarding and step—inside.

And then she felt her face being taken over by a wide, childish grin, because of all the horses.

In the shadows below that round roof, the bright-painted wooden ponies stood in ranks three deep, first the prancers, then the jumpers on their poles, motionless, yet always leaping, heads tossed high, mouths open in a soundless prophecy, eyes rolling, wooden manes always flying, hooves lifted. And the trappings, the delectable carved nonsense on their necks, their narrow bodies, their curving crests! Pomegranates clustering under the cantles of long, absurdly impractical saddles, cabbage roses cascading down brown flanks like confections on chocolate icing, and the candy-colored bas-relief ribbons. . . . As her eyes grew accustomed to the dim light and she could see where she was going, Cally stepped up onto the platform and moved from one carousel horse to another in delight, her bony hands reaching out to touch gilt angel wings clinging to shoulders, streaming manes, jeweled foreheads, the dusty carved stars and crescent man-in-the-moons ornamenting a caparison, a diabolical bat-winged gargoyle perched above a tail. Lollipop spangles, a delicious-looking pulled-taffy mane and another full of golden bells lured her from the chargers of the outer rank to the smaller, more graceful jumpers inside. Then she looked up, for her eyes, trained to read anything, saw words. On a panel of the inner cornice that covered the driving engine, at the hub of the machine, someone had fastened a sheet of heavy paper, hand-printed:

> So it must have been after the birth of the
>   simple light
> In the first, spinning place, the spellbound horses
>   walking warm
>   Out of the whinnying green stable
>   On to the fields of praise.

"Dylan Thomas," said Cally in wonder, her soft voice echoing inside the carousel pavilion. " 'Fern Hill.' Who the devil put that up there?"

Then she startled like a deer, and turned to look behind her as if expecting to see someone between her and the way out, a distant oblong of light. But between her and it stood only the dusty, shadowy, looming horses, eerie in the old-barn filtered light from cracked wallboards, wedding-cake horses with flanks iced with white lime; birds had been nesting in the place. Birds and other things, rodents, snakes perhaps . . . Sojourner Hieronymus said that nests of rattlesnakes lived in the hollow wooden bellies of carousel horses, ready to come out their gaping mouths like tongues of poison—

"Bullshit," Cally muttered to herself. Sojourner Hieronymus also said that snakes came up garbage disposals to hide in kitchen pantries behind the home-canned succotash. Sojourner was full of it. Nevertheless, Cally touched no more painted ponies. She looked around her, looked at the posted Dylan Thomas poem again; the paper on which it was calligraphed looked new. Who had put it there? Something larger and more human than birds and rodents had been nesting in that place. At her feet Cally saw a stash of store-brand peanut butter, bananas and Stroehman's Sunbeam bread. Blankets lay in a heap nearby. An old cardboard suitcase must have held someone's few belongings.

Cally saw the suitcase, took three steps to look closer. Her movement carried her in front of a mirrored panel, and the time-stained, glinting surface drew her glance—

She saw herself. Yet not herself—she saw a virtual skeleton wearing her clothing, her rich-looking paisley shirt, her sleek riding breeches, her black boots.

A skull-like head capped with her black riding hat and puke-colored hair peered out of the mirror at her. Her fingernails, painted Pepto-Bismol pink to please Mark, capped fingers gone nearly to whip-thin bone.

She jerked away and started back toward the hole in the wall in a tightly reined panic, snaking at a rapid walk between horses, careful not to touch any. Without really seeing them she passed a warlike mount in pseudo-medieval fish-scale armor, a gaudy pinto with gravy-yellow mane, a white—

Though nearly at her exit, she stopped and stared at the white, heavily-ornamented lead horse of the carousel, while a slow knowledge crawled through her. The maraschino-red caparison, the glass-jeweled breastplate with fringed and crenellated velvet flowing down, the spangled crupper, drapery upon drapery under the saddle—but it was not the trappings Cally recognized, or even the polished brass designation plate on the bridle, with its number—666. . . . It was the horse itself she knew. That straight, almond-eyed head, high-flexed neck, that short, level back and narrow body—she knew them. The horse she remembered had been warm, white hide over hard muscle; this one was white paint over wood. But they were the same.

It was the horse she had seen on Main Street, under a woman too beautiful to be real.

Slowly, calmly, almost dreamily, Cally turned and left the carousel, left the shattered building that sheltered it, walked out again into the late-May sunshine pooling like melted butter on the ground between cloud shadow and locust shade. The black horse she called her own was still grazing nearby, placid as an old plow nag. She went to him without hesitation, pulled his head up unceremoniously and mounted. "Devil," she said in the tone she used to her children when she expected to be obeyed, "get me out of here."

At a smooth, ground-covering walk he took her back the way they had come, down what had once been the trolley line, over the barricading tree in a high but easy leap, and along the steep ridge above the town: the town far from anywhere, huddled in its valley as if in a pit. As if the network of orange river, rust-brown railroads, slag dumps and potholed streets and power lines and drag lines and, underneath, deep mines—as if they had all snared it to hold it down, hold it fast. It still looked utterly strange to her from this unaccustomed vantage, but she knew it. The water tower crouched over it. In the winter the yellow cheap-coal smoke had hung heavy over the rooftops. Snow had sprawled black on the ground. Children had been beaten black as the snow. There might not be a winter to come.

Cally knew the name of the place now. It was Hoadley.

Mark knew he was getting old when he had to agree with his mother. When she put him onto something, even. But in this one isolated instance he had to admit she was right. "Anorexic," Ma Wilmore had declared to him over one of the hot, heavy lunches with which she periodically plied him. "Cally is getting to be one of them there anorexic nervosities." And looking back at his mother's round, detested face over reheated pot roast, Mark had felt it all click into place. A nervous disorder. Of course. That was why Cally had been acting so strangely. She was sick with an insidious disease.

It was imperative that she be made to get better.

He canceled his afternoon golf game to make the

arrangements. When Cally came home from riding, he was waiting for her, and he saw at once when she entered the apartment how tired she looked, and on edge, and so thin, so frail, and he felt guilt slosh through him; why had he not seen before that she was pitiable? Quickly he got up and went and hugged her, softly, carefully, as if hugging eggshell and not wanting it to break. She had been about to say something, but she blinked and accepted the hug instead. Surprised. God forgive him, how long had it been since he showed her he—he loved her?

"Cal," he told her huskily, "look. I got you a doctor's appointment." He stepped back enough to hand her the card. "I want you to go, get yourself fixed up. You're not well."

"What the—" She jerked away from his touch. "Mark Wilmore, you louse, how dare you? I don't need any doctor! Who the hell do you think you are? Stop trying to run my life!"

A shouting fit. It proved his point. "You're not yourself, Cal."

"Which fucking self is that!"

She was overreacting worse and worse. Gentle, kind, patient, and feeling better about himself, he tried reasoning with her. "Cal, just look in the mirror and see. You're nervous as a cat, and you're way too thin. When's the last time you ate?"

She quieted, or so he thought; he did not recognize her parody of his reasonable tone. "I'm on a diet. See? People don't eat as much when they're on a diet."

"You've dieted enough. You're turning into a skeleton."

She flinched as if he had struck her, then flared at him, "Fuck you, I am not!" She had never said anything that harsh to him. He could not help reacting almost as loudly.

"Quit the damn diet!"

"I will not! Since when do you tell me what to do with my own body?"

"Cally, go to the doctor, he'll tell you! You're anorexic."

"Right. Thank you, Hawkeye Pierce."

She didn't believe him. Maybe she wouldn't believe the doctor either. Mark felt fear start to gnaw. "Cal," he said softly, "anorexia can kill you."

She looked at him.

He said, "I'm really worried about you." He meant it, and made sure she could tell he meant it. Then, movie-star-style, he tried to lighten it into a joke. "Hey, Cal, I've got corpses enough downstairs. Got no desire for one up here."

"Mark," she told him, wearily but gently, "I'm fine. I'm not going to die. I just like being slim."

He said, "I've got no desire for a skeleton up here either."

It was the wrong thing to say, seemed to set her off for some reason. She glared at him, then stomped out. Dammit. A minute before, he knew, he'd had her almost talked into going to the doctor to reassure him.

She came back an hour later, with an armload of library books. That evening after dinner (of which she ate a little, grudgingly, to please him) and after the kids were in bed, she brandished one of the books at him.

"Read this. You'll see I don't fit the profile of an anorexic at all."

"You shouldn't try to diagnose yourself from a book, Cal." Immediately and guiltily realizing that he had done worse; he had diagnosed her from a comment of his mother's. Better never let her know that.

She went on, ignoring him. "It says here that an anorexic thinks about food compulsively. And I think about plenty of things beside food. And the encyclopedia entry says that anorexics don't feel hunger. But I'm hungry all the time."

"Shouldn't that tell you something?" said Mark mildly, immediately recognizing a mistake. Patient. He was going to have to be very patient, and practice his active listening skills with her, if he was going to get her anywhere at all.

She shot a sharp look at him, but continued. "Every one of these books says that an anorexic is stuck in childlike thinking and behavior. I am certainly not childish."

The heck you're not. But Mark restrained himself from saying it.

"Insecure. Attention-seeking. And overly compliant. I'm not any of those things."

He wished she were, in fact, a bit more compliant.

"The bottom line is, all these books say an anorexic is a browbeaten adolescent in hidden rebellion against her family. And I'm not an adolescent any more, my dad is dead and my mom is hundreds of miles from here."

"Cally," Mark said, "just go to the doctor. Please."

"Why waste my time?"

"Cal, please! Something's wrong." He humored her by deferring to her research. "If it's not anorexia, maybe it's something else. Something just as bad." He let his voice shake. "Cancer, maybe."

She had always yielded to him when he begged. . . . She stared at him, and he saw that he had scared and touched her. Then he saw a struggle he did not understand tightening the muscles of her lank face.

Face he no longer felt that he liked any too much . . . She was going to be stubborn again.

And he saw her decide against him. Just sheerly obstinate, like a kid. She wasn't going to do what he wanted her to. He knew it even before she said "No. It's my body, and I think it looks nice even if you don't, Mark Wilmore."

Tears, hot and angry. At least there were still tears in her.

CHAPTER SEVEN

My family always joked that when I was little my
Ma tried to clean my ears with one of them Kirby
vacuum cleaners with all the attachments and it sucked
the brains right out of me. I thought it was true for a
long time, but I didn't hold it against my Ma none.
She was always good to me. And she didn't do that
with the Kirby, I figured out when I was in high
school. I could figure things out if I cared. I had
brains. They was just real slow.

So the next time I go to hear Ahira, a couple
nights later, I was still waiting for whatever it was I
was trying to think about her.

So I was standing there with all them other misfits, bighead Garrett and the twitchy men who smelled
like garbage and the old women with mustaches and
the old guy they tooken to the hospital once for
something weird and the girl with green skin and all
the rest of them. We was all waiting for Ahira, just
like we was regular people who had a right to get
together and do things.

So Ahira come like she done before, in a long

white dress and all, and starts to talk to us like she done before, and her voice is silky warm, telling us we're her people and she loves us, and I'm standing there half believing her or at last wanting to believe her and half waiting and watching for something strange to happen, the bandstand to go around or something like it done last time, but what happens is that another different kind of misfit comes butting in from somewheres behind me and shoves his way to the front, and Ahira sees him and stops talking and gets this strange, quiet smile as if her lips ain't ever going to move again, and looks more beautiful than ever. It was that big-bellied, white-shirted asshole, the Reverent Culp.

I knowed just why Joanie always hated him so much. He was the sort of fat-ass always pushing himself forward, like he just done. And always thinks he's right, when most of us don't hardly never know when we're right about nothing.

And all the time he's bulling and pushing and shoving crippled people to the side he's yelling. "Antichrist!" he's yelling at Ahira. "False prophet! You are the beast out of the pit, the treacherous beast come to lead the people into captivity, the people of God down into perdition!"

And she's just standing in the bandstand and smiling at him, real still, and he's sweating and turning red above the tight collar and tie grabbing his neck under them three chins of his.

He yells at her, "Satan! Demon woman! Your appearance is fair, but your bowels are foul as the pit you wallow in! You look like a lamb and speak like a dragon and blaspheme the name of God! You come to kill with the sword. You come to whirl the world down to Armageddon!"

He run out of breath, standing at the bandstand

steps, ain't got enough breath left to take them, and he's lunging at the railings as if he wants to shake the place, standing at Ahira's feet, and she finally moves that quiet mouth and says to him, sweet as honey and just dripping with hate, "You're right, of course. You're always right. I am the Antichrist, and I have come to be worshipped and to destroy all you preachers."

Then all of a sudden his red face turns white like a john tank with the sweat still on it, and instead of shaking at the railings he's grabbing onto them to hold himself up, and Ahira says to him, almost friendly, "Why so sick? Armageddon is what you always wanted, isn't it? Don't you Christians say that after the end days comes the kingdom of God? Won't you get to go up to God in glory? Isn't your name written in a book somewhere?"

Then I wasn't looking at Reverent Culp no more. I looked back at Ahira, and something come together in my head, and I seen her different, and I seed who it was.

I just knowed, clear down to my bones. It was something about what she just said or the way she talked or moved her hands, the way her head tilted or something. You stay around somebody for a long time, you get a feel for them. Maybe it was her voice. She always had that classy voice, and it was just the same except that squashed-nose tone was gone. I don't remember no more of what she said, but I knowed it was her, right to my heart. Not no monster like Reverent Culp was trying to make out. It was Joanie Musser. My Joanie.

"It's her!" I yells out loud, and I was shoving forward just like Reverent Culp did. I almost yelled her name, but I knowed Joanie wouldn't like that. She wouldn't want nobody in that town to remember her the way she was before, not now that she was beautiful.

She hears me, and she sees me, and I guess maybe she thought I was saying she was the Antichrist. She smiles at me sort of soft and points me out to Reverent Culp, and she says to him, "There's one who already bears my mark."

He's still white like a china plate, and he just sort of slides down the railings and lays on the ground, and I knowed just looking at him that he was dead. I seen enough dead people, I should know. But Ahira talks to him like he was still alive. "I'm not surprised you knew me," she says to him. "You have always been good at recognizing demons. You should know the devil right away when you meet him."

The people in the crowd are sort of edging away, because they see Culp lying on the ground and they don't want trouble. Though I bet Ahira could of got them to stay if she wanted. But she didn't want. She looked at me and beckoned me to come up to her, and then she sort of lifted her hands at the rest as if to say, That's okay, go on home for now, and then she come down the bandstand steps and walked off, and I followed along after her. Generally there would've been a bunch of us misfits trailing along, at least for a while, but this time there wasn't nobody but me, because everybody else was scared. But I wasn't scared or nothing. Whatever Joanie wanted or did was okay with me.

Except I was scared to say to her, Hi, Joanie. She was so beautiful, I was afraid she wouldn't like it.

She says, to herself or me, "Damn preachers. I hope they notice I never ask for money like a goddamn preacher."

She swirled along like some sort of wild dream in that white dress lifting like wings and them beautiful bare feet of hers, and I just followed along and watched her. I waited until we was clear out of town and she'd turned off the street and was walking on the railroad tracks, and then I come up and walked closer behind her. "I'm Barry Beal," I says to her, and all the time I'm telling myself that I'm going along with her game for fun, so I can surprise her later. But deep in my gut I knowed the truth. I was scared.

I was scared, now she was Ahira, she wouldn't want me or like me or need me no more.

And the way she looked at me didn't help none. She looks at me like she's sizing me up, and then she chuckles deep in her white throat like she's laughing at me. I guess she was worried at first I really did know her, and that's why she invited me to come with her, but now she's fooling me. I didn't really mind, I was so glad to see her again. Though I wasn't exactly seeing her again. Because she looked so different, I mean. But it didn't matter, because I knowed it was her.

She says, "Would you like to come home with me and see where I live?"

And I says, "Sure."

We was out where all the slag heaps was, them black mountains the old folks calls bony piles, and Joanie went off the tracks and ducked behind one of them. I followed her, and I couldn't figure out why she didn't limp or cut them new pretty feet of hers on the clinkers, because that is rough stuff. But it didn't seem to bother her none. Anyhow, she took me around back of the slag heaps where the woods started, and there was her white horse, waiting for her, and another horse beside it, like they knowed I was coming.

I can tell you now I don't think much of horseback

riding. I knowed Mrs. Wilmore done it all the time and said it was real fun, but I sure as heck don't know why. Them horses run us up the mountain through them woods in the dark, and I don't know about Ahira but I got my knees banged against trees and my face bashed with branches and I got shook around so I thought I was going to lose my teeth. And I got my balls banged against the saddle every jump. Course Ahira didn't have that problem.

The only good thing was it didn't take long. Pretty soon we was there, and I slid off.

I could see a little bit because them woods was more open, and I seen them horses jump away into some sort of big building. Ahira motioned me to come on and went in after them. It was dark in the building, and I stopped walking, and Ahira come back to me and took my hand. That surprised me. I didn't want to touch her or think she'd want to touch me because she was too beautiful, even though she did say she loved all the misfits.

She led me around all them things in the way to where she had a flashlight, and then she turned it on, and I seen the things she'd led me around was wooden horses, and I knowed where I was. The old trolley park. I'd been up once or twice with a bad girl, but didn't nobody generally go up there except kids. And I hadn't never been inside the merry-go-round before.

Ahira says, "You want something to eat?"

Now you got to know I'm most always hungry. So I says yes. And then she pulls something out of a cardboard box and offers it to me. Of course I should of knowed what she would have to eat. "Have a banana?" she says. And I could of spit, because then I knowed for sure that she was really playacting, even with me, that she didn't want me to know she was Joanie, and she hadn't brought me there to tell me. Joanie knowed from way back that I don't like bananas.

"No, thanks," I says.

So we sets down there on the floor of the merry-go-round, and she eats one of them damn bananas of hers, but she don't offer me nothing else. "How'd you come to live here?" I asks her, and she tells me a little bit about it, and over the next few days I figured out some more from what I knowed already. And I figured out the rest later on. A lot later.

Here's the way it was:

Before she left Hoadley with my welder's mask and my five hundred dollars she'd got good and mad and made up her mind that if Culp and the rest of them preachers and her mother and all were going to say she belonged to the devil, because her face was so ugly, and if they was so sure they wasn't going to hell the way she would've liked them to, well, she'd just go there herself and thumb her nose at them and their God. She didn't want to be noplace where they was. Any God would put her in hell was a rotten God and she wouldn't brown-nose him no more. Their God hadn't never been no use to her and she didn't want no more to do with him. She'd go to the old gods, the ones that had been around before there was a fat-ass God, and maybe they'd be better friends to her.

There was two things she wanted real bad. One was to be beautiful for once in her life. And the other was to get back at all them people had made her miserable.

I didn't understand till later that she meant to kill them, kill the whole town, kill Hoadley. I was still thinking Culp had give himself a heart attack. And she didn't say nothing about none of that to me. She just said about deciding to call up the spirit of deep earth and fire, black and orange, the old Halloween god who had been around longest of all.

What she did, she took the bus toward Pittsburgh just so's everybody would think she'd left Hoadley, but she got off at one of them gas stations with a little food store in it and bought a bunch of food with some of the money I give her and started walking back, cross country. Joanie was a big strong girl but she still got awful tired with all the stuff she was carrying and she didn't get to the trolley park until way after dark. Which was okay, cause it had to be dark for what she was doing.

"I knew it had to be a spinning place," she says to me. She says all the poets and them prophets in the Bible says so. "Yeats and the gyres, Ezekiel's wheels and all that. And I knew this carousel was up here, not that far from town but isolated. And I had a good idea what to do."

She'd come up with some spells to try by doing the opposite of them Christian spells in the pow-wow book. Turn the sign of the cross upside down and like that. Take the three highest names and say them backwards. Plus she had my welder's mask for protection, plus she had this weird snake she hadn't never told me nothing about. She stood in the trolley park beside the carousel and told her snake to crawl all around her in a circle, and it done it. And she put on the welder's mask, and told her snake to stay between her and the merry-go-round, and she said her strongest spell.

"Next thing there was this crash," she says to me, "like the earth splitting apart, and a big ball of fire came out of the carousel. Broke out through the wall like it was something solid and came rushing straight at me, and poor old Snakie just turned belly-up and died." She gave a sort of chuckle deep in her throat. "I was so scared I about wet my pants." For a minute there she sounded like the old Joanie.

The earth god was in the fireball. She could see him a little bit in the middle of the fire by looking through the welder's mask. He had horns. And he was mad as hell because she'd interrupted his dessert or something, dragged him away from a good dinner. But he couldn't come across the snake line to get at her. And he couldn't see her face through the welder's mask, to see how ugly she was, and that made her feel better.

So they talked, and he calmed down when Joanie told him what she had called him up for. She wanted him to take people and burn them for her. Lots of people. He liked the sound of that, and he invited her to step outside her snake circle and come into the carousel with him.

"You're crazy if you went," I says.

"Of course I am." She give me a little smile. "So I did, and he stood where we are now, and even in the mask I could see the whole place lit up brighter than the sun. He lifted his hands and said, 'The hub of the universe and time now turns in Hoadley, just as each Hoadley soul believes.' "

I says, "That's Hoadley, all right."

She throws back that beautiful head of hers and laughs out loud, and I'm happy cause I made her laugh. But she didn't tell me the rest of what the earth spirit said.

And she didn't tell me most of what happened then, because she was pretending she was Ahira and beautiful all along, and she never told me she was wearing my welder's mask, because then I would have knowed who she was. That beautiful new face of hers was so perfect it was almost like a mask itself, and it didn't show me none of what she was feeling, especially in the dark, with just the flashlight to see by.

"He touched me," she says. "He reached over and touched me. I put my hands up to try to keep him from doing it, and I burned them. I felt my hair go up in flames." Joanie shuddered in her voice. I couldn't tell nothing from her face, but I could hear everything I needed to know in her voice, and I knowed later, when I got time to think about it, that he had pulled that mask off her. "I felt my eyes go blind, and I wanted to scream, but I felt like I couldn't move or scream. He turned me toward the hub." The middle of the merry-go-round, she meant. "And I could see the mirror; it was the only thing I could see. And I could see myself in it." Her voice got hushed, and I knowed the bad part was over.

"And I was Ahira."

And I knowed something else: she really wanted to tell me, tell old Bar, just that one thing. How she changed, got the face she always wanted. How it felt to look in the mirror and see herself more beautiful than anybody had ever been.

Except then she'd have to be Joanie to me.

So instead she says, real casual, "You say your name is Barry Beal? Barry, stand up."

I done it, and she says, "Look in the mirror. Let's see what you really look like."

She was shining the flashlight on me, in my eyes practically, so couldn't see nothing, I felt half blind, but I looked anyways, and I could see one of them mirrored panels on the merry-go-round hub. And I could see a reflection in it.

It didn't look a thing like me. It didn't have no clothes on, and it was a really good-looking guy, like a movie star, except not so tight-ass, if you know what I mean. Not so squeaky clean. This guy looked like he'd been places movie stars never go to. He looked like he could have kissed a person or killed a person. He looked like he could have done anything.

But he was me anyways. I knowed he was the same way I knowed Ahira was Joanie Musser. There was something the same about us. With her, it was that voice, and the eyes. She still had the same eyes, them big greeny-brown sad-mad eyes. I knowed them eyes. I thought they was pretty even when everybody else was calling them frog eyes.

She was laughing somewheres behind the flashlight in the dark, and saying, "I knew it! I knew I got it right. Just right!"

"What you mean?" I says.

"Never mind," she says, and she set the flashlight down and come and stood beside me, and I could see her in the mirror beside the movie-star guy, and she was Ahira in all them filmy floating clothes, but she was looking at him like she was daring him. And he turned and smiled at her greasy, just smiled, didn't even kiss her or nothing before he put his hand on her breast like the clothes wasn't there, and she slapped his hand away. I didn't see no more. I looked away, quick, and Ahira, not the mirror Ahira but the real one, was standing beside me watching me and ready to laugh.

"Barry Beal," she says, "don't go getting any ideas." She says it like she was joking, but she still sounded just like Joanie used to when I would come back between the library shelves with her.

I only got one idea, because I figured Joanie wouldn't want no jam-faced Barry Beal no more. I says, "How do I get to be the guy in the mirror?"

She says, "What makes you think you can do that?"

And I forgot I wasn't supposed to know about her

getting herself a new face, and I says, "You got to be Ahira, didn't you?"

I didn't get no further, because she started to glow white hot. All over, like she was made of white fire. Since I knowed she was Joanie I'd forgot she was Ahira, sun child, and Estrella, daughter of the stars, and all the rest of it. I'd forgot the things she could do. I ain't too bright. But I was bright enough to be scared, and I stepped back from her.

"Barry Beal," she says, the good old angry Joanie-voice coming out of that spook-fire stranger, "you're a stupid fool. You don't know me, and you don't know where I've been or what I've been through. You don't know the first thing about me."

"So tell me," I says.

She looks at me, and the angry fire fades out of her, just the way I was used to, except I wasn't used to *seeing* it happen. But she still can't tell me she's Joanie. "Some other time," she says, like she's tired. "Barry, you'd better get on home."

So I done it. But I wouldn't take one of them damn weird horses again. I walked down the mountain and back into Hoadley. By the time I got to my car it was real late.

At least I'd had a lot of time to think. But it didn't make me feel no better, thinking. Now I knowed where Joanie was, but it still didn't do me no good. She might as well have run away and stayed away. Now she was beautiful, she didn't need old Bar no more, not even to loan her lunch money. And she didn't want me. She didn't even want me to get beautiful like her.

Maybe if I was like the Barry in the mirror, if I wasn't ugly no more, maybe she wouldn't mind so much the way I wanted to be with her, the way I—

Loved her.

Boy, I was dumb. Of course I loved her. I should've knowed it a long time before. I should've told her a long time ago, when we was still really dating, before she left Hoadley. If I would've told her then, when she was still ugly, she would've knowed it was true. Maybe it would've made her feel better. Maybe she wouldn't of left. Now she was Ahira, now she was beautiful, I didn't know if I could ever tell her.

Hell.

Jesus shit, what could I say to her? Joanie, I love you? All them misfits loved her. Joanie, I want to be your friend? She had all the friends she needed now. Joanie, I'd do anything for you?

Joanie, I know who you are, and I love you anyways?

Hell, I should've told her that before, too.

Instead of keeping her doctor's appointment, Cally went to see Gigi.

She walked. In any event she would have walked for the exercise (burn those calories), but this day she had no choice; Mark had taken her car to the dealership for service. With ulterior purpose, she felt sure. He had said nothing, but the message was clear: she could not get to the stable that day, but the medical center was within easy walking distance. That air-conditioned Hoadley mecca, that much-frequented place where entire families, cousins and grandparents included, gathered in the communal waiting room and discussed symptoms, was centrally located for the convenience of everyone in the town. Why not join the crowd? Why not use the nice appointment he had made her?

She did not. Instead, she walked downslope toward the creek (the color of dark urine in its concrete flood-control embankments) a couple of blocks until she came to Railroad Street, then turned and trudged past blocks of wooden mine-company houses utterly without architectural distinction to Gigi's similar house near the other end of town.

She had phoned; Gigi would be there. Gigi, liked by scarcely anyone else in Hoadley, was therefore, like Sojourner Hieronymus, one of the women Cally admired. But Cally went to Sojourner to listen, not to talk. With Gigi she could talk. Sojourner disapproved of everything. Gigi scarcely seemed to disapprove of anything.

Approaching, Cally saw Gigi's typically sparrow-brown mine-town house as toffee, the high chain-link fence (not so typical) that stockaded her back yard as white chocolate lace. Lord, she was so hungry all the time the whole world looked good to eat, even Hoadley, even the candy-bar-brown dog poop on the sidewalk. . . . Gigi was on her knees, puttering in her garden. Odd, Cally thought; she had not considered Gigi the gardening type. Yet most of the hard old woman's yard was in flowers, and they grew lush and thick and tall, even the five-foot fleshy-leafed canna root. A primitive tropical beauty which disliked Hoadley's thin soil, it nevertheless grew strong and barbaric in Gigi's garden. Soon it would bloom, blood red.

Gigi saw Cally, called a greeting and came through the house to let her in at the front door.

"I thought maybe we could talk outside." Gigi sounded rather formal for her; she seemed not as much at ease in her home as in the stable. "It's such a beautiful day."

"Yes, it is. Good day for riding, right?" Sullen,

Cally tried to joke; her bitterness tinged her voice so clearly that neither woman smiled, though Gigi might have felt, as always, her sour and private amusement.

"Have something to drink? Diet cola?"

"Well . . . okay." Glad the older woman had diet soda on hand, should have known Gigi would. Though not fat, Gigi had the blocky, thick-waisted body fated on her by her German genes, and it was a minor heartache to her that even in stretch-fabric riding breeches (which she wore as commonly as other women of her age wore housedresses) she could not achieve a truly deep, legs-down-long-around-the-horse riding seat.

Cally trailed after Gigi to the kitchen.

She had been in the house before, and thought of it as a comfortably neutral sort of place, exhibiting neither the worst of Hoadley decorating taste nor anything Hoadley would find offensive. Homer's hunting trophies, an eight-point buck, an antelope head from some long-ago western foray, hung on the living-room walls, staring with sorrowful glass eyes. A ripple-stitch Afghan (an African, Ma Wilmore would call it) in candy-corn colors lay tidily on the back of the cracker-tan nubbly sofa. There was little else to look at. The place was sparsely furnished and very clean, almost sterile; some of Gigi's nursing training must have taken hold, that she kept her place so clean. Not until that day, waiting while Gigi clinked ice into glasses and poured beverage brown and limpid as deer eyes, not until then did Cally realize how Gigi (out of character in ham-pink Jamaica shorts) undertook the protective coloration of a secretive animal in her own home. Despite the old woman's passion for horses, there were no equine knickknacks on the end tables, no photos of Snake Oil on the walls. Nor was there any sign of Gigi's cynical sense of humor about the place. No hang-in-there posters or scatological pronouncements or plaques proclaiming, "A woman's place is on a stallion." Nothing to say "Gladys 'Gigi' Wildasin" about the place at all. Except, perhaps, that in one corner, almost as if on display, stood a huge vacuum cleaner, a Hoover upright.

"Homer got taken to the hospital with that attached to him once, years back," Gigi remarked when she saw Cally looking at it. She handed the younger woman her glass and led the way out into the flower-thick air of the back yard.

"Attached to him?"

"Yep. You've heard the expression, 'beating the meat'? Well, Homer took it into his head one night to use the beater bar on the Hoover." Gigi sat down on a lawn chair and gestured Cally to another. "He got his penis sucked right up inside and couldn't get it out. They took him to the hospital on a stretcher with the Hoover sitting on top of him like a giant dildo. Bet he's never felt so big."

Gigi chuckled, deep and astringent, as she told the story, but Cally blushed cherry-red.

"Used to embarrass me too," Gigi added, observing her.

"I should think so!"

"I couldn't look anybody in the eye, there for a while. But then I figured it was Homer's problem, and I let that be known. He could go his way and I'd go mine."

And that was when she stopped loving him, Cally thought. Flower gardens crowded all around her, wildly thriving and choking thick. Even Oona's cosmos and snapdragons and salvia never grew half as rank. Cally wondered what in the world Gigi did to her gardens.

"So how's Mark?" Gigi veered with shrewd insight to the substance of Cally's visit.

In church, on the street, anywhere else in Hoadley Cally would have said, Fine, Well he's worried about things in general, There's a lot of pressure on him from business, He's a good man. And she would have felt a pang of misery at their estrangement. But to Gigi she said, "Mark is a pain in the butt."

"Still doesn't believe the things you tell him?"

"Worse."

"What'd he do now?"

"Wants me to go to the doctor." With both bony hands Cally gripped her cold, chemically-sweetened glass. "Says there's something wrong with me. Guess he thinks I've got 'nerves,' like his mother. Asshole." Cally had never spoken of her husband so harshly, but Gigi nodded as if at merest self-evident truth. In another moment Cally burst out, "If he'd just take me—if he'd just accept me the way I am!"

Gigi said, "It's not Mark making you starve yourself."

Cally goggled. Gigi, disagreeing with her on the infamy of a man? "But that's part of it, don't you see? That's me! The way I want to be."

"But that's it, see. That's the problem. There's no point being the way you want to be, not in this town. What you got to do is be the way Hoadley wants you to be."

Something sere as cicada husks in the old woman's voice. Cally stared. Gigi stared back with her hard little grin, teeth edge to sharp edge.

"And Mark's Hoadley," she added. "Hoadley born and Hoadley raised. You can't forget that."

"Aren't you the same?" Cally reminded.

"I'm a special case. Been different since I can remember." She was convinced of that, and she blamed it on the radiation somehow. Radiation did

things to people. "Mark's more what I would call
normal for Hoadley."

In her thoughts Cally sprang to Mark's defense.
How could this arrogant old woman think she knew
him? She remembered a time not so long ago when
Mark had worn a spaghetti colander on his head,
clowning, and pulled tendrils of his hair through the
tiny holes so that he looked like a Martian. She
remembered the cadaver jokes from embalming
school. She remembered Mark down on his hands
and knees on the living room carpet giving horsie
rides to the children when they were smaller. But
also she remembered that she was angry with Mark,
and said nothing but, "So what are you saying I
should do?"

"Go along with him! That's all. Just play along. It
isn't hard." Gigi's grin spread and narrowed into a
tight-lipped smirk. "I been doing it for years. It's
fun. You keep up an act that you're like the others,
but underneath you got your own little secrets, see?"

Cally eyed her, wondering what were the secrets
in this blunt-spoken, tree-tough old woman, then
shook her gaunt head hard. "I'm not giving up my
diet."

Gigi shrugged, not caring enough to argue long.
"Well, hell, Cally, what does it all matter anyway?
You know what they say. Tomorrow we may die."

Another ear would have heard "Eat, drink, and be
merry." But Cally knew at once that Gigi was not
speaking of the universal human condition, but of a
threat more specific and imminent.

"Especially if nobody does anything," Gigi added
dryly.

Thinking of a naked fetch in the woods and of
hungerbug wail, Cally burst out, "That's another thing.
Why do I feel like I'm the one who should do some-

thing? I feel like I'm to blame somehow. For everything." Her hands started to shake, disturbing the brown liquid (clear as Eros's eyes) in her glass. "Is that sick? To feel like everything depends on me?"

"What sort of everything?"

"Everything! The heavy air. The hungerbugs, even."

"The cicadas?" Gigi smiled thinly amid the dense perfume of her many flowers. "Now how could you or I or anyone else be to blame for them?"

CHAPTER EIGHT

"I didn't know him that good, what I mean," one middle-aged woman was saying to another, "but he was my neighbor and all, and when his Sunday paper laid on the porch three days I called the police. I didn't go over there myself because he had that shotgun, what I mean, and run them teenage boys off his yard with it that once, forgot he wasn't sheriff of Lower Salamander Township no more, and went and pulled the trigger on them."

"Goodness," said the listening woman obediently. "I hope he didn't hurt nobody." She was permed, with aggressive lipstick but such a homely face that she looked no prettier than her acquaintance, who wore a triangle of scarf tied over hair that hung relentlessly lank.

"He couldn't hardly see to hit nobody that far away, what I hear, but he might have close up. What I mean, that's why I didn't go over there myself to check on him. So anyways I called the cops, and when they come I went over and peeked in. And there he was, laying on the floor, been dead about three days, in this hot weather we been having, and the smell was enough to revolt a goat."

"I can imagine," said the permed woman as the other paused for dramatic effect.

"But that wasn't the worst of it," the peasant-scarfed woman went on. "You know all them cats he kept, they'd got hungry, shut in the house with him dead for three-four days." The speaker let her voice sink to a horror-movie whisper. "And they'd been eating on him. I seen his face, where they'd been eating on him."

"Oh!" The other put her hands to her mouth in appreciative shock. "Don't that beat all."

"Isn't nobody talking about it," said the woman with lank hair in the same low tones, "but I know, because I seed. This here is shaping up to be a bizarre year, what I hear. Did you hear about that baby in them apartments down on Eleventh Street got chewed at by rats? Poor little thing's mother had gone off and left it in the crib. What I hear, they taken it from her, for neglect, but it ain't never supposed to be right. Its lips is gone."

Cally, eavesdropping, put syrupy canned pears (for the children) in her grocery cart and moved on before the conversation was done. Generally she loved to drift along the aisles of the store, a supermarket specter, so thin and so rootless in Hoadley that she had become nearly invisible. Hoadley women astonished her; in the supermarket they greeted each other with cries of joy and thick-armed, stumpy embraces that blocked the aisles for moments at a time, while other shoppers waited patiently—even if they had seen each other only a week before, nevertheless they embraced. Though hardly anyone ever thus accosted Cally, she liked grocery shopping; she loved to buy cartloads of belly-filling food for her family, dreaming of food as she did so, vicariously eating, and she loved to nibble at the edges of the community as well, listening to Hoadley women talk. The flood of their words and the trickle of their intellects invariably left her awed and aghast.

But this time, this shopping trip, the chitterings of the women in the supermarket aisle reminded Cally too strongly of the conversing of the bizarre bugs in the woods just beyond the town. Bizarre, yes, it was indeed shaping up to be a bizarre year, so much so that Cally felt she could not listen any longer to the stout women with their casual tales of the routine horrors of Hoadley. These people, though perhaps not evil, were on familiar, shrugging terms with evil. She had heard them discuss the details of a rape-and-mutilation and the price of margarine in much the same tones. As if the devil himself was no more than another neighbor to keep an eye on. Cally knew that the tale of the man whose face had been eaten by his cats was true. Mark was in the Perfect Rest basement workroom as she shopped, intent with wax and photographs, trying to restore the man's features for the burial. He considered this particularly decrepit corpse, gnawed and decomposing, the greatest challenge of his career, and Cally, though she was scarcely on speaking terms with him, had left the children with his mother so they would not disturb him—with Ma Wilmore, who had once told her one of those by-the-way tales of Hoadley's incredible cruelty: how when she had been a young wife and pregnant with her first child, when she and Elmo were still living with the senior Wilmores on the farm, she had felt the labor pains start and wanted to go to her bed, but her mother-in-law wouldn't let her; there were twelve pies to be made on that torrid August day for the field hands haying. Not until the pies were baked

and the dinner served and the dishes steamily washed
was the young mother-to-be allowed to lie down and
the doctor sent for.

The baby had been born dead.

Somewhere in the underbrush just beyond Hoadley,
babies with the bodies of cicadas wailed. . . .

Cally loaded her grocery cart with bananas, cinna-
mon buns, toaster pastries. School was out, and the
kids were home for the summer, which gave her
plenty of opportunity to offer them treats and watch
them eat. When she had filled the cart to above the
level of its steel-wire sides, she turned toward the
checkout, pushing hard, a featherweight waif trundling a world-size load, a breaker boy struggling with
the coal trolley.

Old Luther Wasserman, who cleaned the church,
limped painfully in dank or chilly weather, of which
Hoadley had plenty. He had told Cally once that his
father had started him in the mines when he was
twelve, and the first year a car full of coal had run
over him, smashing his legs against the rails. And his
father had refused to have the doctor set the legs,
because of the expense. The boy had lain in bed
until the legs mended on their own. "With no more
care than if I was a barn cat," old Luther had told
Cally. "And they ain't right to this day. I got pain all
the time, and I hold Dad to blame. But he died
coughing his insides out with the black lung. Maybe
he done me a favor. At least I couldn't go work in the
mine no more."

Cally paid for her groceries and motioned away
signs of assistance from the bag boy, wondering why
the pimply kid offered; she wasn't old, pregnant, ill
or feeble—was she? The store bulletin board, along
with for-sale notices and empty refund pads, carried
a poster for home nursing care. By the doors, next to

the video games, stood a blinking red machine that declared, "Check it out! How's your health? Heart/stress analyzer measures basal cardiovascular rate and electrodermal response. Insert quarter, grasp handles." Cally wheeled her overloaded brown bags past it and past the thin man who stood outside panhandling for the cancer association.

She took the groceries home, and if home smelled of death, she did not notice. All of Hoadley smelled much the same.

Commotion in the night, sirens, people in the street, woke Sojourner Hieronymus, and she sat up, swung her desiccated old feet over the edge of the narrow bed and stayed that way for a moment, letting the blood come to her head so she would not be dizzy and fall when she got up. The people from the hospital had been to see her, wanted her to wear one of them new inventions, a sort of electronic bracelet that would take her pulse all the time, and send them a signal if anything went wrong with her, and dose her with something to keep her alive till they got there. Century meter, they had called it, and they had a slogan: in the next millennium, everybody could live to be a hundred. She had sent him away. When it came time for her to die, she would die, and meanwhile she would live the way she always had, by the rules.

Rules. People were such fools; if only they would follow the rules they would be safe, they could lead long and orderly lives such as hers. But they failed to follow the simplest rules. The young girls played ball like the boys, and got their new breasts bumped, and what happened? Thirty, forty years later they got breast cancer, sure as sunrise. Sometimes cancer of the ovaries, too. And it was their own fault.

Sojourner said a quick prayer. After a seemly interval had passed she shuffled her feet into her waiting slippers, stood up and put on her dressing gown, buttoning it up to her neck, with the two nighttime braids of her long, gray hair inside; it would not do to have people see her with her hair down her back, even at midnight when they were all roused from their beds by fire. It had to be fire of some sort. In her darkened room she could see the orange glow on the black window glass.

Holding on carefully, first to the handrail and then to the doorjamb, Sojourner went down her steep, narrow stairs (innocent of smoke detector; she would not have such a cowardly device in the house) and out onto her front porch. From there she could see what everyone was gawking at. In fact, it was in plain sight of all the town.

Under the water tower, swinging from one of the horizontal struts, a limp thing all in flames—in spite of herself, Sojourner pressed her hand to her mouth. It looked like a human, hanging by the neck and burning up there.

"Who is it, Mommy?"

"I don't know."

"Is it really a person, Mom?"

"I don't know. We'll have to wait and see what the police say."

Glad of neighbors to disapprove of, Sojourner turned her pewtery old eyes away from the burning horror on the hilltop and toward the voices in the street. There stood that little fool Cally Wilmore, with her two youngsters, letting them look at what was happening in the night. Irresponsible. Didn't she know that the children should be in bed, no matter what was going on, unless it was their own house burning down? Cally wasn't from Hoadley, hadn't been raised right, but that was no excuse. The parents these depraved days were all alike; they let their children run wild. When she, Sojourner, had been raised, the child that gave trouble or disobeyed had its fingertips burned on the hot stove, a foretaste of hell fire, and cried for hours, and went to school with the pain and embarrassment of blistered hands to show that it had been punished. Children had been taught how to behave, back then. Sojourner would have raised well-behaved children had Mr. Hieronymus given her any. She had married him hoping to have a good influence on him. But the man had been weak, irresponsible; he had killed himself with rat poison after only a few weeks of wedlock with her.

Oona, in a wrap bathrobe sloppily tied, came out onto her porch next door, nodded her disheveled head and smiled and asked the questions appropriate to the occasion. Oona was a good neighbor, but lax in her housekeeping, letting the window curtains go unwashed year to year, and Sojourner believed she had spoiled her children. Certainly she spoiled her grandchildren. She hardly ever punished them, and punishment was the essence of learning what was right. Take toilet training. In Sojourner's day, a child that messed its pants was sat in a tub of scalding water to be cleaned and taught. It usually hadn't taken more than a few such lessons before the child learned, though now and then a child died. Its own fault, if it did.

An unmistakable, stomach-wrenching odor of burning fat and hair and flesh reached Sojourner from the thing on the hilltop. She did not let it trouble her. She stood straight, taking the posture her mother had taught her, strong against fire, fires of hell, fires of discipline.

"Phew!" yelled little Owen with boyish enthusiasm. "It stinks."

"Quiet," Cally told him without raising her voice.

"It does, Mommy! It smells like—"

She shushed him by putting one hand over his mouth, and she leaned down to whisper in his ear. Sojourner saw a flash of pale skin and took another look, cocking her head like an ancient bird of prey, reptilian eyes glinting. The chit was standing out in the street in a negligee nearly down to her bosom, and the peignoir she had thrown over it concealed nothing, being open. Sojourner smiled, suffused with a quiet, happy sense of scandal. She intuited why Cally was wearing the filmy, low-cut nightgown, and she suspected it was doing no good. Mark had not come out to watch the fiery spectacle with her. It was no secret to Hoadley, the town with a sixth sense for people's troubles, that Mark and Cally were quarreling. That was no reason, though, for Cally to show off what little bodily endowment she had to the whole town. She was likely to end up like the girl who had been raped. Not that frog-faced girl. Sojourner had heard whispers about the father doing it to that one, but that was not really rape; that was just incest. This girl, a pretty little goldilocks who had made the mistake of walking past the municipal building by herself, had been knocked down into the back stairwell by the parking lot and there beaten and raped. And once a woman got herself raped, she might as well brand a big black "R" on her forehead and have it done with. Nobody would ever look at her again without remembering what had been done to her. Sojourner knew what had been done to the girl who had been raped, in detail. She knew what three bodily orifices the rapist had used, and how often, and in what order. She knew the family. She knew how the girl had been hospitalized with a nervous breakdown afterward. She had half a notion to tell Cally what might cure her of wanting her husband. The girl who had been raped had not wanted the conjugal act with her husband since, so Hoadley said. Moreover, Hoadley said (with a romantic sigh) that the husband planned to wait for as long as it took. Sojourner expected he would wait until he died. Once a woman understood what men were really like, she wouldn't want "that" any more as long as she had an excuse. Sojourner had been honest to start with; she had never wanted "that" except insofar as it was unpleasantly necessary in order to procreate children (to be raised as a credit to the family, with all due discipline). And though the event had denied her the children, she had been just as glad when Mr. Hieronymus disposed of himself, especially as he had left her the house and wherewithal to live in it.

The blazing thing hanging from the water tower had been doused, first fading to an indeterminate shape glowing ember-orange against the smoggy nighttime sky, dull as coal; then blackening to a sizable cinder gleaming watery white in the light of firemen's lanterns. Cally, Sojourner saw, was talking to a man in a car, one of the firemen returning to the station, indecently stooping as she did so. Then she straightened, stepped back and waved and said to her children, "It wasn't a person. It was a bear."

"A bear!" From the expression on young Tammy's face, this was a more shocking and unsettling event than if it had been a neighbor. People killed each other routinely on TV, but bears were Paddington and Pooh and Theodore; bears were for hugging.

"A bear. Somebody shot a black bear and put dungarees on it, hung it up there, poured gas on it and set it on fire. God knows why." Cally saw Sojourner standing straight and gray on her shadowy porch, waved, then herded her kids back toward home and bed.

Sojourner watched after her retreating neighbors, but her mind remained on the girl who had been raped, whom she no longer remembered by any other title but that. The girl had worked, she remembered, at the sewing factory. After the rape there had been an arrest, and after the arrest, while the girl lay in her hospital bed, a mob of women from the sewing factory had stormed the jail and demanded that the man be handed over to them. Some of them had kitchen knives, wanted to take care of him so he wouldn't rape anybody again, and some of them had ropes, wanted to string him up from the water tower where everybody could see, though Sojourner doubted they would have set him on fire with gasoline. A nice touch like that they weren't likely to think of. Still, it would have taught rapists a lesson if they had got their hands on the man. But the pigheaded police wouldn't let the women have him. The man had been put away as mental. Just put away, with his pecker not cut off or anything. What was the good of just sending him away? Suppose he got loose, what might he do?

Sojourner sighed for what might have been and for the foolishness of humankind, took one last look around the quieting town, then before going indoors turned her eyes heavenward and surveyed the moon. A ring around it. Bad weather coming. Weather hadn't been right, hadn't been the same since the confounded government and the know-it-all scientists had messed around with the moon.

*   *   *

"What I mean," said borough council President Wozny, "we got to find out who is doing this all."

Like everyone else in Hoadley, he had found the night of the blazing bear oddly unsettling. Something about the incident seemed like a threat. More than a threat. Deviant. Sick. So much so that he had called a special meeting of the town council to address the problem, if there was one.

"Isn't it a police matter?" Council Secretary Zephyr Zook challenged. Looking at her, Wozny knew why some of these daunting old women still wore those long-out-of-date, rhinestoned wing-shaped glasses; they glinted hard and sharp as spearheads.

"It's a matter for all concerned citizens." The president, who planned to seek re-election in the fall, looked around nervously, not sure whether he would come out of this meeting with his prestige enhanced or ruined. "It's everybody's concern when there's rumors like there been." Council President Wozny let his voice sink to a dark and serious tone. "What I mean, there might be a panic if we don't do something. Everybody been seeing and hearing strange things. I hear there's talk about a witch been doing things."

The response was far more forthright than he expected. "If there is a witch," an outspoken old German snapped, "it's easy to tell who. That Ahira woman."

The council had discussed Ahira at a previous meeting—or, rather, not at the council meeting itself, but at the real meeting of minds in the parking lot afterward—much as it had discussed barking dogs, without reaching any conclusion. The attitude of most upstanding Hoadley citizens toward Ahira was to ignore her as a nuisance and hope she would go away. The council had adopted the same attitude up until Gerald Wozny had mentioned witchcraft. Neither council nor president remembered in any conscious manner that the witchcraft idea had been brought before them first by Shirley. They had discounted her, and therefore regarded the concept as their own.

There followed one of those peculiarly circuitous and nonparliamentary discussions characteristic of governing boards of the town. The more important the matter under discussion, the less likely it was that a formal motion would be made. Herd instinct prevailed in Hoadley. No one wanted to stand apart from the crowd; therefore courtesy demanded that no member be required to ascend to the block and assume the neck-out position. Moreover, the tacit rule was that the council as a whole would not care to stand on record concerning any matter that was likely to come back to haunt it. Witch hunting qualified splendidly as such a specter. Zephyr Zook, finding in the nebulous swirl of talk no statement on which to hang her note-taking, laid down her spiral-bound notebook and Bic pen while the council, like a convocation of starlings, began without any discernible leadership to move in unison.

"Take her in for vagrancy?"

"What I mean, didn't none of this start to happen till after she come here."

"Police say they can't do nothing."

"They could, but they don't want to."

"You don't want to get in a pissing contest with a skunk, what I mean."

"Can't blame them. Look what happened to Reverent Culp."

"Coroner said that was heart attack."

"It don't matter. She done it to him all the same."

"No great loss."

"That's for sure."

"Two of a kind, what I say."

"Seems to me Father Leopold might could do something about her if we asked him."

"What I mean, a town can't go letting a witch walk around like regular people."

"What about Reverent Berkey? We could get Reverent Berkey to go talk to her."

President Gerald Wozny sat by and nodded and tried not to let his mouth come open like that of a mutt hanging out a car window. He had never known the council to move with such speed. Within the single evening Ahira had been reclassified from annoyance to public enemy, from a gnat to a pestilence-carrying rat to be driven out or extirpated. In fact, the main problem was likely to be one of choosing the appropriate exterminator. Roman Catholics outnumbered Protestants, on the council, as they did in Hoadley proper, but simple majority would mean a vote, and a vote would mean a motion, on the record and therefore unthinkable. An accord had to be reached.

Wozny had opened the meeting intending to play the part of the rumor-scotcher, the level-headed, public-spirited leader paternally telling the citizenry to be calm and law-abiding. But the proper politician takes credit as credit comes. Wozny was equally pleased to find himself the nominal head of a righteous crusade. With rising excitement he realized that someday he, a Protestant, might be able to run for mayor if he could keep himself in the good with Protestants and Catholics both. He said, "How about Father Leopold *and* Reverent Berkey?"

It was settled, of course, after the formal meeting was over. The more important the matter, the less was actually said at the end. There were a few grunts and a soundless chorus of nodding, and it was understood that someone, eyed but unnamed, would speak to each of the divines, and that something was to be done about Ahira.

The priest came to the park in full liturgical regalia, in cassock and embroidered, lace-edged surplice, his heavy pectoral cross glinting on his white bosom, the symbols on his stole glimmering gold in the dusk. He progressed like a battleship under billowing sail, and in his wake an altar boy in alb and cincture swung a thurible giving off the smoke of consecrated incense to drive away demons. At the priest's side walked the Brethren pastor, hollow-chested and craterous of face, in soot-black suit and severe tie, black zippered Bible in hand. Behind the holy and ecumenical duo, but keeping a cautious distance, crowded the town council members and a few other clergy, nuns and church hangers-on, including Pastor Berkey's secretary (decently attired in skirt and sensible heels), Cally Wilmore.

The assembled misfits stared when they saw this strange congregation approaching, but Ahira laughed out loud, a lovely, ringing laugh out of her proud and lovely mouth.

The priest sketched the sign of the cross in her direction. "In the name of the Father, and of the Son, and of the Holy Spirit," he and the Protestant pastor intoned in unison.

"In the name of the earth, and of the moon, and of the stars!" Ahira shouted back, still laughing. "You people can do nothing against me."

Father Leopold carried an Occasional Service Book containing a text for exorcism, which he began to read in a droning voice, to no effect except that Ahira stopped laughing and listened with her head cocked catwise, smiling. "Old man in drag," she interrupted after a while, "I like your dress. Where could I get one like it?"

The grim-faced Brethren pastor was growing angry, and impatient with the priest's droning. "Witch of Satan!" he shouted with thunder force, "Begone from this place!"

"The best lack all conviction," said Ahira quietly, "while the worst are full of passionate intensity."

Listening, Cally Wilmore startled like a deer, completing in her mind Yeats's next lines: *Surely some revelation is at hand; Surely the Second Coming is at hand.*

Yet Ahira veered away from prophecy into mockery. "Old crow," she jeered at Pastor Berkey, "why don't you wear a pretty dress and a necklace, like your friend?"

The individual in question lifted his Bible, directing its cross-embossed cover toward the enemy, and shook it at her—or else his hand shook with fury, as did his voice. "*This* is my clothing, my shield, my armor!" he cried. "This, the cross of Christ and the word of God!" It was a dramatic moment, and the priest did not wish to be left out. He abandoned his droned exorcism and lifted his pectoral cross in his hand, stepping forward. The Protestant minister was quick to step forward as well. Ahira addressed them sweetly.

"You two righteous fools," she said, "don't you know why you can do nothing against me? It is because you are a pair of frauds." Her voice rang out over the listening crowd. "You pretend to come here in 'Christian love,' but you hate each other."

Her people, the misfits, stood gathered around

her feet, their numbers sufficient to fill the park, and none of them had deserted her, though many of them had flinched back from the pastor, the priest and the attendant pillars of Hoadley.

To the two divines Ahira said, "I know what you have called each other in your prayers."

They shouted at her, the one in English, the other in Latin, their mixing voices incomprehensible. Ahira spoke nearly in a whisper, yet her words carried throughout the crowd.

"All you fat-ass normals in this smug town, listen to me: there is not one of you fit to face me. Not one pure of heart. Hypocrites." Ahira included all the intruders in her glance. "I know your secrets. I know how you fondle yourselves in the dark. I know which ones have latches on the outside of the bedroom closet door, and where you keep the whips and shackles. I know which woman sucks her little boy to give him a hard on. I know which man locks himself in the bathroom to sniff his daughter's underthings waiting for the laundry there. I know which men go to whores, and which ones go to other men, and I know which ones love their neighbors, and which ones love other women. I know which man likes to touch little girls. I know which man likes to beat little girls. I know which men have done rape and gotten away with it, and which woman has done murder and gotten away with it, and which one of you has killed animals and set them afire, and would love to do the same to neighbors."

The crowd of the righteous had gone utterly silent, the council members and churchgoers and pastor listening intently to a soft, low, shocking voice, even the priest leaning forward to hear, and in the dusk above the grass of the park the bronze horseman sat silent, immobile, impotent, and the many fireflies winked slowly, like the myriad eyes of God—or the devil. One or the other, Cally Wilmore thought hazily, was in Ahira. What God knew, this woman seemed to know. Or what the devil knew, for why should the knowledge of the devil be any less than that of God? Though, thank God or the devil, Ahira had not mentioned mayapple or a love god like white sugar or Cally's own humiliating secret.

There had to be at least one pure and courageous person, one Galahad in Hoadley. . . . Mark? No, Mark was just an ordinary, whining man and no savior, at least not for her, though half the town looked to him as their white knight—but there had to be at least one truly good person, Cally thought. Reverend Berkey? She would have sworn Reverend Berkey was a saint, yet even his ascetic back, to which she looked, appeared bent, rusty black and defeated. What was his weakness? Did everyone, everyone in the whole world, have a dark secret and a hidden shame?

"Not one of you is fit to face me," said Ahira.

The priest, the ship of the church, who had been listing badly, straightened and swelled, his sails full of stung pride. "Insolent sprout of Satan!" he intoned. "The might of the Lord God Omnipotent—"

"Is not in you. Is as nothing, compared to the might of those your God has trampled into dirt. Watch, priest." Easily, casually, Ahira reached over the gazebo railing and touched the misfit who stood closest to her. It was the bald girl, who screamed, not in fright or pain, but in sheer startled ecstasy, for the touch of Ahira's hand put hair on her afflicted head: richly curling, shoulder-length fawn-brown hair, properly accessorized by eyebrows and eyelashes in the appropriate places. Her undistinguished face, awash in hair and alight with joy, looked very nearly

beautiful. With a gentle hand Ahira turned her to
face the onlookers.

"Can you do this, priest?"

A gasp and babble had gone up from the crowd,
but the priest did not add to it or silence it; he
seemed unable to speak. He had witnessed a healing, a miracle. The devil could quote Scripture, but
only prophets and saints and messiahs were supposed to be able to do what he had just seen done.

"And the Antichrist," Ahira added pleasantly, as if
she had heard his thoughts. Like Jesus coming down
from the mount she came down the gazebo steps to
the bottom one and beckoned the erstwhile-bald girl
to her side. With the same offhand but tender grace
she lifted the plenitude of hair at the youngster's
temple. There, just at the zygomatic arch, showed a
dark red mark.

"All of you whom I touch must wear my mark,"
she said, her eyes not on the intruding townspeople
but on her own people, the misfits. Her glance on
them, soft as twilight. "You are my people, and my
mark is the seal of our bond. Who wants to come to
me and be healed?"

Already they crowded around.

The bent woman straightened, and smiled, and
wore a dusky mark on the side of her thin face. The
blind man threw down his white cane, tore the paper
bag off his head, and he was handsome with seeing
eyes and a dark, romantic scar. The woman who was
so fat she could scarcely move laughed and cried; her
dress dragged to the ground from her new, thinner
shoulders, and even her shoes no longer fit her. She
pushed her hair back from the burning mark and
wore it proudly. The man with stumps stood on legs
again, and yelled aloud like a football player running
in the winning touchdown, and leaped about the

park with fists in air, shouting. His plain face bore
Ahira's mark.

Priest and pastor and most of their followers turned
and left, silent, too horrified to converse, doing their
best to censor from their minds what they had seen.
Magic, they told themselves, an illusion, like on TV.
Had to be. There was nothing like any of this going
on elsewhere; the world was circling in its same old
rutted round. Therefore what had happened could
not have happened, or how could Hoadley go on
with its routine, its stagnation, its life? They would
not make anything they had seen real by conversing
of it.

They left, but Cally Wilmore stayed, keeping to
the outskirts of the crowd, picking crumbs and sweet
specks of icing from the edge of some huge forbidden
ceremonial cake. She saw Ahira touch people who
seemed to have nothing wrong with them, putting
on them her mark—was it blood, or fire, or wine? In
the nightfall streetlamp-and-firefly light Cally could
not decide. But she saw the smiles, shouts, sometimes glad tears of those who received the mark, and
knew that Ahira had healed something in them.

The green girl (made that way by jaundice plus a
prescription drug overdose) came, and her skin returned to the Dresden shepherdess beauty she had
been born with, and she wept. Garrett came to
Ahira, received the mark and a subtle change in his
head, his face, the mind behind the face, and he
pulled out of his pockets hundreds of dominoes and
tossed them black-flashing into the air, and left them
where they landed. Barry Beal came to Ahira with
him. But Ahira looked at Barry—watching, Cally
could not understand the look. Something of the
lover in it, but also something of scorn. Ahira would
not touch him.

She told him, "You are mine the way you are. You wear my mark large, and you wore it before any of the others." Ahira's voice rang out into the dark and hubbub as she gave the accolade, and Cally saw Barry Beal straighten, his particolored face parted again with his wide smile, quartered, as if he wore a harlequin mask. Tall and cocky he stood, proud to be Ahira's possession, proud of his birthmarked face for perhaps the first time in his life.

Cally looked at broad-chested Barry Beal, and thought of Eros in the forest and her own sullen Mark home in his house of death, and felt the ever-present ache in her gut grow harder. As if she belonged there she went and took her place in line.

Close to the strange woman Ahira, very close, Cally could see only beauty. But though she could not find a flaw in that poreless glowing veneer of flesh, she knew if for what it was: somehow, a living mask. She knew it because she stood close enough to smell Ahira amid the stale-beer and bird-cage odors of the misfits. And though Ahira did not smell strongly, what odor Cally discerned belonged to Hoadley.

When Ahira's chamois-soft hand reached toward her, Cally stopped it with a frail, defiant gesture.

"No, thank you," said Cally. "I just wanted to look at you. I wanted to see what sort of woman would kill an animal and hang it up and set it afire."

Ahira reacted with a faint smile. "But I did not do that," she said. "One of you did it."

Cally felt unease crawl like a mouse through her puny shoulders. The woman was telling the truth; she felt it. "But the rest of it," she challenged, "Mrs. Zepka and the naked man and the—" At last she knew what to call them. "—the hungerbabies, you did."

Ahira's smile quirked a shadow wider in qualified

assent. "Hoadley helped me," she acknowledged. And only after she spoke did Cally feel the profound depth of the understanding between her and this—this unnatural woman, this ungodly beauty, this frightening fetch. Ahira had known of what she spoke. What else did Ahira know about her? What was Ahira? It did not matter. To the marrow of her nearly-fleshless bones Cally knew the most important thing about Ahira.

She whispered, "You mean to end us. End us all."

Ahira's smile faded into the tender-eyed frown of concern. "Cally," she said, though no one had told her Cally's name, "let me touch you, let me stop your hurting, let me put my mark on you. You are one of my people. You must be, or you would not understand."

Her exquisite hand lifted again, and Cally watched it for a moment, fascinated, almost assenting, before she stepped back in horror.

"You!" she accused. "You mean to destroy Hoadley."

Ahira smiled again, the same dusky-soft smile. "I will not need to," she said. "You will do it."

Tingling with fear and anger and eerie insight, Cally used her strongest weapon. Ahira was not the only one with unaccountable knowledge and the poetry to couch it in.

"O rose," Cally breathed, "thou art sick. The invisible worm—"

White fire flared up. Ahira had turned to embodied lighting, and fury spun off her with sirocco force. "Get away from me!" Her voice crackled, a thunderbolt out of the darkness.

Cally departed like a dried leaf blown away before the force of that storm. If she had been in boots—but she was not. She scurried homeward, hating the skirt, the insubstantial shoes that would not let her

stride out, strike out. In something other than her
Hoadley-approved clothing—the uniform that crippled heart and soul and mind as much as body—on
her own terms she could have been a worthy antago-
nist to Ahira, she felt sure of it.

What had Ahira meant by that last odd pronounce-
ment? "You will do it." She, Cally, would drive
Hoadley down into the pit?

Pit? What pit? And of course Ahira had not meant
that. She meant people in general. It was a joke, the
sick joke of a starved mind, Cally's own. Cally's lips
twitched back from those skull protrusions called
teeth, and she smiled.

CHAPTER NINE

Tammy had just that warm early summer hit upon an ability to produce a liquid flute-note sound between her lips. The new knack pleased her no end. All day every day she went about her arcane preadolescent business whistling melodiously but randomly, like a yellowthroat warbler, and she softly whistled herself to sleep at night. The fluid, atonal sounds of the child's rapt self-possession touched off in Cally a rush of yearning affection. Tammy had been her first baby, and Tammy was growing up. . . . Tammy seemed like the one right thing in her life at the time. Everything else seemed to forebode. And nothing was ever again going to be right with Mark, she felt. Some devil in her would not let it be. She could have swallowed her anger and smiled through her teeth and made up to him with food offerings and conciliatory words and tears, as Hoadley wisdom advised, as Cally's hungry heart urged her to do, as she had often done before. But some new and obdurate self-will would not let her do it this time. She had stayed home from church on Sunday—because the hard pews hurt her increasingly bony body, but she would not say as much—she had put a face of defiance on the act, and had sat out on the apartment porch reading the newspaper while the churchgoers passed, for no reason except to shock Hoadley and annoy Mark.

Locating Tammy by the constant stream of her whistling, and Owen by the gunfire bursts of the morning cartoons he watched on TV, Cally called both children and got them moving out the apartment door and down the sidewalk toward Ma Wilmore's house. She was going to leave them there while she went riding. Every day since her most recent quarrel with Mark she had gone riding for hours, dawn, dusk, high noon or after dark in the moonlight, sometimes two or three times a day, and sheerly by constant riding she had reached an accord of sorts with her rebellious black horse, though that was not the reason she went. . . . Passing Sojourner Hieronymus's stark gray house, she greeted the old woman on the porch with no more than a wave of one attenuated hand, flouting the convention that she must stop and talk. She did not care any longer what anyone thought of her. Least of all that stubborn Mark. She would go riding amid the delectable hills, she would enjoy her life, what was left of it, and to hell with him and all of them.

Owen aimed his forefinger at Sojourner and made pistol-shooting noises at her; Cally did not attempt to stop him. Tammy skipped past the gray porch, her soft hair bobbing, and whistled notes as liquid as her gazing eyes.

With percussive force, as if someone had struck a bell of clay, Sojourner's voice rang out: "Whistling girls and crowing hens always come to bad ends!"

Tammy smiled the brave smile of a good, forgiving

child, and skipped on, whistling. Cally called ironically, "Right."

Then, three strides down the pavement, she turned her eyes to her daughter and felt her heart shiver.

The change was so subtle, perhaps only a mother's glance could have caught it, the scrutiny of a mother as intent and besotted as she. Cally saw. What had a moment before in Tammy's wide-eyed gaze been that peculiar blend of sweep and focus, of essential wildness and fierce dependence, of fawn and fox cub, that we call innocence—it had all turned to something . . . other. Tammy whistled and looked back at her mother thoughtfully, like Eve calling up the serpent for his sup of milk.

"No," Cally whispered.

"No, what?" Tammy wanted to know. Her voice, piping and bratty, sounded much the same as ever.

"Nothing." Cally hurried both kids to her in-laws' place and left them there, taking no time to exchange courteous pleasantries with Ma Wilmore. Heading home, she took the back alleyway so that she would not have to deal with Sojourner, and she ran, her riding boots thudding on the asphalt. A bizarre, feverish, unnatural energy filled her, though she had not eaten more than a few mouthfuls of food in days.

Instead of getting in her car and roaring off at unsafe rates of speed toward the stable, as she had planned, she invaded the hush of the deep-carpeted funeral home with her booted feet, looking for Mark.

She found him atop a step ladder, removing the crystals of the Peach Room chandelier so that he could clean them. He loved to do that; when nothing more urgent pressed he would sit for hours, waiting for a death call and soaking and scrubbing and polishing the small swords of glass.

"Mark," Cally told him without preamble, "I am going to send the kids away from here."

He looked down from his perch without replying, wary, exasperated by too many surprises from her, unsure how to react. Cally, intent on her own agenda, saw his face only as unresponsive, an angry mask.

She said, "They'll be better off somewhere else."

"Why?" Mark found his voice. "Because you've made up your mind to drive me as crazy as you are? You can fix that."

She swung her head, eyes narrowed to slits, wanting to charge him, trample him under hard feet; the jackass, he would not understand! "No, I can't," she stated, words hard out of hot lungs. "The world is going crazy. I'm just riding it. I want the kids out of here. Hoadley's going first."

"I see." Sarcastically, though he did in fact see, dimly, as if out of the corner of his brain. Too frightened to see more, he blinkered his stare on his wife. "And where do you propose to park the kids? With your mother?"

She had in her hasty planning thought of sending the youngsters to stay with an old friend, a college roommate. But the way he said "your mother" sent adrenaline of primal defense surging through her. Family. Hoadley was spelled f-a-m-i-l-y. It was the sacred word. And by damn she had family of her own, not Hoadley, not Mark's family, but her own; at the mention of her mother Cally grew determined to have this. Thinking of her parents as she had seldom thought of them in all her Hoadley years, Cally could not call their faces clearly to mind. It was as if a haze of Hoadley yellow cheap-coal smoke had gotten in the way. Nevertheless, she was suddenly the child of her parents again, filled with a child's blind anger.

"That sounds like a very good idea," she said. Every word was an edged weapon.

"Cal, you're not thinking straight." Mark saw his mistake, and tried reasoning. "Your mother kills plants. She can't even remember to feed a cat."

"She's my mother! Don't you bad-mouth her. You've never liked her."

"I'm just telling it the way it is! Cal—"

She took a step forward, thrusting her pointed jaw toward him; still on his stepladder, he looked down on her, the king of the dead in his wholesale-furnished palace, elevated, enthroned, wearing the chandelier like a megalomaniac's crown. She wanted to knock the props out from under him, bring him down where she could level her glare at him. Instead, she had to glower up into his nostrils as she said, "I can send my kids to visit with my own mother if I want to."

"Cal, they're my kids too." On his own Mark came down from his pedestal in order to make better eye contact. His embalming school dealing-with-the-distraught classes had taught him all about eye contact. He stood in front of her and kept sincere eye contact with her as he said, "You've told me a hundred times how she never gave a damn about you as a kid. Why do you want to send her Tammy and Owen?"

Cally could have sent the children elsewhere, at that point, with little or no argument from Mark. But she refused to see and press her advantage. She loathed Mark's pop-psychology games—how stupid did he think she was?—and she had discarded the original direction of the argument. She felt herself hell-bent on vindicating her family honor, as if her own worth somehow depended on where she came from. On having definitively come from somewhere.

"At least my mom'll give them room to breathe! Let them do some things on their own, let them grow a little. She'll be better for them than that— that octopus mother of yours, with her tentacles into everything."

Mark flushed rage-red to his hairline. He forgot that he had ever professed to detest the narrow-minded woman who had given him birth. He clenched his fists, stepped to within inches of his wife, bulled his face into hers; playground and locker room had taught him the masculine arts of intimidation. "You leave my mother out of this," he warned.

"I will not. She's an anal-retentive old fart. Kindly remember that Tammy and Owen have more than one grandmother! Where is it written that they must visit only your mother and never mine?" As if riding her black Devil in full career and out of control Cally rode the surge of her own rage, thrilled, exhilarated. "You've always been jealous of my mother because she's got some brains and independence. And because someday I might just leave you and live alone like her. Can't stand an independent woman, can you? Your mother spends all day nattering in her kitchen, crawling up her own behind, and—"

Mark hit her.

She was hysterical, he told himself afterward. He had slapped her to stop her shouting. And in fact the open-handed blow was little more than a swat. It knocked Cally sideward, but startled her more than hurt her. She took only two gasping breaths before she shouted again.

"Beast!" she screamed, echoing something she had once heard her mother shriek at her father in a late-night quarrel she was not supposed to have known about. (Theirs had not been a very good marriage, she had decided when she was grown. Chilly in the light of day, quarreling in the dark. Was hers any better?) "You brute! It's just like they say, all men are brutes. No better than animals. How can you be such a beast!"

"Cal, I'm sorry," Mark said, contrite and furious; she could see in his face how red rage came and went, leaving pale shock behind. "Stop it. You're hysterical. I just want you to stop. You shouldn't shout at me like that."

Before he was done speaking she had passed beyond shouting into action, and swung at him. He stepped back, ducking, and she missed. She glared at him like a Halloween skull, lurid—he had not noticed before how the small muscles were beginning to show around her eyes as if skin had melted away entirely, as if she were intent on becoming an anatomical chart. She bared her teeth, panted something inarticulate through that nearly-lipless rictus, and turned away, running out with a thud of boots and a crashing of the heavy funeral-home door.

She would go ride her horse, Mark knew. Briefly he hoped she would break her thin, stubborn neck. It bothered him that she had not cried. Not that he was fond of tears; Lord, no, not in his line of work. But he would have felt better, somehow, if she had cried.

Not knowing what else to do, he went back to his chandelier and its pretty swords of glass. "Beast," he said bitterly to the glinting blades. "Great. Lose my temper once in ten years, and I'm a goddamn beast."

"You know, Bar," Ahira says to me, setting up in that merry-go-round house of hers one night, "I could really screw up a certain person's mind."

I knowed she could, all right. She was really screwing up my mind, Ahira was. She knowed I loved her,

I figured, cause it seemed like she knowed everything them days, and because sometimes she looked at me like she was laughing at me. But maybe she didn't know I knowed she was Joan Musser. I hadn't never let on. And she didn't seem to care that I loved her, not to let me touch her or nothing. The couple times I tried to touch her, she pushed me away and made fun of me. "Barry Beal," she says, "I can tell, you never in your life did know how to make love to a girl, did you?"

Mostly I was scared to touch her, I didn't feel like I could never touch her or talk to her or nothing, because she was so beautiful and so spooky-strong and I was just ugly old Bar. Sometimes I wished she hadn't never come back, not like Ahira. I just wanted the old Joanie back, and course I couldn't tell her the way I felt. So that's why my mind was in a mess, because I felt like a stray dog hanging around. But what the hell. I knowed I was always going to be there for Joanie, no matter what. Come hell or whatever.

By this time I had figured out that hell was what Joanie had planned. She figured on sending Hoadley down into it. I couldn't blame her, but I was glad my folks lived outside of town.

I says, "What you mean, screw up a certain person's mind?"

"That self-righteous Norma Musser. You know her. Don't you think her mind needs something done to it?"

Then I knowed she meant her own mom. I didn't say nothing.

Ahira says, "I know all her buttons to push. She knows I killed her precious Pastor Culp, and she's heard I'm the Antichrist, and she's heard I put the mark of the beast on the people I've healed. And I bet you even so I can make her do whatever I want."

"Like what?"

She didn't say nothing, only smiled the same way she smiled at Culp that once. And Culp was dead. I didn't think she meant to kill her mom, not right away, since everybody in Hoadley was supposed to die pretty soon anyways. But I figured she had something planned that was maybe even worse, and I didn't really want to know what it was. Even though I'd just asked.

I says, "What you want to mess around with anybody for?"

Joanie didn't answer me right then, but her smile went away. I couldn't tell nothing from looking at that Ahira-face of hers, but I got the feeling something was bothering her. Finally she says, "We're going to see her."

I says, "Not me."

"Yes, you are."

I says, "I got to get home."

But I end up going along with her. I ain't never been able to say no to Joanie. She gets me on one of them weird wooden horses of hers, a black one, and it comes alive like her white one does, and the two of them takes us down the mountain and clear around Hoadley so we comes at the Musser place the back way, across Trout Creek, and probably ain't nobody seed us. It's past midnight by then, ain't nobody around.

Once we gets across the creek Joanie gets down and motions me to get down and the horses go off somewheres, and we go up to the Musser place on foot. Joanie don't go in right away. She stands at the bottom of them rickety steps looking up at the place, and she says something, like, to herself.

She says, real soft, "O rose, thou art sick. The invisible worm that flies in the night in the howling storm has found out thy bed of crimson joy, and his dark secret love . . ."

I says, "Huh?"

"Does thy life destroy," she says, softer yet.

"Huh?"

She didn't look at me or say nothing more. She just goes in. She rooted around under the steps first and finds the key, acting like she don't know right where it is on account of I'm there watching her, but it turned out the door wasn't locked anyways. She just touches it and swings it open and goes in soft and wiry like a cat, and I follows her.

There was shadowy white light from the street coming in through the windows, but no noise except somebody snoring. It's old man Musser, old Roland, passed out on the kitchen table. Joanie don't look at him. She stands still in the middle of the front room and looks around her. It must have felt funny to her, coming back to that place. There was cracked floorboards coming loose and old wallpaper coming down in drips and old furniture with the stuffing coming out through the rips in the goods like guts out of a road kill. Joanie, Ahira I mean, she was so beautiful in one of them floating blue-white gowns of hers, she looked like an angel got into the wrong place by mistake. She made that shack look even more like soot and nose snot than I guess what it really did.

On the old lumpy davenport lays Joanie's mother with one of them ratty knitted blankets over her, sleeping. She was a sort of skinny, worn-down-looking woman to see her on the street, but there on the sofa in the streetlamp light she has that special look people get when they're sleeping, like they're younger and better than what they really are. Mrs. Musser looked almost pretty like Ahira laying there sleeping, and Joanie just stands and looks at her for a while before she goes to her and takes her by the hand.

"Come," she says, that's all, and Norma Musser sets up, startled, and Ahira still has her by the hand.

"Come, Mary of the Millennium," Ahira says, low. "Prepare to be raptured. The bridegroom awaits."

Norma Musser's mouth fumbles open, and she don't look pretty and holy no more. She looks like somebody in a horror movie gasping for air, and she hollers, "No!" only it comes out a croak. She says, "You—"

"I am she who is sent," Ahira says, low and smooth, in that silky warm voice of hers. "Oh woman of little faith, if the devil can quote Scripture, cannot the Almighty speak through the mouth of a sinner? I tell you, you are the chosen one. You are she who is to bear the most holy son, the messiah of the Parousia."

Joanie had spoke no lie, she knowed which buttons to push, all right. All her life Mrs. Musser must've wanted nothing but that Chosen One business. Her eyes got big and soft and watery, and she wasn't afraid no more. Not the same way, anyways. She looked scared, but it was holy scared. She says, "But—but why? Why me?"

"Why Mary of Nazareth? Why Cinderella for the prince?" Ahira stood up, and Norma Musser stood beside her in a big old faded nightgown blue-white in the streetlamp light, and they almost looked alike.

"Why not you, foolish woman?" says Ahira with a twitch in her voice. "Are you not worthy? Are you not pious and humble and holy?"

"But—but—I am barren!" Norma Musser is holding onto her daughter's hand with both her own, tight, like she don't want to let go, no matter what her mouth is saying. But she never knowed it was her daughter.

"So was Elizabeth, mother of John the Baptist," says Ahira. "So was Sarah wife of Abraham and mother of the nation of Israel. Come, no more talk. Have you no faith? Do you not know the power of the One who has sent for you?"

Ahira leads her out the door by the hand, and I follow a little ways after, and I don't think Mrs. Musser ever seen me, she was so wrapped up in what was happening to her.

Up Hoadley Joanie takes her mother, up to the right side of the tracks, where some of the better houses starts, them yellow brick ones. Right along Main Street there's a big yard sloping up with one of them shrines of the Virgin Mary at the top, the kind people set up with a plaster Mary and an old bathtub sticking up half out of the ground. Our Lady of the Lavatory, Joanie and me used to call them when we was in high school. Joanie takes her mother right up to the plaster Mary and stops. Me, I stay by one of them big spruce trees around the edge of the yard, watching.

"The mother of our lord Jesus welcomes the mother of the new messiah," says Ahira. She does a sort of bow in front of the plaster Mary, and Norma Musser does the same. Then Joanie looks at her mother.

"It is said that Mary of Nazareth was impregnated by a dove flying into her ear." Ahira has that twitch in her voice again. I guess Mrs. Musser didn't know what it was, but I knowed. It was Joanie laughing at somebody inside herself. She done it to me sometimes. "Or by a sunbeam, or a shower of gold. But the mother of He Who Is To Come must do more truly. She must be impregnated in rapture by the bridegroom himself."

And out from behind the bathtub shrine he steps.

"Oh, Jesus," I says to myself, because it's him. Not Jesus, I mean. Him. Me. The one I saw in the merry-go-round mirror. Except I never knowed he was real, and I never knowed he went around buck naked from the waist down too. And I never knowed his thing don't look like mine. He ain't never been made civilized down there. Though no reason why that should surprise me. The rest of him ain't all that civilized neither, because he's gorgeous and weird, and even though I ain't no woman I can tell he's a real turn-on. I guess women dream about guys like him at night the way I dream about women.

I looked at Joanie, quick, to see if she's turned on by this guy, and she ain't even looking at him. She's looking at her mother, and there's something in that mask of a face of hers I can't figure out.

Then she gets down on her knees. "Mother," she says, "your blessing."

As soon as I heard her voice I knowed what it was in her face. I could always tell what was going on inside Joanie from her voice. There was two feelings in her, fighting, shaking each other, shaking her voice, and they was hurting and hate. Joanie Musser still hurted, still wanted her mother, no matter how much Ahira hated her. Joanie Musser wanted Norma Musser to put her hands gentle on her, say soft words, even if it was because she got tricked into it. And Norma Musser done it.

She put her hands on Joanie's head. Her face looked like she was already making love, because she knowed she was the mother of the whole new world. She never knowed what Ahira meant when Ahira called her Mother. "Bless you, my child," she says in a whisper, and she ain't saying it to her own child at all. Except she was.

And Joanie bows her head, then gets up and comes over to stand beside me, half hid in the spruce trees.

Norma Musser is giving the strange guy a look like a deer about to get shot and go to heaven, and I see his hard-on start, and I know this guy can make love to anybody, anyplace, anytime.

"Jesus," I says again, and I look away.

"All right," says Joanie, real low but hard-edged. I tooken a quick look. Mrs. Musser had her nightgown off, she's standing there as naked as the bridegroom guy, and he's just starting to curl his hands around her saggy old behind.

I looks at Joan, at Ahira I mean, standing next to me, and she's beautiful, and she's watching what I'm too embarrassed to watch without her face even moving, but I can see her shaking all over like a steel engine housing, and them sweet hands of hers is clenched into fists.

"All right," she whispers again, and all of a sudden for the first time in my life I understand what sort of hating it is makes people spray-paint on somebody's garage, Fuck You.

I didn't want to watch no more, or mean to, but I kept taking quick looks, then turning away until I got to look again. I couldn't help it. So them two was all tangled up in each other and the night and the slantwise shadowy white street light, and I seen them in flashes, like a peep show. And that stranger guy, the bridegroom, my double, everything he done was so smooth, so strong and wild and soft, he could even make sex with old Norma Musser look good. And all the time I knowed it wasn't just women I dreamed about at night when I'd wake up sticky wet. It was only one woman. Ahira. Joanie, I mean, except she's Ahira, beautiful, making slow, wild love to me in my sleep. To me, ugly old jamhead Bar.

And she's standing next to me, shaking with hate and hurtness. Hurting for love.

"Joanie," I whispers to her, "I can love you like that. I can love you good as that guy. You give me a chance sometime. Joanie."

She didn't hear me at all. She's glaring off at her mother laying in front of Our Lady of the Bathtub. And I looks that way too, and the slantwise light has gone flashy red, so I seen them two white bodies in front of the plaster Mary in flickers, like in a bad movie. A cop car is pulling up the curb. Course it would. Decent people in Hoadley was asleep, but a Hoadley cop would find his way to a show like this like a dog to a bitch in heat.

Joanie smiles and sort of blinks, hard, her whole face tight for a second—and that bridegroom guy is gone like he was never there. Joanie's mother is laying naked on the ground in somebody's back yard, in front of their lawn shrine, with her feet up in the air fishy white and a crucifix hugged up to her flabby old breasts.

I started forward, I was so surprised, but Joanie grabs me and pulls me back in the spruce hedge and through it out the other side, and her and me walks away up Hoadley, and that cop was so tooken up by what he was finding I don't think he ever seed us.

They put Norma Musser in a hospital mental ward, and the story was all over Hoadley what she done, except nobody had never seen the reason. So when Norma Musser come home from the hospital in a few days, she didn't stay long. She couldn't hardly walk for shame in that town. She just put together a box full of clothes or whatever and got on a bus and left. Didn't nobody know where she went, not even her

husband. Least he never made no sense whenever
anybody asked him. Probably was too drunk when
she left to care or pay attention.

So Joanie had got back at her mom for all the
times her mom had called her a whore of Babylon.
Them times her mom had accused her of fornicating
in the house was nothing compared to being caught
making love naked with a Jesus cross in front of a
Mary shrine. I didn't like what Ahira done. It was
the meanest trick I had ever seed. Next time I seen
her I couldn't look at her straight no matter how
beautiful she was, I was so ashamed of what she done
and shamed I had been there to watch. But when I
thought about it, it sort of made sense. Getting driven
out of town was the same like what her mom done to
her.

Then I thought, Now Joanie's mother is out of
Hoadley. Now she won't go down to hell when the
rest of the town does. She got showed up bad, but
she'll be alive after the rest of them is dead.

And maybe that was what Joanie intended all along.

Plus I remembered Joanie on her knees, begging
that blessing.

Plus I got to thinking about that bridegroom. Something about him being my double and all bothered
me. There was lots of questions I wanted to ask him.
The main one was about him and Joanie.

Next night around dusk when I knowed Ahira
would be down the park I didn't go there. I went up
to that merry-go-round place of hers instead. It was
the only way I could think of to try to see the guy.

I started walking up the hill right after work and it
was still pretty light by the time I got there, but it
was dark inside the building. I found Joanie's matches
and lighted some candles she had setting around
stuck in Mogen David bottles she'd picked up some-

wheres. I lighted them until there was enough that I could see myself in the mirror. Him, I mean.

There he was looking back at me all right, and he smiled kind of a shit-eating grin. "Come out of there so's I can talk to you," I says.

He don't come out, but he answers me right back. "Why are you so worried?" he says. "I am only your shadow. You know that."

I didn't like being told I was worried. It was true, but I didn't like him saying it. "Where'd you come from?" I says.

"Where do you think?"

"Did she make you?"

"Who?"

"You know who."

"Yes, she made me. Out of her dreams of you."

The way he said it, dirty like, didn't make me feel no better. Only later I got to thinking, dreams of me? And then I figured he lied. No way would Ahira dream about me.

I says, "How did she make you?"

He just grins. Now I know I'm more jealous than worried. I says, "Did she do it with you?"

He laughs. I didn't take that to mean she done it, not really, but something about the way he laughed, like he was making fun of me or Joanie or maybe both of us together, it made me mean-dog mad. Quick I picked up one of them wine bottles to heave it at the mirror. I figured if he was just my shadow, I had a right to get rid of him.

He stopped laughing and gave like a gasp, and before I could do nothing else he was out of the mirror and standing beside me among all them wooden horses, and he grabbed my wrist. His hand was strong, and he stood taller than me, and even naked like he was I knowed I couldn't take him down. He held onto me until I dropped the wine bottle, and then he let me go.

He says, "You should ask her, not me."

I was still plenty mad at him, and I says, "You'd do it with anybody, wouldn't you? Anytime. Anyplace."

"That is my nature. Though with some it is more pleasure than with others." He don't act mad at me. He's looking at me straight and quiet, and he says, soft, "You are my eidolon, my paradigm, my model and my mirror. You are my better self. With you, it would be the greatest of pleasures."

Good God, he was a homo too. And I ain't never been propositioned by no homo before. But the weird thing was, for a minute I almost felt like it would be right. Good, even. I wasn't mad at him no more. Him making love to me—well, who the hell ought to love me? He was me. I could love me, couldn't I?

Then he put one hand on my shoulder, and I seen the hungry look in them brown eyes of his, and I knowed if he was me it was just too bad. I didn't like him very much. I pushed him away, and I started to shake at the idea of what I almost went and done.

"There's no need to be afraid," he says, still looking at me the same way. "You are my master. I am as nothing without you."

"Go away," I says, hoarse.

But I guess I wasn't so much of a master to him after all, because he didn't. He just stood there looking at me with them eyes like a beagle dog's, and I'm the one went away. I stumbled out of there, didn't even blow the candles out, and I run down the hill in the dusk and didn't stop until I was under the street lights down in Hoadley. Damn lucky thing I didn't burn down Joanie's merry-go-round, leaving the candles lit that way.

Later on I noticed that guy never answered none

of my questions, and I had a thought. Maybe he didn't want to answer no questions. Maybe whenever anybody come near him with too many questions he made love to them. One way or another that would shut them up.

Well, maybe that was part of what made him do it to me.

If he done what he done to keep me from asking him stuff, it was working. I wasn't going near him no more.

And I felt sick, because I still didn't know what was going on between him and Joanie. I dreamed at nights, sometimes, about him doing her the way he'd done her mother, and I'd wake up shaking mad.

Cally Wilmore heard about the poor woman who had gone ga-ga. Some sort of religious frenzy, with wonderful overtones of sexual neurosis. Perhaps an exotic variety of millennial fever.

But she was too preoccupied with getting her own children out of Hoadley to pay much attention to Norma Musser's problems.

Within a few days all the arrangements had been made. At about the same time as Ahira Estrella Amaris Anona Joanie Musser's mother was disgraced, Cally Wilmore talked to her own mother over the cicada-buzzing long-distance line, and assured her that everything was all right, she just thought it a good idea that the children should spend some time with their other grandma for a change. And about the same time as Ahira's mother left town, Cally Wilmore turned over to her mother a gift, or a burden, or a trust: Owen and Tammy.

CHAPTER TEN

The cicadas came to Hoadley on the day the girl who had been raped died.

Cally was sitting with Gigi in that austere individual's high-fenced back yard when a shadow came across the oleo-yellow sky, and stayed, and thickened before she could squeak, and engulfed her, and she saw the pudgy black-jellybean bodies, heard amid the humming din and the rattle of a million wings the now-familiar wailing cries.

"Well, I'll be damned," Gigi remarked, getting up hastily.

The two women fled into the house. The few baby-faced bugs that entered with them they carefully expelled, opening the door a crack to do so, then slamming it. Despite their efforts, one wailing mite got smashed in the door and gave a glassy scream as it died. Cally started to shake, but Gigi said angrily, "To hell with them."

The hungerbabies clung to the melba-brown, nurtureless walls of Gigi's house and cried and cried and cried. The two women sat in the kitchen and

found that they had nothing to say to each other.
Later Cally, who was afoot, had no choice but to
walk home amid the cicadas. She found that at first
they had come solely to Gigi's house, but they followed her, spreading throughout the town. They
rode in her hair like half-grown opossums riding on a
milk-swollen mother's back; they crawled along the
gaunt line of her collarbone and explored the dark
hideyholes of her blouse. Outside the Perfect Rest
Funeral Home they clustered in the laurel and aza-
leas, singing their strange slide-flute song.

They swarmed the small town as if it were a grove
of sumac, clutching with their orange claws to clothes
on the clotheslines, to children in the sandboxes, to
wooden siding and yellow brick house walls and the
black shirts of clergy on their way to monthly fellow-
ship. They zinged through the air on orange-edged
wings or clung black and pudgy to porch railings,
sighing, crying. Because they were everywhere, the
fact that they had the faces of babies could not be
ignored. The town hummed louder than they with
talk of them. Some people seemed to recognize departed loved ones in the black faces of the cicadas
and were afraid to kill them; a woman burst into
tears in front of the Handi-Mart because she stepped
on one by mistake. Other people perceived them as
an affront and bought out the local supply of insecti-
cides. The Lutheran, Methodist, and Brethren pas-
tors were inclined to interpret them as a plague, a
punishment sent by God, but among the fundamentalists
and the Roman Catholic majority there was talk of
demons. Special ecumenical community prayer meetings were called, and a special meeting of the borough council. Talk of witchcraft reached a new height,
and quarrels erupted for small reason, even among

the men, who were not as exhausted by the hunger-babies as the women.

No woman in the town who had ever mothered a baby could sleep properly those days. The sound of those weak, yet ever-continuing, dying cries put their nerves on constant emergency alert. A salient exception, Sojourner Hieronymus, who had never borne a child, took broom and did battle with the cicadas invading the sanctity of her tidy yard and front sidewalk. Oona Litwack, who had mothered many children and hugged many grandchildren to her cushiony bosom, shooed the black-and-orange bugs gently off her peonies, her plastic chipmunks and wooden propeller-winged ducks and the potted impatiens hanging from the edge of her porch. Ma Wilmore cowered in the heart of her house, the kitchen, talking nearly all day on the phone, though she would not open a door or a window. The talk was of the hungerbug onslaught. Amid that phenomenon, the death of the girl who had been raped went undiscussed and almost unnoticed by Ma Wilmore and Sojourner Hieronymus and the others.

The girl who had been raped—or rather, the young woman, though women in Hoadley remained "girls" until they were in their graves—the young woman was not hospitalized, but died at home while her solicitous and unsuspecting husband slept at her side. The coroner easily determined the cause of death to be a cancerous tumor nearly the size of a basketball pressing on her internal organs. Undressed, she gave the appearance of being perhaps three months pregnant with death. Her husband, who had not seen her undressed since the unfortunate occurrence which gave her her epithet in the town, had known nothing of what she was carrying. The doctor who signed the death certificate clicked his tongue, for the cancer was of a slow-spreading sort and would have been operable if caught even so much as a few months earlier.

Barry Beal, who arranged the blanket over her at the Perfect Rest Funeral Home, was probably the only person in Hoadley more than ten years of age who did not think of her as the girl who had been raped. He knew her only as the pretty blond girl from the drugstore, the one who black-lacquered her eyelashes into spikes and curled them so that they stood up above her eyes like a wrought-iron fence. The one he had seen a few times amid Ahira's misfits. He checked the side of her face for Ahira's mark, but it was not there. This one of Ahira's people had chosen not to be healed.

Cally Wilmore knew she was the girl who had been raped, and was surprised to see her young body lying in a casket (a sixteen-gauge steel Perma-Sealer casket, top of the line) in the Blue Room, the color of which matched that of her palisaded eyes. She wondered if the girl had somehow died months later of the rape, but couldn't ask Mark. Though she and Mark were occupying the same apartment, with no kids around to keep them from talking out their problems, they seemed farther apart than ever.

Cally wanted a reconciliation. The carousel of her personal agenda cycled on a constant hub of hunger for Mark. Other needs—for independence, adventure, growth, selfhood—loomed up from time to time and flashed by in a blur of mirrorshine and sky music and rainbow candy color, to cycle away again, but that one remained. Always before it had been possible; therefore Cally had thought she could go to Mark, duck her head, put her hand on his shirt, offer a few tears perhaps, and then their marriage would be all right again—or at least as right as it had been for some time—as long as she behaved herself, kept her mouth shut, did errands, cleaned the apartment and made good dinners. (How she was to maintain this Hoadley-woman facade while the world was ending, she did not question. She would manage somehow. The love hunger took priority, as it always did.) So she had presented herself to Mark the day before, contrite. But it had not worked as she expected. Mark had turned his back on her with a hard laugh she had never heard from him before. Mark had changed. Was changing.

Standing in the Blue Room next to the corpse of the girl who had been raped, Cally felt as always the tug of two urges. Wryly she knew she was like the house cat who, when let out, wanted to be in, and when in, wanted to be out. For the most part she wanted to be with Mark. He was around the funeral home somewhere; she had come into the place to be near him. But also she wanted to be away from him. Family was the thing that held a person down . . . she wanted to be far, far away, on her own adventure of living, free. Like a bird in the sky.

Neither seemed possible. Instead, she went riding.

"She good as killed herself," Gigi declared to Cally, out on the trail. "No reason the cancer should have killed her. A person can live with cancer. I should know. I got six kinds of cancer."

Gigi had known, of course, what had killed the girl in the Blue Room. Hoadley born and bred, Gladys Gingrich Wildasin knew what happened in and around the town as naturally as if she breathed in gossip along with the polluted air.

"I got more parts missing than a stripped car," Gigi bragged. "Cancer took 'em. First thing was, I had to have skin cancers removed. Then I got both breasts taken off, right to the armpit. I got a kidney taken out, had a tumor in it. All my female organs are gone. I got a section of bone missing out of my arm, the one that had radiation when I was a baby. Now they're talking about taking the rest of the arm, so's I'd have to ride Western, left-handed. There's a shadow starting to show up on my backbone. By rights I ought to be dead, but here I am, walking around."

"Riding around," said Cally. She glanced at pale, dust-brown-roaning-out Snake Oil, no longer in envy but with covert satisfaction, knowing that she had one-upped Gigi in the stable hierarchy by riding Tazz Man. On the black gelding, she was indisputably more the daredevil than Gigi.

As if in acknowledgment, the black horse plunged his heavy head, without provocation, to buck. Cally pulled on the huge curb bit—there was not much strength in her starved arms, but the bit acted as a lever on the tender parts of the horse's head and mouth—and kicked hard with booted feet. Devil's head came up as he leaped forward, and Cally hauled him in several rapid circles until he condescended to walk on. Devil was never happy on a trail ride unless he was running away.

Gigi watched impassively. "How's Mark?" she asked, perhaps not entirely tangentially, as Devil began to come to order.

"Worse than ever."

"Cicadas got him down?"

All around them the tar-baby bugs chorused in tragic soprano voices, lurched through the air, crunched under the horse's hooves, sighing Doom, Doom. The women paid little attention. They had accepted the cicadas and their glissando song. Doom. It was a given in the Hoadley summer, easily accepted, because it had been a tenor, a refrain in Hoadley conversation for years. Since forever.

The previous night another animal had burned, hanging from the water tower. A stray dog this time. At least so Hoadley hoped, that it was a stray and not someone's house pet. The carcass was charred beyond recognition. Gigi and Cally accepted the burning dog, also, and scarcely spoke of it.

Answering Gigi's question, yet not answering it, Cally murmured, "I don't know why I stay around."

"I would never leave Homer," declared Gigi cheerfully. "Kill him if I could get away with it, sure. Make him miserable, all the time. But I'd never leave him. He foots the bills."

"Right," said Cally, recognizing Gigi's familiar cynicism, wondering briefly what would happen if she got a better job, could support herself and her horse; would she leave Mark? The thought left within a breath, because it was no use making plans. The cicada song told her that.

Only after she was out of the woods and off her horse and had returned to Hoadley, to her house that happened to be a funeral home, to what should have been the bosom of her family, did the love-hunger return to her and she remembered, aghast, some of the things Gigi had said. That callous old woman, hard and hollow as a rotten tree, as Devil's black hooves—all her female organs were gone; had cancer taken her heart, too?

Cally found Mark in the apartment flipping through mortuary supply catalogues, contemplating the dry shampoos guaranteed to remove tobacco stains from moustaches, the New Improved Weldit Lip and Eye Sealer, the No-Mold crystals for use in humans, the Sur-Kill fungicide. Glowering, he did not look up when Cally came in. When, a moment later, someone rapped at the door, she answered it even though she had been on her way to change her clothes, rather than asking him to do so.

At the door stood Barry Beal. Darkly he stared at her from under heavy brows, and for a moment she expected him to ask her if she had seen Joanie. But he had not been asking about Joanie lately. He must have gotten over Joanie since he had been spending time with Ahira and her band of misfits. Maybe he had fastened his childlike devotions on Ahira instead. Had she put her mark on him? Who was to know one way or the other? thought Cally with skewed and sour humor. Ahira's mark would not show on Barry "Jamhead" Beal's pinto-patch face.

Barry's somber stare deepened. "Mrs. Wilmore," he said with the unprefaced directness of the mentally slow person, "somebody messed up my layout." He peered at her as though he thought she might have done it somehow, though she had been miles away at the stable.

"Huh?" said Cally, even though the words had been perfectly clear. The girl who had been raped, he meant. There was no other layout in the Perfect Rest at the time.

"Somebody messed up the blanket, and her dress and everything." Barry shifted his suspicious gaze past Cally to Mark. "Mr. Wilmore, you was around all afternoon. You know who done it?"

"I wasn't watching, Barry." Mark came to the door, and Cally moved away. "Probably some prankster," she heard Mark tell Barry. As indeed it probably had been, especially since the deceased was the girl who had been raped. Certainly her funeral would bring out the worst in people—though after every funeral, even the least likely funerals, Mark had to make sure to search the guest book for sick-sense-of-humor entries before he presented it to the family. "Could have been anybody," Mark was saying. "Some old gossip curious to see what she looked like under her things. Whoever. Just fix her up again before the viewing this evening, would you?"

Barry's mind was still stubbornly fixed on the injustice that had been done, not to the girl, but to him. "You mean I got to do her blanket all over again and everything?"

"I'm paying you to do it, right? I'm paying you by the hour. So what's the difference?" Mark's voice did not rise. He was really very good with Barry, Cally knew from many past occasions. He was kind to children, gentle with people in general, patient with the rambling mental processes of the elderly, supportive of the bereaved; he was really a very good man. She was surprised to remember how she had married him partly because of that goodness.

"Just pretend it's another blanket," Mark was telling Barry. "A whole 'nother job. You don't have to get it back the same way again." Mark went out with Barry to look at the damaged layout.

A good man. She knew he had always been faithful to her; he would have been paralyzed with remorse if he had slipped. She remembered his wincing guilt whenever he became annoyed with the children to the point of shouting at them, making them cry. Yet he had showed no such guilt after hitting her that one recent time. And even a few months before, such a scene would have been unthinkable.

Outside the cicadas sang their dirge. The keening voices loudened to Cally's ears when the door opened and Mark came in again.

"The beast is hungry," Mark announced to the air of the apartment. "The beast wants his supper."

Making a mirthless joke of their estrangement. . . .

Cally felt so starved for the sound of his voice that she didn't mind. "Would the beast perhaps care for some spaghetti?"

Made the day before, it could be warmed tomato sauce and all in the microwave without undue cooking odor to disturb the mourners who would soon be gathering down below. Anxious to please her husband, already moving toward the kitchen, Cally tried to speak lightly. But Mark did not answer.

She warmed the spaghetti and sat across the table from him, watching him eat. Even a few weeks before he would have offered her some, argued with her when she refused, coaxed or bullied her, trying to make her eat. But now he forked spaghetti impassively and did not speak.

Afterward he dressed for the evening viewing and went out into the cicada-chanting dusk. Hiding in the kitchen, Cally gobbled leftover spaghetti. She had meant to put it away in the refrigerator, but handling the food she found herself suddenly unable to keep control; hunger had gotten the better of her at last. She lifted gobs of cooling spaghetti to her mouth with her hands, licking the blood-red sauce off her fingers. It was not enough; would anything ever be enough for her hunger? There were iced sweet rolls in the cake saver. So much neglected food in the house since the kids were gone. She ate the rich pastries, all of them, then went on to assault the contents of the refrigerator. Cold gravy with the slab of congealed fat on top was as good as the cold chicken; cold soup and cold baked beans no more disgusting than the cold raw wieners. She bolted whatever food came to hand until she was gorged, until her stomach swelled as if she was pregnant with her own obsession, until she could not stand up straight. She sat on the kitchen floor amid droppings and splatters of sauce and juice and gravy, amid a devastation of greasy, empty Tupperware, with slimed face and filthy hands, and hated herself.

After a few moments she heaved herself up, walked bent over like an old, old woman to the bathroom, stood at the john and made herself vomit. She disgorged until nothing was left, until she felt light again, like a bird, as if even her bones were hollow. Then she rinsed her mouth, and washed, and went out to scrub the kitchen and all the evidence in it. She washed herself at the bathroom sink, then again in the kitchen while doing the dishes, then once more in the bathtub afterward, and still felt dirty.

When Mark came back from the viewing his wife was sitting on the bed, waiting for him.

"The beast is home," he announced dourly to the apartment when he came in. Then, entering the bedroom with suit coat and tie in hand, he saw her.

The fragrance of her perfume covered the lingering odor of vomit. In an absurdly tiny black lace teddy, low below spaghetti straps to show off what Cally seemed to think were breasts, high-cut above her thighs—Mark saw picket-fence ribs, saw hip bones grotesquely jutting, angular as those of a concentration camp victim in some *Life* magazine photo. Her legs, coquettishly folded, reminded him of nothing so much as broomsticks. Yellow broomsticks; her skin had gone sallow as her hair. Muscles twitched transparently around her nervous mouth. Her nose had thinned to a beak, the juncture between bone and cartilage plainly visible. Wispy fuzz covered her broomstick legs, her dowel-rod arms, as her abused and frantic body tried to warm itself; and despite all that, the crazy woman was trying for a *Playboy* pose, thought she was attractive, when she was starving herself to death. The nut case. He was done shouting at her, worrying about her. His lip curled as he hung up his suitcoat.

"What wonderful timing," he said.

She essayed a smile. Shy, it looked sweet and touching even on her hollow-cheeked, fleshless face. Despite the smile, or perhaps because of it, Mark saw that her bony shoulders and fiddlestick arms were shaken by a fine tremor, nearly invisible, her fragile body a violin under a rapid vibrato. He knew that she was always cold those days, always shivering. He knew that her trembling at this time might not be due entirely to her airy outfit and to chill. Neither fact moved him. The sight of her in no way pleased him.

"I know what you want," he said to her. Her presence on the bed was not an act of sensual desire; it was an act of fear and desperation and raw need. She did not want sex; she wanted him. She wanted to wind around him, a parasite, to entwine him, possess him, to draw her strength from him. She would be his succubus if he let her, like all the rest of them with their tentacles on him, their despairs leeching away at his life. She would suck him dry, she would take his essence, his soul.

She interpreted his statement as playful, and he saw hope lift her bony head with its careful cap of permed hair the color and texture of dead grass. He had known plastic junk-store dolls with softer hair, and someday soon when she was fussing with it he would tell her so. But for now he would tell her what he thought of her idea for his evening. With his next words he swatted down her hope as surely as if he had swatted her flyweight body down to the floor.

"You stupid airhead," he told her, quietly but with the joyous hardness that was new to him, that would protect him from whatever threatened to hurt him, that might yet deliver him from Hoadley's incessant demands; where had he gotten this wonderful hardness? "You total idiot. Look at yourself! Who would ever want to make love with you? You're like something out of a freak show! The walking skeleton; come see the walking skeleton girl! Who'd want to screw a skeleton? If I want to fuck a dead cunt, I know where I can find one."

He saw her shrink, trying to cower into her useless scrap of nightgown—but then, as if knocking her down with one hand and picking her up with the other, he lifted her head again with a sudden smile. He knew how to do that, smile. He could show his teeth as well as anyone.

"Tell you what," he said. "I've got an idea how we can do this. I finally found something that really turns me on." His smile broadened, became a boyish grin, but his voice turned knife hard, honed to stab. "You go into the bathroom and run yourself a tub of cold water and soak in it for fifteen, twenty minutes. Then come back out here and just lie real still."

He watched it hit her, watched it all become clear in her ever-so-intellectual mind. Watched the horror take her face, gape her mouth, she could not speak, she could not yet breathe—and he twisted the knife.

"You got any soft little baby blankets left around here? We'll cover you with one. Lay it on you in pretty folds. I can't do it as well as Barry Beal, but it doesn't have to be perfect. It'll just get messed up again when I lift it."

She scrambled back from him, spiderlike on the bed, her adrenaline surge giving her back her breath, her voice. Though the voice spasmed in her throat. "Oh. Oh. You. You—you beast!"

"Right," said Mark, and he started to take off his trousers.

Cally plunged off the bed, banging her emaciated knees on the floor, then found her feet and scuttled from closet to dresser, snatching clothing, clutching it against her half-naked, famished chest. Mark, hanging his trousers, stood in her way and laughed at her as she hesitated to come near him, to push past him.

"You were right, you know," he told her. "This town is going down the tubes. Bears burning on the water tower, crazy bimbo preaching in the park, dead babies coming back as bugs, and now there's a beast. It all goes to prove you were right. I admit you were right. We've got nothing to argue about any more."

"Get out of my way," Cally ordered in the same strangled tone, as if her own fury was a noose around her throat, turning her face red and threatening to kill her. Mark winced and pouted in mock pathos.

"You don't approve of the beast?"

"Go to hell." Goaded into courage, Cally reached past him to claw her jeans from their hanger. The movement pressed her against him, against the good smell of his tee-shirted neck and shoulders. If he tried to grab her . . . but his hands did not lift. He stood laughing deep in his chest as she turned and ran into the bathroom to dress where he could not see her. Even above the sound of his own stony mirth he heard the cold-metal sound of the bolt sliding shut.

He followed and stood outside the door, still laughing to make sure she heard him there. She was no longer entirely terrified of him, just wildly angry. He knew what would have thrilled and terrified her: if, after all, he had wanted her. But he preferred her anger. Standing there in his jockey briefs, he preferred to show her what she could plainly see: that even a corpse had roused him more than she.

Bolt slid again, door opened, she stood there clothed, the slim-cut jeans baggy on her, hanging in folds from her protuberant hipbones. Seemed like she was going to turn into an old bag, a craggy-hipped cow, no matter what she did. And too intent on herself to know it.

She said as if she expected him to care, "I'm getting out of here."

"Where? Going home to Mummy?"

"None of your business." She scurried circles around his large, half-naked presence in the bedroom, slamming things into a suitcase. A sizable suitcase, but not nearly large enough to hold all the baggage she was going to have to take with her. And she was in a wild hurry, and everything she laid hold of, panties, dreams, shirts and jeans and pain, makeup, break-up, purse and money and memories, they all went in jumbled, confused. Mark knew smugly that she was going to have a mess to sort out and clean up later. When the suitcase was only approximately full, Cally closed it.

"Here," said Mark with exaggerated solicitude, "let me help you carry that. Wisp like you, arms like spaghetti noodles, you can't possibly handle—"

She glared, silencing him—she almost frightened him. Her set teeth between thin, thin lips gave her the look of a death's head, spectral. But she was too much in a rush and tumult to notice how Mark blinked; she snatched up the suitcase, heaved and blundered it out to the door and into the car, an ant carrying away what was left of the picnic. It was in fact very nearly too heavy for her.

"Toodle-loo!" Mark stood on the front lawn in his underwear and waved as she drove away.

                    *   *   *

"What I mean," said Borough Council President
Wozny, "we've got to do something."

Since the animal-burning incident the night before
he had called yet another emergency council meeting. Though nebulous council opinion had long since
condensed into a consensus: no longer was it a question of whether there might possibly be a witch.
Instead, it was a matter of eradicating the obviously
extant witch.

Everyone sitting in the room knew, without Gerald Wozny's needing to stick his neck out and say it,
what he meant by "do something." Ahira had been
proselytizing and healing in the town park three or
four times a week, and the council members had
their informants; the number of her band of misfits
had steadily grown, including even the "woodchucks,"
the people who lived in holes and were scared of
shadows, from the mountains surrounding the town.
People like Bud Zankowski, the crazy coal mine hermit, and the otherwise-nameless Bicycle Man, who
rode his eponymous vehicle from house to house
sharpening knives and scissors, who slept no one
knew where, somewhere so far back in the woods
even the deer hunters hadn't found it. And who was
rumored to be a rapist, kidnapper and child mo-
lester. These were the sorts of people Ahira at-
tracted. The Hoadley majority, who liked their
religion served with coffee and doughnuts, looked
on with a queasy, motion-sick sense of indecency at
what Ahira was doing, rather as if they were seeing
their town roll over like a shit-eating coon hound and
show its verminous underbelly and spraddle its legs.
Ahira's band of followers had passed the five hundred mark and was creeping toward the ominous
six-six-six. Ahira had to go.

And every day the cicadas wailed.

"Reverent Berkey and Father Leopold don't want no more to do with it," President Wozny admitted. "It" being the silencing of Ahira. He would have said more, something inspiring about the secular leaders of the community taking upon themselves the threats facing the community, but he didn't like the way the council secretary was looking at him through her aliform glasses. The woman lived to contradict him.

"Something you want to say, Zephyr?" he inquired with a show of resignation.

She laid down her notebook on the table in front of her and crossed her hands atop it; the nails were enameled into blood-red bone-hard spear points much the same shape as her glasses. "I been doing some checking," she said. "And what I say, that Ahira ain't your witch at all." Zephyr paused, waiting for prompting from another council member. It would have been immodest for her to continue without urging. Reluctantly Wozny provided it.

"How come not?"

"She ain't from around here. Ain't none of us never seed her before. The 'cyclopedia says a witch is somebody from close at hand." Zephyr produced a tiny fold of tablet paper from her purse, displaying it as proof of research done, though she did not open it. "It says this here kind of town is perfect for a witch. Any kind of backwater. Places where people just stay, got to put up with each other, one of them gets to be a witch. So what the 'cyclopedia says,"— Zephyr took care to cite opinion greater than her own, authority of Right Here In Black And White potency—"the witch is somebody we knowed from little on up, somebody we'd look right past. Somebody that's got a secret, somebody—" Zephyr affected a delicate hesitation, but her eyes glinted salaciously behind her rhinestoned glasses. "Somebody different, been hiding it. Light in their loafers, what I mean."

The other female council member pressed for a clarification of terms. "You mean somebody what's a sissy, like?"

Tapping at her evidence, Zephyr came right out with it: "Says in here witchcraft's got to do with all them wrong kinds of—sex." On the significant word her voice dropped to a nasal leer. Measuring the reaction, she allowed herself satisfaction. Even Gerald Wozny was listening with greatest interest. A well-done presentation, she knew, really very well done.

The council indulged in a murmur of scandalized appreciation for a moment, until its blunt old German member brought it back to business. "Don't make no sense to me," he complained. "Didn't none of this here locusts and stuff start until after that Ahira come."

"That's what I say," Wozny declared. But then he hastily mollified the opposition by adding, "Maybe this Ahira's funny and we don't know about it." And at once, like any well-fed herd animal, the Council was off on the enticing scent of deviant sexual practices.

"What about that one the cops found the other night?"

"Oh, Norma Koontz! Musser. Wasn't that something? But there ain't no harm in Norma."

"What about that there fellow rides a bicycle, rings the bell at the children? I always did say—"

"I got a better one than that for you," said Zephyr. She kept her voice suggestively low, and the council came to immediate attention.

Zephyr had been doing some checking other than

in the encyclopedia. She started, as Hoadley story-tellers generally did, at the outer rim of the topic, spiraling in toward the center. "Do you remember old man Witherow? Lived up Olp's Dam Hollow."

Some of those present remembered him.

"Had a daughter Blanche, run away with a fellow from Hoople. Remember? Then she come back, had a baby, finally married a Wertz." The Wertzes were a solid, unassuming Hoadley family, Catholics turned Lutheran because of a mixed marriage. "Todd Wertz. And he adopted the baby."

Nods. "It was a boy," volunteered the other female council member—women were in charge of keeping track of these things. Men participated in gossip, but women were in charge, the guardians and promulgators of Hoadley's values. "Their oldest. Peter Wertz." Her eyes took on a deep look as she dredged memory. "Seems to me he didn't do too well."

"I remember that boy," a man offered. "He was one of them didn't—didn't—he didn't do sports, or—"

"He didn't fit in," said Zephyr smoothly, "and he went away."

"To California!" The other woman pounced into the center of this circling dance, the nugget of information like a trophy between her teeth, a mouse in a cat's mouth. "He was one of them hippies, like."

"Sure," said Gerald Wozny. "I know his father at work. He says they don't know what become of him. Don't never hear from him no more." This statement caused shock and smug pity for the parents; it was an unaccountable thing, such an ungrateful child.

"Well, I know a woman knows his mother," said Zephyr, "and I just today found something out."

Council gave her its most interested attention.

Once again she prolonged the suspense by starting roundabout and spiraling in.

"You know how them pesky bugs are getting on everybody's nerves?" she asked rhetorically. "Well, they work on Mrs. Wertz something awful. Seems like she hears them reproaching her. And she got to crying and went and told her neighbor lady something she hadn't never told nobody."

Zephyr paused until urged to go on.

"They hear from Peter all right," she said finally. "They heard he had him one of them sex change operations."

A gratifying hubbub followed this statement. Zephyr, with a seasoned performer's sense of timing, waited (thinly smiling) to cap the story, to put the icing on the cake. And Wozny, of all people, served as her foil.

"What's all this got to do with anything?" he demanded, irritated that she had created such a sensation, suddenly aware that the council meeting had gotten out of his control. And Zephyr leaned forward, her spear-tipped fingers tapping and crawling on the tabletop, and opened her mouth, and spake.

"Why, what it's got to do is that this here Peter Wertz ain't in California at all." A pause, sufficient for effect but not allowing for interruption. "He's back here, he's right outside of town, only he's a woman now. And he lives with another woman."

Uproar, topped by a common-sense blast from the German farmer. "Why, then what the hun did he have the operation for?"

That no-nonsense question went unanswered, because Wozny, along with half a dozen other council members, was clamoring for the culprit's name.

"Well, he changed his name," said Zephyr with tantalizing slowness.

"We can figure that!" the other female council member snapped.

"Uses his real father's last name," Zephyr divulged at last. "Danyo. Shirley Danyo, he calls himself now."

Go home to Mummy? Not hardly. It was in fact the last place in the world Cally wanted to be, with her indifferent, ever-preoccupied mother, even if Owen and Tammy had not been there to ask questions, which they were. She would go—she would go where her heart was: where her horse was. And where her friend was, her big-voiced, generous friend, the only person she could think of who seemed to like her just as she was, for herself, and not want anything of her, and not tangle her in any of the complicated meshes of sex and love and duty and role. And she would keep it from Mark as long as she could, where she was going. When he found out he would make something dirty of it somehow. Hoadley would make something dirty of it somehow. She sensed that.

A good thing it was so late, very little traffic on the roads, because she could not seem to help driving like a crazy woman. . . . Cally started to sob and drove more recklessly than ever.

Down, down, screeching around the sharp curve and rocketing through the single-lane stone railroad underpass, the dark and dripping tunnel . . . Around the hairpin bend and up the steep hill beyond. The night, the road were a mine tunnel flooded with stagnant tears. Tarry pavement melted seamlessly into dark forest unseen against a soft-coal sky. Headlights lit only blackness. Behind them, Cally jock-eyed over the steering wheel and pressed, forcing her puny way over the hill and down again, down,

down into the pregnant depths at an unreasonable rate of speed.

Weeping, and observing herself from a small distance, Cally began to realize that she really was sick, that perhaps she should indeed have gone to see the doctor. . . .

Shirley heard her coming—the wild whine of Cally's overtaxed engine woke her up, for not many people came near the place at that time of night, and even fewer driving so fast. She heard the car plunge to a stop, got up (hearing the snick of the opening door), pulled on a bathrobe (the somewhat delayed clunk as the car door closed) and looked out to see Cally lugging her suitcase through the gate in the junk-horse fence. Shirley had her front door open before Cally knocked, and took the suitcase from her, hiding surprise, hiding consternation at how Elspeth would react to this particular houseguest. Elspeth would just have to go screw herself. It didn't take half an eye to see that Cally was hurting.

"I had to get away," Cally explained, or tried to explain without telling too much. "Mark . . ." The name seemed to choke her; she tried again. "Mark . . . and . . . I . . ."

"Sure thing," Shirley hushed her. "No problem. You're welcome to stay long as it takes. Cup of tea?" Her raucous voice had gone uncannily gentle, and instead of accepting the tea Cally clutched at Shirley's sleeve with starved hands that scratched against the chenille with a sere, bony sound, like claws. Shirley embraced—there was hardly anything to featherweight Cally to embrace; it was like holding a Rice Krispie, a dry leaf ready to fly, a husk, the shell an insect leaves behind, something hollow-boned and brittle-thin and so fragile that a hug might cave it in. Nevertheless, Shirley hugged—cautiously—and Cally rested against her warm bosom, sobbed tenuously on her shoulder, and against that sturdy shoulder Cally's wails sounded ghostly frail, like the wailing voices of the hungerbugs.

CHAPTER ELEVEN

Elspeth found Cally in Shirley's house in the morning, went back to her castle tower and did not come out again until suppertime. She had seen the pain in Cally's face, and even, somewhat, felt it. She wanted, if not to befriend Cally, at least to avoid hurting her more. To be a good person, as Shirley was. Or at least to let Shirley sit and talk with the little twit. But it was a hollow effort. Though Elspeth laid out for herself a soft-hued palette and tried to paint, she felt always the sharp dark thing hard and restless just below the surface of her mind.

Reporting to the house at sunset for something to eat, she found Shirley serving lasagna and Cally sitting at the kitchen table looking more literally like death warmed over than any living person Elspeth had ever seen. Cally had accepted a small portion of Shirley's excellent homemade pasta. As Elspeth watched, Shirley's houseguest took a corner of one noodle, hardly larger than a fly speck, on her fork, and lifted it to her mouth, then gagged as if it was indeed excrement. Shirley observed anxiously.

"You're all upset, is why you can't eat that." As her own portion of lasagna cooled on her plate, Shirley pawed at the contents of a cupboard. "Maybe something else would slip down better."

"I don't think so," said Cally thinly.

"Soup? They say chicken soup is good for whatever ails you."

Shirley heated the soup. Elspeth snorted softly, like a horse in the stall, and stood beside her lover at the stove, getting herself a slab of lasagna. They did not speak. Elspeth sat down by Cally and ate, feeling the substantial pasta lump in her slim toast-brown throat and congeal to bulk heavy in her stomach; her gut had to be almost as tight as Cally's. She forced herself to eat nevertheless, gazing levelly at the intruder.

"Try this here." Shirley set a small portion of soup in front of Cally. But Cally gagged even at the odor of the rising steam.

"I can't."

"Cally, you got to eat!" Elspeth had seldom heard placid Shirley speak with such obvious alarm. Though Shirley did not say it, they both knew what she was afraid of: Cally would die on her hands. "You ain't still thinking of this diet of yours, are you?"

"No. I want to eat. I ate last night. And then I threw it all up."

"You got the flu? Maybe we better get you to a doctor."

"It's not the flu. I made myself throw up."

Shirley sat down and stared at Cally over her cold dinner, trying to comprehend. Her expression said, though her mouth didn't, Why the hun did you do that? Cally met the look levelly and answered it.

"I couldn't help it. I know I've got to start eating, but I just couldn't stand having all that food in me."

So starve, thought Elspeth, helping herself to more lasagna. It did not escape her notice that she was serving herself while Shirley hovered over Cally.

"Mark's right about just one thing," said the latter in somber tones. "I've got anorexia."

"Well . . ." Shirley faltered, out of her depth. Elspeth, who considered that Cally should have grasped the just-mentioned fact months before, gave her lover a sardonic look and offered no assistance.

"And Hoadley's to blame for it," said Cally.

"How you figure?" Thrown off balance after having heard Cally blame Mark all day, Shirley wore the troubled, patient look of a horse on slippery footing. She still had not touched her lasagna. Disgusted, Elspeth took it. And Cally, she noticed, was looking down at her hands, hesitating, making a heart-touching show of what she was about to say, as if she was confessing her previous sex life to a fiance. The nose-picking dork.

"You know, I loved Hoadley at first. Everybody was so nice, I felt like—you know, my family wasn't that close." Cally's hands twitched at her paper napkin, clawing it apart. "I mean, I never really felt like my parents—cared much. But Hoadley—even people I hardly knew seemed—so warm."

"Hoadley's like that," Shirley promptly agreed.

Not in Elspeth's experience. But then, she had not married a Hoadley boy.

"It was like I had family," said Cally with weary amazement. "I mean, I never put it to myself that way, I just now realized, but it was. It was as if I had real family for the first time in my life."

"Well, that's good, ain't it?" said Shirley. Shirley had patience and goodness the way some people had social diseases. Elspeth had neither, not when it meant having to listen to this sort of thing. She could not sit by Cally and look at Cally any longer; she got up to find herself something to drink.

"It was, until I—I guess that's why I started starving myself. I saw the writing on the wall. I learned the score."

No cola, no fruit juice, no milk in the fridge, only a glass jug of water. Damn. Elspeth felt the sharp knife of anger nudging inside her ribs. She had not spoken a word to Cally since she entered the kitchen.

"I found out how much this family really—really loved me. Oh, they loved me to pieces—as long as I behaved. As long as I did just what they wanted me to. Dressed the way they dressed. Went to the right church. Said the right things." Cally was gaining volume. "As long as I was just the Cally they wanted to see, it was all hugs and kisses. But let me get out of line once, let me have a thought or a dream of my own . . ."

"No go, huh?" Shirley sounded sympathetic, if somewhat bewildered. The system sounded normal to her. Naturally people liked you when you did what they wanted. Naturally they resented you when you didn't. No big deal. "But why starve yourself?"

"I was starving anyway." Cally looked up with tragic eyes huge in her thin, thin face. "That's what the books say," she explained softly. "The anorexic comes from an oppressive family. The anorexic is starving for love."

Silence.

"That's me all right," added Cally after a few dramatic moments. "Except I adopted Hoadley as my family, and it turned out to be just as abusive as the real one."

"Jesus shit!" Elspeth could stand listening no longer. "Jesus fucking knee-deep shit!" She slammed the ice-water bottle down on the countertop so hard that

it shattered under her hand, never hearing Shirley's
protest. "You call that abuse?" She advanced on Cally,
feeling her curling fingers tingle with her own rage,
swordpoint inside her prodding hard. "You are a
spoiled brat. You don't know abuse; you never came
close. Abuse is when they tease you with lighted
cigarettes for fun, places the burns don't show. Abuse
is when they pinch your nose closed and pour hot
tabasco sauce down you. Abuse is when they throw
you in the dark closet and don't let you out even to
go to the bathroom, and then they punish you for the
mess. Abuse is when they—when they—"

Elspeth's voice cracked. Cally curled up almost
fetal in front of her, and Shirley sat with her mouth
open soft and gawking, but Elspeth scarcely saw
either of them; she was seeing the man, the one they
called her father, coming at her with the leather
strap—again. . . . Abuse was when you prayed to
God they weren't in fact your parents, that it was all
a mistake somehow, that somewhere, someday, you
would find the cradle from which you had been
stolen, and your real father would be a prince with a
golden crown. . . .

"Elspeth," Shirley was saying, "*Elspeth*," and getting up, stepping clumsily in the broken glass, and
ignoring it, coming over to put her big hands on
Elspeth's shoulders. "You?" asked Shirley gently.
Because Elspeth had never told her any of this.
Elspeth, the young beauty, the exotic, there had
been no past to her except a discarded name.

"Who the hell do you think?"

Even the name under which Shirley had first met
her, not real. The beautiful young people who came
to California to find their futures often hid their
pasts.

From what seemed like a great distance Cally said,

"I used to daydream that they did things like that to me. Then someday the prince would come and take me away. Somebody would—love me. . . ."

"You are a goddamn asshole," said Elspeth savagely, and she tore away from Shirley's quiet hands and thrust herself out the door.

It was nightfall. And Elspeth's mood matched the night, so charcoal-black it could almost have been seen as a smoldering hot, feral aura around her in sunlight. Head thrust forward, she strode toward the barn. She wanted to kill something, right away; she did not want to take the time to stalk and shoot a bear, as she had done the first time the mood came on her, the cunning, chill, stealthy killer mood that numbed her like black ice. Killing the bear had been good, a long, leisurely self-indulgence; the mood had sated itself slowly throughout the days it took her to stalk and dispatch her prey. And killing the dog; that had been quicker, less satisfying. Her hatred for Hoadley had been more urgent by then, had not let her take the time she needed—but still her war had been merely with that kissing-itself town, not with anyone to whom she felt so tied, so tangled in meshes of shared passion as she did with Shirley. But this time her sneak assault was to be on her lover—her diatribe had been at Cally, but her rage was mostly for Shirley, Shirley, the one she loved, the one who would therefore, according to the pattern of her life, brutalize and betray her—and she lusted for a victim as she sometimes lusted for Shirley's breasty, golden body, lusted so strongly that she could not withstand delay. She would kill. At once.

The horses stood in their stalls, looking out stupidly at her past their own long noses. Horses were cherished, infuriating, feeble-minded animals. It would hurt Shirley if she killed a horse, Elspeth knew. But mere killing, mere hurting were not quite enough; her mood demanded manifestation in fire. And she would not be able to drag a horse to a hanging place as she had dragged the bear. It had worn her out, dragging and lifting the bear.

She climbed to the loft and hunted out the stable cats much as they hunted the birds and rodents that inhabited the barn along with them. Atop the highest bale, looking rather like a perched eagle, sat the biggest cat. Not fat—no stable cat ever grows fat— but big, battle-scarred, bony, tough. He jumped away when he saw her coming toward him—he trusted no human except Shirley—but she had anticipated the direction of the jump; quick as a cat herself, she cornered him, grabbed him despite his hissing and biting, despite his vehement clawing, which tore her tunic and bloodied her arms. She throttled him with her slender sepia hands until he went limp, then swung him by the tail and bashed his head against the wall to finish him. Her sword hung at her waist, but she did not use it, did not think of using it, did not want to use it. Though she knew the day would come when she would use it.

Dangling the dead cat by the tail, she went out to the shed where the manure spreader and tractor and lawn mower were kept, and the cans of gasoline. It did not take much gasoline to soak the small carcass. Shirley was a trusting sap; Shirley had never missed even the huge amount it had taken for the bear. Elspeth felt in her pocket for the matches, found them—she had kept them there lately, like a Boy Scout, prepared—and headed toward the farmhouse. She would hang the cat from the fence. Her lips, the soft, faintly pouting, exquisite lips of a consummate lover, thinned into a grim smile. Shirley would be surprised. Had been already, and would be sur-

prised some more. Shirley knew nothing of the secret Elspeth, the real name, the court records:
prostitution, malicious mischief, cruelty to animals,
assault with a switchblade. . . . As long as she had
been with Shirley, as long as she had felt sure Shirley loved her and only her, she had been able to
keep that ice-black aspect of herself under control,
under wraps, hidden. For the most part. But lately
there had been Cally to contend with . . . and Ahira,
that Ahira woman, scared her. Something in that
Ahira woman called to her. The worst in her. Brought
it out of her so that she had gone and done what she
had not done in years.

The memory of the smell of burning fur would
sicken her once the mood passed, she knew. But she
could not or would not desist. She couldn't think
what might stop her. . . .

Coming past the farmhouse, she found out.

Still outside the fence and just past the porch
corner Elspeth stared, hearing the roar like cicada
roar only louder, coming nearer, seeing dimly in the
night the swirling of the approaching swarm—Elspeth
reacted within an instant. There was enough of a
black person's instinct and training in her that Elspeth
knew a hostile mob when she saw one. Or heard one.

She dropped the dead cat and ran forward, rounded
the fence corner—the plastic ponies floated at her
eye level on their posts—sprinted toward the gate,
Shirley's gate that swung perpetually open, and
reached it and closed it before the Hoadley natives
blundered up against it. Then she stood at guard just
inside, panting, waiting, one hand on the pommel of
her sword.

The borough council, as Gerald Wozny had made
clear in the parking lot after the formal meeting,

intended nothing more than to go out and talk with "this here Wertz, or Danyo, or whatever" and see what was what, "see if he can't call off the damn bugs, what I mean." The very next evening had been agreed upon, despite a conflict with summer reruns of "Family Ties." The fact that the council members did not hesitate to make the necessary personal sacrifice showed the depth of their dedication to public service. Indeed, their zeal made them forget discretion; they spoke with their families and neighbors and co-workers while the orange-eyed bugs with the black faces of babies hummed and whined and incessantly wailed . . . and the idea that the cicadas and all the other perversities that plagued their beloved town could be blamed on one unnatural person was too much for the average Hoadley person to stomach without strong action. The logic was simple, seductive, infuriating: drive out the witch and the world would be well. Half of Hoadley, hoarsely shouting as if at a softball game, accompanied the council to confront Danyo that evening.

Through the frail wire fence Elspeth faced men— and some women, stalwart old farm wives, the black-jacketed young women who lifted weights and clung to the backs of motorcycles—Elspeth faced a mob armed with lead pipes, baseball bats, lengths of heavy chain, the biggest wrench in the tool box, blunt instruments of all sorts. These were not gang warriors or knife fighters, Hoadley people. Their stabbing was generally verbal and in the back; up front, these were blunt-force folk, verbal or otherwise.

"What do you want?" Elspeth demanded through the fence.

The young exotic in pseudo-medieval garb, hand on sword, made them uneasy enough by her sheer wild-eyed oddity that they stopped and found something to laugh at. "Not you, sweetie!" one man yelled.

"Why not?" someone retorted. "She's just as much of a queer as the other one."

"Not by a country mile, she ain't!" With a bark of hard laughter.

Elspeth had no time to wonder what that last meant. She had grasped the essentials: that the mob wanted Shirley for some reason, and that only she, Elspeth, and a chicken-wire fence stood in their way. Already some of them were banging and prying at the flimsy barrier with their weapons. "You call this here a fence?" one lifelong farmer yelled. "What fer kind of fence is it? Wouldn't hold a chicken in!"

Elspeth said fiercely, "It's meant to keep Hoadley out."

"Won't keep nothing out for long! Least of all us!"

Elspeth's dark hand shook briefly on the pommel. Then, slowly, she drew the sword. That unmistakable long, downsliding metal sound, glassy-smooth as a cicada's wail . . . The sound sliced through the rah-team shouting so that it subsided to a mutter, a near silence, and into that uneasy lull Elspeth thrust words meant to cut.

"It's to keep out windbags. Bigots. Slogan shouters. Hypocrites. Narrow-minded old bitches. Judgmental old farts. Pompous assholes. Backwoods, thick-skulled, no-neck shitheads. It's meant to keep you all out."

A fence topped with bright-colored little horses, some with silver-painted shoes on their plastic hooves . . . Muttering crescendoed to an angry shout. Blunt weapons loomed high as the horses. Like a huge

snarling dog the mob pressed against the fence so
that the wire stretched.

Elspeth stood erect like a warrior of old, waiting
for them with the sword.

Odd, thought Shirley, watching through her limp
and dusty curtains, odd how Hoadley had called her
and called her and called her home from so far away,
even though once she had hated it. Even though she
knew it would never accept her. A clutching, clinging place, Hoadley, its tendrils deep in her heart.
She pitied it, but even now, facing the worst Hoadley
had to offer, she could no longer hate it as she had
when she was young.

Elspeth had drawn her sword. Shirley knew she
could put it off no longer; she had to face them. She
made her body move; she went out, letting the front
door slam behind her so that Elspeth would hear her
coming and not slit anyone open, not yet. . . . "Hey,"
she called to her fierce little lover, "watch what
you're saying to my relatives." Shirley tried to sound
jovial, voluble, at ease. She did not quite succeed,
but her appearance diverted the mob for the moment from action into invective.

"Fag!"

"C'mere, queer!"

"He-she," declared the councilwoman with the
lethal-looking glasses, Zephyr. She carried a heavy
flashlight; a weapon, or a tool? She shone the powerful beam in Shirley's face.

"Hey, Peter! What did you do with it?" Laughter
at the shouter's wit. "Did they throw it in the garbage after they cut it off?"

Shirley felt her smile slide away, leaving her wide
mouth naked, indecent. She squinted in the flashlight glare, knowing she was ugly when she squinted—

and homely even when she did not—knowing she
was pale in that white spear of light, knowing she
was sweating. The flashlight beam followed her as
she moved to stand beside Elspeth. As best she
could, she ignored it.

"What do you people want?" Shirley asked the mob
with a conscious effort to keep her voice calm and
quiet, as if she were a storekeeper trying to please a
difficult customer. But a roar and a babble assaulted
her in answer.

"We want you out of here, Peter Wertz!"

"Pervert!"

"Bringing this, what I mean, evil on us all—"

"Get out of town and take your bugs with you!"

Shirley said, "Whoa! I never done no harm to
none of you."

"Weirdo!" They seemed not to have heard her; the
voices had grown angrier. All laughter had ceased.
"Get out, witch!"

"Oversexed sissy whore!"

"Did you let them cut off your balls, too?"

And Elspeth, listening, had turned to stare at her,
had started to shake, and the tip of her sword drooped
until it dragged on the ground. And the mob, sensing that it no longer needed to be afraid of the jig
with the knife, roared and surged against the fence
to trample it down.

"I wouldn't, if I was youse." Shirley could speak
calmly, for she felt numb, wooden. This was her
worst-case scenario, and she was living it, and in a
way she had planned for it, in nightmares, in her
instinctive fears whenever she had thought of her
home town throughout the years of her self-imposed
exile. She knew what to say. "Youse don't want to
splatter my blood around. I got AIDS, what I mean."

Her level voice had carried throughout the crowd.

Roar dwindled to an uneasy mutter, and the mob stood still. Elspeth had not stopped staring at Shirley, but Shirley was looking at the others, many of them her former neighbors, people she had known since she was a little boy.

"What's more," she reminded them gently, "last I heard, things were getting so's AIDS could take regular, upstanding people like youse. Not just deviants like me." Shirley glanced at Elspeth and smiled, a flat smile that strained her mouth; it was the best she could do. "We both got AIDS," she declared. "Both us queers. Right, Elspeth?"

Be with me on this, Elspeth, she willed her. But Elspeth stared back at her without replying.

And from the crowd a voice shouted, "She's lying!"

They all knew she was lying. The awkwardness of her voice and Elspeth's lack of response told them that. A woman in the night yelled shrilly, "Get her!"

Like a single huge, many-legged and many-limbed beast the mob lurched forward, snapping the wire or trampling it. Shirley flinched and stepped back, one hand to her face—the nightmare response, to make her eyes stop seeing what was happening—the other reaching out to grab Elspeth by her left arm, dragging her back toward the house; Elspeth had not moved, did not seem to care what happened to either of them. Elspeth had not lifted her sword, and unless they could barricade themselves in the house, could fend them off that way for a while, it would all be over as soon as the roused representatives of Hoadley had cleared the fence—

Something else was roused.

The fence, the fence itself was moving.

Not the wire; the horses! Shirley blinked and stood gawking, and by the sudden stiffening life she felt in Elspeth she knew that Elspeth saw it too: the hooves,

the dainty black-and-silver-painted hooves darting
to strike, the handsome little heads snaking out,
ears flattened, teeth bared. And swinging hard
and heavy and biting as spiked maces—heavy? Was
there weight in those hooves, those heads? Could
not have been. These were hollow plastic horses on
wooden posts, nothing more. Yet people were falling, people were screaming and struggling to push
back against those behind them who had not yet
seen—the weirdness.

And the posts and their ponies, the posts themselves were moving.

Drawing in, pulling down, tightening their line of
defense until their rectangle had turned to a ring
around Shirley and her house, until the painted ponies ran at chest height, the nose of one less than
half a length from the tail of the next. They looked,
Shirley thought profanely, like a fucking merry-go-
round ride. When they began to move forward in
their circle and bob, some up, some down, in alter-
nation, she considered that she had had enough for one
evening. She turned her back on the mob (which was
retreating in consternation, as was she) and on the
smoothly springing horses, and pulled Elspeth along
with her into the house.

Cally was in there, looking out a window from
behind a veil of curtain. Shirley did not hold it
against Cally that Cally had hidden herself from the
mob. No sense letting Hoadley call Cally a monster/
deviant/witch too. Poor skinny kid. Came to find a
friend, and found a lesbian transsexual instead. Shirley felt sure that until that evening Cally had seldom
given a thought to what went on between Elspeth
and herself. Cally was too smart, thinking about other,
important things, to nose into people's lives the way
Hoadley did. Cally was a hilltop, sky-looking person,

not interested in sniffing the crotches of life. And Elspeth would never understand that, how Cally could be innocent without being dumb. Elspeth was a jealous little cunt, practically primed to kill Cally. Keeping Elspeth around was in more ways than one like keeping a panther for a pet. Shirley hated to bring her into the room where Cally stood.

But Cally stared out the window at the fence-cum-carousel, only glancing at Elspeth, and said to Shirley, "How'd you make it do that?" The blank, staggered look on Cally's face, Shirley knew, matched her own.

Shirley's wooden calm cracked, and she said with unnecessary vehemence, "I didn't have nothing to do with it!"

And Elspeth, at her side, spoke for the first time since Peter Wertz had emerged like a specter from the woman she thought she knew as lover.

"You didn't tell me."

Shirley looked. Elspeth's sword, bare and dangerous, still dragged from her right hand. But Shirley could see that she did not need to worry about what Elspeth might do or say to Cally. Elspeth did not know where she was, and there was no room in Elspeth to think about Cally, or Hoadley, or the fence weirdly carouseling outside, or the weapon in her hand, or anything but this haunt, this fetch, this doppelganger, the ghost of Peter Wertz.

"You didn't tell me you were a man."

"I'm not a man."

"But you didn't tell me that you *were*." Elspeth was worse than blank and staggered; she was a zombie. Worse than walking wounded. Elspeth was walking dead, and Shirley looked at this one whom she loved and blazed into vehement life.

"I'm not a man! I never was, I never wanted to be.

Nobody asked me, dammit. I like *women*." Shirley took Elspeth in her arms, hugged her, shook her, tried to warm some response back into her. "I wanted to be a woman. I always knew I was a girl, from little on up. Somebody goofed when they gave out the bodies, that's all."

Elspeth stood dead as a parking meter, except for her mouth, which moved, robotic. "I thought I knew you."

"You do know me! You know everything that's true about me."

"Five years, and all a lie."

"I've never lied to you!"

"Faking in bed . . ."

"No! What we had—have—is real!" Shirley made up in passion and volume all that Elspeth lacked. "Being a guy was a lie. That wimp Peter Wertz was a walking lie."

"Did he like dressing up in his mommy's clothes?" Elspeth came to sudden, vicious life. The long steel blade in her hand trembled, slowly lifting, hard lights glinting and slithering along its blood groove. "Did he like jerking off in her undies?"

Shirley felt her face tighten, her gut muscles tighten as if she had been punched, and in spite of herself she stepped back, just as Peter Wertz would have stepped back from the inevitable playground bully. "No," she said. "El, you don't understand. That thing was a piece of meat fastened on me by mistake, is all."

Elspeth seemed not to hear. "Boys? Did he like doing it in his ass with other boys?"

"No. Elspeth." Shirley backed a step farther away. Hurt, she knew she was going to be hurt, and her body wanted to avoid it even though her mind wanted to face it. . . . "Get to the point."

"The point?" Elspeth raised her sword and laughed, if anyone could call such a cold sound a laugh. "This is the point." The steel swordtip wavered in front of her face. She focused on it, nearly cross-eyed, seeming to examine it, to see it deeply, and she started to tremble. Shakily, needing both hands to guide the blade, she sheathed it.

"I don't know," she mumbled, not looking at Shirley. "I don't know what to do or think."

And still gawking out the window, seemingly unaware of what had been going on a few feet from her, Cally exclaimed, "Look! You've got to come see this!"

"I don't give a shit!" Shirley had never spoken so savagely to Cally, and did not care. She went to Elspeth, tried to put her arms around her, but Elspeth shied back from her, almost whimpering, like a scared little girl with her cotton underpants down around her bony knees.

"Let me alone!" She pulled away from Shirley's embrace. Shirley had been a man.

All Cally's pain had left her. Nothing about her erstwhile wife-and-mother life with Mark seemed real. She felt an exaltation, a sense of purification and moral superiority; she was moving on another plane of existence, only vaguely aware of Shirley and Elspeth quarreling behind her, and she knew herself capable of seeing visions. But the scene outside the tall farmhouse window was no vision. Its colors, its music, its lights were so vivid to her that she muffled her ears with her hands, wished for dark glasses.

"You guys," she insisted, "you've got to *look* at this. I don't believe it."

Silent, Shirley came and stood by her side.

In the darkness beyond the windowglass sheen the little horses still bobbed in their defensive ring. Cally felt a vague sense of something wrong about the way they were circling, but did not pursue it; the truth would come to her in time, in the cycling fullness of time, as light came to the sky. . . . Rapt, she watched the wheeling spokes overhead, girders made of small amber lights sweeping past in synchronization with the majestic cavortings of the plastic ponies, spreading into an ornate rim, a cornice, over the fence posts. From the night floated the somewhat asthmatic treble notes of a Strauss waltz. A carousel waltz.

Shirley blinked and shook her head hard as if to clear her hearing. "Locusts?" she said, querulous, after a moment.

"And lightning bugs." It had taken Cally an indeterminate span of time to realize that the lights were fireflies, the calliope music cicadas—or the all-too-human cicada creatures Hoadley called locusts.

A voice spoke. "How incredibly bizarre." Elspeth, with some of her exquisite scorn back, had chosen her own window to look from.

Like an Apache boy fasting on a mountaintop, seeking truth, Cally turned her thin face and spoke to her across the room: "It's happening because you told it to."

"Me!" Elspeth was startled out of her scornful pose by Cally's oracular tone. "I didn't tell anything to happen!"

"You said the fence was to keep Hoadley out. This is the way it took to do so. Shirley." Cally shifted her glance, seeing Shirley as almost unbearably golden, Amazonian, goddesslike, just as the lights of the night's extemporized carousel were eye-throbbingly bright to her, the spiritous music as loud and clear as if a Wurlitzer thumped and ground a few feet away, in Shirley's kitchen. She apprehended existence and essence so clearly, so intensely that even time seemed almost visible to her, she could almost hear its dopplering rhythm. "Shirley. You should never have said you have AIDS."

Elspeth came and stood staring at her lover. If Shirley was a golden Amazon, Elspeth was a dark-eyed Gypsy, the colorful one, the mysterious wanderer, the perpetual stranger, a small presence but as vehemently, unaccountably eternal as Shirley.

Speaking to Elspeth's look more than to Cally's words, Shirley protested, "You know I can't have AIDS! You know we both tested clean." Therefore, if they had been faithful to each other since, logically Shirley could not have contracted the pestilence.

Elspeth didn't answer, but Cally averred, knowing that logic had nothing to do with it, "You should never have said you did. Lately things people say have a way of coming true." Cally stared out the window again. Speaking, like Shirley, to Elspeth's silent fears, she said, "I'd go out and sleep in the barn, leave you two alone, if I had the nerve to get through that fence."

Not even Elspeth expected it of her. She slept in Shirley's spare bedroom, or watched out the window more than slept, and all night the plastic-pony, fence-post and firefly carousel kept up its impossible circling around the house. But sometime toward dawn Cally dozed, and come daylight, when she looked again, the firefly lights were gone, the music stilled, the fence motionless and in its accustomed place again, the plastic junkyard horses belly-stretched in full frozen career above their locust posts as always. The fence wire sagged broken or bent from the pressure of the mob, but no mark, no furrow, no weird circle showed on the turf of the yard.

CHAPTER TWELVE

The next day in the Perfect Rest Funeral Home's mailbox was a letter addressed to Cally. Mark had to look at the return address to recognize it as coming from her mother, so rarely had he seen that elusive woman's handwriting. Cally's mother never wrote. Why this missive? It had to be about something serious, perhaps something she didn't want Mark to overhear, or she would have phoned. Or something she didn't want the kids to overhear? Concern for his offspring overrode Mark's suspicions, and once he felt himself ennobled by a worthy emotion he was Mark the White Knight of Goodliness and Service to Mankind, he could not open someone else's mail, even though in the grip of jealous spleen, as Mark the Beast, he had been about to do so.

Mark the Goodly reached a compromise with Mark the Beast, and snooped. He held the envelope up to the light. It contained a brief note, folded only once; therefore he was able to make out a few words: "Tammy . . . the doctor says . . ." And later, "quite concerned." This from the woman who could scarcely be concerned about anything.

Mark put the letter in his pocket, phoned his mother and made arrangements for her to answer the funeral home calls, then instructed his telephone to forward them to her home. Then he strapped on his beeper, so she could summon him if necessary. All this so that he, the funeral director, could sally forth from his establishment. He would drop the business end of the beeper off at Wilmores' on his way to find Cally.

By the time Mrs. Wilmore run away I was real worried about Joanie. She changed a lot after she done that mean trick to her mother. She didn't have nothing to say to me, but she didn't mind me hanging around either, which wasn't no good. She didn't seem to care about nothing. She didn't hardly ever go out noplace except to them park meetings of hers. Not even to get stuff to eat she didn't go out none. A lot of the time I come up the hill and found her just laying in that merry-go-round camp of hers, in the dark, with nothing to eat. I'd bring her stuff to eat. It reminded me of the way Joanie was that last year, except the old Joanie would've growled me. Ahira didn't growl me none. That bothered me.

If I'd been thinking, I would've knowed she needed me, I would've told her I knowed she was Joanie. But I'd got in the habit of her being Ahira. Another thing was, she had me half scared of her since I seen what she done to her mother. So I just brought her food and left her be.

It seems like things always go by opposites. Seemed like the less Ahira come out of her hole, the more all the Hoadley misfits come out of theirs. Of course a lot of them was healed and didn't feel so bad or look so bad no more, except for the marks on the sides of their heads, but that didn't matter. We was still misfits, and we knowed it. Being a misfit don't depend on how you look. It depends on what the world has done to your insides. Only now, see, we was proud of them scars, the ones people could see and the ones nobody could see, because them scars had made us Ahira's family. So instead of hiding ourselves away like we used to would, we was out on the streets all day, early in the morning even, just walking around Hoadley and sort of looking at it in the daylight like we wasn't used to seeing it and hugging when we met up with each other and then walking with each other and smiling. It was like we owned the town. Hardly nobody else come out that didn't have to, either because of us or because of them big black bugs all the time yelling like babies. We didn't mind them bugs none. We even carried them around like pets and sweet-talked them black baby faces of theirs. Them bugs was kin to us, and we knowed it. Them bugs was misfits too. The girl who used to was bald wore a whole nest of them in her hair. She give them names and loved them like they was her children and kept them with her wherever. A lot of us done the same.

And when Ahira come down at dusk to the park, we wouldn't just sort of creep out when we seed her to stand around like we used to. We would all be there waiting for her and sort of partying even though there wasn't no drinks or nothing, and we'd yell hi when we seen her coming, and bunches of us would run to meet her and hug her. And when she would start to go away again, we wouldn't let her go. We'd make her walk around Hoadley with us, and we'd sing stupid stuff and crack bad jokes, and a lot of us would walk in a big line with our arms around her

shoulders and each other's. I never done none of
them things with Ahira because I thought they would
make her mad, but I was glad when the others done
it and it didn't make her mad. I saw her eyes, her
face, sometimes, and it looked like she wanted to
cry. That was okay. People got a right to cry
sometimes.

Like I said, I was worried about her, but I never
would've guessed the crazy thing she would do.

The morning after one of them nights—a bunch of
us and Ahira had walked clear out to Mine 28 and
spray-painted "666" on the railroad bridge—the next
morning early, before I had to go to the funeral
home to work, I tromped up the old trolley line to
Joanie's place. I had a bunch of bananas and some
jelly donuts and some sweet bologna for her. But as
soon as I stepped in that hole the earth spirit had
blowed in her merry-go-round house, I set that stuff
down, because I knowed something was wrong.

I knowed it because I seen hard little glitters of
glass all over the place. Then I seed Joanie. She was
laying on the floor between some of them wooden
horses. She wasn't dead or even knocked out, cause I
seed her eyes, hard and thin and glittery, like them
pieces of glass. She was watching me the whole time,
but didn't move or say hi or nothing. And her eyes
was looking out of dark stuff. And it was blood.

"Joanie," I says, all shook up, not thinking about
what I'm saying, "oh damn, Joanie, what'd you go
and do to yourself?" I looked around and walked a
few steps and grabbed her flashlight, turned it on so
I could see her better. And her eyes was on me
wide, and her mouth moving under strings of blood.

"Bar," she's sort of whispering, "How—who—how'd
you know—"

I'd went and called her by her real name, see. But

I ain't worrying 'bout none of that. I'm worrying about her. I scrooched down beside her with the flashlight, and I can see she ain't bleeding no more, she'd been laying there awhile, the blood drips on the floor beside her are dry, and it's just sort of sticky on her face. But she'd cut her face all to a mess and busted her nose flat. She hadn't hurt her hands; they was folded on top of her. She had herself laid out tidy as a corpse.

"Bar," she's saying, "how'd you know who I was?"

I ain't paying attention. I can see now what she'd done. She'd broke them big mirrors in the middle of the merry-go-round, all of them. There was splatters of blood and sharp pieces of broken glass everywhere. And she must've done it with her head. She must've rammed her beautiful face right into them mirrors.

I went and got her plastic milk jug she kept full of water, and I found a dishtowel or something, I don't remember what, I was so fussed, and I come back and set beside her and started trying to wash the blood off her face without hurting her worse than she was already hurt.

"Joanie," I says, "Joanie, are you all right?"

Then all of a sudden she pushed my hands away and set straight up, and when she yelled at me she sounded like the old Joanie. "Barry Beal, you are so dumb!" she yells. "Of course I'm not all right! I—" Right then I put my arms around her. I should've done it before. She snuggled up to my shoulder and started crying. I held her as comfortable as I could. And I wasn't glad about what she'd gone and done to herself, but I was glad about one thing: I knowed right then that she needed me after all. Joanie needed me to love her.

"You're so damn skinny," I says. She felt like a

baby bird I held once, shaking and all bones. "You
ain't been eating enough," I says. She didn't answer
me. She was too busy bawling.

"God damn, that hurts!" she cusses between gulps.

"What does?" I let go a little, scared I had been
hugging her too tight, I'd smashed her nose worse or
something. Even her voice sounds more like the old
Joanie, because her nose is smashed.

"Not you. The tears."

"Tears is good for you."

"They're getting in the *cuts*," she yells. She kept
on crying anyways, until she was calmed down, and
then she pulled away.

"I've made a real mess of your shirt," she says,
dull. She looked like she wanted to cry some more
but she was too tired.

"You made a real mess of your face," I says. I can
see it better now it's mostly washed. There was a lot
of shallow cuts, and one cheek was sliced open pretty
good. "We gotta get you to a doctor."

"No." She lays down on the floor again.

"Joanie—"

"No," she says. "I hate it. Let it be."

"I ain't going to let it be. It's getting all swole." It
was, too, especially around the eyes and lips. I started
putting the cold water on it again to keep the swelling down. "What was wrong with it?" I says. "I
thought it was real nice."

She smiles, sort of stiff because her mouth is sore,
and she says, "Barry, you'll never change. How long
have you known who I was?"

"A good while. Since that first night I was up
here."

"Lord. I wish you'd told me."

I wished too now that I did, but I said, "I didn't
think you'd like it."

"Maybe not," she says, real low. "I was pretty stupid."

We was quiet. I kept working at her face with the cold cloth.

"But maybe I needed it," she says.

"Didn't look to me like you needed me for nothing no more."

"I need something. Maybe a brain transplant." She started trying to tell me what was wrong. "It's like—Bar, it's like I'm two different people, and they each want different things. And then there's all those— all those misfits together in one place, treating me as if I'm really special. . . ."

"Well, ain't you?" I says.

"Sort of. I did what I had to do. I made myself into Ahira. Made a name for myself. Started something. I'm better than other misfits." She sounded like she was making fun of herself. "That's what I was thinking."

"Well, that's okay," I says.

"Yeah, sure. So you say." She sounded dead tired. "Everything I do's okay with you. It's okay with them, too. They're a lot like you, Bar. They're sweet, gentle people. Most of them, anyway. I want them to—I want them to like me."

"They do like you!"

"No. They like Ahira."

And I'm staring at her, I didn't understand, and all of a sudden, like it was inside her all the time but it just busted out, she was really upset. "They don't know me! I might as well have a goddamn mask on. It's just Ahira they like. Gorgeous Ahira. And all the time there's a—a child inside me, crying and crying. . . ." She set up, and her hands were in the air, fluttering like doves.

"Huh?" I says again.

"She made me let her out."

"Who?"

"Joan Musser! She made me smash the mask to let her out. I—I had Joan Musser hidden inside!" she yells. "Like in a dark place, a closet, a cellar, under my damn face, where they couldn't see her, and she was screaming—" Joanie was shaking so bad, seemed like she shook them wooden horses all around us. "—all the time screaming and crying, like a child in the dark, crying 'Please, please, *like* me, l-l-l-love me,' and they're sweet people, they just might have liked her even the way she was, and Ahira yelling no, no, dead thing, smelly thing, stay where you are, hateful, hateful—"

I tried to get hold of her to calm her down, but she scooted away from me under one of them wooden horses.

"I'm all ugly inside!" she screamed.

I couldn't think of nothing to do, so I patted the only part of her she was letting me reach, which was her leg. She had her face turned away. "Joanie," I says to the back of her head, "you ain't ugly. You're talking *ugly*, I mean, have a look at me."

"Shut up," she says, crying.

"You come out of there and look at me once," I says, and I keep at her till she done it. She looked at me fit to kill. And she looked like hell, her nose broke and her face cut and her eyes and mouth all swole and the eyes already turning black.

"Okay, so you're ugly," I says. "We can be ugly together."

She almost laughed, and choked on it, and then she says, "You don't understand."

"That's true." Didn't bother me none. It always tooken me a while to understand things. "Lean on me anyways?" I snuggled her up against my shoulder again, and she let me.

"I ain't so smart," I says. "If I would've been smart I would've knowed I love you. I would've never let you go off and leave me."

"Huh?" She sounded tired.

"I love you, Joanie. Always did."

She stayed quiet a long time, not moving, not looking at me. "That doesn't help as much as you might think," she says finally.

"It's the best I can do."

I just set there holding her, both of us on the floor of the merry-go-round with them wooden horses pawing at the air all around us, spooky looking because there ain't much light in that place. They made me feel like I wanted to get out of there, and get Joanie out of there, even though she was letting me hold her, and I says to her, "Joanie, c'mon, let me get you to a doctor. There might be some glass still in them cuts."

She moved her head a little without looking at me. I could just feel it against my shoulder, her shaking her head no.

"Joanie—"

"I don't care," she says.

"Look, I care."

"Stuff it, Bar." She set up and looked at me out of eyes that was just slits between black-and-blue swole-up lids, like she really was looking out of a mask. "You want to care about me. . . ." She broke off, and then she didn't say what she meant to at first. She says, "Did my father drink himself to death yet?"

"Not yet," I says, because I would've knowed if he did, because he would've come in the funeral home, I would've did a blanket for him if he was dead.

Mussers was Protestants, sort of. But it was a weird question for Joanie to ask, because she would've knowed too. Everybody in Hoadley knowed everything. "How come?" I says.

"I want him to die," Joanie says.

"Well, I guess he will soon enough, won't he?" I says. Either drinking himself to death, or when she took down everybody in that town.

"I don't want him just to die," she says. "I want him to scream. I want him to shake and know he's going to die and know why. I want him to shit his pants and hurt and die."

I set there not looking at her beautiful, messed-up face, not looking at Ahira, just listening to her voice, just listening to Joanie. I could tell she hated her father a lot worse than I thought.

"I didn't know you hated him so bad," I says.

"I'm the rose that's sick, Bar. And he made me sick."

I didn't remember about her poem, and I probably wouldn't of understood even if I did. I thought she meant, like, the flu or something. "You ain't feverish or nothing," I says.

"You can't see how I'm sick. Bar, I never told you. I never told anybody." She ain't looking at me while she talks, she's just staring, and I begun to get a bad, crawly feeling about what she was going to say. "All those times my mother called me a whore, said I was a filthy sinner, said I was fornicating whenever her back was turned, whenever she was out of the house—it was true. Except it was him doing it to me. And there wasn't a damn thing I could do about it."

It was so awful I didn't understand for a minute. And while I was setting there like a dummy she kept talking, just looking at the board floor and talking like there was a machine inside her making her talk.

"I wasn't any older than ten when he started. I know I wasn't, because when I first got my period, I saw all this blood on my panties, nobody had explained it to me, the first thing I thought was that my father had hurt me."

"Jesus," I says.

"I tried to tell her a few times what was happening to me, but she called me a liar. Slapped me so hard she knocked me over, then prayed at me. I got pregnant three times. There's a woman back Railroad Street I went to for abortions. The first time I was only thirteen, I almost died."

It was all finally sinking in, and I was on my feet with my hands all balled into fists, and I says, "Why didn't you tell me? I would've killed him. I'll kill him now. I'll go do it right now."

She says in a funny, soft voice, "That's why."

"You don't want me to kill him? You want me to, I'll kill him all right!" I was so mad my chest was pumping. "I'll do him any way you want. You just tell me what you want."

"That's the problem," she says, real soft, real calm. "I thought I wanted him dead. I thought I wanted them all dead except the misfits. This whole reeking Hoadley town. Screwed me just like my father screwed me. That's why I did what I did. I thought I wanted my mother dead, too."

Then I began to get it, what her problem was, and cooled down some, and set down on the floor beside her again.

"It worked on me too," I got to admit, "what you done to your mother."

She nodded at the floor between her knees. "Now I'm not sure what I want anymore."

Wasn't sure she wanted her father dead, she meant.

"Well," I says, "let me go beat him up, anyways. I can tell him why from you."

"Barry," she says, sort of desperate, and I got cool all the way and looked at her and listened hard for whatever it was she had to say.

"I'm not sure I want anybody dead anymore," she says.

"Well, that's all right," I says, not really getting the point. I just knowed whatever Joanie wanted was all right with me. But she jerks her poor bashed face up and yells at me.

"It's not all right! Don't you understand what I've done? I've called up the Devil. The hell god. The fire lord. Satan himself."

Then I finally understood. It took all the brains I had, but I understood, and I knowed she was in deep trouble. We all was.

She says, "I offered him souls. Lots of souls. A world's worth. I don't think just a town's worth would have convinced him. He's greedy. But I invited him to begin the end days right here in good old Hoadley, and he sort of sniffed the air and tasted it with his tongue, like a hunting dog." I heard the shiver in her voice. She was finally telling me the truth about that day, and she was talking like it was a bad dream she had to get out. "His tongue was a lick of fire. And he smiled like a dog showing its teeth, and said it was as good a place as any. 'Much evil has been done here,' he said. And that's when he made this place the hub, and he pulled my mask off and made me look in the mirror and gave me this face." The way she said it, you would've thought he'd made her into a toad. But there wasn't nothing I could do about that.

She says, "I promised him every son-of-a-bitch normal in Hoadley to take and burn."

"He ain't going to stop with Hoadley," I says, because that's what the real problem is.

"No. He doesn't like to quit."

Oh, God. My ma, my pa, my brothers—but that wasn't what worried me the most, not right away, anyways.

"Joanie," I says, "Joanie," joggling at her leg with my hand, I was so scared. "Joanie, he got your soul?"

She didn't answer me. She wouldn't look at me. She just pulled her knees up to her chest and wrapped her arms tight around them and laid down her head on them with her face turned away from me, and she sort of rocked, back and forth, back and forth. And she sort of moaned to herself, like a baby does sometimes. Only there was words in what she was moaning. She's crooning to herself:

". . . the invisible worm
Has found out my bed
Of crimson joy
And his dark secret love
Does my life destroy
My life destroy
My life destroy. . . ."

It did not take much for Mark to guess where Cally might be. He knew what was important to her; in fact, he had often thought that the damn horse was more important to her than he was. Certainly it was more important to her than his priorities: his death calls, his deep carpets on which she pertinaciously tracked manure, the dusting she was supposed to do in the parlors between viewings. He supported her, so certainly she ought to give him some cooperation and assistance with the business. She could never support herself, not in Hoadley, not at women's wages. Let alone support a horse.

Let alone the kids.

The kids; what could be wrong with the kids?
Mark sent his vehicle—the Going Home To Perfect
Rest Van, the one in which he brought the bodies to
the discreetly-screened-off-from-prying-eyes back basement door by the embalming room—sent it swaying
around a single-lane dogleg turn under a railroad
bridge, one of those damn old redstone bridges built
low and narrow, like a tunnel, with a redstone wall
and a streambed tucked under it for good measure,
just to make it more dangerous. He should have
blared his horn going into it in case someone was
coming the other way. But he hadn't. And he didn't
at the next one, either, and going around the hairpin
up the hill he pushed the accelerator to the floor,
rocketing into the wrong lane.

At the stable he found Cally's car but not Cally.
Not anyone else, either. Mark hammered angry-fisted
at the farmhouse door, glaring at the plastic junkyard
horses on their posts—these horse-crazy women, what
overgrown children they were. Mark had heard something about this place, some sort of leer, some scandal, not paying much attention, as he had not been
able to pay much attention to anything in the two
days since Cally had left him. All he remembered
was that the speaker had been frightened of these
women and their horses. Ridiculous.

Not finding anyone at the farmhouse, he went and
knocked at the door of the remodeled silo—a make-
believe castle, might as well be a child's playhouse.
Fine bunch of nuts Cally had taken up with. He
blamed her recent stubborn rebelliousness on them;
he blamed her thin, thin, reproachful death's head of
a face on them, he blamed his failing marriage on
them. Best to blame everything on them.

No one answered his pounding, though various

vehicles stood parked nearby. Mark shouted into the barn and found no humans there. He scanned the pastures; not knowing one horse from another, he saw little to help him, but it seemed to him conceivable that Cally and the others had gone riding. How could she go riding at a time like this? Yet of course she would. It was just what she would do.

Too full of resentful energy to sit down and wait, or even to pace and wait, he set off with a long, hard stride down the trail that ran past the pasture toward the steep downslopes and valley bottoms of the woods.

A deep-throated vibration filled the woods to the treetops, seeming to catch on the myriad small branches as did the ever-present cicadas scoring the tender bark with their orange claws. The twigs minutely trembled. A massive organ, a huge rasping tomcat, a monstrous *basso continuo* beneath the treble chorus of the hungerbugs, the mine was roaring in the valley.

Even before he plunged into the woods Mark had almost forgotten where he was going and why. In fact it made no sense for him to be searching for Cally along this particular trail. She was just as likely to be riding somewhere else, across the road perhaps. And even if she had gone this way—Mark saw hoofprints everywhere, maybe recent, maybe not— even if she was somewhere ahead he was not likely to catch up to her. It would have been far more sensible to wait at the stable. But Mark strode on, veering off the trail, tearing his way through poison-green bramble patches, snapping branches, lunging down the steep side of the ridge between trees. The woods were lovely, dark and deep. . . . Crashing along in that wild place, Mark was able to forget who he was, what he cared about, or nearly forget; his relief was physical and immense. He reveled in the rush of air through his pink spongy lungs, the feel of his own elastic muscles, the hot pulse of his blood, the thud of his feet. His beeper sounded; he tore it off his belt and flung it against a rock. Black plastic smashed, tiny metal parts scattered, the insistent noise stopped; Mark felt as satisfied as if he had shattered a black hungerbug and silenced its babyish wail.

Pausing at the bottom of the ridge for breath, he pulled the letter from his pocket, tore it open and read it.

The chesty tremolo of the mine was in his ears, his mind; the words meant nothing to him. Tammy, displaying deviant behavior? A prepubescent girl approaching strange men like a streetwalker? Hospitalized for observation? Owen, showing stainlike, reddish patches of insensitive skin and loss of feeling in his fingers, the classical symptoms of—leprosy? Leprosy. Absurd. Who were these people? What were they to him? He could not remember their faces; he could not remember his own name. Who was this hysterical woman writing in such a heightened tone? Another one demanding his help, his heart, his soul. Well, they had taken his soul, Cally and all the Hoadley poor souls between them, and they could keep it for their very own. He felt much better without it.

And speak of the devil, there was Cally on that damn black horse of hers, along with those other damn women she liked to pal around with, on their own ridiculous animals.

Mark laughed—or thought he laughed—and started forward.

Elspeth jerked her head up at the first stutter of that sound, looking for a charging bear. She knew a

bear when she heard one, and she knew there was
nothing more dangerous to a rider on horseback than
a bear; any horse would go crazy at the mere smell of
one. The horsewomen, riding along the black brickle
mine road, reined in their mounts sharply when they
heard that coughing roar, but had no time to do
more before Mark burst out of the woods. Clinging
atop their rearing horses, the women gaped; the man
lunging toward them was running berserk, his name-
brand polo shirt nearly ripped off his torso by snags
and briars, his skin torn, his eyes as wild as his
knotted hair, but—those things were the least of
what made them stare.

Mark flung the letter at Cally as he had flung the
beeper at the boulder, but the letter did not satisfy
him by hitting with a smash; it swayed in air and
fluttered wimpishly to the ground. With a snarl Mark
turned away and loped off down the mine road. He
was so bizarrely changed that not until he was out of
sight did Cally realize who he was.

"Mark!" She started after him.

"Wait," said Shirley in a voice so stunned it entirely lacked its usual volume and resonance. "You
sure that was Mark?" Shaken, distressed by the events
of the past few days, she felt sure of nothing, but she
thought she had seen claws, a stirring of horns in the
wild man's hair.

Cally wasn't waiting, though Devil fought her at
every pace. With hard black boots she kicked him
into a run. With her own peculiar grim glee, eager
for trouble as always, old Gigi sent Snake Oil after
her. Shirley cursed and trailed after. Elspeth, last of
all, slipped down from her plunging Warrior and
picked up the torn envelope lying on the ground
before mounting again and following.

She galloped, then, to catch up with Shirley, who

had galloped and caught up with Gigi. Cally, on runaway Devil, was still somewhere ahead. Incredibly, Mark—or whatever it was they had seen—seemed somehow to have run faster than them all. And trees lay strewn on the black gravel mine road as they neared the tipple, half-grown trees broken off above the ground, their trunks splintered or dangling. The place looked as if a twister had savaged it. Yet no storm had struck, and the trees had been trembling skyward an hour before.

No one could hear hoofbeats, splintering trees, the thunder of her own heart; the clamor of the mine superseded all other sound. As if some chauvinist man had dared them on, the horsewomen galloped through the devastated woods, jumping treetrunks when they could, dodging others, impatiently circumventing the rest, fighting their way through the bewilderment of downed timber like ants through a pile of jumbled pick-up-sticks—

The mighty cat-purring nose of the mine abruptly ceased, leaving the woods in deathly silence. Even the cicadas had fallen silent, listening for the scream— the first scream of that apocalypse day.

It came.

Mark had known in an instinctive way where he was going. A beast needs a lair.

CHAPTER THIRTEEN

Gigi had arrived at the stable on that day wanting to go horseback riding, and the force of Gigi's presence generally impacted on those around her. The thick corpse-white callus of her scarred skin seemed to define her, let her walk hard, talk like dropped stones and take her own way. She found Cally and Shirley and Elspeth in the farmhouse still dazed in early afternoon by the events of the night before, and with the tug of dry words and cold fingers she pulled them out to go riding with her.

Once Gigi had gotten them moving they were glad enough to oblige. Each deadlocked, wrestling with her own devils, they welcomed the riding as a talisman of control, of mastery; once they had ridden a while, they would feel a sense, however illusory, that all was well, and they would be able to talk with one another again. Though that was not their aim, to intercommunicate, to act as a phalanx of four. They went, each one, as a personal venture, in search of a personal answer.

Saddling Devil in his stall (since he would not

stand in the stable aisle) Cally could look at the others without her scrutiny's being noticed. Gigi, so wonderfully self-possessed that the mood of the others could not squelch her, chirping baby talk to Snake Oil; if there was any tenderness left in her, it was all for the horse. Elspeth, darkly shaken, saddling Warrior in silence. Like Cally, Elspeth and Shirley had not eaten that day. Cally had cooked bacon and hash browns and raspberry-jam omelette, urging the heavy brunch on the others in order to vicariously feed herself, but no one had eaten. And Shirley, also silent, pale even in the honeyed afternoon light: big-boned, hearty Shirley who had always laughed loud, whose flushed face had always resembled the round, peach-hued, nodding bloom of a manure-grown German rose . . .

"Shirley," said Cally, the name surprised out of her by her own shock at what she had seen on the pale skin in the sunlight.

Shirley came wordlessly to the stall, looking over the dusty partition at her, and even though she knew everyone could hear her, could see what she had seen, Cally spoke softly.

"You've got spots."

Shirley glanced down at the hard, elderberry-blue lumps on her arms and nodded.

"They're not just bug bites or something."

Statement, more than question; Shirley did not bother to shake her head. As well as Cally did, she knew that the small meek-looking bumps were not spider bites or pinpricks or zits.

"I heard you coughing in the night. Sounded like smoker's cough. But you don't smoke."

"Never did," said Shirley.

They looked at each other. Cally felt the small muscles twitching and blinking around her eyes.

"Go ahead and say it," Shirley told her. "It's starting already."

"What's starting?" Gigi sang out with cheerful insensitivity from the end of the stable, where she was standing, waiting, with Snake Oil. Elspeth and Cally looked down at the horse muck on their boots, but Shirley answered.

"AIDS." Curtly. Elspeth's dark eyes flashed up, outraged and pleading.

"Don't say it any more!"

Shirley retorted, "Don't make no difference now, does it?"

They rode. They mounted their horses: the black, the gray, the blood bay and Gigi's mount the color of parchment. Four women far too old for juvenile pastimes, they rode: Gigi half eaten away by her own impending death, Cally starved nearly to a skeleton, Shirley with the raven of AIDS skulking sharp-clawed on her shoulder, and Elspeth with a weapon as yet unbloodied. They rode down the ridge and along the valley amid the shaking shadows and the nattering of the mine. They talked about men and mobs, telling Gigi some of what had happened in the night, skirting the subject of what Shirley had been; odd, their feelings toward a woman who had been a man. Even the weird carousel-circling fence seemed easier to deal with than Shirley now that they knew what she was. They felt unsure of how to treat her, no longer willing to trust her with their thoughts, their confidences, though she was the same person she had always been. . . . And the Lord God of Misfits only knew what would become of her might-as-well-be-marriage with Elspeth.

And on the way back from their ride they encountered a man, perhaps mad, perhaps merely a representative specimen of his gender, wild with a primal rage that grew visible on his body in claws and bristling fur and horns.

And a few moments later they heard Mr. Zankowski scream.

In the middle distance they heard him, his voice echoing, clarion, through the woods. "Armageddon!" he trumpeted, in the reverberating word as much triumph as fear. "Arr-mageddon! Arr—" The victory call ended in a cry, cut off.

Cally reached him first, fell off over Devil's shoulder—the horse spooked from the limp-rag thing strewn on the brickle, from the smell of coughed-up blood, of death—Cally landed on her thin back beneath Devil's wild-eyed, wide-nostriled head grotesquely snaking down at her, beneath his lifted forehooves, but kept hold of the reins. Falling over the shoulder was almost routine to her. By the time the others rode up, she was kneeling by Mr. Zankowski's body (as flat and untidy as if it had been dropped from a tall building), holding Devil's reins in one hand and feeling for the prone man's carotid artery with the other, but finding no pulse, no sign of life. Mr. Zankowski's dead face stared up at the stained and murky Hoadley sky with a look of rapt repose, as if he had seen the glory of the coming of his Lord.

Shirley and Elspeth kept to their horses and hung back; they considered Cally their death-professional-by-marriage, and wanted no share of her expertise. But Gigi rode close, glanced down and said bluntly, as if out of sure, almost casual knowledge, "He's *ferrecht*." Broken, wrecked, irreparably ruined, the old German word meant. Dead. Once, generations before, use of the term had been someone's idea of a euphemism or a joke, to say that a dead person was out-of-order beyond fixing, like a smashed watch, burned-out wiring, a dropped telephone, a vending

machine permanently on the fritz. *Ferrecht.* "Let him
lay."

Cally stood up, aching from her fall; she would
admit to herself now that it hurt her far more than it
would have months before, when there had been
some meat on her ribs, her spine. Even the saddle
hurt her now that there was no flesh covering her
sit-bones. She stood wobbling with pain and hunger,
and all around her blades of raw yellow wood knifed
up, kris-edged, from their stumps; poised flame in its
near-primal form, one step removed from the sun.
Flame. People said the world would end in fire.

Amid the splintered trees the mine mouth showed,
a gaping, shadowy, stony rictus, as it had never
shown before.

"How did he die?" Elspeth asked, keeping her
distance and her perch on horseback, yet stretching
her head and shoulders toward the body like an
exquisitely beautiful vulture, as if the smell of blood
drew her.

"How should I know?" Cally had not realized until
she snapped the words how afraid she was. Of what?
Mark? Of whatever had happened to Mark?

Did she still care about Mark?

"Let the coroner worry about it," she added more
temperately, trying to sound sensible. No, sane. By
Hoadley standards, sane.

But Gigi declared with grim, gleeful, utterly crazy
certitude in her voice, "The coroner ain't ever going
to get this far. Coroner's going to have lots to worry
about."

"Let's get out of here," begged Shirley.

Despite the panic lying just beneath the bravado
of her loud voice, she reached over and held Devil
while Cally mounted. Cally might not have managed
to get on the tall horse otherwise; the last of her

unnatural, flesh-burning energy seemed suddenly to have left her, and she was shivering with cold in the heat of late June.

Something moved black on the black brickle, and the horses violently shied. Like an emanation out of Hoadley coal the black snake wavered to the hermit miner's body, where it tested the poplin terrain with forked tongue, then laid itself in a spiral on the shabby, concave chest.

"Let's get out of here!"

"Out of here" meant home, to the stable, to safety; horses and riders felt fully in accord on that concept. They fought their way through the tumbled treetrunks again, and once again at reckless speed. Even Shirley seemed to have no sensible caution left in her. They lunged up the shortest, steepest trail over the ridge; the women clung to their mount's manes as if to lifelines, and once again in the clutching, clawing twigs just overhead the cicadas with human faces were chanting, chorusing, wailing: "Doom. . . . Doom. . . ."

"My God," said Shirley in a dead voice.

She had stopped her big gray thoroughbred at the pasture's edge; they all stopped behind her to stare. "My God," said Shirley with something more of personal affront, of umbrage, in her voice. "Skulls. Just what I love best in the whole wide world."

Around the farmhouse the fence was once again circling, merry-go-twirling, round upon round, and the plastic ponies serpentined up, down, all colors in the sunlight—but their heads were skulls. Horned skulls, grotesquely large for their small bodies; the bone was dull black, the horns, hard mustard yellow or pumpkin orange or pink. Cally shaded her starved eyes from the buzz of that neon pink.

"Lord," she said with a dazzled look, as if she was

seeing the world whirling, multihued, flashing before her eyes like a life to a drowning swimmer,
"Lord Jesus, is it to keep us out or keep us in or save
us or kill us?"

"I don't want to find out." Shirley's big mare was
shaking and sweating, and so was her rider. With
unspoken accord the four women turned their mounts
and started away. Two cars, Cally's and Gigi's, sat
outside the circling perimeter of the fence, but no
one wanted to approach the weird thing even that
close. Their horses now were no longer their playtoys,
but their vehicles.

Where to go? There was only one place to go. The
hub of the universe. Hoadley.

Devil had pushed his boorish black head into
the fore, as always, so that Cally led the way
through the abandoned strip sites between the stable
and the town. Along the gravel road—hooves striking
crisply on the black cinder surface—

The world turned hollow underneath her.

She heard Devil's hoofbeats sound deep, deep, as
if vibrating a great earthen gong. Hastily she pulled
the horse to a halt, and for once he obeyed her
without a struggle; he too had felt the sudden void,
the elephant trap, the thin and treacherous footing
underneath, and he stood spraddle-legged and still,
ears uncertain.

The others had stopped some distance behind Cally.
"Must be a mine shaft under there," called Gigi
briskly. "Nothing to worry about."

"It was never there before," said Cally. Her words
fell blunt and stark as stones into a chasm, silencing
Gigi.

From a mile ahead, where Hoadley lay in its river

valley, came a rumbling sound. Dust rose over the trees.

"Hell," Elspeth spoke up suddenly, her tea-colored skin draining to gray. "Let's go back."

"To what?" Nodules of bruise-purple had proliferated on Shirley's face and arms, painfully livid on her pale skin. "We've got to go on."

Gigi found her voice again. "One at a time," she said, "and we'll be safe enough over that hollow place. Devil hasn't fallen through yet. Cally, move that horse's butt."

Cally touched her legs lightly to Devil's sides. But instead of walking on, the black horse swung his head and pawed with one forefoot, as if he had decided to return to the hell from which he, or his namesake, came. The striking hoof rang the ground like a great bell of clay. "Hey!" Cally yelled, terrified, and she kicked him hard. He jumped from a standstill into his runaway gallop.

Devil swept down on Hoadley like a black angel. And the other horses were of like mind with him, and the other riders as reckless as starving, half-suicidal Cally (hanging on with her aching, rawboned hind end in the air, riding by balance and stirrup and knee, like a jockey), as daring as old ever-dying Gigi. They crossed the dangerous span with a single leap and ran like wildfire. Sometime during the few moments of that hurtling ride, Cally comprehended: the hidden hollow, the empty place—call it coal shaft, worm hole, beast lair—had been on a straight line between Zankowski's mine and Hoadley.

Between the tarpaper shacks of the outskirts and into the town proper, where the mouse-brown mine-town row houses minced down the hill like shabby dowagers on steps, the four horsewomen rode at daredevil speed. "Yee-hah!" Gigi yelled, enjoying herself. Hoadley matrons, brought out of their kitchens and off their porches by thunderous noises and fire-siren clamor and shouting voices farther downtown, stood crowded on the sidewalks, chittering like locusts; Gigi lifted a hand and thumbed her nose at them. Elspeth, feeling a similar defiance, smiled darkly, but Shirley—who had more cause for rancor than any of them—would or could not smile; this was her home town, and she thought with bittersweet longing of estranged family, of old friends who were friends no longer. Face blotched and taut, she pressed heels to Shady Lady, keeping up the breakneck pace. Cally, whose horse needed no urging, rode as if in a trance.

Down Main Street, four abreast, the four horsewomen swept: Shirley with the claws of pestilence marking her skin, Gigi grinning like a skull, famished Cally, and Elspeth wearing a sword.

Ahead of them, dust had turned to a pillar of smoke reaching toward the yellow clouds of the Hoadley sky. And in a moment Devil slowed his headlong gallop, and shied, and stopped, not because he wanted to but because he had to. And the others stopped and looked; the four horses stood in a row with ribs heaving, nostrils wide and heavily blowing, and forehooves near the edge of a precipice.

A sinkhole had opened at the center of Hoadley, a black abyss, gradually widening. From where they stood the horsewomen could see no bottom to it; perhaps there was none to be seen. The Municipal Building, the gargoyled redstone structure housing the borough offices, had already disappeared into it, along with the town's only traffic light. Thick wires writhed up over the lip of the town's wound like worms, sparking, and from somewhere came the sound of rushing water; mains were broken. A fire truck swayed on its belly, half in the chasm, and heavy-booted firemen had given up on trying to save it or the Tropical Beauty Tanning Salon splintering and burning, slowly dropping portions of itself like torches into the darkness below. Shouting, the firefighters scrambled away or made small, futile sorties along the disaster's rim. Townspeople gathered to look at the coal-black hole—a huge mine shaft with no lift cage—alternately hurrying to look down the gullet of hell or screaming and scrambling to run away from it. In the park nearby, six hundred sixty-six misfits wearing Ahira's mark had gathered near the gazebo, where they huddled, waiting for a leader who had not yet arrived.

With shouts and screams the spectators surged back; another portion of pavement was dropping away, sending baritone reverberations through the town. Over the hollow bowels beneath Hoadley now swayed a row of parking meters and the corner of the only modern brick building in the town, the Post Office. Foundation cinderblock and bricks broke away and fell without a sound to tell that they had struck bottom. From somewhere inside, envelopes post-marked with the date of the rapture day fluttered down like white butterflies into the depths.

"That reminds me," said Elspeth as coolly as if she had ridden into Hoadley merely to check her box; the artist, the observer, she had distanced herself from the bizarre events going on around her. She was watching; in a sense she was watching herself, her own superbly aesthetic aplomb as in a tunic pocket she found the letter she had meant to give Cally when returning to the stable, passed it over. But as she did so, her glance caught the name to which it was addressed.

"Apocalypse?" she demanded, poise lost. "That's what 'Cally' stands for? Apocalypse?"

"Don't call me that!" Cally ordered, heartily and irrationally annoyed that her secret had been found out, afraid she would have to battle the unattractive name now for the rest of her life in this place. She took the envelope without much comprehension, too harrowed by the events of the day to wonder how Elspeth had come to have a letter for her, knowing only that it was from her mother. No one except her mother called her Apocalypse.

"God!" exclaimed Gigi with a horror she had not showed for the body of Bud Zankowski or for the town going down into the belly of hell. "Who would name a poor baby Apocalypse?"

"My mother would." Cally held the envelope in her hand, noting the torn flap but not yet pulling out the message. "She was in a sort of Pentecostal phase when she had me." She glanced around her as if looking for a quiet place to sit down and read. Beneath her horse's feet, the pavement was starting to shake.

"Let's get out of here," Shirley said abruptly and with something of passion. "Not just out of this mess. What I mean, all the way out. Over the mountains." Out of Hoadley, the town with the long memory; away from what it had made her: a misfit, a freak.

No one answered her, though Elspeth backed her red horse, looking to Shirley to lead off. But Cally sat where she was, gazing down into the black pit taking the town.

She said, "Mark's down there."

"Huh?" Tabling her own agenda, Shirley inched closer to the edge, leaned and looked. Through shadows, dust, and eye-stinging, tear-inducing smoke, she could see nothing. "You sure?"

"Sure."

"But how can you—"

"And who the hell cares?" Gigi interrupted with sudden violence. "He's a goddamn no-good man. What do you care what happens to him, Cally? I'd kill him if I was you."

"Right," replied Cally tonelessly, and she turned her horse. The four women rode down a narrow alley to Railroad Street, which put them a block downslope of the devastation taking the genteel shops and homes and funeral establishments along Main Street. On Railroad Street were bran-colored houses again and boarded-up corner stores and wide-open corner taverns and the ethnic lodges: Slovak Eagles, Polish Club, Fraternal Order of American Italy. Men in Sears work coveralls were spewing out of the bars and clubs. The earth was trembling underfoot. Steel horseshoes slipped on the cracking asphalt, and the horses tossed their heads in reined-in panic, wanting to run.

To Cally it seemed only natural that earth, footing, certitude were collapsing and sliding away underfoot. The fundament of her life had been quaking since the night she had left Mark; she scarcely questioned the undermining of Hoadley, so condign, so apt, so inevitable did it seem to her. Sluggishly she felt moved, however, to remonstrate with Gigi. Mark was not one to whom something was going to happen, however richly deserved. Rather, Mark was the agent of the disaster. Watching at the edge of the abyss, she had recognized a technique. Mark was dispatching Hoadley methodically, joyously, gluttonously, relentlessly, the way he would go through a greasy paper bag of roasted peanuts.

*	*	*

Sojourner Hieronymus sat straight-backed in the cold metal chair on her gaunt, gray front porch, refusing to be coaxed down to the sidewalk, drawn into the panic. She disapproved of panic, messiness, untidiness; she disapproved of most of what she was seeing. Because there was so much of which to disapprove, she could not help thinly smiling. She felt very nearly cheerful, watching her foolish neighbors.

From the direction of the commotion downtown a whirlwind, a dust devil, came spinning up the street. No one liked to walk through a dust devil—it was choking dirty, and reputed to be bad luck—but on this day people cried out and scrambled away from it without dignity. Sojourner watched: one of them candy striper girls coming home from the hospital, crossing the street, was cut off from the sidewalk and caught by the edge of the thing. It lifted her skirt all around, blew it up above her waist, no matter how she tried to hold it down with her hands. Everybody could see her panties, them indecent skimpy-cut silky-lacy kind. Some old folks would have said her boyfriend was thinking about her, but Sojourner knew better. The Devil was thinking about that one. The Devil knew what she had on under that prissy-sweet mint-candy dress. The Devil had come to have a look and take her as his own. Sojourner knew. The girl shaved her legs, too, Sojourner felt sure of that, and everybody knew shaving any part of a woman just made the hair grow back thick and bristly, like a man's beard—

The teenager screamed, because as her hands had smoothed down her skirt after the dust devil's mischief they had felt, she had looked—hair, dark and thick and curling, sprouting from her legs, bursting out through her pantyhose. Already it grew so thick it hung like pantaloons, swished like fur trousers as she ran, still screaming, toward the somewhat-refuge of her parents' house.

Sojourner laughed out loud, a surprised, delighted squawk of laughter, and turned quick gray eyes, beady-hard and pitiless as a bird's eyes, toward another victim. That Jessie Rzeszut, the beefy woman from down by the corner, the one who dyed her hair straw blond, she tanned herself until she looked like a nigger, all winter running to that Tropical Beauty place, spending hours under them money-wasting machines, cooking herself like in a microwave—

The woman shrieked and fell to the sidewalk, where she lay on her back, her heavy bosom tilted skyward, savory-brown and crisp as a turkey on Thanksgiving.

All her life Sojourner had felt frustrated, helpless to rectify or understand the evil of the world, of her community, of her neighbors; the rush of rapture, the long-awaited joy of consummate power, the ecstasy she felt at that Apocalypse moment shook her as strongly as the collapse of Hoadley was shaking the porch on which she sat. She shouted aloud as if seized by the holy spirit, and from her snapping-turtle mouth her word issued forth, creating misfits to replace those Ahira had healed.

"You play with fire, you're gonna wet the bed!" She bounced on her chair, her head thrust forward, her old eyes gleaming with the glory of the coming of the Lord. "You women wear men's clothes, you're gonna get hair on your breasts! You men play with yourselves, you're gonna get hair on your palms!"

Every man in sight looked startled and clenched his hands. So compelling, though, were the events downtown that no one paid any further immediate attention to the hair or the manner in which it had appeared.

Uplifted, Sojourner teetered to her feet. "World

ain't been the same since them government fellows messed around with the moon!"

Oona Litwack, who was standing out front of her half of the house wearing her customary polyester slacks, and who had felt a peculiar prickling on her bosom—her comfortable bosom, soft as the cotton fiberfill cushion on her living room sofa, the one embroidered, "Ewe's Not Fat, Ewe's Just Fluffy," with a fleece appliqued sheep in the center—Oona Litwack, who had lived next door to Sojourner Hieronymus for twenty-one years, turned and looked carefully at the lean, gray old woman standing on the lean, gray porch, then came up her front walk toward her own porch.

"Step on a crack, break your mother's back!" Sojourner shrilled at her.

Oona proceeded in her plump, flat-footed fashion between her American Beauty rosebushes and a row of plaster ducks, stepping on numerous cracks. "My mother's dead, so she don't care." No doubt the spine had shattered in the casket, six feet underground in the old town cemetery. No doubt at all. Oona stopped at the top of her porch steps and looked across the dividing rail at Sojourner.

"You sneeze on Sunday, or what?"

Ignorant people said that if a person sneezed on Sunday, the Devil would be with that person all week long. Sojourner didn't hold with such superstition. She had, in fact, sneezed the Sunday past and didn't feel any different than usual.

"Them impatiens of yours is hanging over my porch and dropping leaves," Sojourner accused.

Oona ignored that. "Instead of saying things about people around here, better you should say the sea is gonna turn to blood, things like that," she gently advised. "Sea's not around here."

Sojourner gave her a hard look. "You wish on a white horse, you're gonna cry," Sojourner snapped. "You dream of a white horse, you're gonna die."

Far down Main Street, horses appeared, their hooves clangoring on the pavement, four horses clattering out of smoke and dust and whirlwind and thunder sound like an omen. On them rode four women all the town knew: four persons, rather. That addlebrained Cally Wilmore, and Gigi Wildasin, and that there Elspeth no-name, and that there Peter Wertz called himself Shirley Danyo. Oona Litwack saw Sojourner's glinting eyes, the same cold color as her milk box, fix on them. Oona saw the stark old woman suck breath to speak.

On the rosebushes the cicadas sighed, Doom, doom.

Oona did what she had been wanting for twenty-one years to do: "Shut up," she said, and without effort or rehearsal her hand found a flowerpot, a heavy ceramic one in the shape of a potbellied lion, and hurled it over the porch barrier, violating Sojourner's air space and Sojourner's skull. The old woman fell and lay still. Knowing how frail these lank old ladies with no padding were inclined to be, Oona felt satisfied she would not get up again.

Going into her house, Oona felt the hair on her breasts itching against the inside of her blouse and made a sour face. Just because she wore slacks. Good Lord. Probably it would get bristly if she tried to shave it. No matter. Her husband would never notice it.

Oona grudgingly thanked her luck that Sojourner had not said men who masturbated themselves would go blind. Even though there didn't seem to be much time left for Hoadley, she wouldn't have wanted to spend it leading her husband around by the hand.

*   *   *

In passing on her snorting black horse, Cally noted Sojourner's body lying on the porch. The sight did not affect her other than with uneasy second thoughts. She had always respected Sojourner, because Sojourner was the only person in Hoadley who seemed to think and live in lean, terse, uncompromising lines, who did not smother her lawn and house with cuddly-cute icons of sugar-coated life, who did not messily overeat of life. It occurred to her, glancing at the body (lying like a wintertime corn husk the wind would soon take away) that she was the only person in Hoadley who had thought much of Sojourner. Yet seeing Sojourner dead, she felt nothing for her. And she wondered if she had been right to admire her, or if she had admired her for the wrong reasons. As she had admired Gigi maybe for all the wrong reasons.

She had asked Shirley (who may have been a man once, but was a nice, obliging person just the same) to exit Hoadley via the funeral home, and as was expected of her Shirley had agreed. Arriving at the Perfect Rest, Cally looped Devil's reins over the top spire of the three-tiered fountain on the front lawn and ran inside while the others waited for her. She was not at all sure what she was looking for—Mark? But she knew where Mark was. Nevertheless, she trotted from Blue Room to Peach Parlor to Rose Room, peeking in. In Rose the body of Mr. Mundis, a former coal miner, awaited the ministrations of Barry Beal, who would arrange over it a blanket of a texture and hue that would have appalled the man in life. Barry Beal was not there, had not been there, Cally noted, the everyday portion of her mind automatically wondering where he was. Meanwhile, the world, like the rest of her, was going insane, and the corpse was slowly sitting up in the coffin—casket, rather; never say coffin—the dead man was sitting up, but still unmistakably dead, the eyes blank, the face flat and pork-pink with makeup and embalming fluid. Mr. Mundis did not push himself up with his hands and complain of his poor wind and his arthritis, as he would have in life. He sat up woodenly, as if the hand of God had pulled a string attached to his head. Cally fled.

With frenetic energy hers once again she ran up the steps to the apartment. No Mark there, either. But once in the cluttered and familiar living room, already forgetting the dead man downstairs (too much was happening for one overactive corpse to matter very much; the late Mrs. Zepka's leer, evidently, had been the merest hint of things to come) Cally knew why she had come home. Comfortably, as if someone had put a cup of tea in her hand, she sat down on the sofa and read her letter.

Tammy, acting strangely, hospitalized for evaluation? Owen, showing symptoms of—leprosy?

Her children. Getting them out of Hoadley had not been enough. Like a pestilence, Hoadley had afflicted them before they had gone; Hoadley was in them, a poison in their blood. Hoadley would kill them.

Her children; all the children . . . In the bushes outside, the hungerbabies keened.

Cally got up with eyes as fixed and lifeless as that of the corpse; with a stride that had lost all impulsion she went downstairs and outside to join the Elspeth and Shirley and Gigi. What else was there for her to do but to be the horsewoman who rode the black steed?

"My house next," Gigi demanded, not bothering to look at Shirley for acquiescence; Shirley would not argue. "I want to see if Homer's got himself dead of a heart attack yet. And if he hasn't, I want to kill him."

No one smiled or so much as blinked. Gigi had always matter-of-factly talked about murdering Homer.

"What better time?" she added. "What's one more body in a mess like this?"

They had to backtrack. Shirley trailed in the rear, stoical but pale. The sinkhole taking the town into the bowels of the old mines had grown; they had to skirt it. They discovered that on their mounts they could move around what remained of the town as no one else could; they could cut through the narrow spaces between houses where cars could not go, they could canter across back yards and jump the fences that separated them. On the streets, they could traverse the broken pavements between the abandoned cars, and the panicked crowds fleeing the catastrophe on foot made way for them, frightened of the lathered, wild-eyed horses. There was an undeniable thrill in their unaccustomed freedom, their power on horseback in that stricken town. Gigi, trampling flowerbeds under the hooves of her pale appaloosa, gave a high-pitched bark of laughter. Never, Cally thought, looking at her with repugnance and fascination, never had she seen the evil old ever-dying woman so alive, so youthful with excitement, as she was on that day of doom. The strong, sweaty smell of terror in the air must have suited her.

The old Wilmore house had gone down into the abyss, Cally noticed. Mark's birthplace and childhood home was gone, cactus named Fred and all. She saw Ma Wilmore in her customary crocheted hat (the cactus had worn its own headgear down to its demise) standing in the crowd at the edge of the chasm, looking after it. Those Hoadley people who remained by the great pit looked and screamed and looked and shrieked but seemed unable to move away, these old-timers, as they had always felt unable to move away from Hoadley, as if held by some hypnotic black-snake gaze of God.

Cally looked, from the vantage of Devil's high-horse back, and saw something dark moving in deep earth—a shadow, a coal-colored stirring, nothing more distinct—and murmured without feeling, "Mark."

"God damn! There goes my house." Gigi sounded outraged. Cally knew the old woman felt no affection for the house; her dudgeon must have been because she had wanted to send Homer with it.

"Mark," Cally whispered again, her taut, thin gaze fixed downward, into the smoky black emptiness under Hoadley, hollow as her belly, hollow as Gigi's heart, and she did not look up until she heard an odd sort of dry, coughing scream from the woman next to her—Shirley. Then she looked.

Gigi's house and high dog-proof fence and incredible flourishing flower gardens all sagged at the edge of the abyss, breaking apart. And out of those thick, thriving gardens, boiling out of the dense roots and falling into the void—came babies, long-dead babies, falling without a cry, by the dozen, the hundred. Tiny, frail, some skeletal, some curled and tan, like so many dead birds and insect husks they drifted on the heat of infernal fire, on the updrafts of smoke yellow as chicken fat. Babies—or what had once been babies—or what could have been babies. . . .

The children, Cally thought, all the children . . . And loud on the wind sounded the wailing, dying cries of those other babies who had boiled out from underground, the children who wore coal-black faces and translucent, orange-trimmed wings. The hunger-babies. And Cally remembered Gigi declaring, to hell with them. . . .

"Abortionist," said Elspeth in a flat, dispassionate voice, studying Gigi with an artist's narrow eyes.

"Murderess," Cally said, or tried to say, her voice sounding tenuous, strangled, as if a snake had her by the throat. But Gigi only grinned, showing her teeth like a skull.

"I am what I am," Gigi said, "and so are you. You are Famine. And you, Shirley Peterless Danyo, can't-have-a-child-or-make-one-either, you are Pestilence. And you are War, Elspeth, whether you like it or not. Poor Elspeth, never wants to get involved." Gigi stared until Elspeth looked down at her sword, then turned on Cally, her grin gone between thin lips. "Don't get sniffy with me, Ms. Famine Apocalypse Wilmore. You're no better than me. You're nearly the same as me."

"I hate you," Cally whispered.

"Do you? Seems to me—"

"Gigi—what are you?" interrupted Shirley, to quell the quarrel.

"Damn it!" Elspeth exploded at her lover—or former lover. "Must you always have everything spelled out? Now—"

"Now," Gigi said, "it is my turn. And I am Death."

CHAPTER FOURTEEN

I guess Mr. Wilmore didn't mind none that I didn't show up for work that day. He had other stuff on his mind. Course at the time I didn't know what all was going on down in Hoadley and I figured I was in trouble, but I couldn't help that. I couldn't leave Joanie the way she was, and I couldn't get her to go with me neither. So we both just set in the merry-go-round and tried to figure out what to do.

I says, "Did the Devil say how he was going to . . ."

"He said he wouldn't have to do much of anything. Once he got things started, people would do all the work themselves."

Like Garrett's dominoes.

"Destroy themselves," Joanie says, "just like they always did, with half a chance."

"Joan," I says, "you got to talk to him again and tell him to make it stop."

She gave a hard sort of snort, like she would have laughed at me if she wasn't so discouraged and tired. "Sure," she says, sarcastic.

I says, "You got to at least try. What's going to

279

happen to my Ma and my Pa and my brothers?" I heard my voice go up high, like a kid's, and I tried to calm down. Joan had set up straight and was looking at me. Ahira, I mean. She had that Ahira look in her eyes.

"Barry Beal," she says, real slow and soft, "I will never understand you. You've asked about what will happen to me, and your family, and everyone in Hoadley, and never once have you asked what will happen to you."

That didn't seem so hard to understand. "I'll be with you," I says.

"If I'm going to try to summon Satan again," she says, "you've got to get out of here."

"No," I says.

"Bar, you'll get killed!"

"I'm staying with you," I says.

"I don't have Snakie to make the circle any more!"

"It don't matter. I'm staying."

"Bar, what the hun do you think is going to protect us?"

We could've argued about it a while longer, but then into the merry-go-round come footsteps, and we both looked, and it was that weird guy, the one that looked like me but too damn perfect and would have had sex with a dead person if they asked him. He came in cocky naked and set down with us and smiled at me like a cat.

I says, grumpy, "What the hell is he doing here?"

"I called him." Joanie used her Queen-of-Sheba Ahira voice on me. "I can do that, you know."

"I guess you could send him away, too."

"He might be able to help us. Bar, stop being so jealous." She sounded grumpy as me but more like Joanie again. "It's silly to be jealous of yourself."

"Huh?"

"I'm you," the big dick says.

"In a pig's eye!"

"He is!" Joanie says. "Mostly. Whenever you left part of yourself around my place, I saved it. He's your hair and nail trimmings and—and nose tissues and stuff." Joanie's voice went a little pale. "And a piece of wood. And some junk food. Vanilla Tastycakes and things."

"Jesus," I says.

"It took a lot of doing," Joan says, stronger. "So have some respect."

I made a snotty sound in my nose and says, "I don't care what you say, he ain't me. I'm right here."

But the hunk's looking at Joanie, and he says, "What have you done?"

Her face, he means. She says, "Never mind that."

"But why? You were beautiful."

"Never mind! I want you to just—just mind your own business and help me."

Them's two things impossible to do both at once. But Joanie's naked friend don't say so. He just says, "Help you with what?"

So she explains it to him. And after she's done, he sets real quiet. Then he says, soft, "Why should I help you?"

"I made you."

"Your mother and father made you. Would you do such a thing for them? No, because they did not love you. And you do not love me. I disgust you, and you are afraid of me. You know how I have ached for you, but you will not so much as kiss me or touch my hand."

This here was good news, sort of. I perked up, listening.

"Now you have made yourself no longer beautiful," he says. "Why should I stay and put myself in danger for you?"

And Joanie don't have no answer. And I think, Well, that's it, and I guess he will get up and go. I sort of hope he will, and I sort of hope he won't. But then he turns them deep brown eyes, like a ten-point buck's eyes, on me.

"But for this one I must stay," he says, soft as his eyes.

I feel my chest get tight, I don't know why, and I says, "How come?"

"I have told you, you are my second self. I cannot do otherwise. I will stand between you and Satan."

I can't argue with him none. It's our only chance. I look at Joanie, and she looks at me and nods, and we get up.

We should've went outside, maybe, but we didn't. We just done it right where we was, in between the horses. That nude dude drawed a circle on the floor around Joanie and me with his finger—it showed on them planks, red, like blood—and then I seen it was blood. His finger was dripping when he stood up. He looks at Joanie.

"I have a name now," he says, hard. And then he looks at me.

"I want you to know my name," he says, soft. "It is Eros."

"All right," I says. "Thanks." For what he was doing, I meant.

He takes a stand on the rim of the circle with his back to us, and Joanie started the spell. She stood by one of them wooden horses and said words didn't make no sense to me, and she made her voice sound fierce but the rest of her was shaking. But Eros didn't shake none. He was cool. He was like some movie star facing the firing squad without a mask or a cigarette. Rock solid beautiful.

Me, I just stood there like a dummy.

First thing I noticed was the smell, like Trout Creek, all sulphur. But I didn't hardly have time to smell it before the devil come busting out in front of us like a blast furnace, so hot and fierce I just about couldn't stand it. I put my hands over my eyes and looked right through them, red, and I could still see him. He didn't look like no Sunday-School devil with red tights or a pitchfork or nothing. I wouldn't of been so scared of him if he did. He was big, maybe twice as tall as me, he was a big swaying snake of fire with the face of a person, except the next minute he wasn't no more. Next he was a person all the way, grinding his hips like a peep show dancer, except his face was a politician or a mine owner or a television preacher, I ain't sure which, and his hands was burning bones. And he had a big hard-on and big breasts both. But then he was one of them nosy old ladies from Hoadley. All at once, sort of. Trying to see him was like watching shapes in fire flames, and trying to touch him would have been like grabbing a bonfire, and I knowed why he was like that. He was the devil. You couldn't get hold of him.

And before he even said nothing, that hot dog Eros, the one who was supposed to be protecting us, just melted away. Not like when he disappeared before. This time he made a puddle on the floor. Little bits of fingernail and hair and dandruff and cookie crumbs, melted icing and stuff floating in something like hot motor oil. And a big old chunk of wood. It flared up and burned like a firecracker. He was gone.

And the devil says to us, "How dare you." His voice was like the whooshing sound a welding torch makes, but I understood him okay, right down to my bones, and I was shaking worse than Joanie. Old Satan, he was plenty mad. Or she was. Sounded like a she, just then.

Joanie may have been shook but she had guts. She didn't give him time to say no more. She says, "Call it off." She tries to say it like she's got a right to order the devil around, but I guess she don't fool nobody. Her voice ain't behaving, and it keeps getting worse. "Make it stop," she says. "Call it a day. I've had it. I don't want any more of this Ahira business. I don't want the world to end. I don't even want Hoadley to end. I just want. . . ." Her voice shook so bad she couldn't finish. Or maybe she didn't know what she wanted.

Anyways, when the devil heard what she was saying he let out a blast-furnace roar scared me so bad I about peed my pants, until I figured out he was laughing. Laughing!

Yukking it up so hard he could barely talk. "You ridiculous humans!" he hollered. "You poor, wide-eyed, wishful, muddleheaded, muck-footed, absurd fools! You call on me!"

"Yes," says Alita. "You gave me the power. You gave me this face. Take them away."

Old Satan is still laughing, jiggling and shooting off sparks; I can't look at him. "You simpleminded twit," he says to Joanie, "don't you know what that is lying in a puddle in front of you? Like dog pee?"

"It's just the doppelganger."

"Ninny. Pudding-faced, hyperventilating coito-phobe. It's your dream lover."

I still had my hands over my eyes, trying to look at the devil, but now I wanted to look at Joanie. I squeezed a peek at her between my fingers. I couldn't see her real good—it was like she was a black person standing there. But I could tell she had stopped shaking. She was standing real still with her hands stretched out a little like she was dizzy or floating.

The devil says, "He was your dream of the way your lover should look, and you are your dream of the way you should look, and now look at your dreams!" And he laughed some more.

Joanie says, "So my dreams are melting. So what else is new? Listen to me! I want you to stop what is happening in Hoadley."

"But I have nothing to do with that!" He's still laughing, and Joanie gets mad and yells at him.

"You make it stop!"

There's a sort of angry rustling, like fire in a dry woods, and Joanie shuts up. We was all quiet for a little.

Then the devil says, "Ill-mannered twerp, I will tolerate no more insolence from you. I have done nothing but what is expected of me. You called me here to put flesh on your dreams, and I have done what you wanted. You invited me into Hoadley, and once there I listened. All I have done is what Hoadley people said. What they wanted of me. I have fulfilled their expectations." He snapped his fingers, the sound popped and hissed and crackled like a green log in a fire. "What makes you think I can leave just like that? People are making use of me."

Joanie whispers, "You are hideous."

"Me! Don't you see? It's all up to them, not to me."

Down in Hoadley, the water tower teetered like a huge, stilt-legged, swollen-bellied spider at the edge of the cave-in. From somewhere down in the blackness a broken water main was spraying up a fountain as artistic as that which had once graced the immacu-

late lawn of the Perfect Rest Funeral Home. But that
lawn and fountain were gone, along with half of that
Victorian edifice. Rose Room and Peach Parlor, broken open, sent down pale, chaste statuary, lurid
amid shards of chandelier. Blue Room and basement
storage dropped darkly shining, blimp-shaped caskets like bombs, like overlarge Easter eggs to crack
open and spill their contents against some still-unseen
bottom. And from the remains of the Homer and
Gladys Wildasin yard and all-too-fertile gardens, the
long-dead fetuses continued to sift down. Watching
them, watching the coffins fall, knowing what Easter-
morning treasure might be in them, the crowd
swerved from panic to a deeper desperation. Only
Gigi was happy.

"I am Death!"

Staring at her, dumbfounded, Cally thought she
had never seen the heartless old ever-dying woman
so alive, so vital.

"I am Death, and I've got you all in my pocket.
You all come to me in the end." Sitting on her pale
horse and looking across a small space at Pestilence,
Gigi grinned the tough little grin Cally had once
loved. "Right, Shirley?"

Paler than Death's horse, her skin appaloosa-spotted
with raisin-colored sarcomas, Shirley did not answer.
She seemed not to have heard, not to be aware of
much around her; blue-eyed and blank, she stared at
the dead things falling, falling, falling into the pit.
But Elspeth sucked in a sharp breath, nudged Warrior forward and fingered the hilt of her sword.

"Let Shirley go," she told Gigi.

Grinning, the old woman said, "Why, I haven't
done anything to her. She did it to herself."

"Let her go!"

"Why, what do you care?" Gigi curled her upper

lip; grin turned to a sneer. "She was a man, remember? She lied to you."

"You old hag." Elspeth's hand tightened on her sword hilt. "I don't care what she is, I don't care what she's done. You know I love her."

Shirley's staring blue eyes widened; she turned to look at Elspeth. But Elspeth's fierce, dark scowl was bent on Gigi.

"Let her live." A small, tea-tan hand, the delicate hand of an artist, gripped the sword hilt. "Or shall we see if Death can die?"

Gigi threw back her iron-gray head and crowed with laughter. "You sneaking jig! Poor excuse of a War. I've never known you to draw that sword against anything except blackberries!"

"Wrong, Gladys." Shirley spoke, and not to quell the altercation; her voice was weary but her eyes were shining. "When I'm in danger . . ."

Elspeth reached out briefly to touch her lover, then drew the sword with a long swish of metal against metal. Gigi's grin widened; her old eyes lit as if with fire, for one is never so alive as when one is dying. . . .

And under Cally's gawking person, black, tempestuous Devil rocketed suddenly out of control.

Cally felt the horse leap, felt the reins snatched from her famished hands by that leap, grabbed for mane, and only then realized that there was a crowd of people all around her and the others; the horse had noticed them before she did. Uplifted hands pulled at her clothing, her legs, trying to unseat her. The mob wanted the horses. The good citizens of Hoadley attacked each other as well as the horsewomen for the mounts that could carry them away from destruction. Something, perhaps a rock or a brick, struck Cally painfully on her thin, stooped shoulder; she ducked her head and kicked hard, not at Devil but at the people clinging to her boots. Devil was fighting like a hell-horse already. He reared—Cally gripped with hands and knees, flat against his neck. She saw bodies go down in front of his striking forehooves, saw blood, shockingly red, saw a vaguely familiar face shout something then turn pale and topple into the abyss—Wozny? The borough council president? It didn't matter; it was war, there was blood brighter than Zephyr Zook's fingernails. Cally saw the flash of Elspeth's sword; Elspeth stayed close by Shirley and slashed at the people menacing them both as if she cut down briar bushes. What became of Gigi, Cally did not see or care. She and Devil had kicked themselves free, and the black horse thundered away, choosing his own path, out of Hoadley.

Cally was aware of the things they passed in flashes, unbearably acute, dazzling as the light shattering from Elspeth's sword. A flash: the park gazebo, still with multicolored Christmas bulbs decorating its posts and eaves, still standing like an island in the midst of pit and devastation (although the pigeon-chested bronze general on horseback who had once reared near it had gone down without striking a blow); on it and around it the six-hundred-sixty-six, all those misfits of Hoadley who wore Ahira's mark, stood stolidly waiting for her, quite safe in their expectation that she would save them. Then a span of pounding hooves, and in a flash again the place Cally remembered from another wild, runaway ride: the abandoned cemetery (never say "graveyard") where white violets languished in the rank grass. Devil had carried her to the hill above Hoadley. From behind her and below her, rising on the updrafts of inferno, came faintly the odors and clamors of extremity. She could have looked back and seen the town, or what remained of it, and seen down into the pit, perhaps. But she did not, for her hypersensitive stare was caught on the cemetery, horrified: the graves were opening. Under the weathered white marble shafts, under the crude fieldstone blocks carved with tulips and hex circles, under the more recent gray granite markers inset with sepia-tone oval portraits of the deceased, under them all the unshorn grass was parting, the violets fainting, six feet of moist violated earth opening, dark as the fundament of Hoadley.

Cally hid her assaulted eyes; Devil carried her on.

But just beyond the cemetery the black horse stopped short, nearly sending his featherweight rider over his shoulder; a different roar in the clamor rising from Hoadley, a different fetor in the updraft's stench, turned him in his tracks. He stood with spraddled forelegs, with pricked, trembling ears, looking. Cally looked as well, over his black crest.

So painfully vivid was everything to her starved eyes that she had to nearly close them in order to see. . . . She saw. On the water tower. It had toppled but still clung with its metal feet; it hung over the edge of the chasm on its long spidery legs, bulbous body dangling in the darkness. And climbing up that attenuated metal carcass, that arachnid, feeling its way up and out over the lip of the abyss, out into Hoadley, came something as big as its bloated belly and black as the pit. And it seemed to Cally, watching, that the whole day turned storm-lurid-dark; something more than smoke had blotted out the sun.

From the locust trees brushing Cally's neck with long-fingered leaves, black-faced hungerbabies cried, "The beast! The beast! The beast!"

Devil vented a snort of terror, whirled and sprang into a flat-out gallop again, up the graveled trolley line. Though she had caught hold of the reins again, Cally let herself be swept along, caught up in the black tempestuous horse's assault of the hill, in his fateful momentum, in the headlong curving sweep of his leap as he challenged the fallen treetrunk. She rode with her frail body hovering airily above the horse's withers, her shoulder blades jutting from her fleshless back like inchoate wings.

At the hilltop trolley park, as before, Devil slowed and stopped of his own will, though he did not graze. On what must once have been the barker's strip he stood puffing, nostrils flaring; the smell of sulphur hung in the air. Then his ears swooped forward and he spooked. Two people were coming out of the carousel building, arms around each other. Lovers? Perhaps—but peering between her horse's black, pricked ears, Cally saw that their mood seemed more desperate than loving. Their embrace was to keep one another from falling. They were stumbling. Barry Beal and—and that Ahira woman. . . .

With a horse-snort sound a lick of flame sprang from the peak of the carousel house and wavered there like an ethereal pennant. Devil spooked again, springing backward, but Cally did not go with him. Half dismounting, half falling, she left the horse and staggered toward Ahira on stiffened legs. She stared; the stranger woman's long hair, once a honey-sleek flow, now hung lank, ropy, around a face ugly with cuts and bruises. With drooping head Ahira sank to a seat on the ground, and Barry Beal sat beside her, his arm still around her, protective, loving. . . .

Cally had not heard Barry Beal mention Joan Musser's name since he had met Ahira. And she knew it would have been reasonable to suppose he had forgotten his Joanie and fallen in love with Ahira like the rest of the misfits. Reasonable, but . . . in that moment, starved for love even more than for food, and with the heightened perceptions of a fasting visionary—or of a person soon to die . . . Gazing, Cally knew the unreasonable truth.

"Joan," she said, standing in front of her. "Joan Musser."

The woman lifted her head. Looking into her green eyes, Cally perceived the mud-and-algae pop-eyes of the woman Hoadley had called Frog Face. Looking into her exquisite, injured face, Cally saw Joanie's bent and hating face.

Cally nodded and said without passion, "So you are the witch."

Barry Beal said, "Hi, Mrs. Wilmore. I'm sorry I didn't make it to work this morning. There was things I had to do." His arm tightened around the drooping woman at his side, and she leaned against him, but neither she nor Cally looked at him.

"You are worse," said Ahira to Cally. "You are Apocalypse."

Cally stared at her; how could she have known the name? Out of beautiful, blackened eyes Joan Musser stared back. "What the devil knows, I know," she said.

And the fire flared brighter on the roof of the carousel building. Cally's gaze shifted there. "Burning this down?" she complained. "Why?" As if watching a play from an excellent box seat she felt righteously, abstractly incensed; the destruction of Hoadley seemed a mere spectacle to her, but the destruction of such a beautiful thing, the carousel, had to be ontologically evil.

Joan twisted herself to look back and up at the blaze. "The hub," she muttered. "The whole—the whole macrocosm will go next, the whole world."

At the same time Barry Beal said earnestly. "It

wasn't her, Mrs. Wilmore. It was him, Satan. He set it on fire."

Cally half heard him, half heard Joan Musser, and understood hub, Satan, whole world, and knew that her children would not live to survive her, and felt her theatre seat drop her back to Hoadley earth, hard and obdurately real, with a jarring pain. For a moment, as if she had physically fallen, she couldn't move. Then,

"My kids!"

She strode toward the carousel.

"Yo! Mrs. Wilmore!" Barry Beal yelled after her. "What you doing?"

She did not hear or answer. With temerity worthy of Gigi she intended to tell the devil to let her children alone, to make him let them alone, somehow. She speeded her stride to a run, passed into the shattered mouthway of the place, leaped onto the platform.

The hub of the carousel stood like a giant, ornate candle with flame at its top, and small orange snakes of flame lazed along the spokes of the ceiling as if venturing out from a nest at its center, and above the wheel-like carousel frame the peaked roof and rafters of the housing had begun to burn, making a spider-web of fire. Under the flames the wooden horses flung up their heads, eyes rolling, manes wild, mouths agape and teeth bared in silent screams, like horses trapped in a barn fire, and like them they did not move; panic froze them to their places, their poles. The bright paint of their trappings and curved necks and deep-cantled saddles glinted all the candy colors in the gaudy light, but the world over them was only orange and black, orange and black, fire and shadow. Cally saw nothing resembling a devil. Of course the old bastard was gone. Barry and his girlfriend wouldn't have been limping around talking with her other-wise. Stupid.

Nevertheless, Cally stood looking, seeing fire flicker, remembering fireflies over a wheeling uncanny carousel at night . . . . And the gazebo in the park, turning, turning with blinking bulbs. . . . And the great, doomed, spinning, starlit world. . . .

"Joan!" she yelled with such fierce authority that the woman who called herself Ahira came to her, into the shadows of the carousel house, under the burning roof, with Barry Beal following like a dog at her bare heels.

"What spell have you put on this place?"

Joan looked back at her dully, too soul-tired to care much about Cally's misconception. "It's the hub. . . . It's the center of the universe."

"And of time?" There had once been a song or a poem or a book called Carousel of Time, and Cally's mind was leaping, leaping, like a strong horse over all the barriers on the uphill way. Joan did not answer. Her answer did not matter. Cally's eyes glittered with feverish vivacity in her gaunt head; she turned to Barry. "Can you make it go backwards?"

"Huh?" Barry could not follow such a logic-leaping path, and Cally showed none of her former patience with him.

"Barry, we've got to make the carousel go backwards! Get a move on!"

"Oh," Joan breathed, her great, shadowed eyes coming alive in her still-lovely face. She understood. "Bar, she wants us to make time go backwards! Far enough so none of this ever happened."

"To hell with all that! I just want my kids back." Cally's voice started to shake, and she toughened it. "Barry! Get busy!" The moron, he was good with cars and things, what was his problem?

In the splotched side of his face the white of his eye showed wide, frightened, lurid in the flamelight. He could barely talk, but managed, rapidly, stammering. "M-Mrs. Wilmore, the-there ain't no motor in this thing no more! And even if there was, the gears—" He broke off, scared. Cally did not know that she was the horror confronting him, that all the too-plainly-visible muscles in her face were moving, jerking, red in the firelight and shining with her tears, as if they had no skin.

"Then push," she said, and she put her frail shoulder against the sturdy wooden shoulder of the nearest carousel horse, a bay. She planted her feet just outside the platform and strained every starved muscle of her body—what little body she had left herself. Strained to move the great, inert wheel.

"Wait a minute!" Barry hurried to the horse behind Cally and began pushing; it was either that or watch Cally break herself in half. After a moment Ahira bent her shoulder to the next horse and did likewise.

The carousel had not moved for a long time—since 1955, in fact. It did not take kindly to being aroused from its long slumber. Cally strained far beyond what should have been her endurance; Ahira pushed until salty sweat stung her cut face instead of salty tears. Barry Beal started to pant curses, stood up suddenly, shouted, "Fucker!" and kicked the platform.

With a groan and an angry screech it started to turn. Slowly, slowly, but Barry said in surprised tones, "Son of a bitch!" and bent to work again, pushing against the white shoulder of the richly caparisoned lead horse, the one with the brass number plate etched "666" on its bridle. A little faster. Painted ponies spinning tail first into time. Ahead of him Cally made a hoarse noise she meant to be a cheer; even to her ears it came out more like a death gasp. Overhead, the fire had spread and grown hotter. Burning embers were falling. One of them sizzled on Cally's thin arm; she noticed the noise and shook it off, but did not feel it.

Yet the next moment she let out a startled squeak as something touched her shoulder, something alive.

She jumped back—the carousel moved on without her, faster, faster, speeding up, but she saw clearly enough the snake oozing out of the carousel horse's ever-gaping mouth. Thick as a horse's tongue, bluntheaded, phalluslike, it was orange-bellied and black of back, with orange eyes. They met hers as its head wheeled past her head, and Cally screamed.

There were snakes coiling out of the mouths of every horse on the carousel. Cally caught at Barry's arm as he trotted past her, pulled him away from the white lead horse he was pushing, and he stood dumbfounded, for the carved animal had a thick serpent hanging down from between its teeth, down to its knees, and it was changing as he stared into something not white and not carousel horse at all—

Black and orange, orange and black, it was a cicada as tall as Cally, its translucent wings rattling—but it had the tail of a scorpion. And its face, human, all too alive, looked down as it swung by, a face deeply lined, arrogant and cold of eye under a golden crown. Gigi's face! Yet, the face of an ancient king. And the snake still hung from its mouth.

"Oh, Jesus!" Barry shouted, bursting out of astonishment. "Joanie!"

She had jogged past him and Cally, head down, pushing at her horse—it was still a horse, though its eyes blazed fire, yellow smoke puffed from its nostrils, a serpent extruded from its mouth and its tail had turned to a cluster of snakes that lashed angrily against its back legs. Ahead, Cally's bay carousel horse had changed into a red dragon. All over the platform she saw grotesque beasts instead of the pretty painted ponies. She saw something with the body of a leopard, the feet of a bear, the head of a lion—the fanged mouth gaped wide open, serpent-tongued. She saw an ox with three sets of wings. She saw an eagle with hundreds of eyes covering its body like smallpox. She saw a black angel sitting stolidly in place of a chariot. She saw an armored horse galloping with a breastplate of fire. And overhead, fire, fire, the whirling of the carousel fanning it so that it lifted a thousand orange-maned heads and roared like a lion.

"Joanie!" Barry cried, his voice cracking, like an adolescent's, into a scream.

She had seen, but too late, what was happening. As she raised her head the cicada with a tyrant's stony face had lumbered from its place on the carousel. With black, clawed forelegs it reached over the back of her carousel horse; the animal shied and whickered aloud in terror, and Joan tried to stop, let go, stumble away—but there was a clack of harsh wings, and the cicada caught her in its narrow grasp. It spraddled its two pairs of hind legs, pulling back, and tugged her past lashing serpents onto the carousel platform. She screamed—Barry Beal was running toward her, shouting; his shouts and the sound of his thudding feet and even the roaring of the fire above were drowned in the sound of her screaming.

Cally saw the cicada drop its victim to the merry-go-round's floor as if she were something not good to eat. Then the carousel whirled her out of sight beyond the fiery column on which it turned—turned now faster than Barry could run, and Joan's cry wailed away.

"No! Oh, no. No. . . ."

She spun into view again from behind the blazing hub. Sprawled flat, clinging to a pole at the platform's edge by the fire-eyed horse's skittish heels and venomous tail, her head down so that her long hair trailed, her face hidden—Cally could not at first comprehend what had happened, except that Joan's dress had turned blood red. Then the cicada laughed out of its tight-lipped human mouth, a laugh like the creaking of insects in the night.

"Welcome, Whore of Babylon," it said in the same creaking voice, the king of death said, looking down at the one who lay at his feet beneath the orange flames.

Joan lifted her head like someone drowning in fire. "Stop this thing!" she cried out. "Make it stop!" In a flash piercing as swordlight Cally saw her face, saw how it had changed, and felt as if she could not breathe; she felt faint, and the blaze overhead seemed to take all the air.

"Where are your babies, Whore of Babylon?" the king taunted.

"Please . . ." Joan passed and was snatched away again by the carousel careening backward into doom.

Embers fell, stinging worse than betrayal, and Cally did not feel them or move, and at a small distance from her Barry stood as stupefied as Cally. It was not they who stopped the carousel's tailward turning, but the fire above them. For with a rain of burning coals and a noise worthy of a hundred uncouth beasts the roof began to fall, and the first timber jammed the spinning platform like a sprag.

CHAPTER FIFTEEN

When Elspeth first swung her sword the shock as it struck through flesh to bone reverberated up her dark-skinned arm and shook her soul. A person, a man with sunburned ears and a balding head, was cut down, dead by her doing; how could that be? How could any of this day be happening? It felt unbelievable, unreal, like a mad dream, as bizarre and floating as a certain carousel night. . . . Only one thing was real: Shirley. And Hoadley was trying to destroy that large golden verity, the mob was pulling, pounding at Shirley to drag her down, and Elspeth struck with the sword, and again, and again, clearing a way to take her to the big, blond woman's side, where she and Berrysmiter and her plunging horse could clear away the people who attacked—

Her beloved.

Elspeth lifted her sword again, needlessly. The crowd around Shirley wanted a horse, a means of escape, not a swordfight; though they felt desperate enough to risk the slow death of AIDS, they did not care to be killed on the spot. They pulled back at the first sight of the long, bloodied steel blade. But in that moment Elspeth was no longer a butterfly floating in a nightmare. Her sword grew tangible in her hand, her arm bone-hard and strong-muscled to her unquaking soul, and she hated them, hated them all who had ever hurt Shirley or despised Peter Wertz; she was no longer merely Elspeth, her more proper name was War, and she would kill, kill them all. Warrior felt her mood and shrilled, reared, mane and tail flying. Mount and swordswoman lunged, and the erstwhile mob, helplessly pressed together, shrieked and scrambled to escape War's sword.

"Yo!" Astonished, aghast, Shirley exclaimed, "Elspeth!" The easy-going woman, strapping-strong from her farm labors, had not much minded being mauled by the crowd, not enough to kill for it. She had been holding off her attackers absentmindedly and watching Devil carry Cally away when War swept down, a vengeance. "Elspeth!"

Her general called and must be obeyed. Sighing, War turned away from the scene of carnage before she had struck down more than three of the enemy. Dripping sword held low, she trotted smartly to the one who awaited her on the tall gray horse.

"Come on," said Shirley, "let's get out of here. Where's Gigi?"

The general was not her general after all, but her captain and comrade in arms, and Gigi was the traitor who had called her a jig. War didn't know or care where she was. "Gigi can go to hell," she said.

"Probably will," Shirley admitted. "Come on. This way." She led off, and War followed at her side, menacing from time to time when townspeople failed to scatter from her path with sufficient alacrity. Shirley kept an eye on her. "No," she protested once when War's sword came up, and she was relieved to see that the word had its effect.

They made their way around the still-standing gazebo and the tightly-packed crowd of misfits gathered near. War gave these people a glance and found them no threat. Obviously, they were refugees. At the far side of the pit, though, were enemies again, screaming and fleeing from something—but not from her sword, to War's chagrin—the fools were blundering into her very path! With an irritated snarl she lifted her weapon, awaiting the word to attack. Attack! Why did her captain not give the command? But when Shirley spoke, it was in a voice from which all her usual volume and confidence were missing.

"Oh, my God."

War followed the direction of Shirley's gaze and looked, and saw: the beast was coming up over the lip of the pit.

Not the sleek black of black horse or raven wing, but a dusty coal-black, a choking, smutty, lung-disease black, and huge: To Shirley's eyes the beast was an unhealthy growth such as she had once cut off her gray mare's chest; a melanoma, but one the size of the ever-growing manure pile behind her barn; a monstrous throbbing cancer coming toward her on legs like draggles of blackened blood, entirely too many of them and entirely too quick for such a gross thing. . . . War saw something resembling an immense, rotting, warty fungus, alive, regrettably real, coming at her and seeming to grow as she watched.

Not even War wanted to attack that. War changed back into Elspeth with a shudder, and her sword hung limp from her trembling hand. The beast—it was of a curdled black, a perverted color, a color gone wrong, misconceived, misused, an artist's horror. It was enough to harrow her heart.

"Time to run for it," said Shirley. "Come on!"
Shady Lady was plunging into a gallop as she spoke.
The horses were exhausted, but their first whiff of
the beast's fetor on the air sent them into a frenzy of
fear. They ran at top speed, Warrior lagging only a
little behind the taller thoroughbred, up Cemetery
Hill and out of Hoadley. Shirley tried to guide her
mount past the people in the way, but the animals
were running out of control. The gray mare knocked
down a woman and child; Warrior, following at the
thoroughbred's flank, leaped over the child but trampled the woman, and Elspeth moaned and dropped
her blood-smeared sword to the dirt.

"Elspeth, are you all right?"

Shirley glanced back, saw Elspeth turn ashen under the tea-tan skin of her face. The steep hill had
worn out Shirley's horse to the point where she
could attempt control. She hauled hard on the reins
with one hand, leaned sideward and clutched Warrior's bridle by the cheek strap with the other, intending to wrestle both mares to a halt. The horses
swerved with her and tossed their heads and tried to
pull apart, and in that frightened moment Shirley realized she was not as strong as she had been a day
before. She cursed; she left a trail of imprecations
along the path of the two ignorant, mule-mannered,
pea-brained fathead animals, and she thought she
was dead more than once before the horses stopped
and stood still on the grassy hillside above the old
Hoadley cemetery.

In scrub locust trees just behind her the baby-
faced cicadas wailed and chanted their dismal song,
less with abandonment now than with a certain fierce
fulfillment: "Doom . . . Doom . . ." With a buzz of
wings three orange-and-black hungerbabies flew to
Shirley's shoulder. She glanced down at them, shud-

dered and let them stay. Let them crawl down her shirt if they wanted to and huddle between her pestilence-spotted breasts, if that could comfort them. She would not deny anything to anyone now. At her horse's feet the graves stood open, empty, each in mute rictus, as if they had a story to tell Shirley could not hear. Death . . . What would it be like? Sooner than she had ever thought, she would know. . . . She wished the horses had stopped anywhere but there. Then she pushed the thought and her horror aside. Elspeth was sick.

The erstwhile War was clinging to Warrior's mane, and as soon as the mare stood still she leaned over her shoulder and retched. There was not enough in her stomach to let her vomit as she needed to do; she heaved and strained, trying to rid herself of what troubled her.

"Yo!" Reaching over from Shady Lady, Shirley patted her friend's back anxiously. "You all right, woman?"

Elspeth quieted, panting, spitting, lying against her horse's neck to recover, and Shirley did not hurry her. From where she sat she could see the pit like a great open mine far below, and the beast still moving about near the edge as if searching for something to eat. Though Shirley felt a chill of remembered terror crawl up her spine and into her chest as she looked at it, the beast seemed no more than a dark and featureless, blindly questing insect at the distance. They had left it far behind.

Painfully Elspeth straightened, rubbing her mouth with her hand. She looked not at Shirley but down at Hoadley, what little remained of it. "I wanted to kill them all," she said in a low, strained voice. "I wanted to take them apart."

"No kidding!" said Shirley tenderly.

"Don't joke about it."

"Who's joking? You don't want to talk about it, you don't have to."

"I've got to! I killed people. I hate them." Elspeth turned to face Shirley, her dark eyes narrow, taut. "I still hate them. I hate them all. They—people from Hoadley, they talk about how they're all family, all friends, but it's like Cally said, they only like you as long as you do what they want, say what they want, think what they want. They want to own your soul." The words were bursting from her, Elspeth the scornful, Elspeth the self-possessed, and when she said "you" she meant Shirley; it was Shirley who had suffered from Hoadley's stranglehold, not she. It was Shirley who had come back to live as a stranger in her own home town, and how anyone so big of heart had ever come out of that meager-minded place was beyond comprehension. . . . It was Shirley who was sitting pale on her horse, the sarcomas growing on her by the moment, and smiling faintly with rueful affection.

"That's the way they are, all right," Shirley admitted.

Elspeth's eyes widened, became liquid, shadowed, gazing. "But you, Shirl—" A gulping pause. "You—you've always loved me no matter what."

"Sure thing!" Shirley blinked; how else could she love Elspeth? Love anyone? It was the only way. Lord, to think that Elspeth had to say something about it, as if it was something new to her. . . . Shirley's big hand went out to her, because the little brown beauty looked like a stricken deer.

Their hands clasped across the gap between their horses and their lives. Hands gripped, the slender brown hand of the artist in Shirley's larger one, far too pale. "Sure thing," Shirley repeated. "What about it?"

"I've been thinking the least I can do is return the favor."

"Hell, Elspeth—" Shirley was not used to talking about these things and could not find the words to say that love demanded no such favors returned. Love asked nothing. But surely Elspeth understood that?

Maybe not. But the little sword-carrying fool understood something else. "Let me say it!" Elspeth lifted her exquisite head. "It shouldn't matter that you were born a man. It shouldn't matter that you didn't tell me everything. You're you. Who you are. The person who brought me home." She raised their clasped hands into a salute, a soldier's gesture of sisterhood. "That's all that matters. I'm not going to let anything else matter to me."

Emotions in Shirley ran deep and needed no theatrics. Her hand tightened on Elspeth's and she nodded, but she answered the pledge only with a sensible caution. "It matters that I got AIDS, though."

Elspeth looked straight into her eyes. "No. It doesn't."

"The hun it don't!"

"Shirl, we're all going to die soon anyway."

It was a matter to be accepted like love, like hatred, like Hoadley. Shirley nodded again. Hand in hand, the two women looked down on the town. Then Shirley gasped.

"Son of a bitch! Look at that beast!"

The creature of coal dust and shadows had come around to their side of the pit, come nearer, so that they could hazily see the workings of what appeared to be its feelers, or whiskers, or tentacles. . . . It was searching, not for food, but casting about as if for a scent. And as they watched, wide-eyed, it threw up the forepart of its shapeless body in what might have been exultation and bellowed forth an uncouth noise like the baying of a hound. Then it lowered its—its sensors, whatever they might be called, and snuffled again, and trundled rapidly up the hill, coming closer.

Elspeth exclaimed, "Jesus Christ, it's tracking us!"

"I don't want to die that soon!" Shirley disentangled her hand from Elspeth's with unromantic haste and grabbed her reins. "Come on!" They kicked their horses into a headlong gallop up the hillside.

They had not yet gone out of sight of the cemetery when Shirley's panicked mind cleared and she understood. The beast was not tracking Elspeth and her. It was trailing Cally. Had to be. And Cally had to be warned. But she said nothing to Elspeth. Shirley was ever the pragmatist; she knew the limitations of human nature. She would not test Elspeth too far.

Instead, she began to watch for the hoofmarks Devil had left, plain on the brickle, even plainer where he had leaped the fallen tree blocking the trolley path. Cally had come this way.

And then Shirley saw the flames rising ahead.

"Elspeth! Hold up!"

Already the trees had thinned, they were in what was not quite a clearing, becoming a young forest, the trolley park of yesteryear, with small tumbledown buildings all around and a larger one going to blazes not far ahead. The horses reared, panicked not only by the sight and smell of the fire, but by the snakes—many snakes fleeing the hilltop inferno, darting out like black rays from a dying sun. And there were people coming out as well, three people, crawling like the snakes from under a shattered wall, then staggering up. Shirley recognized Cally—

Shirley's weakening muscles gave up their struggle

to stay on her terrified horse. What did it matter, anyway? What did any of it matter? She let herself be thrown. Elspeth shouted, she heard that through the air rushing around her ears, and the next moment the young woman was crouching beside her. Elspeth had scrambled down from Warrior and let the blood bay mare plunge away.

"Shirl! You okay?"

Shirley lay flat on her back, looking up into tree-tops and Elspeth's anxious face. "Sure. I'm just laying here resting. Why shouldn't I be okay?" Aside from a minor detail called AIDS. But she didn't say that.

Blood rushed to Elspeth's cheeks, and she glow-ered. "Up!" she snapped. "Get up, you idiot, before a snake bites you!" She hauled at Shirley's arm, not at all gently, and the blond woman heaved herself up, feeling her pale face break into a grin; Elspeth, at least, was back to normal.

Cally coughed and blinked smoke-bleared eyes, trying to see—Barry, had he gotten out all right, had he gotten Joan out? Not that it mattered. But it did matter.

There they were, standing near her, and Joan Musser was coughing as hard as she, the tears stream-ing down from her protruding eyes, down her de-formed, freakish face, that grotesquely familiar face. . . . And Barry was saying, "Joanie. Joanie," and putting his arms around her, and kissing her skewed temples, her weeping eyes, and nestling her head against his shoulder. "Joanie, I can't believe it. I'm so glad you're back. Joanie, I love you." And the Musser girl was holding onto him as if he were the only solid thing left in the world.

And through the flame-tinged haze Cally saw the coming of the horsewomen, saw dark Elspeth, saw

Shirley, golden, taking to the air like an angel for an instant before thudding to earth. And the blood-red mare and the gray one running away God knew where, and black Devil raising his head scornfully from his grazing to watch them go, never stirring for the orange-and-black snakes passing between his hooves.

Joan Musser also turned her tear-blurred eyes toward the thud, the hoofbeats, and Shirley stared back as Elspeth pulled her up. "Yo!" she exclaimed. "It's Whatserface. Musser, ain't it?"

Joan hid the face in question against Barry's shoulder, and he rocked her in his arms and whispered and kissed the uneven parting of her hair the color of soiled straw.

Walking unsteadily toward Shirley, Cally began earnestly to talk, as if an explanation was due. "I thought I had the answer," she soliloquized. "I was so sure. I thought the carousel was the key. We turned it backwards, to turn back time, but it didn't work." She glanced over her shoulder at the flaming wreckage behind her, then at the preposterous young couple embracing in its light. "Well, it sort of worked. . . . It didn't do what I expected. Then I thought, what a dummy I am. That carousel around your house, Shirley, it was turning backward the whole time. The horses were facing the wrong way. And the gazebo, when Ahira made it spin, it was going the wrong way. See what I mean? Turning the thing backwards just made monsters."

Shirley didn't care about any of this. "Cally—"

"If only I could turn it forward again. . . ." Cally's voice trailed away like a torn cloud, and she had gone very still, and somehow transcendant in her stillness, her wide eyes fixed not on Shirley's face but on something—beyond.

"It was stopped," Cally whispered. "Like Hoadley. It was all the fun, all the venturing, all the growing up and leaving home and going forward, and they stopped it and locked it up in the dark. If we—"

"For God's sake, shut up!" snapped Elspeth. "Hoadley's wrecked, and so is your carousel. The problem now is—"

"*Cally,*" Shirley interrupted, "Mark's coming."

Elspeth swiveled her head like a hunting cat and stared. That was not the way she had been going to state the difficulty. To her the problem was one of getting away. The horses were gone, goddammit, and the beast—

"He's been looking for you," Shirley added.

Cally said, "I see." And watching her thin, rapt face, noticing the way she turned toward the forest where her husband would appear, they knew that even with smoke-blinded eyes she did, indeed, see.

"Cally," Elspeth demanded, "are you going to use your horse? Because if you're not . . ."

"No." Tranquilly. "I'm not going to use him."

"C'mon, Shirl." Elspeth grabbed Shirley's hand and pulled her toward the black horse, the four-legged means of transportation big and strong enough to carry both of them.

From down the hillside where the windfall blocked the trail, not far away, came a hollow roar and a shriek of splitting wood. At the sound, Devil flung up his head with a snort of terror and plunged off to disappear over the hilltop. Gone for good.

Shirley and Elspeth froze where they stood as the dark destroyer entered view, as the beast came to the trolley park. But Cally walked to meet him.

The beast—he stood twice as tall as she, bulky, grimly furred as if with coal fiber, and in the fur, clinging, keening, rode hundreds of the human-faced cicadas, perhaps six hundred sixty-six—but these were old-news horrors, were nugatory, as nothing, to Cally's eyes, compared to those other living things, the protuberances, the—she did not know what to call them. Some were horns, some clawed limbs, some the busy heads of snakes or frogs or lizards or reptilian birds, some were feelers or perhaps stingers, like catfish whiskers—it was because it was so many things, mixed, schizoid, unclassifiable, that the beast was a monstrosity. Yet overall, it reminded Cally of nothing so much as the louse she had once seen under an elementary school microscope. A big thing with far too many legs and antennae. A louse, she thought. I guess I did call him that, or think it. More than once.

"Mark," she said.

He lumbered toward her. He had no human eyes for her to look into, no human face for her to study; in no way could she know what were his intentions for her. Yet some of what he felt she did know.

"You are hungry," she stated.

He lifted his forepart—evidently his head—and bawled hoarsely like a bull, so that amid smut-colored fur his mouth appeared, a red-gulleted rictus big as a grave. Seeing that gape, Cally nodded.

"I understand hunger," she said. "I am always hungry. I used to eat, but no matter how much I had there was something inside me always crying for more, more, like a baby crying for the moon. Insatiable. Until I wanted to kill it. So I stopped eating."

Bawl darkened to a roar. The beast leaped. Shirley wordlessly shouted, Elspeth screamed, and Cally squeaked more in reaction than in fear—there had been no time to be terrified before the thing was on top of her, knocking the breath out of her—it made a reedy oboe-squeak in her throat. She noticed subliminally, as the beast sent her staggering backward, that the creature did not smell bad, not bad at all, no worse than a tweed-dressed pipe smoker. Then she noticed that it had not hurt her. Was not hurting her, rather. Its forelegs drove her back toward the flaming carousel, then bore her down to the ground, but their claws had not opened to tear. Breathless, unable to move, she lay flat between those great clawed legs, far too near the fire, far too near the soft soot-colored fur of that huge underbelly, but the beast did not pin her to earth with his great weight. Like the water tower teetering spider-legged on the brink of hell he hesitated over her.

"Mark." She struggled to speak. "Mark. Not hungry for food only. I was—hungry for you. Hungry for—love."

"You ass-tucking sap," came a bitter voice out of the fire, "don't talk to him that way!"

At the sound of the words Cally moved, scrambled out from under the beast's belly and staggered to her feet. She knew that voice, or thought she did. . . . Between the beast and the blazing carousel she stood, so close to both that the heat of the fire drove her back nearly into the bosom of the beast, as if for comfort. But her frightened stare was on the fire. And out of the flames, but unscorched by the flames, walked the great devourer, the locust, the cicada with the tail of a scorpion and the head of the Prince of Darkness—and the face of Death, Gigi's face. Horrible on black bone-hard legs, the thing came and stood beside Cally as if beside an old friend and comrade in arms, and Cally could not retreat to avoid that unwelcome intimacy, for the beast stood at her back.

"Stop the bullshit," complained Gigi—if it was Gigi. "Tell him what you really think of him."

Cally shook her head. "No bull," she said, "Just the truth. I love him. I want him back. I have forgotten what it was we were fighting about."

"Then remember! Have you forgotten what men are like? The tyrants, all they want, all they attempt, is to master us. Turn, look! There's one right behind us. You can see what he is."

Cally did not move. Her gaze remained unwavering on the speaker, the Gigi-thing. "I can see what you are," she said.

The carousel creature hissed; its orange eyes blazed like the flame from which it had come.

"What Mark is, I have made him, for the most part," Cally said. "What you are, you have made yourself."

"Apocalypse!" Death's voice grew terrible. "Obey your destiny!" And listening, the beast opened its huge mouth and bayed, or belled, a fearsome and melancholy sound. Cally shivered, feeling the hot wind of that howl on her back.

But she said, "Destiny? Do what you say, you mean. You want me to obey you, is all. There are no destinies." Her steady gaze took on a visionary sheen. "There are only decisions and dreams."

"Fool!" The cicada creaked forward on armored legs.

"Yes, I am a fool!" Cally's words crackled out angry, hot as orange fire, hard as black bone. The menacing insect-king swayed back a moment in surprise, and Cally spoke on. "I am an idiot: I listened to you far too long. Your way is the way of hatred and despair and death, and I followed it. Now look at me!" For the first time her gaze lowered; she scanned herself, holding up her own clawlike hands in disgust. "I am hardly better than a skeleton. I let myself become nearly the same as you."

"How dare you speak to me that way!"

There was more, but Cally did not listen; deliberately she turned her back on Death.

She heard the snake-hiss of rage, heard the rattle of the scorpion tail raised to sting, but she did not look at her enemy. She looked at the beast, so near, so huge that she had to tilt back her head to see him, or as much of him as she could encompass. She saw other things: beyond him, a young couple in tight, frightened embrace—Barry and Joan. And off to the other side, another pair of lovers, holding hands, just as frightened and staring—Elspeth and Shirley. She saw many things: the hungerbabies in the beast's fur, the shadow of a passing bird, the slow wheeling of the sky. But what were the feelings of the beast, she could not tell.

"I choose the way of life," she said softly to the beast. "I have put away my hunger. I intend to eat. I want to feast of life."

"Apocalypse!" The bitter voice spat like fire.

She ignored it, speaking only to the beast. "And I know now. I have seen. The way to find nurture is to sow it. The way to receive is to give."

"Apocalypse!" Death's breath seared her shoulder, panting with passion at her neck. "I, too, can give. I give you one last chance—"

"Go to hell," Cally commanded.

Something or someone shrieked. The beast trumpeted and reared.

"I love you, Mark," said Cally starkly, tenderly as he leaped.

Gigi, struggling with the mob, had seen Elspeth and Shirley ride away and had reacted to the sight with a screech of outrage; the sword of War had not been bloodied to defend her! They cared nothing for her. No one did. Even War, Famine and Pestilence shunned Death.

The four horsewomen had scattered; she was alone. (The thought caused her rage more than heartache.) Or, rather, left behind, fighting fifty people to keep her seat and her horse—and losing. She felt herself pulled off balance, falling; she screamed—some who heard might have thought they heard fear, but it was fury. She hit the ground, indignant, and a hundred hands grasped at Snake Oil. But these were not horsepeople. They did not know how to catch a frightened horse. Their clutchings and importunities sent the gelding into a frenzy. By the time Gigi had struggled to her feet, cursing, ten people lay flattened, and Snake Oil was a pale, high-tailed blur disappearing into the smoke, with a straggle of men running after him, pitifully slow by contrast.

"Assholes!" Gigi vehemently yelled. "You're scaring him!" Her shouts had no effect, as she had known they would not, but the men would soon tire and give up the chase. And maybe Snake Oil also would tire and stop after a while, and graze; it had been an exhausting day. With not a glance for the trampled people groaning on the ground, Gigi trudged off to find her horse.

An hour later, Death was in tears.

She had followed Snake Oil's trail clear out to the old garment factory, and it looked as if the horse had disappeared into the woods behind it. He might catch his bridle on a snag and strangle himself or starve before she ever found him. . . . Doom hung heavy as the smoke in the air that day, and Gigi gulped and wept and fretted like the mother of a lost child. Up at the trolley park at that moment Shirley and Elspeth were watching their mounts whisk away, more concerned with Cally, Joan Musser, Mark. And when Cally saw Devil snort and take off toward the sunset a few moments later, she accepted his desertion without even a shrug. Devil owed her no affection, no loyalty, no love; people were for love. But to Gigi, losing Snake Oil was as if that overinflated sonofabitch, God, had reached down from his high horse in the sky and taken away the only thing she cared for.

Besides, it was humiliating trudging around when a person was used to riding. They had brought her low, those mobbing Hoadley yokels, and they knew it; they were probably laughing at her. . . . And her new riding boots, so spit-polish swaggering on horseback, were torture to walk in. Her heels were blistered, the backs of her knees rubbed raw by the stiff black leather.

Nevertheless, limping and weeping, she rounded the corner of the abandoned factory—that yellow brick corner, yellow as the Hoadley sky—and then she stopped weeping. Things had just gotten bad beyond the reach of weeping.

Between yellow brick wall and scrub woods lay the appaloosa, still saddled and bridled, flat on his side with his head stretched out and a tinge of blood in his nostrils. Dead.

Just beyond Snake Oil, with leveled rifle, stood Homer. "Always wanted to kill that horse," he said.

Gigi wished death on him with her look. Her nostrils—nearly as gray as her steely hair, from shock or her long sickness—her nostrils flared in time with her hard breathing. Nearly within her arm's reach, the rifle bore faced her chest like a devil's eye, so that she could not help looking at it. So black. Intensely, implodingly black, that hole. Like a dead coal. Like her soul.

"Disappointed, wasn't you," Homer jeered, "not to find me at home."

Gigi knew what besides her horse he had for a long time wanted to kill. Her chest hurt as if someone had cut out her heart. . . . But she did not even think of pleading with him. Heedless of pain, she drew herself erect. "Beast," she averred. "Tyrant. Monster."

Homer smiled. "Yep," he agreed, and he pulled the trigger.

The beast leaped.

Atop the hill, by a carousel's dying fire, the beast out of the pit roared and attacked, hurtled, lunged to kill the one who had angered him. Cally fell nearly into the flames. On the air, along with the smoke, rose a scream—but not Cally's scream. Not at first.

Then she screamed.

CHAPTER SIXTEEN

I'm a God damn coward. Maybe if I wouldn't of been so scared I would've understood what was going on, I would've knowed like everybody else did, maybe I could've helped somehow, and maybe none of it would've happened.

Joanie knowed all right. She screamed when she seen the beast jump. I thought it was on account of Mrs. Wilmore. For a minute it looked like the beast was going for her to kill her and maybe eat her or something, and I thought that was why Joanie screamed, and I wanted to run and help Mrs. Wilmore but I couldn't because of Joanie. I had been cuddling Joanie in my arms till then, see, and she didn't seem to mind, but when she screamed she pushed at me, she wanted me to turn her loose, and I was afraid she was gonna go and get herself hurt, and I couldn't let her. I just couldn't, even if Mrs. Wilmore died. I'd just then got Joanie back, the old Joanie I mean, ugly, like me, and I'd just got to finally tell her how I loved her, and it seemed to me if she stayed around a while and let me love her she might come to feel different about things. About her life and stuff. I couldn't let her go tackle no beast for nothing.

And it wasn't Mrs. Wilmore the beast was after anyways. I seen it knock her down, but she must've just been in the way. The beast went over top of her and jumped that monster out of the carousel, that locust thing with the stinger tail, and Mrs. Wilmore rolled off to one side, away from the fire and the fight, then sort of half set up and looked, so I knowed she wasn't killed or even much hurt. And I was watching—the beast had pinned that poison tail to the ground first thing, and all his snake heads and stuff were biting and hissing like fire, but they come up against that bug like it was made of sheet metal and they didn't do no good. And the beast couldn't do no good with them big jaws of his neither, because the other monster had hold of him with them black clawed legs—them things looked strong as iron struts. I didn't know which one looked meaner, the beast or that bug thing, and I was hoping they'd both kill the other one, and I was so glad they was fighting each other and not none of us that I forgot Joanie might not feel the same way. And I forgot to hold her real tight.

And then hell happened.

Mrs. Wilmore screamed. And Joanie busted away from me and run straight toward the fight. And I'm so shook by what I see going on that it's a second before I run after her.

What's happening is, the beast is changing, right then and there. Getting smaller, weaker. Snakes, claw, horns, all going away. Fur, smoothing out into skin. The beast was turning into a man. Just regular man not even as tall as me, and that other monster still holding him in its claws.

"Mark!" came a scream.

See, I didn't know till I seed what was happening that the beast was Mr. Wilmore, or the God-awful danger he had put himself in, attacking the thing that was threatening his wife. But Joanie must've knowed all along. What the devil knowed, she knowed, she said. And I guess she just didn't want no more bad things to happen. So she run like hell to help.

"Mark!" his wife is crying and screaming, trying to get up and go to him. But she couldn't. Seemed like she didn't have no strength left since she got knocked down that last time. And even if she could get up, what could she do, skinny little starved thing like she was?

And I was running too, more on account of Joanie than Mr. Wilmore—I liked him a lot, he was a good boss to me, but I ain't sure I would've fought no monster just for him—anyways, Joanie was flying along in front of me in that red dress of hers like wings and I was running fast as I could but I seemed to go slow, so slow, I would never catch her or get there in time, and that poison stinger tail was coming up, I could see it, Mr. Wilmore had his foot on top of it but that wasn't no use, nobody could be that strong to keep that thing down with their foot. It was all hard shell and muscle and it was as big as him. And the locust had him around the neck with its black bone hands, and I seen a horrible grin on its old gray face, and its tail come up in a curve like a wrestler's arm, in half a second it would have him—

And Joanie thrown herself right on top of it.

She took that hard sharp stinger and pressed the poison spine of it in between her breasts and hugged it there like it was—like it was her lover. And she rode the rest of it like she was riding a horse. And I knowed she'd killed herself as much as saved anybody else, and it drove me crazy that she'd do herself that way. I didn't even try to stop running. I piled into that helldamn black murdering stingertail death king and tried to take it apart with my bare hands. I remember snapping off its wing like the cruddy thing come out of a cereal box. I remember ramming my fist into its creepy old face, into one of its hateful eyes. I remember breaking one of its black arms and kicking it in the gut. Other than that I don't remember much until I was wore out and done being crazy. Then I stood there panting and I seen them other women standing beside me. They was holding tree branches they been using like clubs, they been helping me. And that goddamn killer locust was laying there good and dead.

I thanked them women later. I guess maybe them helping me was what kept me from getting myself killed. But there wasn't nothing nobody could do to help Joanie.

She was laying sloppy with blood and pieces of bug shell and stuff, like she couldn't move, but she wasn't dead yet, because I seen her eyes on me, and I went to her quick. "Joanie," I says, "God damn, why'd you have to go and do that?" Right away I knowed it wasn't the right thing to say. There wasn't no time for yelling at her. "Does it hurt bad?" I says. "Joanie, say it don't hurt."

Her eyes told me no. Seemed like she couldn't hardly talk or even move her mouth. Since I knowed it wouldn't hurt her, I got down beside her, I wanted to hold her. But her eyes looked a warning at me, and then I understood why. The stinger was still laying beside her. She was scared it would poison me.

"I won't touch it," I says, and then she lets me take her into my arms. I cuddled her head in my lap and kissed her face. "You're beautiful," I says. I guess maybe she wouldn't have looked beautiful to nobody else, especially all messed up with blood like she was, but she did to me. Except I meant beautiful in a different way, too. I wished she wouldn't of died, but if she had to, it was beautiful the way she done it. Saving somebody else. A real normal, too. Wasn't nobody more normal than Mr. Wilmore, him being a funeral director and all. I guessed Joanie'd stopped hating normals.

A little ways away is Mrs. Wilmore holding Mr. Wilmore the same way I was holding Joanie. She has his head in her lap. I think maybe he's dying too, and he better not. It wouldn't of been no use Joanie should die if he would die too.

Joanie is still breathing, slow, real slow, she's having trouble, like her chest don't want to work. The poison, see, it's shutting her down one thing at a time, first her arms and legs, then her chest, and next her heart—and after that it would be up to me to shut her eyes for her. She must've knowed, too, what was happening, because her eyes blinked fast and her mouth moved. I could tell it was all she could do to make her mouth move. I could tell she really wanted to say something, and I put my ear down close to her lips. Her voice was just a breath. I could just barely hear her. I still ain't sure she really said what I thought she did.

"Bar—I—love—you. . . ."

Maybe I was just hearing what I wanted to hear. And anyways I didn't believe her none, not for a minute. I knowed if I'd heard her right, she was just saying it. The way things was for her, maybe she'd done what was best, getting herself killed. I knowed she had too much pain to love nobody. And I was crying anyways, didn't even know when I'd started but there was tears dripping down on her from my face, pink tears, because that damn bug bashed me some and I got blood on me. And I was looking at Joanie, and she was looking at me, her eyes was still looking at me even though she stopped breathing, and then all of a sudden even though they was still open her eyes wasn't seeing me no more. But I held her a while longer before I laid her down and straightened her out and closed them for her.

Then I made myself stop crying. What she said there at the end, she meant that to stop me crying. She at least cared about me some, as much as she could care about anybody. I could tell them things. I could most always tell what she was feeling from her voice.

God, I'd never hear it again, ever.

But look on the bright side. The way things was going, maybe there wouldn't be too much ever for me to get through.

"There's something I've got to say," Mark Wilmore told his wife. "How right you were about all this."

Holding his head on her lap, Cally stroked his cheek (her hand, so soda-straw tenuous as to seem nearly insubstantial) without replying. She gazed off over the treetops at a yellow sky turning black with Hoadley smoke. All this: death and pestilence, famine and war, fire and tumult and a black pit, Hoadley's destruction and world's end. . . . Her thinking had changed so much it took her a moment to comprehend that Mark remembered how the long quarrel had started and wanted to set it straight. Wanted to mend it before the end.

"I'm not so sure," she said finally. "Seems to me that I almost made it happen. The crying babies I heard, they were me, but then next thing there were hungerbabies in the trees. I made up my mind that men were monsters, and . . . Mark, about the girl who was raped—did you really—you know. . . ."

He did not know. He looked up at her blankly.

"You don't remember?"

"The blond one, worked at the drugstore? I don't remember a thing about her. What did I do?"

"Nothing."

"Cal, I've got to know what I did."

"No, you don't. Trust me." It was a better outcome than she could ever have hoped for, that this gentle man her husband was not ridden by such bedeviling memories. She smiled like sunrise as she gazed down at him. "And you don't remember—" She hesitated, afraid to say "beast," and found a euphemism. "You don't remember going down under the town?"

He shook his head. He did not recall coming up out of the pit either; he remembered little of being Mark the Beast. "I just remember—coming back. Knowing that I loved you."

His love for her had brought him back to human form, or hers for him—it didn't matter which. She put her cheek next to his and hugged him. She had twisted her knee, but he was not injured. He lay in her lap merely because he felt a bittersweet lethargy, as did she. These last few hours of their lives, of their world, they would spend together.

"You were right to send the kids away," said Mark after she had sat up and found his hand with hers. A tremor in his voice told more than the words did; he was wishing he could be with the children one last time. But he believed they would live after he was gone. Cally's hand tightened on his, but she said nothing. No use making him suffer what she was thinking: that Tammy and Owen might as well have

stayed in Hoadley for all the good she had done.
World's end would come to find them soon after it
had found Mark and her. There was no way she
could save them for long.

The carousel burned low. A small distance away,
Barry Beal hulked bearlike and motionless over Joan
Musser's body. No one tried to speak to him.
Downslope, someone moved between the trees: Shirley and Elspeth returning, coming up the trolley
path, arms around each other. They had gone to
have a look at Hoadley, and perhaps to be alone
together.

"The pit keeps spreading," Shirley reported to
Cally, keeping her loud voice low, as if it mattered
who heard. Not wishing to disturb Barry, perhaps.
"The town is all but gone. And there's a beast down
there, scouting around."

Mark blinked and sat up with a faint scowl, as if
his franchise had been invaded. "A new beast?"

"It makes sense," Cally said. Hoadley had been a
town where women were bitter and men wore their
egos on their sleeves; why would there be any lack of
beasts? The new beast would carry on to the other
side of the mountains what had begun in Hoadley,
the hub. Perhaps the beast was Gigi. Perhaps the
children, Owen and Tammy, would die as other
children had died, by her hands.

The sky was darkening, the shadows growing even
darker than the smoke had made them. Others might
have thought that it was the dusk of a long, long day.
But Cally knew it was not just another twilight. It
was the falling of a final night.

Only the carousel gave light, and its fire had dwindled to embers. Cally looked to see how soon it
would be dark. . . .

She grabbed at Mark's shoulder. "The horses!"

He gazed at her, seeing how her lips had slightly parted, seeing how vulnerable and potent she was. "That black horse of yours is gone," he said. "You could have ridden away from me on it. I remember that much."

She was staring beyond him. "Not those horses!" Cally felt an impatient lack of regret that the four snorting horses of Death and War and Famine and Pestilence were gone. "Look!" She pointed. "Mark, there!"

He swiveled and saw: shining in the dusk, the white horse of the hero, with mane and tail of gold. And others: palominos, and pintos with yellow saddles, and pearly dapple grays with hooves of silver. His jaw dropped. Nothing was distinct except the horses standing there, and they seemed to glow; at first he did not understand.

"The carousel!" Cally gasped. "Mark, it's not destroyed!"

The building that had sheltered—or shadowed— and hidden it was gone, burned away to black coals. Even the round framework of the carousel was gone; clouds of smoke wheeled over it instead of a cornice and girders. But the horses stood forth in the twilight lucent, uncharred, changed and freed. Airily poised, amid dark of smoke and nightfall and doom they shone like dawn's dew, like newborn winged things rising from the ashes.

"Mark!" Cally breathed. "If we can make it go . . ."

Somewhere behind the smoke, the cloud, stars still lit the sky.

Gawking, struggling with the sense of what he was seeing, Mark complained, "Cal . . ."

"*Forward*, don't you see? It has to go forward."

He swung around to protest, but the sight of her stopped him. In the thin carousel light, purifying as moonlight, her fleshless face was ethereal, spiritous, not that of a skeleton any longer but that of an angel.

Using his shoulder to take the weight off her injured leg, she got up from the ground. Through her hand he felt her trembling excitement, her urgency, and he hurried to stand beside her, holding her arm to prevent her falling; already she was limping forward. "Shirley! Elspeth!" she called.

They were huddled not far away, arms around each other, oblivious to anything but each other until Cally's cry recalled them. There was clarion in Cally's voice. "Come on! We've got to get Hoadley moving again."

"Hoadley?" Shirley blinked at her. "Hoadley's gone."

"Not yet. Listen."

"Listen to what?"

"In the air! Listen."

The plaint, the timeworn familiar sighs ever trundling in the same rutted circle. . . . In the benighted trees all around them they heard the cicadas with the faces of aborted babies, of dead souls, of bad memories. "Crossed knives mean a quarrel," wept one.

"Go out the same door you came in," quavered another, "or someone will die."

"Whistling girls and crowing hens—"

"Always come to bad ends!"

"Looking at the sky will drive you crazy . . . crazy . . . crazy . . ."

"Doom," they wailed, "doom."

"That's Hoadley, all right," said Shirley with rueful tenderness in her voice.

Already Cally led the way again toward the carousel. "Come on!"

"Lord," said Elspeth, some of her old scorn back. "If that's Hoadley, why do you *want* to save it?"

"Because if it goes, the rest of the world goes soon after."

None of them disbelieved her. In the dark the cicadas crooned.

The white wooden lead horse, the hero horse of the carousel, no longer carried an ominous brass disc or a bridle to wear it on, but instead wore his wild golden mane like a crown. On his back was no saddle, but instead a kingly mantle of white and gold cloaked his shoulders and sides, fastened by a silver breastplate beneath his neck. It was to him that Cally limped. But when she pulled her arm away from Mark and put her hand on a white hock to urge the carousel into motion, she snatched it away again.

"Hot!" she exclaimed.

"Well, of course," Mark grumbled, laying hold of common sense and hugging it to his mind as a child hugs a flannel blanket. Embers glowed like small earth-fettered stars all around his wife, stirred up from under ashes by her feet. There had been a fire; the horse would be hot.

Though it should also be charred to ruins. "It's not that," Cally said, and she hitched to the horse's head, looked up into blue eyes in a proud white face.

"What is wrong?" she asked him. "It's true, I mostly want to save my kids. I want to see them again, and have another chance at my life. With Mark. And we need a world to live in, and I'd like it to be what's left of this one. . . . What is wrong?"

Sapphire glass eyes, clear, remote, gave her no answer. Gold forelock, real gold, not just a splash of paint, made a frontlet between them, and the eyes themselves seemed so transcendent they could have been the sky-born eyes of a god; who would make a carousel horse's eyes blue? The white horse's mouth, unlike that of most carousel horses, was closed and calm, giving its long head an expression of nobility and sadness. Cally went to one knee in the ashes, as if facing her Lord on Judgment Day.

"Hoadley," she said softly. "It's Hoadley I have to want to save, isn't it? But how can I? I hate it. I made it my family, but it's a family full of guilt and abuse. . . ."

Mark had grown restive, listening to the crying of the soul-lost cicadas in the night, watching his wife talk to a wooden horse. "For God's sake, Cal," he grumbled, and she turned her stark head to look at him. Tears shone on her cheekbones.

"I told you," came an unexpected, faintly mocking voice, "you don't know what real abuse is. And even if you did . . ." Elspeth hesitated, lost her fine-tuned disdain, and when she, of all people, gave the answer, it came quietly as the flying of a lacewing in the night. "Even if you did, the hell of it is, there's still love. Mixed in with the hurting."

Cally heard, though she did not look at the speaker, and she whispered, "It's true, I want them to love me. . . ."

In the night, on the mountain sides, in the scrub trees, Hoadley ceased its crying and fell silent, listening, waiting. Mark felt the world stop breathing, felt his mind go blank and his heart plod bare in the wilderness of his chest. Above Cally's head glass eyes the color of true sky shone steadily as a blue candle flame where no wind stirred. Beyond the clouds, somewhere, had the lonesome wheeling of stars come to a halt?

Cally said, "I have to love them. I want to—I will love them. I am Apocalypse, and I will forgive them and feast of their lives. I will live and hunger and eat, and I will give no more thought to whether they ever love me."

And the white horse reared up in triumph so that his mantle lifted from his shoulders like wings.

Cally took Mark's hand and stood up, and somewhere the stars were making a canopy of lights for the carousel. Cally stepped back. "Never mind," she said to Shirley and Elspeth as they moved forward to help. "We don't need to touch it. It will turn."

Mark rolled his eyes, Elspeth looked dazed, but Shirley nodded as if she understood utterly. "Sure thing," she declared. "Once you've got hold of that feeling, it all comes together."

From every direction in the night small voices started to sing, soft as mist. "Round, around, up and down, all the pretty little horses. Hushabye, hushabye . . ."

Slowly, slowly, in the lullaby night, the wheel of gleaming horses started to move, to turn. And from the bushes as the hungerbabies laid themselves down to sleep chimed the notes of the great circling waltz of time. And still crouching by Joan Musser's body, Barry Beal gave a soul-deep sigh and looked up at the sky.

The clouds were clearing away as if before a strong wind, though no wind blew. Stars were showing through.

By gentle degrees the carousel spun faster. Barry Beal looked at it as if seeing it for the first time, seeing with a childlike wonder the moon-dapple grays and the sunbeam palominos and the starlit white leading the dance, its gleaming gold crown of mane flying . . . Barry stood up and came and stood by Mark in mute curiosity. It was Mark who spoke for both men.

"What's making that thing turn?" he demanded.

Cally said, "Hope."

*   *   *

I didn't expect no sunrise ever again, but up it come, and I seed it, and I ain't never seen such a sky, all stained glass butterfly colors. I hadn't slept none. I was setting by Joanie again, and them others was off someplace for a while but they come back and set by me, so we all seen it. And that weird merry-go-round was still going round behind my back.

I took notice of a couple of special things in that sunrise. That big blond lady, the one with her skin all pale and spotted up, was setting near me, and when that sunrise light touched her skin it flushed sweet as a baby's and all them spots was gone in a minute. Then she started crying, and Mrs. Wilmore come to see, and I took notice that when that light touched her Mrs. Wilmore plumped up some even though she hadn't ate nothing yet.

Then I looked at Joanie, kind of holding my breath, kind of hoping. . . . But didn't nothing happen. Joanie was dead all right and would have looked pretty ugly even if she wasn't the color of old porch paint, which she was. When that sunup light touched her she should have looked like gold and roses, but she didn't. She looked like all a big bruise. I wished I had something to cover her.

And I didn't want just any something to cover her, neither. This here was Joanie. And if she lived, she would've been . . . would've done . . .

Mr. Wilmore and them others come around me, trying to talk gentle to me, but I ain't listening. I don't want to go nowhere or do nothing or eat nothing or see nobody. I don't give a damn about nothing or nobody but Joanie then. I just put my head down on my knees and tried to think what was next, now Joanie was dead. And then it come to me. I knowed where there was something good enough to cover Joanie.

I gets up and looks, and sure enough it's just right, all white and gold mixed up like cream, with a white flower border and a long gold fringe. And I can see just by the way it drapes around his shoulders and back that it's heavy and thin and rich, like a cover for a king. "Hey, white horse," I says, "Hey, can you come down here a minute?"

"Barry, no!" Mrs. Wilmore yells at me, cause she told me later she was afraid I was going to stop Hoadley again, and Mr. Wilmore wants to know what the hun I'm trying to do, but I ain't paying no attention to them. I'm just trying to get Joanie a blanket to cover her dead body. And the white horse took an easy jump off that carousel and come prancing over to me, and I says to him, "I want this here blanket of yours for Joanie."

And he arched his neck like a new moon and bowed his head to say yes. See, he knew. And after I undid the clips and took the blanket off him he went back on the carousel and neighed like he was glad to be rid of it, and he made that sunrise sound like a big yellow bell ringing.

The blanket was just like I thought, soft and silky-rich all at once, and I knowed it was going to lay great. Once I get it on Joanie I feel some better about everything, and I start to make it look pretty on her, and I don't care that the rest of them are all standing around staring at me.

"Barry," Mr. Wilmore says to me. "Should we maybe take the deceased home first?"

Down to Hoadley, he meant. What was left of it. That made me look up at him. "No," I says. "I think she liked it better up here." What home she had, I figured this carousel was it. And I didn't want none of them people looking at her.

"Did she have a church?"

"No." I knowed what he was thinking. "No, not in no graveyard you don't put her. She wouldn't like that none."

"Where, then?"

I just kept on pleating at the blanket, and it was coming along pretty good. I liked the way the white flowers was worked right into the stuff. They give it heft.

After a while Mr. Wilmore says, "Did she have family?"

"Her ma. Left town. Her pa." If he was still living. "Probably so pickled he don't care if she's dead." And just thinking about Mr. Musser and what he'd done to Joanie I felt everything all of a sudden go hot and red, and I thought, that's the next thing for me to do, is kill that fucker. I didn't care what happened to me. He'd be setting on that rickety front porch of his with a bottle, and I'd walk right up to him and shove it up his nose and kick him till he broke open like a Halloween pumpkin. I wanted to kill him so bad it hurt. And my fists was clenched and my chest huffing, and everybody saying to me, "Barry. Barry, what is it? What's the matter?"

And then I think, it don't matter what I want. It just matters what Joanie would have wanted me to do. Suppose Joanie don't want him dead no more?

See, I knowed a couple things about Joanie. I knowed life had hurt her bad. And I knowed she'd changed her mind about a lot of that before she died.

So I didn't say nothing to none of them other people, but, "Joanie, help me think," I says to her out loud. She's laying there dead, but I still hope she can help me. "Just this one time let me get it right."

"Get what right?" Mr. Wilmore wants to know.

Mrs. Wilmore says to him, "Mark, butt out."

So they all set down and waited for me to think.

And it took me a while, but I done it right and good.
I could feel it, like I could feel the blanket shaping
up good under my hands. And then I looked up, and
it was Mrs. Wilmore I was looking at. So I tell her.

"Joanie forgive them all," I says to her. "All of
them. She would've saved them if she could. If she
lived, she would've been the one rode that white
horse."

"Damn right," says Mrs. Wilmore, and she sounds
like she means it. She knowed it, just like the white
horse knowed it. And just looking at her, I knowed I
had a friend. She understood about Joanie.

The sun was up just a little farther in the sky,
slanting down through the tops of the trees, all beautiful in the green leaves, and the sky was clear deep
blue like the white horse's eyes on the merry-go-
round kept circling and circling close by, and it was
all—it was like everything was new again. It was
special.

Mrs. Wilmore says, soft: "So it must have been in
the first, spinning place." And I didn't understand at
first. But later I remembered them words Joanie had
wrote down and pinned over the mirrors inside the
merry-go-round.

Mr. Wilmore says, just as quiet, "Barry. You want
her buried— here."

I didn't want her buried at all. But she had to be,
since she was dead, and I knowed this was the right
place. I nodded. Then I stayed with Joanie while
him and the others went down Hoadley.

Trudging back up the hill with the shovels, feeling
much stronger and somewhat more her former self,
Cally said, "Bet this is the strangest funeral you'll
ever do, Mark." Slipping back already into the role.

Mark said, "It's the last funeral I'll ever do."

She accepted this fact as another petal in the flower of her blossoming happiness, almost as a matter of course. Because Hoadley was all in confusion or in the pit, they had gone as far as Shirley's stable to find shovels (noting in passing that the fence had returned to normal but the castle had fallen; no longer would Elspeth keep herself cloistered in that makeshift tower) and while there Cally had found to her astonishment that Shirley's phone was in working order, and had telephoned her mother. The children were well. All symptoms seemed to have disappeared overnight. As soon as they could arrange it, Mark and Cally would go to join and retrieve the youngsters.

"Oh?" she said to her husband, smiling. "You're not going to be a funeral director any more?"

"I'm not going to be a prop for the tottering any more, I'm not going to be a pillar of Hoadley any more, and I'm not going to be a dutiful son or a take-care-of-it husband." He gave her a grin she remembered from those distant student days when he had been in the habit of secreting a spring-loaded cloth snake in her purse.

"By damn," Cally remarked with zest. "What will you be, then?"

He said, "Alive." And he turned to her, took her by the shoulders and kissed her. Not a formality, that kiss. Rather, an urgency.

Shirley said, grinning, "Watch it, youse." She had brought them most of the way back in the pickup, coming with them to help dig. "Save it for later."

Cally said, "I'm hungry."

"Aren't you always?" complained the dark, intense young woman who walked by her side.

"No, Elspeth, I mean I'm really hungry."

Mark the prosaic in cahoots with Shirley the equally

pragmatic had brought along a paper bag of food from the latter's refrigerator. Silently he reached in and handed his wife an apple, a Golden Delicious, pudgy and yellow. They walked to where Barry Beal still knelt, oblivious to them and their concerns, arranging and arranging a kingly cloak in tucks and pleats and folds and gathers over the body of Joan Musser. As they journeyed, Cally ate her apple down to the core.

EPILOGUE

The media headlined it as the worst case of mine subsidence in recorded history. Questioning the survivors, reporters met either embarrassed silence or hysteria. The latter, expressed in terms of beasts and burning bears, four horsewomen and human-faced bugs, they dismissed as a manifestation of millennial fever. Such reports would, in any event, have been censored from the public record.

Within the first day a decision was made, loudly and unanimously, at an *al fresco* town meeting, to rebuild. It was unthinkable to do otherwise. Friends were in Hoadley. Family was Hoadley. Only the place had to be repaired; the people remained, for the most part. Thirteen had been killed (excluding Bud Zankowski, whose body was not found for months afterward), and Homer Wildasin had been taken away on suspicion of murder when the bodies of Gigi and her horse were found. No one said much about Homer. Quite a few solid citizens had seen the change; they knew who the second beast had been (though

not the first), and the less said about it, the better—
especially in front of outsiders.

By nightfall of the first day the dead were buried,
lying under the bottommost of what were to be many
layers of slag in the pit where they had fallen; it would
become their communal grave. Gladys Wildasin's
body did not lie with the others. She had been taken
away by the police for forensic autopsy, and she was
not missed.

It was a fine irony, unnoticed by most townspeople other than Elspeth and Cally, that the slag heaps,
which had always seemed to shadow Hoadley, shutting out light and air, that those ugly old "bony
piles" should become the easy means of healing the
town's greatest wound. The town leveled them to fill
the pit. Mark and the remaining horsewomen joined
like many other volunteers (including many with
strange wine-colored scars on the sides of their faces)
in the hard labor, and found that in the absence of
Gerald Wozny and Zephyr Zook, and with the shocked
and/or prostrated resignation of other borough council members, new leadership emerged. Few survivors looked down on anyone any longer, but one
person in particular came to be liked and respected
by nearly everyone, and was within a year elected to
public office: Shirley Danyo.

Hoadley had always insisted on managing things
its own way, and despite an influx of federal officials,
Red Cross administrators and various interfering outsiders it continued to do so. Within a respectable
length of time the pit was filled, rebuilding begun
(including the government-financed construction of
Mark Wilmore's new Home Furnishings and Interior
Decorating business), and a suitably ostentatious mon-
ument raised in the park near the gazebo, in mem-

ory of the victims. On it, of course, were engraved the names of the dead:

Rev. Ronald R. Berkey
Beulah G. Coe (Mrs. Elmer Graybill Coe)
Izetta "Wobbles" Enwright
Sojourner Faith Hieronymus
Gustave Delmar Litwack
Fr. Anatole Leopold
Rose Zankowski Kondas (Mrs. Ralph H. Kondas)
Osvaldo "Slug" Pessolano, Jr.
Jessica Sue Rzeszut
Luther Wesley Wasserman
Gladys Gingrich Wildasin
Gerald Q. Wozny
Zephyr Angelica Zook (Mrs. Howard B. Zook)

Near the apex of the obelisk, over the list of names, was engraved an inscription selected by the town's literary authority and new librarian, Cally Wilmore. Something nice, appropriate, from Donne or Shakespeare or perhaps the Bible. No one knew, for no one except, perhaps, Cally ever really read it to remember it.

But up on Trolley Park Hill, engraved on a bronze plaque that huddled flush with the ground, lay another inscription remembered by those Hoadley citizens who read it, though it was read seldom, for few of them went up there; nothing was left to take even the bad girls and the eager boys to that hilltop. A scattering of time-tattered shacks still stood, but no carousel building any longer: nothing but a circular pile of debris out of which rose the charred, black hulks of a few wooden horses.

Barry Beal walked up the trolley right-of-way almost daily, but no one cared about that; everyone knew Barry Beal was simpleminded, and no one gave much thought to his doings. Cally Wilmore rode her new horse up there the white winter day she first brought it home. Other than that, deer hunters went there once an autumn or so. And maybe moonlight strollers in the spring. And from time to summertime, kids camping in Boy Scout tents.

So it took a while. But after a few years the tale began to be told, how if a person came to that place at dawn, and sat, and kept very still—and if the sunrise was of exceptional sweetness and beauty—the listener could hear in the hush, ethereal, the sound of calliope music in three-four time. And if the person then looked toward the blackened ruins of the carousel (and if the mist was blanketing the earth in the sunrise, lying in folds and billows beneath green locust trees) sometimes a white wild-maned horse could be seen over those dark ashes, circling, circling, white and ethereal as the mist. And other carousel horses could be seen even more faintly, yellow and dun and spotted horses, following the lead horse in its ever rounds, circling, cycling. . . . And straight and still on the white horse's back there would be riding a young woman in a dress red as a lover's heart, a young woman the colors of milk and honey and sublimely beautiful—but fleeting as time. For no sooner would the watcher draw breath than she and her horses were gone like the mist vanishing in the rising sun.

And if the person blinked and looked down then, he or she might see the new day's sun glinting off the polished, deeply gleaming plaque set into the ground. Why such a marker in that unlikely place? And who had paid for the expensive thing, and brought it up the trolley trail, and had put it there, and kept the grass clipped around it? And who had chosen the peculiar words with which it was engraved?

Leaning, with the morning sun warm on the back of the neck, the Hoadley citizen could read them:

"So it must have been after the birth of the simple light
In the first, spinning place, the spellbound horses walking warm
Out of the whinnying green stable
On to the fields of praise."

THE MANY WORLDS OF
MELISSA SCOTT

*Winner of the John W. Campbell Award
for Best New Writer, 1986*

THE KINDLY ONES: "An ambitious novel of the world Orestes. This large, inhabited moon is governed by five Kinships whose society operates on a code of honor so strict that transgressors are declared legally 'dead' and are prevented from having any contact with the 'living.' . . . Scott is a writer to watch."—*Publishers Weekly*. A Main Selection of the Science Fiction Book Club.

65351-2 • 384 pp. • $2.95

The "Silence Leigh" Trilogy

FIVE-TWELFTHS OF HEAVEN (Book I): "Melissa Scott postulates a universe where technology interferes with magic. . . . The whole plot is one of space ships, space wars, and alien planets—not a unicorn or a dragon to be seen anywhere. Scott's space drive and description of space piloting alone would mark her as an expert in the melding of the [SF and fantasy] genres; this is the stuff of which 'sense of wonder' is made."—*Locus*

55952-4 • 352 pp. • $2.95

SILENCE IN SOLITUDE (Book II): "[Scott is] a voice you should seek out and read at every opportunity." —*OtherRealms*.   65699-7 • 324 pp. • $2.95

THE EMPRESS OF EARTH (Book III):

65364-4 • 352 pp. • $3.50

A CHOICE OF DESTINIES: "Melissa Scott [is] one of science fiction's most talented newcomers. . . . The greatest delight of all is finding out how she managed to write a historical novel that could legitimately have spaceships on the cover . . . a marvelous gift for any fan."—*Baltimore Sun*   65563-9 • 320 pp. • $2.95

THE GAME BEYOND: "An exciting interstellar empire novel with a great deal of political intrigue and colorful interplanetary travel."—*Locus*

55918-4 • 352 pp. • $2.95

To order any of these Melissa Scott titles, please check the box/es below and send combined cover price/s to:

Baen Books
Dept. BA
260 Fifth Ave.
NY, NY 10001

Name _____

Address _____

City _____ State _____ Zip _____

THE KINDLY ONES ☐   FIVE-TWELFTHS OF HEAVEN ☐
A CHOICE OF DESTINIES ☐   SILENCE IN SOLITUDE ☐
THE GAME BEYOND ☐   THE EMPRESS OF EARTH ☐

THE KING OF YS
POUL AND KAREN ANDERSON

THE KING OF YS— THE GREATEST EPIC FANTASY OF THIS DECADE!

by Poul and Karen Anderson

As many authors that have brought new life and meaning to Camelot and her King, so have Poul and Karen Anderson brought to life a city of legend on the coast of Brittany . . . Ys.

THE ROMAN SOLDIER BECAME A KING, AND HUSBAND TO THE NINE

In *Roma Mater*, the Roman centurion Gratillonius became King of Ys, city of legend— and husband to its nine magical Queens.

A PRIEST-KING AT WAR WITH HIS GODS

In *Gallicenae*, Gratillonius consolidates his power in the name and service of Rome the Mother, and his war worsens with the senile Gods of Ys, that once blessed city.

HE MUST MARRY HIS DAUGHTER— OR WATCH AS HIS KINGDOM IS DESTROYED

In *Dahut* the final demands of the gods were made clear: that Gratillonius wed his own daughter . . . and as a result of his defying that divine ultimatum, the consequent destruction of Ys itself.

THE STUNNING CLIMAX

In *The Dog and the Wolf*, the once and future king strives first to save the remnant of the Ysans from utter destruction—then use them to save civilization itself, as the light that once was Rome flickers out, and barbarian night descends upon the world. In the progress, Gratillonius, once a Roman centurion and King of Ys, will become King Grallon of Brittany, and give rise to a legend that will ring down the corridors of time!

Available only through Baen Books, but you can order this four-volume KING OF YS series with this order form. Check your choices below and send the combined cover price/s to: Baen Books, Dept. BA, 260 Fifth Avenue, New York, New York 10001.

ROMA MATER • 65602-3 • 480 pp. • $3.95 _____
GALLICENAE • 65342-3 • 384 pp. • $3.95 _____
DAHUT • 65371-7 • 416 pp. • $3.95 _____
THE DOG AND THE WOLF • 65391-1 •
544 pp. • $4.50 _____

MAGIC AND COMPUTERS DON'T MIX!

RICK COOK

Or . . . do they? That's what Walter "Wiz" Zumwalt is wondering. Just a short time ago, he was a master hacker in a Silicon Valley office, a very ordinary fellow in a very mundane world. But magic spells, it seems, are a lot like computer programs: they're both formulas, recipes for getting things done. Unfortunately, just like those computer programs, they can be full of bugs. Now, thanks to a *particularly* buggy spell, Wiz has been transported to a world of magic—and incredible peril. The wizard who summoned him is dead, Wiz has fallen for a red-headed witch who despises him, and no one—not the elves, not the dwarves, not even the dragons—can figure out why he's here, or what to do with him. Worse: the sorcerers of the deadly Black League, rulers of an entire continent, want Wiz dead—and he doesn't even know why! Wiz had better figure out the rules of this strange new world—and fast—or he's not going to live to see Silicon Valley again.

Here's a refreshing tale from an exciting new writer. It's also a rarity: a well drawn fantasy told with all the rigorous logic of hard science fiction.

February 1989 • 69803-6 • 320 pages • $3.50

Available at bookstores everywhere, or you can send the cover price to Baen Books, Dept. WZ, 260 Fifth Ave., New York, NY 10001.